Praise for Embassie Susberry

'Loved it . . . A great story of danger and intrigue.'
⁕⁕⁕⁕⁕ **Reader Review**

'A really interesting, well-researched and well-written
book, it captures the flavour of France at the start of
WWII beautifully . . .There are so many people who
dare to try to change the way things are, and this acts
as a nice tribute to them. An excellent read.'
⁕⁕⁕⁕⁕ **Reader Review**

'A riveting WWII story inspired by the real-life
experiences of Josephine Baker . . . Historical fiction
fans will adore it!'
⁕⁕⁕⁕⁕ **Reader Review**

'This story was like being on a runaway train and I
couldn't stop reading.'
⁕⁕⁕⁕⁕ **Reader Review**

'Inspiring and beautiful!'
⁕⁕⁕⁕⁕ **Reader Review**

'Susberry does a great job of not skating by hard topics
and complexities but molding them seamlessly into a
relatable story.'
⁕⁕⁕⁕⁕ **Reader Review**

D1330252

Embassie Susberry is a practicing attorney in Chicago, but when she's not doing her day job, she's reading or writing what she wants to read.

Code Name Butterfly is Embassie's first traditionally published novel. She has over 2000 reviews for her self-published novels on Amazon with average ratings of 4.7 stars.

CODE NAME BUTTERFLY

EMBASSIE SUSBERRY

avon.

Published by AVON
A division of HarperCollins*Publishers*
1 London Bridge Street
London SE1 9GF

www.harpercollins.co.uk

HarperCollins*Publishers*
Macken House
39/40 Mayor Street Upper
Dublin 1
D01 C9W8

A Paperback Original 2023
2
First published in Great Britain by HarperCollins*Publishers* 2023

A catalogue copy of this book is available from the British Library.

ISBN: 978-0-00-859151-9

This novel is entirely a work of fiction. The names, characters
and incidents portrayed in it are the work of the author's
imagination. Any resemblance to actual persons, living
or dead, events or localities is entirely coincidental.

Typeset in Sabon by Palimpsest Book Production Ltd, Falkirk, Stirlingshire

Printed and Bound in the UK using 100% Renewable Electricity
at CPI Group (UK) Ltd

This book is produced from independently certified FSC™ paper
to ensure responsible forest management.

For more information visit: www.harpercollins.co.uk/green

To my father who has imparted his fascination with history onto me and to my mother who instilled in me the love of a good story.
Thank you.

PROLOGUE

"Did you read the new message on the genealogy site?" Christine, as always, didn't waste time on pleasantries. There was never an introduction. There was no layout of the plot. Christine just jumped right in and expected you to know exactly where she had landed.

"Chris, you literally just told me to check it . . ." Gwen paused to look at her phone ". . . seven minutes ago. And I'm at the grocery store." Gwen pushed her cart down the aisle, searching for the brand of cereal her husband liked. He was very particular, that man. "So, no, I have not checked the message we received." The DNA business had successfully captured her family hook, line, and sinker. Although not right away. Their parents had initially been hugely skeptical of the idea. But Chris had been bound and determined to prove that they had the strong Native American blood that a great-aunt insisted they had. And Chris, being the youngest, was able to sweet-talk their parents out of their saliva the way she'd been able to sweet-talk them into extending her curfew by an hour when they'd been younger.

It turned out that they had almost no Native American blood. Their father had loudly denounced the whole thing . . . until they got a message from someone—a distant relative—who had spent years researching their family line. It was amazing how knowing where your last name came from or knowing which plantation your ancestors had worked on, or learning how your family had moved from one part of America to the other changed how you looked at things.

Gwen's day job was in her father's accounting firm, but she filled her free time soaking in history. She'd taken over the running of the genealogy site while Chris bombarded older relatives for their DNA. They'd managed to create quite the picture of their family tree. But that was some years ago. Now, they rarely came across information that they didn't already know. If Chris said the message was worth reading, it was worth reading. And Gwen would read it when she got home.

"It'll take like five minutes to check it. I'm about to send a text to the family group chat."

"Chris. Chris!" But her sister had already hung up.

"This girl," Gwen muttered through gritted teeth as she tried to pull up the website on her phone. The grocery store did not have the best Wi-Fi. The page began to load slowly, one section appearing at a time. Gwen restlessly hummed to the Eighties song playing over the store's speakers about girls just wanting to have fun. Staring hard at the screen, and mentally willing it to move faster, she leaned over the grocery cart as a spike of anxiety ran through her. Waiting always made her feel like she'd returned to the dark ages of dial-up.

Her phone flashed a notice. Chris had sent a message to their family. Two seconds later, one of their cousins responded. Then another. And another.

"Come on, come on," Gwen whispered to her phone. More notices appeared across her screen. One of her uncles responded. This particular uncle never texted. "Must you be so slow!"

Another person in the cereal aisle glanced at her. Gwen smiled and shook her phone in explanation. Her phone dinged. More messages.

And then the page loaded. Gwen scrolled to the most recent note they'd received.

Dear Christine,

This is going to seem like a very strange message, but please bear with me. My name is Ange Marie Preston, and I live in Aix-en-Provence, France. My grandfather died some years back, and it's taken me a while to go through his things. You see, my grandfather was a photographer. And a storyteller. And a Black American. He moved to France in the 1930s, and never left. He has photographed hundreds, if not thousands, of people. It's taken me ages to go through his work.

One of the people he took pictures of was **the** *Josephine Baker. He had the honor of knowing her well for a number of years. I'm sure you know*

3

Josephine worked as a spy to help France in WWII. If my grandfather's stories are to be believed (and I believe them), he was there right alongside her. And he wasn't the only one. In his old age, he would tell us all sorts of stories about fighting against the Germans. But my favorite story was the one he'd tell us about Le Papillon de Nuit, *or as they say in English, the Moth. It took me years to convince him to tell me her real name, but eventually, I learned that she was Elodie Mitchell—who I believe is your grandmother. My grandfather only has one picture of Elodie, and I have attached it here: the front and the back. Josephine Baker is on the left. Elodie is on the right.*

I will be making a trip to Chicago next week for work . . . which is where my grandfather said Le Papillon de Nuit *lived. If you are there or if you have relatives there, I'd love to meet up and tell you the stories I learned of your grandmother from my grandfather.*

À bientôt, Ange Marie

Gwen looked up from her phone, seeing none of the cereal boxes before her. Her phone flashed again. She looked down at it. She now had forty unread text messages from her family. Ignoring them, she opened the attachment Ange Marie had sent. And stared. She played with the screen, making the black and white photo larger. Then she made it smaller. What in the world? She scrolled further down to look at the back of the picture. Written in cursive were the words: Jo Baker and Elly Mitchell, 1940.

It was true. Her grandmother's name had been Elodie Mitchell before she married. And she'd always been called Elly. And the woman in the photo looked just like her. And *Le Papillon de Nuit* was not an altogether unfamiliar name. The hairs on the back of Gwen's arms stood up. Another message flashed across her screen. This time, Gwen clicked on it, opening the family group chat. She scrolled to the top, where Chris had dropped the same photo for everyone to see. Underneath the picture, Chris had written: *The woman on the left is Josephine Baker. Some lady claims the woman on the right is Grandma. Thoughts?*

There is no way that's Grandma. – cousin

Grandma was working it! – cousin

Our saved, sanctified, holy-roller Christian grandmother, a cabaret girl?! Not her. But a very good lookalike. Matter of fact, both women in the picture sort of look alike. – cousin

They don't look alike. Racist. – cousin

That's definitely her! Lmbo – cousin

Who sent you this photo? – uncle

The grandparents met in France, right? Grandpa always said she caught his eye walking in a Paris garden. Perhaps it was a different sort of garden? – cousin

Miz Elly Anne would never! But I tell you . . . these old people and their secrets! – cousin

Who is Josephine Baker? – cousin

Google is free. – cousin

Our grandparents met in France? How did I not know this? Why were black people in France back then anyway? How did they even get there? – cousin

How did you get here? That's what we all want to know. – cousin

It's not her! – cousin

> Are you kidding! The woman standing next to Josephine Baker is an exact replica of Aunt Darcy. Of course it's her! – cousin

> It's her. I have a copy of this photo. – uncle

Gwen's phone rang. Chris. She answered it. "Did you see Uncle Jay's text?"

"Yes."

"It's her," Chris said knowingly. Gwen rolled her eyes. "Grandma knew Josephine Baker. Did you see what she was wearing? Or not wearing, I should say?"

"I saw the picture, Chris." Gwen was still trying to process that the church-going, rule-following, conservative grandmother she knew had once put on an outfit like that and, presumably, performed before an audience.

"We should meet this Ange Marie." Because, yes, most of their family was still in Chicago. "Uncle Jay's been sitting on that photo all this time and saying nothing!" Forget Uncle Jay. Why hadn't Grandma Elly ever said anything? If you'd asked Gwen two minutes ago, she'd have said that there was no topic, no event that she and her grandmother hadn't discussed before her death. They had been that close. Except now she knew that wasn't true. "I just spoke to Dad. He's never seen the photo before, but he said it was her. What do he and his siblings know about the grandparents that we don't? Grandpa never seemed to match Grandma, you know? Except now I'm wondering if maybe he

7

did." Chris paused, taking a deep breath. When she spoke again, it was in a whisper. "Also, the reference to *Le Papillon de Nuit*. Did you see that?"

Pinching the bridge of her nose, Gwen closed her eyes for a second. "Respond to Ange Marie. Tell her we're interested." Gwen wasn't going to pass up this chance to learn about her grandmother. And maybe they could find out why the woman had decided to take this story to her grave.

CHAPTER 1

The man referred to as her husband, made his slow, swaggering walk down the stony pathway along the bank of the river Seine. He always wore a variation of black, her husband, except for the one colorful scarf that would be wrapped loosely around his neck. Sometimes the scarf was a solid color: just midnight blue or a deep forest green. Sometimes the scarf was a lovely array of colors: a veritable sunset. Today, his scarf was gray with hints of gold and silver thread peeking out with every cast of the sun.

Sitting on a bench, tucked under a tree that was steadily losing its leaves, Elodie Mitchell was making slow work of her lemon and lightly sugared crêpe. The ongoing war might be phony, but the rationing was not. Elly watched the man she called husband make his way to their favorite crêperie vendor. Unlike Elly, who preferred to order the same flavored crêpe every week, her husband, who she decided today would be called Jean-Baptiste—she really liked to reach for the hardcore French names—ordered something different every time.

The sound of oars slapping water briefly caught Elly's attention. She watched as a small boat carrying four passengers rowed its way into existence. They were young people—the boys too young for the draft and the girls too young to be worried about the draft. Elly watched them laughing and talking and ostensibly enjoying one another's company. She nibbled on the small thin, lemony pancake and that reminded her that she only had about two minutes left before Jean-Baptiste went on his way, disappearing from her life until this time again next week.

Her husband was tall and very long of leg. He was wearing black trousers and a fitted black and dark-gray checkered coat that tied across his very slim waist and stopped just above his thighs. His dark hat was tilted slightly on his head. She'd never been one to notice men's clothing before she'd 'met' him. What her uncle or her brother or her cousins wore had never held much interest to her. But she always noticed what Jean-Baptiste was wearing. He was a very sharp dresser, her husband. He also spoke fluent French.

Once, he'd been early and he'd beat her to the crêperie. She'd stood in line right behind him and had been pleasantly surprised to hear the bass in his voice. She purely loved a man whose voice was as deep as an ocean. But she'd been even more surprised—and a bit envious—as French rolled off his tongue with ease. He'd spoken so quickly and so effortlessly that she'd only caught a few words. But whatever he'd strung together had set the vendor to laughing. Adrian—for his name had been Adrian that day—had laughed too. He was a happy man, her husband.

She watched now as the vendor handed Jean-Baptiste his crêpe wrapped like an ice cream cone. She was pretty sure it was ham and cheese and egg today. Small movement caught her eye and she watched as several birds no bigger than her hand landed at her feet and danced along the river's edge pecking and poking at things. She checked her watch. Her favorite river taxi would arrive in about twenty minutes. She took another small bite of her crêpe.

"Excuse me?" Elly looked up and a piece of thin pancake caught in her throat. She began coughing. "May I sit here?" Jean-Baptiste asked, pointing at the empty space on the other side of the bench.

She nodded, still coughing. Her eyes were tearing up. *Dear Lord, why now?* She couldn't breathe. She pressed a hand to her chest, coughing some more.

"Here." Jean-Baptiste dangled a handkerchief in front of her face.

"Thank you." The words came out as a whisper. "But I have one." She sounded as though she were about to break down and cry. Lowering the remaining half of her wrapped crêpe onto the bench and after clearing her throat a few times, she reached for her satchel, dug around, and pulled out her own handkerchief. She wiped furiously at her eyes. The first time he'd deigned to speak to her *would* coincide with her very nearly choking to death. What a lovely first impression she was making. Although, she at least looked rather smart in her powder blue reefer coat, hat, and matching pumps.

Face clean, throat clear, she returned her handkerchief to her bag and straightened in her seat. Embarrassment began to slowly fade away as excitement took its place. He was here. Her husband was here, and he was sitting next to her. And he'd spoken to her. She should make the most of this. She should find out his real name and where he was from and why he had left America for France. Because he was American. She'd gathered that much from the few words he'd spoken.

Occasionally, she'd wondered whether he was from one of the African colonies belonging to France, but she'd always leaned toward American because something about the way he moved read familiar. It was nice to be right.

Just as she was mustering up all of her courage to say something debonair, he spoke again. "Young lady?" Elly glanced over, hesitant to look at him full-on because he was beautiful of face. His skin was a few shades darker than her own. His eyes were a brown so deep they resembled black. He had a strong, fierce, determined nose that probably only a few men could carry well. And he was clean-shaven, giving her a view of a pronounced jawline. Once again, she could barely breathe. "You should probably know that I'm significantly older than you."

"I . . . what?"

"Every time I turn down this path, I see you sitting here watching me like a hawk having caught sight of its prey. At my age it's a bit flattering, I'm not going to lie. But, my dear," he said kindly, "you are barking up the wrong tree. I'm probably old enough to be your father."

Elly turned her head, looking straight ahead at the water. She carefully reached for her satchel, placing it in her lap. Her fingers fiddled with the metal clasp. Men. They always ruined the fantasy when they opened their mouths.

"How long have you been in Paris?" he asked, infusing his voice with the gentle patience of a professor or a religious minister of some kind. She felt her cheeks grow warm. Was this a joke?

Still not looking at him, she cleared her throat. "I've been here for nearly five months."

"Oh?" he said in surprise. "What are you here for?"

"School." It was the easiest answer to give. "What are you here for?" she asked politely.

"I've just always liked France. I moved here about thirteen years ago."

Thirteen years ago? She flicked her gaze in his direction. He just didn't seem that old. There was not a gray hair or a wrinkle to be found on his face. She'd put him somewhere in his late twenties at most. She returned to looking at the river. Her shoulders were beginning to hurt from the stiff way she was carrying them.

"School," he said, repeating her answer from earlier. "Do you attend the university just over there?" Would he just go away? Why was he sitting here making this pointless small talk?

"Yes."

"What are you studying?"

"Literature."

"How long will you be here?"

"Not long." God willing, she'd be on the next boat out of this country any day now.

"Because of the end of your studies or the war?" Elly pressed her lips together. *Just leave,* she wanted to say.

"Both." Elly checked her watch. Ten more minutes.

"Where are you from?"

"Chicago."

"I'm originally from New York." Elly frowned. That didn't sound right. She turned and squinted at him. His eyebrows raised in delight and he smiled, revealing white teeth. "I take it you can still hear the accent? I'm from New York by way of Surry, Virginia."

Now that he mentioned it, it was the accent she was hearing. It was very faint, but he drawled his words a bit. And what was that he'd said? Something about barking up the wrong tree. A very southern phrase.

"My wife always said I could never sound like anything other than a Virginian."

His wife! Elly filled her cheeks with air and then released it. He could have just started with that. Or, he could have just never come over here to speak with her in the first place. Ignoring her had always been an option.

Having finished his crêpe, he crumbled the wrapping and then reached into his coat. He pulled out two small pieces of paper and held them out toward her. Reluctantly, very reluctantly, she took them.

"Have you had a chance to see Josephine Baker yet?" She looked down at the first note. Or rather, ticket. "If you haven't had a chance to see a show, you should come tonight. It's the grand finale."

14

Startled, she looked at him.

"Oh. Not with me," he said quickly, lest she get any ideas. "That's just one ticket. For *you*," he stressed, in case she didn't understand. "The second ticket is for another show tonight that takes place right after Jo's. Only come if you feel homesick. And don't worry. This isn't a gimmick. They're real, not fake."

As a matter of fact, she had not seen Josephine Baker perform although the woman was everywhere in Paris. You couldn't walk down a street without seeing her famous silhouette draped over something. When Elly had first arrived in France, seeing Ms. Baker on the stage had been one of her goals. Except she hadn't wanted to go alone. But look, this nice man had given her a ticket to do just that.

"Have you seen any of her shows?"

"No, sir." She added the *sir* since he was so convinced of their age gap.

"Well, Miss . . . what's your name?"

"Elodie Mitchell."

"Miss Mitchell, you shouldn't leave Paris without seeing Jo Baker in action." He said the woman's name as though they were friends.

"You've been to a lot of her shows, have you?" she asked, raising one eyebrow in stark judgment. He hesitated. Body language hadn't worked, her short responses hadn't gotten the job done. It was time to pull out the talent she was famous for. She leaned a half an inch in his direction and lowered her voice conspiratorially. "I hear she dances wearing only bananas as a skirt."

She'd also heard that these days Ms. Baker wore

15

more clothes at her performances and you were quite unlikely to see the revealing bits, but he didn't have to know that.

For the first time since he'd sat down, the man dropped his eyes. "I've been to a lot of her shows, yes. But that's a bit of a misconception. Jo rarely dances in the nude."

"A misconception! I've seen the pictures! The whole world has seen the pictures. Oh," she said, drawing back and placing a delicate hand over her mouth. "Is that how you explain it to your wife? Mr. . . . ?"

"Grant Monterey," he said, his voice slightly cooler than it was before. "And my wife is dead, so I don't think she cares much. It's a *misconception* to believe that she still dances in the nude. She's famous now. She doesn't have to take off her clothes. It's a good show. I thought you might enjoy it. Every time I see you sitting here, you look a bit lost, and you certainly look alone. I was trying to be helpful."

Lost and alone. He was not holding back his punches.

"Mr. Monterey, I'm so glad that I've met you today." At that statement, he reared back, his eyes widening for a second in surprise. "It's been nothing but a real joy. Speaking with you has fulfilled all of my fantasies." At that statement, he made a small noise in the back of his throat. "Oh, forgive me. I forgot—you have no desire to star in any of my daydreams. From here on out, you won't." Elly extended the two tickets toward him. "But I can't accept these. You should give them to someone who really appreciates the gesture."

Grant Monterey did not move to take the tickets. Instead, he folded his arms over his chest, and it was his turn to look out over the water before them. "Which part offended you?"

"All of it." She jabbed him in the arm with his offerings. "Rest assured, Mr. Monterey, I won't ever wait here to see you again."

He released a snort. And then he laughed, and it was such a nice, rich honest laugh that strangely enough she found herself laughing too.

Grant Monterey stood up and collected his trash. "I refuse to take those tickets back. Come to the show. Don't leave Paris without seeing Jo. You'll regret it for the rest of your life if you walk away from this once-in-a-lifetime opportunity. And as for the second show, Miss Mitchell, we've all been a little homesick sometimes." And with that, he turned, tossed his trash into the nearest receptacle, shoved his hands in his pockets, and walked away.

Elly looked down at the pieces of paper in her hand. The first show was at the Casino de Paris starting at eight p.m. It was a very pretty ticket with gold embossing that probably cost a pretty penny in the making. The ticket for the second show did not look to have been printed by any company. If she wasn't mistaken, the information had been written in ink. That show started at eleven p.m. but the address was the same as Casino de Paris except it said 'Door One' written in tiny letters on the side. Very sketchy. What if Grant Monterey was one of those perverts who pretended no interest just so you would lower your boundaries, making it easier for him to attack you?

She pursed her lips. No, he'd seemed very clear about finding her unappealing. She almost tossed the tickets into the trash with the remainder of her very cold crêpe. But for some illogical reason, she jammed them into one of the pockets of her satchel, even though she already knew she wasn't going.

CHAPTER 2

For a variety of reasons, Elly always took the river taxi if she could. She liked to watch the boat cut through the small waves, forming new ones. She liked the cool breeze that sent shivers down her spine every few minutes—and it was cool. Thanksgiving was around the corner. American Thanksgiving, that is. She liked plopping down onto a bench and becoming as silent and small as possible so that she could eavesdrop on conversations she hadn't been invited to. But mostly she liked that it was slow.

Only come if you feel homesick. Deciding against taking a seat, Elly stood next to the railing, eyeing the second ticket again. Homesick. Elly had a very odd relationship with that word. To her mind, homesick had different meanings that all culminated into one conclusion: Elly felt as though she'd been homesick her whole life.

The first time she'd experienced that intense longing for something she could not grasp was after her mother died in childbed trying to bring a third baby into the world. Her mother's death had changed everything and she'd woken up more times than she could count, wishing she could turn back the hand of time. The second time she was introduced to homesickness was right after she'd found her father hanging from the ceiling of their living room. She'd stared up at him, hands fisted at her sides, craving something she couldn't even begin to name.

And now. Now, she was homesick for America. She was tired of hearing French all day. Irritating as Grant Monterey had been, it had felt good to hear English. It had felt good to talk to someone with whom the foundation had already been set. She was tired of having her brain constantly on alert, trying to parcel out different bits as people spoke. She was tired of the sort of rude way the French went about doing things, making her miss the superficial friendliness of her countrymen. She was tired of the stares and constantly feeling like a fish out of water.

She yearned for her uncle and aunt's house that was always filled with people and talk and food. They'd laugh to hear that. She was notorious for hiding in her room whenever guests were visiting. But there were always a lot of guests. That happened when your uncle was a reverend. She missed her brother, Catau, who was always charging into her life with a new idea; her cousins who never finished a conversation but started ten; her uncle's jokes, which weren't that funny; and her aunt's fluttery ways as she moved from one task to the next, the last having never been entirely completed. She missed greens, and sweet potatoes, ham and turkey. She missed red beans and rice and macaroni and cheese. She missed a burger and fries.

Hearing her thoughts, her stomach growled despite having eaten most of the lemon and sugar crêpe fifteen minutes ago. She patted her stomach in understanding. French food, while good, was just not the same.

She looked down at the ticket fluttering in her hand. *Only come if you feel homesick.* Her uncle would argue that there was another sort of homesickness. Six months after she and Catau had moved in with her uncle Minor and her aunt Tabitha, she'd tried to explain to Uncle Minor how she was feeling. It had been late at night when most lights in the house had been turned off and everyone was tucked in their beds. But she had been unable to sleep. Thanks to her father, it had taken her years to find peace in her dreams.

But her uncle studied for his sermons at night, and she'd known she would be able to find him sitting at the kitchen table reading different books and jotting down notes. In a rare moment of vulnerability, she'd tried to describe how she was feeling. It was he who had diagnosed her.

"Sounds like you're homesick to me," Uncle Minor had told her in that airy way of his. "We're, all of us, homesick because earth is not our home. Heaven is." At ten years of age, this answer had been more than a little bit unsatisfactory. She would learn then, as she knew now, that Uncle Minor, God bless his heart, often provided the most disappointing answers to life's hardest questions. Nine times out of ten, Elly just

21

squinted at him in response. Arguing with someone was never her first reaction. She was usually content to just remove herself from the situation and ponder things on her own.

But this time, she pushed back. "Is that why my papa killed himself then? He was longing for heaven?"

Uncle Minor's eyes had narrowed with thought. One thing she loved about her uncle, then and now, was that he took all of her questions very seriously. Even if she didn't care for his answers. "Your father," he had said slowly. And then stopped. "Everyone longs for heaven—for that perfect place where there aren't any more worries. But what keeps you grounded in this place," he'd said, jabbing a finger into the surface of the table, "is doing the thing God has put you on this earth to do. If you can't figure out what that thing is, sometimes you want to go to heaven sooner. So, I guess in his own way, Louis was homesick." He'd said her father's name in that flat American way: Lou-is and not Lou-ie as he'd been called. But then again, Uncle Minor hadn't really known Louis Valcourt. "Find that thing you were created to do, Miz Elly. Then the longing won't be so bad."

That was one conversation Elly held on to with both hands because at the ripe old age of twenty-four, while she still wished she could have one last conversation with Louis Valcourt where she unleashed the fullness of her rage at him, she understood her father now. Sometimes the longing was just that bad.

A sharp wind blew through the boat and Elly lost her grip on the ticket. She lunged across the railing to grab it, but it danced on the air, well above her head, and then sank into the water below. Well, that took care of that. She supposed she would never find out what Mr. Monterey's definition of homesick was.

The water taxi drifted into the eighth arrondissement and Elly exited the boat but not before giving the captain a quick wave. He shook his head in response. The first time she'd ever used his services, he'd lectured her on the importance of knowing French . . . in French. She'd comprehended enough words to understand the general point of his little speech. But her ability to speak French was almost nonexistent. No matter how many French words she knew, under the fierce gaze of someone waiting for a response, her mind's only defense was to shut down, leaving her with words that danced on her tongue but never formed. So, all she'd done was stare wide-eyed and nod every few seconds. And when he'd finished, she'd pointed at herself and said, "*Je suis Américaine.*"

The captain had sighed with deep exasperation, but from that day on he'd tried to be helpful. If ever she had a question about getting around, between her handful of words and his knowledge, she always got to where she needed to be and so she had no problems waiting for whatever boat he was commanding.

Elly carefully made her way down the short, stone path and then climbed the stairs until she was once again at street level. Not too far away, she saw her destination. One could not miss the stars and stripes waving to every passerby that was within walking distance of the U.S. embassy.

Elly crossed the street and headed for the stone building that was relatively new, but built to look like it had been around since the Sun King. Pausing at the wrought iron gate that encircled the embassy, Elly reached into her satchel for her passport before nodding at the military men on duty and walking through the opening.

She supposed it should feel a little bit like home when she walked through the embassy doors and maybe it did. Maybe that was why her shoulders were always a bit tense and she never quite wanted to linger.

"Hello," she called in greeting to the somewhat gray-haired woman at the front desk. Sometimes it was nice not to use *bonjour*. The administrative woman peered at Elly through her glasses.

"I know you."

"Yes, ma'am. I'm Elly Mitchell. I was just here last week. How are you?"

"Listen, Elly, Mr. Passmore will contact you when it's time."

"Yes, ma'am. I was still wondering if I might speak with him?"

"He's a busy man."

"Could you please ask him if he has a moment to talk?" Elly asked politely.

The older woman huffed before reaching for the telephone. "Hello, Mr. Passmore, it's that Elly Mitchell again."

"Please tell him that I've brought cookies."

The woman rolled her eyes. "She says she's brought cookies." There was a pause. "All right." The woman hung up the phone. "He has five minutes to spare."

"Thank you so much! Have a nice day!"

Elly quickly made her way down the marbled floors,

her heels clicking with every step she took. Mr. Passmore's office was on the second floor and so she ascended the nearest staircase, careful not to block anyone's way as they passed her. She ignored the looks of surprise she got. They were always shocked, these Americans, that colored people were also in France.

Elly reached the third door on the right and knocked. "Come in."

"Good afternoon, Mr. Passmore. It's me again, Elodie Mitchell."

Richard Passmore was probably somewhere in his forties. He was tall and thin and had a head full of brown hair with a few streaks of gray. They'd met serendipitously four months ago. Shortly after Elly's arrival in Paris, she decided to make a trip to Versailles. It was an easy train ride, her professor had told her, and on her way back, if she wanted to take in some wonderful views, she should get off a stop early and walk around. A good plan. Except in Elly's newness, she found herself wandering around in circles and getting more and more frustrated with her lack of spoken French. As the sun began dipping below the earth's surface, Elly was still standing in the center of some strange sidewalk and mentally scolding herself for the hundredth time for being spontaneous. Then, she was tapped on the shoulder by Richard.

His first words to her were, 'You look American.' Unbeknownst to him, he'd endeared himself to her in that moment. He walked with her until she finally came across the street that led to the apartment. She learned that he worked in the embassy. His job title was something fancy but he summed it up by describing himself as the transportation man. If she ever wanted to return home and needed assistance, ask for him. She'd nodded politely at the time, thinking they'd probably never meet again. And then France declared war on Germany.

Richard stood up from behind his desk to greet Elly, a rueful smile on his face. "Elodie, how are you?"

"Good." Elly entered his office and closed the door behind her, a bright smile on her face. "Better now that I've seen you."

Richard rolled his eyes. "You promised me cookies."

"Oatmeal cookies with chocolate, not raisins," she said as she pulled the small tin box out of her satchel. Her housemother, fondly known as Madame, and her house-sister, Claire, had been fascinated with the cookies. They had never eaten oatmeal anything before.

"Elodie, you know me so well," Richard said, taking the box from her. He didn't wait. He popped the lid open and shoved a cookie in his mouth. He released a happy moan. "Been dreaming about these," he said, his mouth full. He dropped into his chair. "Sit."

Elly took the seat across from him and looked around the room as he ate another cookie. Richard's office was small but packed full of things. There were filing cabinets, tables, and bookcases. Stacks of paper covered every surface. She turned back to face him. He was eating another cookie. "I just wanted to remind you that, as an American, I think it's time for me to leave this country."

Richard rolled his eyes again. He held up a hand, chewing quickly. "Elodie, I promise you, as I promised you last week and the week before, and the week before

26

that, I will have you on a ship out of this country whether I have to put you on a train to Portugal or fly you to London myself. Every American who wants to leave is going to be able to leave France."

"Every American who *wants* to leave?" Didn't everyone want to get out of here? Why on earth would you stay to be terrorized or killed by the Nazis? Because God bless France, but the Maginot Line was not going to cut it. If they didn't get themselves together, they'd find themselves in the same shoes as Poland.

Richard lifted his hands in surrender. "Not everyone wants to go. I have it on good authority that *the* Josephine Baker has no intentions of returning to the U.S. Believe me, we've asked her." It was the second time within the hour that she'd heard that name.

"Well good for Miss Baker, but this American wants out." Elly straightened in her seat. "You have my address?"

"Yes."

"And Madame's phone number?"

"Yes. I promise I haven't misplaced it. The moment I have a ship available, you will be on it."

Good. That was all she needed to know and the main reason she'd come here. But it was rare that she got to talk politics and she found herself lingering for a second. "They seem to think that Hitler is playing a game. Like this is Russian roulette or something." She thought of Madame and Claire who had bought into the lie of the 'phony war.'

"Tell me about it," Richard said, sounding suddenly exhausted and for a brief moment she wondered what else he did in the embassy besides getting Americans out of France. "I can tell you this much, we believe that when Hitler turns his attention to France, it's going to be nasty." He paused, a very serious expression on his face. "You didn't hear that from me, Elly."

Elly scoffed. "You haven't told me anything I don't know already. Why do you think I'm trying so hard to get out?" With a smile, she stood up. "I think that's been five minutes."

Richard's scowl was fierce. "Ignore that woman downstairs. I swear she's always adding things to my words. You're always a joy, Elodie. I look forward to our chat next week. Please feel free to bring me more cookies."

"Of course."

"I'm also fond of butter cookies."

"Noted." She waved a finger in his direction. "But don't you try and keep me here for my baking."

"I wouldn't dream of it." He stood up and beckoned her to come closer.

She leaned in his direction. "Yes?"

"I make no promises, but I think they'll be the last batch of cookies."

With some pep in her step, Elly left Richard's office. She practically skipped down the stairs. But she didn't leave right away. No, she made a stop at the little post office box. Reaching into her satchel once again, she deposited letters to Uncle Minor and Aunt Tabitha, and to her brother Catau né Albert. Then she wrestled with the large envelope in her bag, which was also known as 'the real reason why she was in France.' She lowered her satchel to the ground, and using both hands, held the envelope up for benediction.

"Lord, let this be the last one," she prayed and then slipped the documents into the slot. She was no longer Catholic, but she still crossed herself.

Giving a generous wave to the woman at the front desk, she left the embassy and hopefully her life as a foreign correspondent.

CHAPTER 3

Deciding to walk back to Madame's apartment, Elly looped her satchel strap over her shoulder, shoved her hands in her coat pockets, and began a slow jaunt through the Jardin des Tuileries. Once a garden that belonged to the palace, the park was large and wide and open and beautiful. When she'd first arrived in Paris, there had been much greenery about the place but now most of the leaves had escaped the trees they'd once resided upon and everything looked just a little bit skeletal. Nevertheless, it was still a lovely sight worth taking and certainly worth capturing. There were a number of painters set up in the garden trying to do just that.

That was one thing Elly liked about France—if the French saw something beautiful, they did something about it. Taking her time, Elly glanced over the shoulder of a few of the artists as they tried to bring the Tuileries to life on paper.

Her mind drifted back to the embassy. Richard would not have told her that her chances of leaving France soon were good unless it was true. That meant her time in Paris was almost at an end. Elly kicked at a rock in her path. This city had been kind to her. It had been everything it promised to be: charming, cultured, historic. And as others had said who had gone before her: safe.

She stopped and, closing her eyes, she inhaled, trying to capture the scent of all that was Paris. A scent she'd hopefully be able to pocket and take back with her to Chicago. As her eyelids fluttered open, she caught sight of a couple kissing on a bench tucked beneath a tree doing its best to hang on to the last of its foliage.

This country was so odd. Who ever heard of kissing in the middle of the day where anyone could see you? And these were not simple pecks on the mouth. These were kisses that taught you things you ought not know. Elly looked away, shaking her head. The first time she'd seen such a thing, she'd had to stop and look around to see if everyone else was seeing what she was seeing. But everyone else hadn't cared.

In her uncle and aunt's house, it had not been unusual for them to show affection in front of Elly and her brother and her cousins. But there had never been full-on kissing—thank God for small favors—and certainly not in front of strangers. And yet, there was something so laissez-faire about it all that after living in Paris for several months it was she who felt strange for not having anyone to kiss publicly while sitting in the garden, or riding on the train, or waiting in line. Ridiculous country.

Twenty minutes later, Elly pulled out her set of keys and unlocked the apartment gates. In the small courtyard, the twin boys who lived above Madame played some form of medieval war game, trying to slash each other with sticks.

"*Bonjour*," she said politely as she passed them. They stopped and giggled as they always did when they saw her. She didn't know if it was because of how she spoke French or because of the sight of her darker skin. Although, Madame and Claire had once told her that when she spoke French, she didn't sound American at all. It was possible they were telling a white lie. Either way, she didn't care.

She climbed the three flights of stairs and opened the door.

"*Bonjour*, Élodie," Claire called out from the living room couch of the Auger home. The large apartment was situated in a rather affluent neighborhood, which didn't match Madame's frugality and need for a constant source of income. Upon their initial meeting, Madame had proudly informed her that the apartment had been in the Auger family since the 1800s, a gift from an aristocrat to his beautiful mistress—her many times great-grandmother. Elly had squinted at that a bit. But her knowledge of French history began at Marie Antoinette and ended sometime around Napoleon so she wasn't going to argue with the woman even though the story didn't quite pass the smell test. It hadn't helped that Claire had rolled her eyes at Madame's story. But no matter how the apartment had come into the hands of the Augers, it was theirs. And they loved it.

"*Bonjour*, Claire. *Comment vas-tu?*"

"Tired, Élodie. Very tired." Claire was a tall, gangly, fifteen-year-old with a massive amount of brown curly hair. She was Madame's only grandchild and had moved into the apartment after her father had been drafted into the army. He was probably at the Maginot Line.

They did not speak French in this apartment. Only English at Madame's request so that Madame could strengthen her grasp of the language and so Claire could continue to learn it. It had not been a hard thing to agree to.

"I don't know why you are so tired," Madame called from the kitchen. "All you did was go to school today. If anyone should be tired, it's me. I went to the market. I washed and hung the clothes. You study."

"*Merci*, Madame," Elly said, taking off her coat and hanging it in the closet. "I could have washed my clothes." Elly always offered, but in the months since she'd lived with Madame, Madame had refused to let her take part in the cleaning. She was getting paid for hosting Elly, let her do her job, the older woman always said. Still, it was disconcerting to let another person wash her underwear. It was even more disconcerting to see said underwear hanging off the clothesline on the balcony, and flapping in the wind like tiny little flags. Aunt Tabitha would have had a heart attack.

"That is a pretty dress you have on, Élodie," Claire told her as she took a seat on the couch across from the girl. The living room of the apartment was spacious and filled with couches and bookcases. There was a piano tucked in the corner and a desk where Claire did most of her schoolwork.

33

"*Merci*, Claire."

"You have boyfriend? You dress for him?" Madame called, teasing. According to Madame, all of society's woes could be cured if everyone found love in another person. Elly had always thought no one was a greater champion of marriage than her aunt Tabitha, but Madame had her beat by a country mile. Although there was a key difference between the women. Aunt Tabitha was always pushing for courtship and marriage. Madame thought Elly needed a good love affair. Two very different things. "No, no, no," Madame said, answering her own question. She appeared in the living room doorway, a spoon in hand and an apron around her waist. "Not boyfriend. Your husband. Today is the day you see him."

A few weeks ago, in a moment of pique and self-pity (and probably after seeing some couple kissing), Elly had informed Madame and Claire that she had finally seen the man she was going to marry just so she could stop being asked whether or not she was trying on purpose to die miserable and alone. She had told them that she saw him every Friday after she got out of her last class.

"*Oui*," Elly said, nodding. "Today, I saw my husband."

"Was he still handsome?" Claire asked, a grin on her face. She was very much amused by Elly's story. "Did you talk to him, finally?"

"Yes and yes."

Madame whooped. And Claire clapped her hands. "What he say?" Claire asked, missing a verb in her haste.

"What he do for job?"

"Did he ask you to go . . . uh . . . somewhere? To meet him?"

He'd told her he wasn't remotely interested in her as a woman. "I don't know what he does for a living." She hesitated. If she told them about the invitation to Josephine Baker's show, they would insist that she go. And she didn't want to go. But, Madame and Claire had been so kind to her.

When Madame had discovered that Elly liked raspberries, she purchased some every time she went to the market until the season changed. Madame had baked Elly a cake for her birthday—an absolutely terrible cake that Elly had had to choke down but Elly still had been very much touched by the gesture. Knowing Elly was in Paris to study literature, Madame regularly went out of her way to bring books home for Elly to read. One of the few lessons Elly remembered learning at her mother's side was to always reciprocate kindness—especially if it cost you nothing. The least Elly could do was pretend to have a date, dress up, and attend the show if it made them happy. She made her voice playful and light. "He gave me a ticket to see Josephine Baker tonight."

Claire and Madame looked at each other and oohed dramatically. For the most part, French people were not particularly kind or welcoming to strangers. But once they got to know you, and you them, there was no one who supported you more.

"What time?"

"Eight tonight."

"You are going to have so much fun!" Claire

exclaimed. Then she leaned forward. "You should wear that dress."

"Oh, yes, wear the dress," Madame agreed.

Months ago, Elly had shared with Madame and Claire her desire to buy a fancy, eye-catching gown for her cousin's wedding that was taking place around Christmas. It had taken a while with the three of them going from store to store but eventually they'd found the perfect thing. But, why not wear it tonight? "Yes," Elly said, nodding. "I'll wear the dress."

And that's how several hours later, Elly found herself in a pale pink and silver dress that had only thin straps to hold it up. The bodice was fitted, mimicking a corset and showing off the tiny waist she'd worked so hard to achieve. There was a bit of ruching just under the waist and then the dress fell loose and long. She'd have to be mindful of the skirt so that she didn't step on it. Not having time to curl her hair, she pulled it up into a neat bun.

"Here," Madame said, entering her room with a thin box. "You need a necklace."

"Oh, Madame, I have one," Elly said, slipping another pin into her chignon to ensure it was secure.

"No, no, no. You need something that brings you, um, *bonne chance*."

"Good luck?" Elly wrinkled her nose. She didn't believe in luck.

Seeing the look on her face, Madame took a step forward. "Not just any luck. This is Sophie's necklace given to her by the *duc*. It will bring you great love and good fortune. Lower your arm, Élodie."

Great love and good fortune? How was being a

36

mistress any of those things? Nevertheless, Elly obeyed, allowing the older woman to slip the necklace around her neck. Elly saw it in the mirror. It was a pearl and diamond choker with several loose charms dangling from it. "Madame," Elly said, bringing her hands to her throat. "It's too much. I'll get robbed."

"You will not get robbed! Wear it. It needs to be brushed off and worn every few years. It won't be worn again until Claire's wedding day in ten years," Madame said, tossing a look at Claire who sat silently on Elly's bed, watching Elly get ready.

Claire's eyebrows lowered. "Ten years? Did I not send you the invitation? The wedding is in ten days. Élodie is just warming it up for me."

"Ha!" Madame said as she finished fiddling with the clasp. She patted Elly's shoulder. "Turn around, let's see you."

Before Elly obeyed, she took a minute to stare at her reflection in the mirror and she loved what she saw. She'd bought this dress, pricey as it was, because of the feeling it had evoked in the changing room. The same feeling she had now. The one that said that she was beautiful and debonair, and she could charm any man in the room. Even if such a thing had never happened before. But more than that, she liked that the dress seemed to raise more questions about her than answers.

Years ago, one of her female cousins had brought home a questionnaire that, when answered, told a woman just how courtship-able she was. Elly had failed that test spectacularly. She was too forthright, too honest, she demanded too much of a man. And more than that she was not mysterious. She would never be able to hold a man's attention long enough for a marriage proposal. She and her cousins had laughed at her results. But when they'd left, she'd taken that sheet of paper, ripped it into tiny pieces, started a fire in the fireplace, and then watched them burn.

"*Très belle*, Élodie. *Très belle*. It's a very good color for your skin."

It was. Pink was sometimes too light, making her look a bit pallid. But this shade with that hint of silver was just right.

"Your husband will be pleased?"

She didn't even know if Grant would be there. But she hoped that he was, if only so he could see her in this outfit and know what it was he had dismissed so easily. "I think he will be. Looking this good, he won't be the only man pleased." All three of them laughed. But several hours from now, Elly would realize with regret just how true that statement was.

CHAPTER 4

The taxi pulled up slowly in front of the theater. The Casino de Paris held that broad stone facade that indicated that the space was a lot larger on the inside than it appeared on the outside. In the very center was a semicircle of glass windows and above that were stone statues of either angels or gargoyles. Elly couldn't tell which in the dim light of the evening but having toured Paris for the past five months, figured it was probably the latter.

The words *Casino de Paris* flashed brilliantly against the dark of the evening and gathered outside the doors were men and women dressed in their best and ready to see *the* Josephine Baker in action. She was most definitely in the right place.

But then a wave of uncertainty hit her. What if for Grant Monterey this was all a lark and the ticket he had given her was fake despite his reassurances otherwise? What if she had dressed up for nothing? Squashing her doubts, Elly paid the taxi driver and climbed out of the car. She might be arriving solo but at least she fit the part. She had draped her long, black coat over her shoulders and added her white evening gloves to her ensemble. She thought she looked rather Hollywood herself. Reaching into her small purse, she pulled out the ticket Grant had given her and she entered the foyer, which was packed to the brim with people talking and laughing and purchasing drinks at the bars that were set up.

The place was resplendent with thick carpet and high chandeliers. And everywhere Elly turned she saw different advertisements of Josephine Baker—the same ones she often saw at the train station or on the street.

There was Josephine and her leopard, Chiquita; Josephine in a green outfit with large green plumes extended everywhere. Josephine here and Josephine there. It was all rather exciting. Seeing a man dressed in the uniform of an usher, Elly approached him. "*Pardon*," she said to get his attention. She flashed her ticket. "*où est . . .*"

The usher's eyes went wide at the sight of her and then he stared down at the words on the ticket. "*Avez-vous famille de Joséphine?*"

"No," Elly said quickly. This man was not the first and he probably would not be the last to link her to Josephine Baker. She had had to, on more than one occasion, explain to different strangers on the street that no, she was not Josephine Baker and no, they were not related. Elly knew it had everything to do with the fact that she was a colored woman and less to do with the fact that they looked alike. Because they did not look alike. "No," she repeated. "*Est-ce que vous—*"

The usher interrupted her, saying something very rapidly in French. Something like she had an excellent seat. A seat for family. "*Pas famille de Joséphine. Je suis* stranger." Elly said the last word in flat-out mid-western English. Patting her chest, she repeated it. "Stranger. No *famille.*"

The usher snatched the ticket out of her hand, turned, and flagged someone else down. This man was wearing a black suit, most likely a supervisor of some sort. The usher pointed to Elly and then flashed her ticket. Was it just because she was colored? Or was there something odd about the ticket? The other man took one look at Elly and bowed in her direction. She swallowed a sigh. "*Pas de famille!*"

"*S'il vous plaît, mademoiselle,*" the supervisor began. He plucked her ticket from the usher and waved her forward. Not sure what else to do but follow, Elly lifted her skirt and did just that.

Along the way, people began stopping mid-conversation or mid-walk and Elly found herself collecting stares like some children collected stamps. She knew that because of the way she was dressed they were trying to make a connection between her and the famous singer. If only they knew more colored women, it would be obvious that the two of them looked nothing alike.

The man she was following opened one of the doors into the theater itself and despite there being people inside, there was a reverent hush as though one were entering a sanctuary. Elly paused in the doorway absorbing the rows and rows of plush seats and the wide stage up ahead that was already set up for the evening's show. "*S'il vous plaît, mademoiselle*," the man repeated when he realized that she'd stopped.

"*Désolée*," she whispered and picked up her pace. He led her down, down, down and she began to understand why they had assumed she was family. Grant Monterey had not only given her a real, legitimate ticket, but one of the best seats in the house. Such a good husband he was!

The man came to a stop next to the third row. As he returned her ticket, Elly caught a brief glimpse of the orchestra below. "Mademoiselle?" She listened as the man asked whether she wanted something to drink.

"No, *merci*." Elly crossed the seats until she found hers and then sat down. She was excited. Why had she never come before? How many people had praised Josephine Baker's shows? When Ms. Baker had last toured in America, Uncle Minor's brother had paid an extravagant sum to see her show in New York. He had declared afterwards that he'd heard better singing on Easter Sunday and seen better dancing at the juke joint down the street. Perhaps with those words lingering in the back of Elly's mind, she'd felt less inclined to make an effort. But she was glad she was here now.

Fifteen minutes later, the lights in the theater dimmed and the stage lit up. And Elly Mitchell saw in person the wonder that was Josephine Baker. Uncle Minor's brother wasn't wrong. Having been raised by Aunt Tabitha who could sing the house down on Sunday morning, Elly thought that Josephine's voice was reedy and thin in comparison. If she'd ever been in a church choir, no one would pick her to sing the solo. She also did that strange vibrato thing white women did when they sang ... much like Judy Garland in *The Wizard of Oz*. Her dancing, while not bad, was not on the same level as what Elly had seen back in Chicago. A lot of it was just cleverly placed bodily movement and shaking: shaking her hips, her chest, and her backside to the beat. It fed into that whole exotic African picture she liked to paint; the same one white people lapped up like puppies. As one of her cousins had once bitterly said, everyone liked to look at the monkey in the zoo.

And yet, there was something so captivating about the woman that Elly was mesmerized by every sequence on stage, and wishing for more by the end of it. Maybe Josephine Baker wasn't the best at singing or dancing or acting or whatever but she was an entertainer and sometimes that was far more potent than any one talent. As the final curtain went down, Elly very happily stood to her feet to clap with the other audience members. And she clapped even louder when for a split second it looked as though the woman smiled in her direction.

Good for her, Elly was thinking, as she made the slow walk up the aisle and to the doors. The woman had probably worked very hard to get where she was. And her French! Elly was pea green with envy. Madame had once told Elly that being French was not a race or a religion, it was a lifestyle. Whatever that lifestyle was, Josephine Baker had it in spades.

Finally reaching the foyer, Elly lingered for a moment.

She felt wide awake and grateful to be alive in the way one always felt after coming across something spectacular. She wasn't ready to return to Madame's apartment and she wished she had come with someone so that they could unpack the show together over coffee and sweets. What a real shame that she had lost that second ticket Grant had given her. She really could see another show. Quite frankly she felt like she could go somewhere and dance herself. And that was when the thought hit her. Maybe she could find somewhere to purchase a ticket to the second show?

Door one at the Casino de Paris, it had said. Looking around the foyer, Elly tried seeing whether any of the doors had numbers on them and that was when she saw a young colored man taking photos. Elly quickly crossed the distance separating them. Coming to a stop directly in front of him, she said, "Hello."

The young man, who had been fiddling with the buttons on his camera, looked up in surprise. Then he saw her and took a step back. A smile lit up his whole face. "Hey!"

Elly's answering grin was wide and nearly hurting—so happy was she to see this stranger and fellow American. She was carrying her coat with one hand and so extended her free one. "Elly Mitchell from Chicago."

"Danny Whitaker from New Jersey." And indeed she could hear that eastern accent. They shook hands like old friends. Looking him over, Elly noted that he was maybe only an inch taller than her. His skin color was a light brown and he was probably her age or a few years younger.

"Do you work here, Danny?" she asked easily. There was an automatic lowering of boundaries whenever Elly ran into one of her fellow countrymen. But, there was something about Danny that felt familiar.

"Yes, ma'am. Photographer," he said, holding up the camera. "You came for the show?"

"Yes. It was wonderful! I actually got my ticket from a man on the street. A colored man," she clarified. "He gave me two tickets and the second one was for a show at eleven p.m. in Door One. Do you by any chance know where that is?"

Danny's grin was rueful and filled with knowledge she didn't have. "Was that colored man walking around in all black, lookin' like the very angel of darkness?"

Actually, she thought Grant looked more like God's gift to the world, but she said, "Yes."

"Grant Monterey?"

"Yes! You know him?"

"Uh-huh," Danny said, nodding. "Don't worry. Giving out tickets to shows is his thing."

"Well, he gave me two tickets and I lost the ticket to the second performance. Do you know—"

She stopped talking as Danny shook his head. "You didn't lose it."

"Yes, I did."

"You have the ticket."

"No," she said slowly. "I was on a boat, you see, and the ticket escaped my hand and landed in the water."

Danny laughed and then tapped a finger against the back of her hand. "This is your ticket, Elly." She looked down at where he had touched her. Then he touched the back of his own hand. And she understood. "Second show doesn't cost a dime to get into. Let me finish up here. I'm going to the same place as you, ma'am. I'll escort you there myself."

"Thank you, Danny. And you don't have to call me ma'am."

"*Pardon*," a well-dressed man said, approaching them. "Mademoiselle Baker?"

"No!" Elly said emphatically while Danny frowned.

Wagging a finger in her direction, in perfect French, Danny told the man she was not Josephine Baker. The man didn't look like he quite believed either of them but did walk away.

"He literally just saw the woman on stage."

"You get that a lot, don't you?" Danny asked, thoroughly amused.

"Yes!"

"You don't look anything like her."

"Agreed!"

"I mean you have the same skin color and maybe you're the same height. But that's it."

"Exactly!"

"You realize that means they think they've seen you naked." Elly's brain stuttered for a second. Danny lifted the camera to his face. "At least they think you look good."

A half hour later, Elly followed Danny to a small closet of a room where he put his photography equipment away. Then he led her outside the Casino de Paris, around the corner, and down an alley. In Chicago, there was no way on God's green earth that she'd follow a man she'd just met down an alley. In

Paris, she trusted Danny from New Jersey not to do her wrong.

"I never would have found this," she muttered as he stopped in front of a door that held the sign: *Door One*.

"Presumably you would have asked one of the ushers in the theater. They know Door Number One," Danny said before raising a fist and knocking.

Another colored man opened it from the other side. "Danny! Where you been?"

"Working. And look what I found?" He waved toward Elly. "Another one of Grant's coins."

Elly looked sharply at Danny but the other man laughed. "Grant be findin' 'em. I swear he's like the Pied Piper of black folks. Come on in, girl. What you waitin' on?"

The second show was not in a theater but rather in a large storage room that was filled with colored Americans. Some were standing, gathered in little pockets discussing the war with great intensity. Others were sitting in the chairs that were set up along the walls of the space, waiting for whatever was coming next.

Elly was easily the most overdressed person in the room and probably the only person who had attended the show nearly an hour ago. She noticed that a few people looked like they'd rolled out of bed just to be here and others who appeared as though they'd just finished a shift on a job. Most were men, which was unsurprising. But she heard accents from all over: southern, northern, eastern, Midwest, and Texas.

A door opened at the very back of the room and

men walked in, instruments in tow. And that's when she saw him: Grant Monterey. He was wearing black pants and a white shirt. He'd removed his suit jacket so his suspenders were visible and he'd rolled up his sleeves. It was the first time she'd ever seen him outside of his usual uniform. In his hand was a guitar.

"He's in the orchestra," Danny explained as he motioned for her to sit in one of the empty chairs. Elly complied and Danny took a seat next to her. "Plays one of the horns in the pit."

"Shut up and sit down," one of the musicians yelled across the room. Dressed the same as Grant, he was equally tall, but probably considered classically more handsome because his skin was very light and his hair was curly.

"That's Grant's . . . hmm . . . how to describe him? Cousin? Brother? Pick one. His name is Pierre Roche. And no, he was not born with that name. You listen to him talk long enough and you'll realize he's from Harlem. But good luck trying to guess what his mama named him. He guards that information like it's the Holy Grail. Polly doesn't even know and she shares his bed." Elly looked at Danny out of the corner of her eye. He was a bit indelicate . . . like Catau when he hadn't gotten enough sleep. She'd have to be careful with what she said to him.

"I said hush so we can get to it!" Pierre yelled out.

"That's the same thing yo mama told me last night!"

Pierre twisted the banjo in his hand and lifted it like a bat. "Boy, don't make me come over there and whip your tail. I'd say like your daddy used to but we all know you ain't got one."

There was hooting and laughter and Elly found herself grinning.

"If we could get started," Grant drawled, his southern accent stronger than when he'd introduced himself to her earlier that day.

Still standing, Pierre began strumming the banjo and Grant joined in with the guitar and behind them was a fiddle, drums, and a few horns. This was not the showy jazz that these men had played only an hour before. This was the kind of music that called to everyone in the room, reminding them of a shared history they all tried to forget but could not escape from.

'The Ballad of John Henry' began to fill the room and Pierre's voice rang out beautiful and rich and carrying all the weight of the legendary man himself. When the song was over, the music switched to a fast and up-tempo version of 'Swing Low, Sweet Chariot.' It being a call and response song, it was clear everyone was expected to sing and clap and tap their feet to the beat. Then the music changed again. This time to the blues.

There was no rhyme or reason to this concert. Just whatever the musicians felt in the mood to play. More than once, Elly closed her eyes, momentarily returned to Valcourt, Louisiana, where she'd spent the first ten years of her life as Elodie Valcourt, daughter of the Creole Valcourts who tried so hard to keep up with the white Valcourts.

When 'Dream a Little Dream of Me' began to play, Elly opened her eyes just in time to see Josephine Baker herself enter the room.

CHAPTER 5

"Stars shining bright above you," Josephine sang, immediately stealing the limelight. She was no longer decked out in sparkles and tassels, but instead was wearing the sort of gown any woman would wear on the street. "Night breezes . . ."

She sang differently back here, in this room. Her voice was still not as strong or commanding as Elly could have easily heard on any given Sunday but it no longer held that vibrato she'd sung with earlier. No, this time her singing was smooth and silky, gently caressing each word as she made a slow turn around the room, greeting everyone who had come using just a glance of her eyes.

Josephine Baker moved with the grace of a woman who had clearly been dancing all of her life. Every step she took, her hips swayed languidly to the beat. All eyes were on her as she sang the entire song. There was thunderous applause when she finished.

"I hope you don't mind me interrupting," Josephine told everyone there. "But when Grant said he'd decided on holding a little concert, I had to come by and say hi." Elly wasn't sure how she expected Josephine to sound when she talked, but her voice was light and airy and she had a way of holding on to a word a second too long as though she could break out into song at any minute. What she didn't sound like was St. Louis, which was where Elly knew she was originally from.

"Glad to have you, Jo," someone yelled from the crowd.

"George, is that you? I haven't seen you for ages." Elly guessed she'd had speech lessons. Or she'd purposely trained herself to lose her accent . . . like Elly had.

Taking her words as a good excuse to either conclude the concert or have an intermission, the musicians lowered their instruments and began talking. Elly watched the famous star glide across the room. Every step was measured, every motion deliberate. Did she ever turn it off? Elly wondered. Did the woman ever just decide that for one day she wasn't going to be glamorous? And then Josephine Baker was in front of her.

"Hello! I don't think I've ever seen you before?"

Elly swiftly stood up. "Oh, no, it's my first time being here. It's a pleasure to meet you, Ms. Baker. I was fortunate enough to see your show earlier and you were fabulous." The words exited Elly's mouth with a tremor. She was unusually nervous. And yet, Elly still found herself assessing the woman, particularly because of the comments from earlier. They *were* the same height and had the same skin color but that was where all resemblance ended. Josephine Baker was more slender than Elly. They had differently shaped features. Elly had longer hair and it wasn't permed so there were always flyaway strands escaping her pins—unlike Josephine's hair, which was perfectly arranged and contained. Josephine looked as though she were perpetually happy. Elly knew for a fact that she went through life looking perpetually annoyed.

"Thank you! Now, you must tell me your name!" Josephine reached for her hand, meeting her eyes as though the only thing she wanted in the whole world was to know Elly's name. It was disconcerting because now the only thing in the whole world Elly wanted was to leave a good impression on this woman.

"Elodie Mitchell."

"Élodie? How French!"

"Yes," Elly said with a quick smile. "I'm from Chicago."

"I know Chicago! I had the pleasure of performing there a few times in my early days." Josephine shivered. "Cold place. The wind can cut like a knife."

"Yes, it's not that far from St. Louis," Elly said, eager to impress Josephine with her knowledge of her, limited though it was.

"No, it's not," Josephine said with a shake of her head. As though old friends, she brought a hand to Elly's arm. "What brought you here to Paris? Are you a dancer? You move with such grace." *She* moved with such grace? And Elly was suddenly reminded of the dreaded ballet classes Ma Mère had forced her to take as a girl where she'd never been good enough and she'd been constantly ridiculed because she'd been the darkest in the room. Maybe she'd acquired some gracefulness from them after all.

"No, ma'am."

"Ma'am! Is that what I am these days?"

"I . . . just . . . well . . . you don't look like a ma'am," Elly said quickly. "But I like to play it safe." Elly felt a rush of embarrassment wash over her. But she'd been raised where anyone older than you was a ma'am or a sir and beware if you failed to address someone correctly. As youthful as Josephine Baker appeared, she was also about ten years older than Elly.

"I'd say you like to live dangerously." Josephine winked. "But I'm just teasing you!"

"I'm here for school," Elly said, returning to the original question. "I'm working on my second master's degree. This one in French literature."

"Wow!" Josephine straightened, looking thunder-struck. Then she took a step toward Elly, closing the gap between them. She placed her other hand on Elly's other arm. And Elly did not move even though every single nerve in her body was tingling. *The* Josephine Baker was touching her. And looking incredibly impressed by her. Just wait until she told her brother about this. "Just wow. And I really mean that. Very good for you, Elodie. That's something to be proud of."

"Thank you, Miss Baker, but it's certainly nothing compared to all that you have accomplished."

Josephine waved a hand. "Just call me Jo. And they're two different fields entirely. I'm honored you came to my show. I so like to meet the smart ones," she said with a laugh that made Elly want to laugh too. "Congrats again to you, my dear." She patted Elly's arm and moved on to the next person.

Elly reached for her purse simply to have something to do. She was trembling. How ridiculous. Josephine Baker put her pants on one leg at a time the same as everyone else. And yet she still could not squash the bubble of excitement that rose within her. She had met Josephine Baker! They had actually conversed! Just wait until she got back to her room. Her next letter home was going to be very long.

"Well, look who made it." Elly glanced up to see Grant Monterey standing just a few feet away from her, his arms folded across his chest.

"Thank you, Mr. Monterey. I've had a wonderful evening." He might not have fulfilled her personal fantasies but he'd more than made up for that.

He smiled, looking a bit pleased with himself. "Grant's fine, Elodie, and I'm glad this was worth coming to."

The handsome man called Pierre appeared at Grant's side, unlit cigarette in hand. "Is this the little girl you found wandering lost around Paris?"

Elly glanced over at Grant whose attention was briefly caught by someone else. There was that word again: lost. And she might be young but she was no little girl. If he was trying to remind her that he was not interested in her, he was doing a fabulous job.

"She's not quite so little," Pierre continued, his voice

languid and his eyes a bit hooded. At first glance, Pierre seemed like a mulatto, and it was possible he was, but there was something about him that made her think that both of his parents were probably just fair-skinned. Pierre's whiskey-colored eyes looked her up and down in a very slow, methodical way that left Elly feeling like somehow he'd seen everything.

When their gazes collided, she raised one unamused eyebrow. He grinned, more challenged, then chastened. Elly watched him reach not into his pocket but into Grant's shirt pocket for a lighter. Grant's expression darkened but he didn't say anything. How had Danny described them? Not as friends but as family. "You might need to get your eyes checked again, old man. It's not just reading glasses you should be carrying." Pierre lit his cigarette and lifted his chin in her direction before handing the lighter back to Grant. "Pierre Roche."

What had Danny said? This man was living with a made-up name. Not surprising. Everything about him seemed staged and Elly didn't care one bit if her judgment of Pierre Roche was harsh. "Elodie Mitchell."

"What brought you to Paris, Miss Mitchell?"

Not particularly in the mood to entertain Pierre Roche, she said, "Can't you tell? I'm French."

Pierre's grin was slow. "Is that so?"

"*Oui.*" There was an element of truth there. It *was* the reason she'd picked France over all the other countries in Europe—not that she'd ever have picked Germany. But she'd been heavily influenced by her own ancestry; by the town she'd been born in where a statue of her many times great-grandfather had been erected.

The grandfather who had been born and raised in France but later lived and fought the British in Acadia. After losing, he was summarily exiled to what was now known as Louisiana. The same grandfather then decided to join the slave-owning community of the South, which led unsurprisingly to the creation of colored Valcourts who passed down sprinkled French like salt onto every generation that followed.

The first ten years of Elly's life had been filled with bits and pieces of French everywhere. French was lullabies and food and names and swear words. It was history and pain and love and bitterness. It was her father, Louis Valcourt, who had held on to his past with both hands until he simply could not hold it anymore.

"I'm French too," Pierre said solemnly, his eyes dancing with laughter.

"We all are." Grant rolled his eyes.

"Look, Grant, one of your lost pennies turned up," Danny said, popping up from nowhere. He'd wandered off after Josephine finished singing. Danny turned toward Elly. "Don't worry, you're not the only one. There's Mark over there. Nancy and Sarah. Will and James." One of the men he'd named heard Danny.

"What did you say, Danny?"

"I said, Grant has a way of finding us in this country."

"What would we do without Uncle Grant?"

"We love you, Uncle Grant!" several others cried out.

"Well, I don't love you!" Grant called over his shoulder, sounding stern . . . and much older than

56

everyone. He hadn't been lying. He probably had more than a few years on her. He was just one of those men who was blessed with a young face.

Everyone in the room laughed at his comment, not believing his words for a second.

Slinging an arm around Grant's shoulder, Pierre whispered, his voice heavy with emotion, "You collect us."

"Oh, shut up, Pierre," Grant said, reluctantly laughing as he shrugged off Pierre's arm.

Elly was proud that she felt only mild disappointment upon realizing that she was not, in fact, special. With a small sigh she released her infatuation with the man. Pierre eyed her. "You didn't say why you're here."

Feeling slightly exasperated, Elly said, "Have you heard of the cousins who traveled to Europe writing articles for the *Chicago Defender*?"

To the average person, this question would have been strange and random. But not to an American Negro. There were two colored papers that most of them read, no matter where they were in the world: the *Chicago Defender* and the *Philadelphia Courier*.

"That's one of the reasons I came here!" Danny said, jittery with excitement. "They loved it here in France." About six years ago, the *Chicago Defender* paid for two young colored women—cousins—to travel across Europe and write about their experiences so that Negroes could know what it was like to be abroad. The articles had been massive hits. The girls had loved France. They'd even enjoyed a Josephine Baker show.

"You're a journalist?" Grant asked, tilting his head

as he eyed her. "I thought you were here to study?" *Ha*, she wanted to say. *I'm more complicated than you think. I am mysterious.*

"I write about my time in France as a student."

"A student," Grant repeated slowly as he tapped a finger against his chin. She also wrote about the international mess that was Europe, but that was a tale for another day.

"It's to encourage study abroad."

"Bad time to study abroad," Pierre murmured.

"Yes, well there was a bit more hope a few months ago. This evening will make for a very nice write-up." She'd draft the article when she was finally aboard the ship taking her home.

"You're lucky. This was our last shindig," Grant told her.

"We keep getting smaller and smaller," Pierre said. "Folks are returning to the States."

"Then, I'm really glad I came. Thank you, again, Grant."

Grant dipped his head. "You're very welcome, Elodie."

"Elly, please."

They exchanged a few more words and brief nods and then Pierre and Grant drifted off in the direction of their instruments. Elly imagined that they were even more tired than she was. She eyed them one last time knowing she'd probably never see them again. Reaching for her coat and purse, she looked at her watch. It was getting late and she'd already seen several people gathering their things and leaving. The makeshift concert was over.

And then suddenly, the door Josephine had appeared through banged open and a young woman stood in the entrance. "Where's Jo?"

Everyone looked around the room for the woman.

"She's gone." One of the musicians pointed to the exit. "Saw her slip out about two minutes ago."

The young woman ran to the door, flung it open, and ran outside.

"Poor Polly," someone muttered. "Always trying to wrangle Jo to the next thing. I do not envy her that job."

"Is that Pierre's girlfriend?" Elly asked Danny. Polly was a very pretty girl with curves in all the right places and still somehow holding on to the tiniest of waists. She could see why a man like Pierre would be interested in her.

"Pierre doesn't do labels." Danny leaned in close. "I'm going to be him when I grow up."

Elly wrinkled her nose. Just like Catau, admiring the wrong people in life. "Why?"

Danny laughed, completely unbothered. "I'm going to be like him *and* like Jo. I want her fame and his joie de vivre."

"Not Grant?"

Danny shuddered. "No." He paused. "Maybe when I'm like fifty and even then I hope life is more exciting than whatever it is he's doing. The happiest I've ever seen him is when he spots his favorite vendor at the farmers' market. Thanks, but no thanks."

"How old are you?" Yes, it was her little brother he reminded her of with that hopeful naiveté that rested in his eyes and that sort of eau de everything-will-work-out-right scent that surrounded him.

"Twenty."

"Well that explains everything."

"Don't be rude. Do you need me to flag down a cab?" Danny asked Elly as he helped her into her coat.

"Would you please?" He cocked his elbow and Elly slipped her arm through his. "Where do you live?"

Elly told him the address. They'd almost made it to the exit when a very disgruntled Polly appeared, blocking their movements.

"You didn't catch her, Pol?" Danny asked, sounding like he would have been surprised if she had.

"Oh, I caught her," the young woman said, irritation lacing her every word. "Please tell me, how am I going to do this fitting when she's gone? *Paris-London* starts in less than a month and I haven't been able to finish the costumes because she's everywhere except where she needs to be!"

"Don't let this stress you out, Polly. You always pull through."

"Shut up, Danny! I just need her body for fifteen minutes. Fifteen minutes and I'm good as gold."

"She needs a body double," Danny joked. "Someone to handle the small things while she takes care of the big things."

"Yes!" Polly said, reluctant amusement creeping in her eyes. "Someone this height." She lifted a hand, stopping somewhere around the top of Elly's head. "And this wide," she created a space between her hands. "And I'd be good."

"Oh. So you mean someone like Elly," Danny quipped, and then lightly nudged Elly's side. And then he stopped laughing and Polly stopped grinning, and Elly knew before either of them opened their mouths that they thought they'd found the solution to their problem.

CHAPTER 6

Elly held her hands up in protest. "I don't think—"

"What's your name?" Polly demanded, peering at Elly as if she hadn't really looked at her before.

"This is Elly Mitchell," Danny said, answering for her. "From Chicago."

Polly touched a finger to her lips. "Move, Daniel."

Danny dropped his arm and took a step away from Elly while Polly began a slow walk around her.

"It's pretty late. I should probably get home." With longing, Elly watched as several people slipped past them and exited the building.

"Ten minutes," Polly said, holding up both hands. "Just give me ten minutes. Please."

"We're not really the same shape."

"You aren't. But you're the same height and that'll get me started. Please. I beg of you."

Put that way, Elly didn't see how she could say no.

And she'd get to see what the Casino de Paris looked like behind the scenes.

"All right," Elly said, hesitantly. She barely got the word out before Polly grabbed her arm in a tight grip.

"Wait down here, Danny," Polly ordered. "We won't be long." Elly almost lost her balance as Polly dragged her quickly to the door she'd come through. Polly released Elly long enough to open the door and then grabbed her again as though afraid Elly might take off and run in the opposite direction.

"How long have you worked with Ms. Baker?" Elly asked, breathless and feeling like they were about to start jogging any second now.

"Years and years. You'd think I'd be used to this by now but it drives me crazy every time." Polly let her go as they climbed a set of stairs.

"Where are we?"

"Behind the theater." And indeed, around them, doors were opening and shutting and people were moving about carrying things and going places. "Just down this hall," Polly told her.

Elly followed but then stopped when she got a whiff of something less than pleasant.

"You smell it, don't you?"

"I smell something."

"It's her zoo."

"Her what?"

"Jo's zoo."

The scent got stronger as they got closer. Polly stopped in front of a door but pointed a finger at a different door several feet away. "There's a pig and a goat, birds, and maybe even a dog or two. I don't know. I avoid the room but you can't avoid the smell."

Pushing open the door in front of her, Polly ushered Elly into a bright pink dressing room. It was filled to the brim with flowers. They were in every corner and crevice possible. "I always ask that Jo's flowers are brought here. The perfume helps cover the scent of whatever is happening in the zoo." Indeed, the room did smell fragrant. But also sour. Because the animal scent was strong.

"Can you change into that dress on the couch? And stand on this?" Polly pushed a small round circular thing into the center of the room.

"I'll need some assistance getting out of this dress," Elly said as she removed her coat.

Polly expertly helped her out of her pink and silver gown and into a long, gold, silk, V-strapped dress that fell past her feet. Then Elly moved to stand on the lifted surface.

"What a beautiful necklace you have on. It's one of those pieces that will go with anything."

"It's on loan," Elly admitted, fingering the shiny charms on Madame's choker.

"Then that's a good friend you've got. I know what you're thinking," Polly said as she retrieved measuring tape. "If I've known Jo for years, what do I need you for? Well, I've got to make sure it falls perfectly, don't I? And that's much easier to do with a body in a dress rather than out of it. If I have to take it up a few inches, I'd like to know now and not ten minutes before her next show."

While Polly hummed and measured, Elly took in the

mirrored dressing table in the corner of the room that held all sorts of bottles and powders, jewelry and fans, and combs and hair pieces. There was a record player next to the dresser and Elly wondered what sort of music Jo Baker found entertaining.

"Can you turn left?"

Elly obeyed, now facing a couch. Above it was a large photo of Jo Baker decked out in a feathery ensemble that didn't cover much. It made her smile. There were worse things to be than proud of your own body. And, well, Jo ought to be proud.

"All right," Polly said, straightening. "I'm going to run and grab the shoes she's wearing with this number. I think your feet might be smaller but the height of the heel is all that matters. Just a few more seconds and we're done. Thank you, Elly Mitchell."

"You're welcome, Polly."

Polly disappeared out of the door. Lifting the skirt of the dress, Elly hopped down from the measuring stand very carefully. Polly had inserted a half dozen pins into the hem of the gown. If she moved the wrong way, a pin would poke at her ankles.

Slowly making her way over to the record player, Elly saw that Bessie Smith was currently resting on the turntable. Tucked just behind the stand and in the windowsill were a number of other records. Elly began to flip through them. Most of them were American artists that she recognized but a few appeared to be songs from operas sung by people whose names she'd never heard of before.

The door opened.

"How many records . . ."

Elly stopped talking as a man she didn't know entered the room. He wasn't wearing a suit but a uniform. Not American. Not French. Not German. The laurel wreath on his hat was so familiar. What country was he from? "There you are, Josephine. I've been waiting to talk with you for so long." Italian. Elly sighed. Deeply. Who was this man who had access to Jo Baker's dressing room and still didn't know what the woman looked like?

"Excuse me, sir. But I think—"

The door opened again and this time it was Grant. She pointed at the stranger. "Grant—"

"Signore Achille, we thought you weren't going to be able to make the show," Grant said, his voice warm as he exchanged handshakes with the officer.

"I did not think I would make it here tonight either, but the meeting did not last as long as I anticipated." The Italian's gaze returned to Elly. "It is always so wonderful to see Miss Baker perform."

Grant looked at Elly and then back at the Italian. "Miss Baker?"

"She is so lovely, is she not?" The Italian was looking at her with his whole heart in his eyes. Too bad she wasn't the woman he was thinking about.

"Excuse me—"

"Miss Baker is lovely, isn't she?" Grant asked softly, a thoughtful expression on his face as he made his way to her side. "Signore, I just need to borrow Miss Baker for a quick second. She'll be right back. Please make yourself comfortable." Grant grabbed her hand and dragged her out of the room.

When the door was shut behind them, she started to speak.

"Grant—"

Still holding her wrist tightly, he pulled her into the room next door. By the smell and the chirps and the grunts, they were in Jo Baker's zoo. Elly only got a quick glance of a birdcage dangling from the ceiling before Grant closed the door and pushed her up against it. He smacked the palm of his hand against the surface next to her head. He was so close; she could smell the faint cologne that he was wearing. She could see the small beauty mark on his cheek and the faint hint of an old scar on his chin. He leaned down, his lips inches from hers. She'd thought he didn't like her. What was happening here? "I beg your pardon—"

"Look at me." The bass in his voice sent shivers down her spine. She swallowed once and lifted her eyes to meet his even though it was strangely hard to do. She had never had a man so intently focused on her in her whole life and she felt a little bit like she might combust. "You are going to go back in that room, and you are going to become Jo Baker."

"I . . . what?"

"You are going to get an invitation to the Italian embassy's Christmas party. Do you understand? That man does not walk out of that room without Jo Baker having been invited. We've worked too hard to get this far for it to all be unraveled now."

An invitation to the Italian embassy's Christmas party? A part of her couldn't believe he had brought her in here to tell her to pretend to be Jo Baker so the woman could attend an event. The other part of her felt like it was trying to put together a puzzle underwater. "I—"

His free hand moved to her back, pulling her up against his chest. Instinctively, Elly wrapped her arms around his waist—probably because she'd wanted to do so for ages. He dipped his head, touching his cheek to hers. His skin was so warm. He needed to shave. He smelled so good. His lips brushed her ear. "This is not a game. In thirty seconds, you will go into that dressing room, and you will become Josephine Baker. You will not let Signore Achille leave without giving you an invitation. Do you understand?"

His words were like being doused with cold water. Elly's arms dropped to her side as Grant leaned back, meeting her gaze. Gone was easy-going 'Uncle Grant'. His eyes were cold and hard and his thoughts were very much on the room next door. Elly felt an instant rush of embarrassment fill her face at the same time everything clicked. A solid weight of lead formed in her stomach. Trust her to stumble into the war. "Who are you spying for? Who is Josephine spying for?"

"So long as it's not Germany, does it matter? I am going to open this door and I need for you to walk into that dressing room and get that invitation." Elly didn't think, she just shook her head. Nobody had to tell her that spying was a dangerous game. And she wanted no parts of it. Grant's eyes narrowed and his lips thinned. "This isn't about you," he enunciated slowly. His eyes were so focused on her, Elly felt like he was reading every thought that crossed her mind. By the pinched expression on his face, he wasn't liking what he was seeing. "This is about the lives you're saving. We've lost time. We're losing time."

"I'm not—"

"All those articles you write about the war knowing good and well what's happening in the world, and you don't want to lift a finger to help?" This second dousing of ice-cold water was different. This one left fear in its wake. How much did he know? How long had he been watching her? Why had he been watching her? Elly slid her eyes to Grant. "Do not think that because you are not from here that you will escape what is coming. If you don't help us, we'll find another way." His voice lowered. "Everyone wonders if they would have been a Harriet Tubman but now, we both know you'd have been one of those folks happily singing in their cabin."

It was a ridiculous comment framed to pack a punch. And she was angry with herself that she felt the sting of it. Her glare matched his as she straightened to her full height. "Okay."

The word exited her mouth through clenched teeth and was barely discernible. But it was all he needed to hear. Grant's taut shoulders lowered slightly, and he pointed a finger at the room next door. "Signore Achille must never, at any point, doubt that you're Josephine Baker. If you mess up, more than one domino will fall, and I don't think I have to explain what will happen next to all of us."

Panic began stirring in Elly's stomach. But she didn't get a chance to think about it. Reaching for her hand, Grant pulled her out of the room. Elly only stumbled once as he led her the few feet down the hall to the dressing room. He opened the door, pushed her in, and shut the door behind her.

Signore Achille was standing by Josephine's dressing

table, tugging on flower petals. Elly's toes dug into the carpet beneath her feet, the skirt of the dress moved gently at her ankles, the needles inside scratching at her skin. Pressing a hand to her stomach, she inhaled deeply, trying to calm herself down. "Such beautiful flowers," the officer said. "Of course, not nearly as beautiful as you."

His words set off a wave of nervous heat and sweat began pooling under her arms. She had never been a very good actress. *Focus, Elodie.* No, she was Josephine Baker. Her eyes darted to the framed photograph of the woman on the wall. She needed that confidence; that *je ne sais quoi*. Elly returned her gaze to the soldier. He was several inches taller than her. His hair was black with gray at the temples. He was probably in his late forties. He turned around to look at her, a smile on his face beneath his thick, bushy mustache.

Pasting a warm grin on her face, Elly beamed, hoping to God there was actual happiness on her face and not something that reflected the sheer terror she felt on the inside.

"Signore, how are you?" How had Josephine greeted her earlier? Elly extended her hands, and he moved forward to grasp them. Forcing herself to make eye contact and keep it, she said, "Please take a seat. I'm sorry about earlier. Let me tell you, it has been a day." She gestured to the couch. "Take a seat. Make yourself comfortable. Would you like for me to play some music? You know I love music." Elly walked over to the record player, fiddled with the needle, and Bessie Smith's voice filled the room. The music instantly took her to Chicago to her uncle and aunt's living room where she danced the Charleston with her cousins. She lost her grasp on the character of Josephine as longing to return home filled her. She wanted to get out of here. She didn't know what she was doing.

She reached for one of the fans on Josephine's dresser and snapped it open. Fanning herself, she tried to cool the flame of nerves that burned bright within her. With a light inhalation, she turned around. Moving to the beat, she gently rocked her hips as she crossed the room.

"Are you angry with me? Don't be angry, Jo. You understand what a tight spot Il Duce was in? Hitler is extreme. But you have been and always will be a favorite of Italy." Il Duce—Mussolini! Elly was proud of herself for not losing the beat as she continued to sway. Josephine, Grant or whoever they were working for was playing a deep game here. *Don't think about yourself, Elly.* "We have never forgotten how we had your support in Ethiopia."

Taking a reluctant seat next to the officer, Elly took this information and decided to roll with it. She was Josephine Baker. The Josephine Baker she'd seen in the show only a few hours ago. Stiffening her shoulders, she said, "But I think he has forgotten."

"No! Never!"

"You come to France, and I don't hear from you anymore. You barely make my show. I don't get invited to anything." Elly closed her fan, suddenly remembering. "You had me banned from Italy. I cannot even visit the Pavilion. And why?" Shrugging with her whole

71

body, she turned away, leaving him only with the sight of her bare shoulders. She cracked open the fan. "It's because I am not beautiful to you."

She heard him shift and then she felt Signore Achille's hands on her skin and his breath on her neck. Something on the inside of her cringed. But on the outside, she didn't move. "That's not true, Josephine. I see you and I can't honestly think of a more beautiful woman."

Elly shrugged his hands off. "You lie. I'm not welcome in Italy for the crime of inciting lust. But what about Mistinguett?" Elly asked, referring to one of Jo's professional rivals. "Is she still welcome in Germany? In Italy? Or is it only I, with my dark skin?"

"Josephine—"

She needed to keep talking because she didn't know the personal history between this man and Josephine. "Words are empty. They are meaningless." Elly rose to her feet. Using the fan, she pointed to the door. "Perhaps you should just leave! Do as Italy told me! Walk away and never look back!" Elly was proud of the way her heart was pounding. She knew she looked worked up because she was . . . She felt like she could be sick any minute.

Signore Achille stood up, standing before her. Once again, he placed his hands on her shoulders. "*Cara mia.*" He cupped her cheek and leaned down as though to kiss her. Elly turned her face to the side, unable to hide her flinch. Achille sighed. "What can I do to fix this? These are careful times. What is said in public is not necessarily how one feels, no?" His hand was in her hair, and she forced herself to relax as he slipped an arm around her waist. "*Mi Manchi . . .*"

"I speak French." Elly pouted. And then prayed that the man wouldn't switch to French.

Achille laughed.

"Did I say something funny?"

"Josephine."

"I suppose I'm just one big joke to you and all of Italy."

"No. Of course not."

"Then prove it."

"How?"

Elly looked around the room as though searching for an answer. "Invite me to the Christmas party."

"Christmas—"

"The one held at the embassy."

He winced. "Josephine."

"Or never say my name again. Your choice." She was so jittery inside it was a miracle that her hands weren't shaking. What if she was saying all the wrong things?

Achille hesitated. "Everyone comes to the Christmas parties. I . . . all right. Of course you can come if it means you won't be angry with me anymore."

Was that an invitation? Would Grant be happy with such a statement? Dropping the fan, she took a step forward, erasing the space between them. Slowly, hesitantly, she placed the palms of her hands on the chest of this man she didn't know. Meeting his gaze, she whispered, "Words. Are. Empty."

"Give me thirty minutes. I'll have my driver circle around for an invitation."

Elly reached up and playfully took his hat off his head, revealing a large bald spot. "Then I'll hold on

73

to this until he gets here. Would you like some champagne while we wait? I'll have Grant fetch us some."

"I just remembered. I might have one in the car."

"Even better. Grant will walk you out to go get it. Please hand it to him." Gliding past Achille, Elly opened the door. Unsurprisingly, Grant was there and he was looking at her as though he had heard every word of their conversation. And maybe he had. "Grant, please take Signore Achille to his car. He has something for you."

When the two men were gone, Elly wasted not one second. She slipped off Josephine's dress and put her own on. She couldn't reach the zipper all the way, but she didn't let that stop her. She put on her shoes and her coat, buttoning it all the way to the top. Then she ran.

CHAPTER 7

Despite returning to the apartment sometime after midnight, Elly was the first person to awaken the next day. She very quietly returned Madame's necklace to her room but not before she wagged a finger at it. "Lucky my black behind."

Then she washed, dressed, and left the house. It was a Saturday, and she didn't have any classes. Not that she would have had them anyway. She had worked out a plan with her professors that would allow her to finish the semester through correspondence. Her last in-person class had been yesterday.

Thinking of yesterday pulled her right back into Josephine Baker's dressing room. Right back to the moment she had knowingly interfered with the war, tiny though her role had been.

And that Grant Monterey! How had she ever liked him? Every time she thought about how she'd slipped her arms around his waist, she wanted to find a hole to crawl in. Elly stomped her way around Paris, wandering aimlessly. So, Grant was a spy. And all evidence seemed to indicate that Josephine Baker was one as well. Very interesting. She would not be the first entertainer to spy for a country and she probably wouldn't be the last.

What did they want with the Italian embassy? Were they trying to discover where Mussolini's allegiance fell? He was clearly going to hitch his horse to Hitler's but Elly guessed the question was whether he was going to support him overtly or subtly—and when. Elly shook her head as the introduction of an article began to form. What did she care about this information? Her journalistic endeavors were over. She was done writing about Europe's problems.

Finding herself near the farmers' market, Elly reached into her coat pocket and felt a small bag. It had become habit to carry one around in case something caught her eye that she might want to purchase. Seeing fresh fruit, she bought a few pieces so that Madame would not feel the need to go out later. They always had fruit as their last course. In the summer, Madame had sprinkled sugar over berries or fruit slices as though that one action suddenly made the fruit earn the title of dessert. It didn't. It wasn't a dessert if two cups of sugar and a pound of butter were nowhere to be found. Nevertheless, Elly didn't complain—the fruit was fresh and sweet.

And it would only be a matter of time until she was home digging into one of Aunt Tabitha's massive pound cakes that put you to sleep for a week. Groceries in hand, Elly turned on her heels and headed back to the apartment. She needed to finish packing. She needed to be ready when Richard called. She was anxious to leave this country.

Mind on all that she hoped to accomplish today, Elly tramped up the stairs to the third floor and opened the apartment door.

"*Bonjour*, Madame, Claire," she called out as she shrugged off her coat and hung it in the closet. "I went to the market and bought some apples and pears and fresh figs." Bag in hand, Elly turned around, and stopped. Sitting there very comfortably settled on the couch and drinking a cup of coffee was Grant. Madame sat on one side of him, Claire on the other.

She dropped the groceries and they hit the floor with a thud.

"Look, *chérie*," Madame pointed to Grant as though Elly could see someone else besides him. "*Ton ami . . .* your boyfriend is here!"

He did wear something else besides black. Today, he was wearing gray pants, a white shirt, and a fitted gray vest. His suit jacket was strewn across the back of an empty armchair. Oh, dear God, why was he here? What did he want? Had his arrival put all of them in some kind of danger? Had she unknowingly put them in danger? It took all of her willpower not to lash out with the words that danced on her tongue. In an attempt to hide her emotion, Elly clasped her hands behind her back. Very carefully, she said, "*Bonjour*, Grant."

"Elodie." He smiled, and his dark eyes lit up, communicating a number of things, one of which appeared to be amusement. His easy expression fueled her anger. He said something in French. Something along the lines of 'it's wonderful to see you again.'

"Oh, she doesn't speak French," Claire told him. Grant shifted to look at the girl.

"She does not speak French?"

"No," Claire said with a shake of her head.

"How long has she been here that she doesn't speak French?" he asked the girl as though Elly wasn't standing right there.

"Five months."

"*Incroyable*."

Elly took a step forward and Grant returned his gaze to her. "What are you doing here?"

Grant leaned forward, lowering his cup of coffee onto the saucer that rested on the coffee table. "I wanted to see you, my dear," he said, in that deep voice of his. "Last night was simply not enough."

"Oh, how was Josephine Baker?" Madame asked with excitement. "My son took me to see her on stage many many years ago."

"Enlightening," Elly answered before Grant could. Elly pointed to the door just a few feet away from her. "Can I talk to you, Grant?"

"Oh, you can use the balcony," Madame said cheerfully and waved in the direction of the rarely used doors. Grant stood up. Speaking to Madame in French, he complimented her apartment and thanked her.

"Elodie?" At ease, he made his way over to the doors as though he had been the one residing here for the past few months.

Slowly, Elly stepped around the grocery bag on the floor and followed Grant outside onto the terrace. She crossed the small space, placing her hands on the railing while he closed the doors behind them. She shivered as a cool breeze wafted in her direction. The sleeves on her dress weren't enough to stand up against the wind. "How did you figure out where I lived?"

"You told Danny. Danny told me."

Fingers tapping against the metal beneath her hands, Elly asked, "Is he also a . . . ?"

"Danny knows things, yes."

Seemingly unbothered by the cold, Grant moved to stand inches away from her. He leaned down, looking out over the railing and at the people walking below. In the distance, through the leafless trees, you could see the Eiffel Tower. "This is a very nice area. Most colored people live in Montmartre," he said, naming a neighborhood. "No wonder we didn't come across each other earlier."

Inching away from him, Elly asked, "Is there a reason why you're here?" She didn't think that she was in any danger from him. He had to know that she was very unlikely to run to the Germans or even the Italians regarding the events of last night. Although, she supposed she could accidentally say something to the wrong person. She shifted another inch further away from him.

"Josephine would like for you to come by the house. She wants to talk to you."

"No, thanks."

"Just like that?"

"Yes, just like that." It wasn't as if Ms. Baker wanted to meet for lunch because she was so taken with their two-minute conversation from yesterday. "You tell her my lips are sealed. I won't tell a soul."

Grant looked unimpressed. "Josephine aside, we're supposed to take your word just like that?"

"You sure didn't seem to have a problem with me yesterday. Now, you're worried?" She rolled her eyes and made sure he saw it.

"Well, you seem like a young lady who is concerned about her fellow man and unlikely to cause any problems." The words were said lightly, but she heard an underlying threat. And she lost any and all trepidation.

Elly raised a finger. "You know what? Don't. I'm gonna keep my mouth shut. And you had better leave me alone."

"It wasn't personal—"

Looking back toward the apartment to make sure Madame and Claire weren't close by, Elly whispered, "You brought up Harriet Tubman. You made it personal. You don't know me. You don't get to say things like that to me."

"I was trying—"

"I know what you were trying to do! I even know why you did it!" Elly took a step toward him, waving her finger under his nose. "Let me tell you something, I recognize that you've lived in this country for a number of years and so you must have forgotten but there are two words in the English language that are more effective than insults and—" she nearly said seduction "—tricks and they are 'please' and 'thank you.'" Inches away from him now, she continued, "And how dare you come here, possibly endangering a young girl and her grandmother!"

Grant captured her finger and leaned down toward her. She got a whiff of soap and cologne. Someone had just gotten out of the shower. The thought was random and unwanted. She pushed it aside and pulled her hand away from his. "Am I allowed to speak now?"

"No," she said, simply because he'd asked. "What you can do is grab your coat and leave. Give my regards to Miss Josephine. She's got a tough road ahead of her." Elly folded her arms over her chest, proud of the way her words exited her mouth so smoothly.

But Grant didn't leave. Instead, he side-eyed her for a second before taking a step forward and gripping the balcony railing. "First off, no one is in any danger just because I'm here. Secondly, when it comes to fighting a war, I won't apologize for the things I need to do to win it, especially if it saves lives in the long run. Now, you're a very smart woman and you did a fantastic job last night. I'm asking you to put aside your personal feelings and meet with Ms. Baker."

"What does she want?" Elly asked, suddenly very concerned that Josephine wanted her to continue her role as her body double.

"She doesn't want you to pretend to be her, so wipe that expression off your face. But I do believe she wants to ask for your help."

"Are you a citizen?"

"Of this country? No."

"Then why?"

"Because they treat me better than my own. And honestly, there's no way America stays out of this. I look at it as sort of preemptive work. Much is accomplished within the shadow war."

The shadow war. It was a good name for those who played spy games.

"I'm leaving for America on the first ship I can."

"I'm not asking you to stay. I'm asking you to speak with Josephine. It's not a hard thing."

"Going to the show yesterday wasn't supposed to be a hard thing."

"Are you always this argumentative?"

"When I'm angry, I'm Joe Louis in the ring."

Grant lifted his eyes to the sky. "What do I have to do or say to guarantee that this meeting will require nothing of you except to listen? What does it take for you to go out of your way to spend a few minutes with the most famous woman in the world?" He said it in such a way that it would make her sound incredibly childish for refusing.

"You're very annoying."

"So are you, actually."

She inhaled. Exhaled. It was just a conversation with Josephine Baker. She glanced at Grant. Unless he was trying to convince her to leave the house so he could murder her and dump her body somewhere it wouldn't be found.

Grant's gaze was steely. "You helped us out yesterday but you are not Mata Hari." The famous spy who had been executed before a firing squad. Elly nearly shuddered at the thought. "Erase whatever fantasies you're conjuring in your mind, please."

It was just a talk. She turned to the doors. "I'll get my coat."

Grant led Elly to a car. Josephine's car, he explained as they approached the black and white Delage.

"I couldn't afford this even in my dreams," he told her as he opened the passenger door for her.

82

"Me either," she said as she slid in. Elly ran her hands over the seats. "This is . . . ?"

"Snakeskin."

"Whoa." He closed the door, walked around to the driver's seat, and climbed inside. There was no cranking for this fancy car. "How long have you known Miss Baker?"

"About thirteen years. Pretty much the whole time I've lived in France."

"You came over here at a separate time than her?"

"Yes. We aren't inseparable. I'm only with Josephine when she's in Paris. As you know, she travels all over."

"And where are we going now?"

"To her house. To Le Beau Chêne. It's just outside Paris."

"It has a name?"

"All of her houses have names."

Elly said no more as she looked out the window. Any other day and this would be the most exciting moment of her life. Here she was riding in luxury on her way to the fancy home of the most famous woman in the world. As it was, her stomach was jumping a bit—not because of fear—but because she did not know what was going to happen next.

And it didn't help that Grant was silent as he expertly navigated the streets of Paris and then the neighborhood of Le Vésinet.

"There it is," he said, his voice a bit hushed as they pulled up to a large three-story home built possibly in the Victorian era. It was all points and angles and reminiscent of a mini-castle. All of this space for one woman. But maybe that wasn't right. "Isn't she married?"

"In the middle of a divorce."

"No children?"

"Not if you don't count her pets."

"She has more?"

"Than the ones she keeps at the Casino?" he asked, knowing exactly what she was talking about. "Oh, loads more. I believe there's a few dogs, a turkey, a couple of monkeys, mice, and let's not forget the ducks."

"Mice?"

"When she lived in hotels, she used to keep guppies in the bidet. If it's living and breathing, she wants it." The car came to a stop. "She told me to tell you she'd be in the gardens, just over there. I'm not going to sit in on your meeting so feel free to talk about me behind my back."

"Oh, I will," Elly promised as she climbed out of the Delage. Ignoring his laughter, she closed the car door shut and carefully walked across the gravel path in the direction that Grant had indicated only moments before. The house was even larger up close. Eyeing the building next to her, she had a change of mind. Perhaps it wasn't Victorian. It was probably built before that era with its sharp spindly look.

Elly caught sight of hedges and a pond and then there was Josephine. It could only be her in the long, dingy pants and somewhat tattered coat. Her hair was covered by a handkerchief and she was tossing small rocks into the water. All the stress and anxiety that had been roiling inside Elly melted away. Less than ten feet away from her was Josephine Baker. And she'd wanted to speak to Elly. She'd invited her to her house; she was welcoming her into her personal space. And it wasn't as if it was Josephine who was responsible for what had happened yesterday.

"Hello?" Elly called out, gently announcing her presence.

"My twin!" Josephine dropped the rocks in hand and waved enthusiastically. "Come on over! I'm so happy to see you!"

CHAPTER 8

They sat on a bench tucked in the corner of the garden. Elly sat on one side and Josephine on the other. Josephine had a small dog in her lap and another one making circles around her feet.

"Do you like animals?" Josephine asked as the dog resting on her legs licked her fingers. She laughed contentedly, patting his head.

"I . . . um," Elly began, trying to be polite, but then decided to go with honesty. "No."

"No?" Josephine raised her eyebrows and sent Elly a furtive glance as though she'd learned something particularly deep about Elly. Maybe she had.

Feeling the need to explain, Elly said gently, "Where I grew up, there was no such thing as pets. Animals were either useful or food." Her parents had barely been able to feed the four of them let alone a dog or a cat. Or a monkey.

"I also grew up poor. But I found animals to be my friends, my source of comfort. Sometimes I find them more reliable than people."

Well. That was what she'd got for being honest. But for no reason Elly could name, she wanted to be nothing less than herself with this woman. And now things were a bit awkward. Elly glanced around the garden, taking in the staid but empty trees and the few, daring flowers. Ducks trotted around the small pool of water, honking gently. It was a very rural picture and not at all what Elly would have thought Josephine would enjoy. But enjoy it, she clearly did.

"I love this country," the woman said as she quietly stroked the dog in her arms. "Sometimes I think I'm more French than American." This was unsurprising. France was treating Josephine very kindly. God bless America, but it would never give Josephine all the love and acclaim that she was finding here. "There's nothing I want more than to give back to these people all that they have given me. And," she said with a sigh as she rubbed her dog's belly, "I'll do anything to stop the Germans. People like that—" she shook her head "—they cannot prosper." Josephine looked up. "Thank you for stepping in yesterday."

"You're welcome."

"Grant said you're a very quick study."

"Is that what he said?"

Josephine grinned even as she reached down to pat the other dog at her feet. "Grant is the kindest, warmest person you'll ever meet except in times of danger."

Josephine shook her head. "Then, you better watch out. But I didn't ask you here to talk about Grant. I asked you here to talk about you."

Was Grant those things? Elly thought about that coldness she'd seen in his eyes the night before. He'd seemed light-hearted and friendly enough this morning but she didn't trust it. She wondered if Josephine really knew this man she spoke so highly of. But Josephine had paused, waiting for a response. Elly nodded.

"Why are you here in France? You could have studied anywhere if you simply wanted to leave the States."

Why France? Elly supposed that she could mention that it was the one foreign language offered at her high school. She'd done well enough in her classes and enjoyed learning it so she'd continued studying French in college. It just made sense that if she was going to study abroad, she would go to France. She could say that she'd heard that the French didn't care about skin color and it was safe for her kind. She could bring up her heritage. She could not trace her African roots. That part of her had been lost in the slave trade, leaving only a gaping wound in its place. France was the only other country she had. Instead, what came out surprised even her. "I wanted to live."

The words were silly and inane and Elly felt ridiculous having said them. And yet, she also felt on the verge of tears. Because it was true. She'd come to France to live. If only for a moment. Next to her, Josephine Baker shifted and stared at her, the dog in her lap forgotten. She leaned in Elly's direction, her eyes lit up with expectancy. "And have you? Lived?"

It all came down to what you thought living was. Whatever that answer might be, Elly had spent the past few months wandering around Paris, stumbling across beautiful sights, and keeping only herself company. None of that was very different from what she did back home. It was a depressing thing to realize.

Perhaps she took too long to answer or perhaps Josephine read her answer in her face because she spoke again. "I started performing at a young age, which meant that I have had the pleasure of traveling all across America. You name it, I've probably been there. And during that time, I tried to sing like Ma Rainey, dance like Bill Robinson, or act like Hattie McDaniel. And it was never enough. I was good. But I wasn't good enough. And then the show I was in received an invitation to perform in France so I came here. And I learned something. They liked me here. Just the way I am. That's not to say that I didn't have some learning to do but for the first time in my life, I didn't have to try and be anybody else. I could just be little ole me." Josephine pressed a hand to her chest. "I could simply live. It's not easy to find that space where you don't have to be anyone but yourself and you are valued for it. If you ever do, you should protect it at all costs."

It was a credit to Josephine that she would acknowledge how kind France had been to her, but it wasn't that simple. "I have a cousin in Chicago who is an editor of a newspaper. That paper paid for me to come here with the understanding that I write about two things: life and education in France and the war. I'm very familiar with what's currently happening in Czechoslovakia and Poland." Elly hesitated. "I think there's a chance that things could get very bad in France. And we're colored, Miss Baker. I have great doubts that the Germans will look too kindly on us despite us being American."

"Oh, there's danger. Make no mistake about that but there is also great reward. How can you not want to be a part of it? What is life if we only put ourselves first?" They were dancing around the question that Josephine had not asked.

"I understand why you would help where you can. I do not understand why you would go down with this ship."

Josephine exhaled, her hands digging into her pet's fur. "You don't think the Maginot Line will hold?"

"No. France seems unaware that this war isn't being fought like the last one. Things are going to get worse before they get better." That was Elly's professional opinion as a wartime correspondent.

Josephine hummed. "You know, I returned to America in . . . 1935. I was not the same small potato that I was when I left."

"I remember."

"I arrived in New York and went to the hotel where my assistant had made my reservation and you know what they told me? They didn't have any room. None. Drove all around that city and there was no room at the inn for me. I ended up having to spend the night in a friend's apartment."

She said the words lightly, but Elly read the tautness in her body, saw the way that Josephine seemed to be clinging to the dog in her arms. "You know why there was no room, don't you?"

Elly squinted at Josephine for a second. Had the woman really believed that America would forget that she was colored just because she had money and fame? But Elly kept her words few. "Money does not change skin color."

Josephine released a humorless laugh. "No, it doesn't. I was colored the day I was born and if I die a queen, I'll be colored when they put me in the grave." Suddenly turning toward her, Josephine asked, "But wouldn't it be nice if we didn't live in a world where everyone was separated by these small, trivial divisions? Wouldn't it be nice if we were kind just for the sake of being kind? If we didn't consider race or religion or sex?"

Elly looked away. Generally speaking, optimistic people irritated her. Naive optimistic people gave her headaches. The world had never been what Josephine was describing and it never would be. Even homogenous societies found ways to erect barriers. "That would be nice," Elly conceded. This was Josephine Baker, after all. She was allowed her delusions. "But that's not the world we live in."

"The world we live in will never change if we just accept the way things are," Josephine said emphatically. To which Elly nodded because it was a valid point. "I want to use my life to be a part of that change. In any way that I can. And I'm asking you to look past yourself and to consider others."

"Help out of the goodness and kindness of my heart, you mean?" Because that was what it boiled down to, wasn't it?

"Well, there's—"

"Will I be getting paid?"

"No," Josephine said after a moment. The expression on her face was one of sharp annoyance. She was not pleased with Elly. A part of Elly winced but another part of her—the part that was calculating the risks— refused to be anything less than direct.

"Will I gain notoriety after all is said and done? Is my name going to be written down in the history books?" Josephine had no response. "But I will get to walk away knowing that I am a kind person? Miss Baker, I like you. Watching you perform yesterday was . . . life-changing. I'll remember it until the day I die. And I think the world of what you're doing for France. You could easily be somewhere safe and sound and far away from here but you've chosen to be right in the thick of it. However, I am not a kind person and I rarely do anything that doesn't, in the end, benefit me."

"If that was true you wouldn't have helped yesterday." Josephine raised a hand. "Yes, I know. Grant had to persuade you. Still, at the end of the day, you were running that show. You had all of the control and you could have exposed us if you had wanted to. You gained nothing by helping."

"It was a small thing." Elly had no idea why she was trying to convince this woman that she lacked all kindness.

"Pretending to be me was not a small thing. It must have been quite a challenge for you."

Elly released a reluctant laugh. "Touché, Miss Baker."

Josephine lowered her dog onto the ground. "You

came here because you wanted to live. That tells me that whatever you were doing back in the States wasn't quite cutting it. The act isn't over; the show hasn't concluded. So answer me this, why are you leaving?"

Grant didn't say anything until he pulled up in front of Madame's apartment.

"Here," he said, waving a torn sheet of paper in her direction. Elly took it. "A number to reach me. When you've made up your mind, give that number a call. Whether I answer or not, tell the person that you'll meet me at the Louvre the following morning. Okay?"

"Okay."

Elly reached for the door. "Elodie." She glanced over at him. "If it makes you feel any better, this is not a lifetime commitment. There can be a time limit. It could be six months. It could be a year."

"Will it be that simple to leave when my time is up?"

"Not necessarily, but neither Josephine nor I have any intention of just letting the Germans run over us. We'll flee this country if we have to, even if Josephine has to fly us out herself."

Elly blinked. "She can fly planes?"

"Yes. Thanks to the soon to be ex-husband. So, if it helps, put a time limit on it. See where you are when that time comes around. If you're ready to return to the States, the route home might be a very long one but we'll do what we can to get you back."

Elly tapped the door handle beneath her fingers. "Why me?" It was a question she'd meant to ask Josephine but they'd both gotten so tangled up in the philosophical that they'd never gotten a chance to discuss the factual before Josephine had to leave to get ready for an engagement.

"Because on paper it doesn't make sense. You're a woman—which Germans greatly undervalue. Then add the fact that you're colored and an American and now you have a recipe for the least suspicious person in the room. Unique to you is your knowledge of the world around you and your ability to think on your feet, which you proved last night. You could be a very valuable asset to France. Why wouldn't we try to recruit you?"

Elly sat with that information for a second. She supposed there was some merit there. She couldn't figure out why someone with her background would spy for France either. "What is it that you would want me to do?"

"I can't go into details until you agree but you got a taste of it yesterday. It would mostly be ferreting out information from different people at events. Josephine is very successful at what she does. But she is only one person in a room often overflowing with information. It would be a boon to have someone else there who can catch what she misses. But we would train you. Last night was a fluke. We wouldn't send you on a mission you were not prepared for."

A mission. The very words made her tense up. Elly's only response was a nod before she left the car.

An hour later, Elly sat on the outside patio of a restaurant drinking a hot cup of coffee and fiddling with the paper that held Grant's phone number. She didn't know why she was dickering back and forth.

Hadn't she already made her decision? Were her bags not already mostly packed?

She gave her coffee a small stir as facts danced in her head.

Fact #1: France was currently at war with Germany.

Fact #2: Germany might not be doing much about that at the moment, but the Germans were coming. And they were frightening.

Fact #3: She was not French, and she owed this country zilch.

Fact #4: If she did this, she would get nothing out of it. Except she might finally live if Josephine was to be believed.

Reluctant thoughts of her father circled her head. The father who had given up his promising medical career for vaudeville. He'd never cared much for book learning but he'd tried to appease his parents until he couldn't do it anymore. The only problem was, her father was not that great of a performer. He'd reached his dream to be on the stage only for it to utterly crush him.

In her worst moments, she wondered whether she could have saved him. Whether the right word or timely hug would have changed his mind. Maybe he'd still be living if she had just been obedient and gone to live with Uncle Minor and Aunt Tabitha when her father first tried to send her away.

But then reason would take over. Her father had been broken in ways that she alone never could have fixed.

Why was she thinking about this right now? What did her father and his broken dreams have to do with spying for France? Elly finished her coffee. Despite the warm drink, her fingers were cold. She could do with a sit by the fire, but her mind was too busy to allow for stillness. Leaving some money on the table, she stood up and left the café.

Making her way across a bridge, Elly came to a stop in the middle of it and looked down over the river. Her father had taken a risk and look where that had gotten him. And yet, she had not been able to answer Josephine's question. Why was she leaving if she had not found what she'd been looking for? There was the obvious answer: France was getting dangerous. But that was not what Josephine had been asking. Had she not come here with her hands open wide expecting . . . something? Hadn't she been hoping to return home different? Settled? Content? Filled with knowledge of who she was and what she wanted from life? Was she willing to risk her life to find it? Because she was not happy. Not really. Like the water that shuffled and flowed beneath her, Elly just went along with whatever life tossed her way. And as she'd begun to recognize over the years, that was not living. If you did the same thing you'd always done, you certainly could not expect different results.

Elly released a small huff of air as she came to a decision. How strange. If she wanted to live, it would seem she would have to be willing to die.

CHAPTER 9

When Elly arrived in Paris five months ago, the Louvre was one of the first places she'd hunted down. Like the Eiffel Tower, she'd heard the name. One didn't study French as she had and not be aware of the famous palace turned art museum. But the sight of the building had completely shattered her illusions as to what a royal home ought to look like.

Now, she knew she had been expecting a castle like those that graced Austria. The Louvre was not that. At first glance, the U-shaped palace looked like an eighteenth-century office building. But one moved past all of their possible disappointment upon entering. It was glorious inside.

"*Bonjour*, Elodie," Grant said, coming from nowhere to stand next to her. Grant's voice, once a mystery, was now becoming something very familiar. It also made her a little bit anxious for reasons she didn't want to linger on. Shoving her hands into the pockets of her coat, she shifted slightly to look at him. He was dressed in black again. Today, the scarf around his neck was a deep, ocean blue and if she didn't already know his name, she'd have called him Étienne.

"Good morning, Grant." His eyes narrowed for a second and she knew it had everything to do with her flagrant use of English but he didn't say anything.

Grant paid for their tickets. As it was a Wednesday morning, there wasn't much of a crowd. In the Louvre, art could be found anywhere; in its high ceilings, in the curve of its doorways, in the crown molding and obviously in the paintings and statues that were littered throughout the building. It was hard to believe that people had once lived here.

"Do you have a favorite exhibit?" Grant's voice was low.

"Jacques Louis David."

Grant's eyebrows rose. "Napoleon?"

"I like the colors." And the size. David's paintings were magnificent. Neither one of them said anything as Grant led them across the expanse of the former palace to the corner where David's paintings hung. They came to a stop in front of *The Coronation of Napoleon*. For a long moment, there was silence.

Twisting in his direction, Elly said, "Josephine Bonaparte is my favorite part of this picture." In the painting, Napoleon was crowning his wife as queen or empress or whatever the female counterpart was to Napoleon at the time the artwork was done. Elly liked looking at the painting. She didn't research it.

"Josephine *Baker* had a few things to say about you."

Elly pursed her lips and focused on the artwork before her. "I like her very much. But we're very different people, Miss Baker and I."

"Yes." She heard a world of amusement in Grant's tone. Out of the corner of her eye, she watched Grant fold his arms over his chest. "When did you first notice me as you sat by the Seine eating crêpes?"

Raising her gaze to the top of the very high ceiling, Elly hummed. "Five weeks ago?"

"I've been watching you for six weeks."

"Six?"

"I've read all of your articles. The ones about life in France and the ones you write as Elliot Valcourt, war correspondent." She'd figured he knew about her pen name because of what he'd said to her on Friday. But she hadn't realized just how long she'd been on his radar.

"Why?"

"Initially, I was looking for Elliot Valcourt. He seemed like a fella who might be able to help. Didn't think he'd lead me to you. It may have taken me a minute to get over my surprise." Elly opened her mouth to speak and then closed it. The question she was about to ask had answered itself.

But as though reading her mind, in a very low voice, Grant said, "I do not work for the United States."

"Yes. I figured as much. They don't believe we have the capability to hold a gun and shoot let alone . . . you-know-what." Spy. She wasn't sure she should say the word aloud.

"The words you are looking for are honorable correspondent. I'm not being paid. I'm just a concerned citizen."

"Except you're not a citizen."

Grant nodded once. "Except I'm not."

"What's the difference between six months and one year?"

Understanding exactly what she was asking, Grant said, "It's hard to say where we'll be one year from now. But a lot of what we do is about establishing relationships and following patterns. And that takes time. Thus it comes down to the types of assignments you would be given."

"For example . . . ?"

"I am working with a department whose sole focus is weaponry. Every assignment I give you would be toward the purpose of stopping leaks about guns, ammo, et cetera. But I cannot say more. If you were caught and tortured, we would want to make sure that you were limited in what you could divulge."

Caught and tortured. At least he hadn't beat around the bush. "No one would rescue me?" she quipped, trying for levity and failing.

"This isn't that sort of job," he said quietly. "If one of us gets caught, the rest of us will scatter like ants. You would be completely on your own." Grant paused, allowing his words to settle on Elly's shoulders like weights. "So, the key is that I train you not to get caught."

"What if there's an invasion?"

"Then everything changes. And I cannot tell you what that would look like."

There was a long moment of silence. "One year, Grant. I'll give you one year and then I want you to promise me that you'll do everything within your power to get me off of this continent." If she was going to do this thing she was going to throw herself into it entirely.

"You have my word." He extended a hand. She looked down at it for fifteen seconds before shaking it.

"I'll have to continue as Elliot Valcourt or my family will not understand." They still would not understand. The Mitchells knew she wanted to come home. None of this would make any sense to them. It was a good thing, then, that letters were well and truly the only form of communication at the moment. One phone call with Uncle Minor and Aunt Tabitha and they would be able to get the truth out of her. Considering that she could so easily cave under such pressure, Elly could hardly believe France was putting any faith in her.

"Just so long as you never mention the other work you'll be doing with me and Josephine, I don't care. Come on, let me take you to my favorite section of the museum." They started down the hall of another exhibit and Grant continued to speak, his voice just above a whisper. "Josephine and I have two different handlers but because Jo and I work together in life, sometimes we work together . . ." Grant didn't finish his sentence. He just waved a hand. "You might think this country is not going to make it because Hitler's war machine is just too great. There's truth to that. But it's also not going to make it because the Abwehr has the run of this place. Whether they like it or not, the Deuxième Bureau has lost control."

He was talking about the spy networks with the Abwehr belonging to the Germans and the Deuxième Bureau belonging to the French.

"There is nothing you can say on the telephone that does not have a German listening in. Don't ever call me or anybody else with information. Understood?"

"Yes."

"Assume everyone you encounter is working with the Germans unless explicitly told otherwise."

"Got it."

"The mutual friend that we have? Let's call her the butterfly."

He meant Josephine Baker. "All right."

"The butterfly is a wonderful asset for a variety of reasons. Because of her profession, she comes into contact with people from all over the world. People who work in all kinds of fields. She is also a people person. You know . . . the very opposite of you."

"Funny."

"Perhaps we should call you, *le papillon de nuit*."

"Butterfly of the night?"

"A moth."

Elly stopped and stared at him, unamused. "One of those ugly-looking flying things that rush into your house at night?" She hated moths. Absolutely hated them. It probably had everything to do with the moth infestation that had occurred one fall at Uncle Minor and Aunt Tabitha's. Unbeknownst to them, a few moths had somehow found a bag of rice, mated, and duplicated . . . into hundreds. Elly still remembered the feeling of being dive-bombed in the shower by baby moths that watched her from the ceiling. She shuddered just thinking about them.

"Moths can be quite interesting in their own way."

She blinked once and then kept walking. "Keep going."

"The butterfly is very smart. Particularly as it comes to her career. She knows what it takes to woo an audience. She knows what it takes to woo a person. If she is given an assignment to get certain information, there is no one better. However, she struggles with the big picture. Case in point, I know you know why she has an in with the Italians."

"Because she praised Mussolini when he invaded Ethiopia."

"Yes, exactly. Mussolini fed her a story about freeing the slaves in Ethiopia and she thought she was standing in the presence of a new Abe Lincoln. When it comes to the international stage, the butterfly can well and truly put her foot in it. She can be surrounded by so much information but miss all of the cues. That is where you come in."

"You want me to be her maid or something?" She'd spent the past few days trying to guess how or why they'd use her.

"No, Moth." She stopped for a second and glared at him. He kept walking. "How can we not capitalize on the fact that you favor her?"

"I do not."

"No, not really. That dog wouldn't hunt in America. Not among colored folks anyway. But we're not there. And here they'll buy whatever we sell. You're her cousin, in case you were wondering. Have you ever been to St. Louis?"

"Once."

"You came here to study. She's been funding your education."

"Has she?"

"She's so incredibly proud of you. The two of you are like sisters. Here we are, my favorite exhibit."

He'd brought her to Africa. More specifically, Egypt. "Isn't this incredible?" He swerved to take a look at a glass-encased mummy. Elly moved to his side. "The French always ask where you are really from."

"I'm familiar with this question. I start off with Chicago."

"I say New York."

"And then they say, no, where are you really from? I say Louisiana."

That got Grant's attention. "You hide your accent?" Elly dipped her head in acknowledgment. "Of course it came out when you were trying to rip me a new one the other day but I chalked that up to you having parents from the South. Well, same. Except I say Virginia and I express absolute surprise and delight that they can pick up my heritage in my voice."

"But then they say, no . . . where are you really from?" Elly said, continuing the imaginary exchange.

"Right. Do they think our ancestors had Sierra Leone or Senegal stamped onto their backsides before they were loaded onto the slave ships sent to America?"

"Or that our ancestors would have even talked of such things?"

"Yes! Were we supposed to sit them down and ask how was that boat ride by the way?'"

"My grandmother would have pretended like she didn't know what you were talking about."

"So would mine." They shared a look of silent understanding. Two people raised in different parts of the United States, in possibly different decades, with the same story. "I can't decide whether they are asking that question because they don't believe that any American is truly of America—aside from the natives. Or—"

"If they don't believe *we* are truly American."

Grant glanced over at her, a grin on his face. "Anyway, my ancestors most likely did not come from Egypt but . . ." He shrugged. "I don't know. It's Africa."

"It speaks to you."

"Yes, it does." He moved away from the glass. "As the butterfly's cousin, you will have an invitation to every party, every function, every event, every show. And you will listen and everything that you hear that stands out to you as important, you will convey. Make sense?"

"Yes."

"Good. Remember the invitation you finagled the other day? You're going to the party. But first, this Friday, you're attending an event at the Japanese embassy."

Elly's brain stuttered. "Japanese?" Her focus was entirely on Europe.

"I told you, the butterfly makes friends with everybody." Now, she was beginning to get a clearer picture of the doors that Josephine Baker was able to walk through. And it was sort of frightening. "This is just to get your feet wet. I need you to get used to speaking with foreign military men and dignitaries. It is my job to narrow down which members of the French military are possibly treasonous. It will be your job, eventually, to finger the exact traitor." The magnitude of such a goal nearly made her take a misstep. It was a bit much for a regular person like her, wasn't it? The insides of her stomach began dancing and she started to feel that nervous heat. "And I report to you? Not . . . the butterfly?"

"Correct. You do not report to the butterfly. Just to me. Although there's nothing wrong with you discussing what you learn with the butterfly. But remember, we have different handlers." Almost she asked him why the French trusted him so much. But then, she decided that the less she knew, the better.

"And I give you a call and ask to set up a meeting?"

"If necessary, yes, but otherwise we will meet every Monday and Thursday in the morning and we'll go for walks and visit museums, et cetera. Have you been to Versailles yet?"

"Yes, I've been to Versailles. Every Monday and Thursday?"

"For our dates. What's that you told your housemother? We're courting."

CHAPTER 10

Once again, Elly was on the river Seine headed to the U.S. embassy and thinking about Grant Monterey. Her boyfriend? She'd countered that point with his own words.

"Aren't you too old for me?"

"I am. Lucky for you, I don't look a day over thirty."

"I had you at at least thirty-two," Elly said, lying boldly.

They continued their trek through the African exhibit.

"Do you want to live with Josephine? That can be arranged."

"No," Elly said quickly. If she stayed with Josephine she'd always feel like she was playing a role. She was going to need some space to breathe. "I don't think Madame will mind if I continue to stay at her house—especially if the paper I work for continues to pay her

107

a fee, and I don't think it'll take much to convince them." She paused. "You *have* to court me? We can't just take walks around town?"

It was going to be stressful enough as it was, pretending to be Josephine's cousin.

Brushing at imaginary lint on his coat sleeve, Grant asked, "Do you think we're being watched right now?" It was a startling question that forced Elly to take a look around her surroundings. "I told you that this country is flooded with German spies and they're taking everything in, making notes for Hitler for when he arrives. And the Germans seem to have an unholy interest in people who don't fit his narrative. Josephine has already been clocked as a 'black devil.' I believe they refer to our kind as *negersmach*. Don't ask me to define that word. Whatever you guess it means won't be wrong."

Grant came to a stop, facing her. She didn't move as he closed the space between them and raised his hands. "May I touch your face?"

"My face? I suppose . . ."

She stood still as Grant's hands cupped her cheeks. It had been a very long time since she'd been touched in any way. It was one of the drawbacks of living away from family. No one hugged her just to hug her. No one touched her shoulder in passing. No one gently bumped into her as they walked side by side. It was very possible that she was starving for the feel of a gentle hand and she felt a shiver go down her spine as he lifted her chin with his thumb.

Her face flushed with something as he'd looked down at her as though he'd never seen a more beautiful woman and it took all of her willpower to maintain eye contact rather than look away. "The Germans are very methodical people," he said, his voice low and soothing. To a passerby, it probably looked like Grant was whispering sweet nothings to his lady love instead of talking about spies. "They are taking inventory of who is who and who is where. Do I think either of us are actual persons of interests? No." He removed his hands and took a step back. Then he extended a hand in her direction.

Slowly, reluctantly, she'd touched her palm to his. He linked his fingers through hers and tugged her to his side. "Let's not give them a reason to take interest. Okay?"

They hadn't talked for much longer than that. At the Christmas party at the Japanese embassy, she was being introduced to society, as it were. She had been given a small challenge: provide Grant with the ranks of every French officer in attendance. Then, she and Grant had picked a time and location to meet the following Monday to discuss things . . . and where he would pretend to court her.

Elly brought her hands to her cheeks, touching her face where he had touched her. She did not completely trust Grant Monterey, but that did not change the fact that he was a very attractive man and her body didn't know whether to fear him or lean into him. Releasing a breath of air, she dropped her hands. She needed to stop thinking about Grant and start focusing on the assignment she had been given: Japan.

She entered the U.S. embassy and asked if Richard Passmore was available to see her.

When she was informed that he was in his office, she quickly climbed the first set of stairs and when she reached the top landing, she leaned against the wall and took in deep breaths. It was all a bit much, wasn't it? Spying, pretending, risking life and limb. If only she could pause this moment, regroup, and then come back, but she had no such luxury.

Hearing footsteps below her, Elly gathered her strength and made her way to Richard's office.

"Elly!" Richard exclaimed as she entered his room. He stood up, hands lifted in excitement. "I was going to call you in an hour. I just got the news that your boat is sailing into Marseille as we speak. You'll need to catch the first train out of Paris—"

Elly held up a hand, stopping the rest of his words. She wasn't sure she could bear to hear them. "I'm not leaving. That's what I came here to tell you."

Richard stared at her, his mouth dropping open slightly in disbelief. "What happened?"

"What makes you think something happened?" Elly asked as she took a seat in front of his desk.

Following her example, Richard sat down as well, but he leaned forward. "I can't think of a single person who wants to leave this country more than you do. What happened?"

"I've decided to stay and keep on . . . writing." He knew she worked as a journalist.

By the dumbfounded expression on his face, he didn't entirely believe her. "Keep writing? Elly—"

"Are you leaving, Richard? Or are you staying?"

Richard exhaled and folded his hands together on the desk. "I am staying to the bitter end."

Elly's smile was small. "I don't know if I'm going to stay that long. But I'm not leaving yet."

"Are you sure?"

No. "Yes."

The room went silent for a long minute. "Elodie, I cannot promise you a way out after January."

"I understand," she said softly.

"The Germans . . . they won't see you as an American," he said politely.

"I understand that too."

Richard sat back in his seat, still looking a bit discombobulated. "If you need any help, I will do what I can."

"I know." She hesitated. "Thank you, Richard. For everything. I know you worked hard to get me home." She leaned forward in her seat. "Changing the subject a bit, what do you know about the Japanese?"

Elly paid the taxi driver who delivered her to the doorstep of Le Beau Chêne. "*Merci*."

Climbing out of the car, Elly reached back and grabbed her small overnight bag. She had been told to plan to spend the night because the party could last until the wee hours of the morning. Bracing herself a bit, she squared her shoulders and made her way up the grand steps of the house. The front door was opened before she reached it. "*Bonjour*."

"*Bonjour*, Mademoiselle Mitchell," the older gentleman, who could only be a butler, said. In French, he told her to come in and that it was so nice to meet a relative of Ms. Baker's. He told her that Ms. Baker was not at home at the moment but he'd been told to

111

show her to the room where she'd be staying and also that Polly was there waiting to assist her. To all of this, Elly provided a simple, "*Merci.*" 'Twas her favorite word in the French language. Right after *bonjour*.

The bedroom was typical of the era in which it was built: small, containing only a bed, a dresser, and a vanity. There was also a fireplace. Large spaces were a real problem when one lived in a time where heaters weren't a thing. But Elly liked the room. She particularly liked the window, which provided a stunning view of the garden.

There was a knock on the door. "Hello?" a familiar voice said on the other side.

Elly moved to open the door. "Hi, Polly."

"Elodie!" Polly lifted her hands in surrender. "I apologize for the mess that was last week. Had I known the Italian guy was gonna show up, I never would have asked you to try on that dress." Grant had informed Elly that surrounding Jo were three other people who knew about her espionage activities and occasionally participated in them themselves. One was her maid, Polly. Another was Pierre. And the last was Danny, the photographer. The three of them did not always know the details but they were willing to dance to whatever tune Josephine had to play at any given time.

"It is what it is. How are you doing?"

"Good. Now, come on. I've gotta find you a dress and get you ready for the party. Jo should have been here an hour ago, which tells me that we'll be pushing it when she comes racing through the door."

A half hour later, Polly had Elly in a ball gown. Josephine had closets full of evening dresses. "You two really are the same color. Everything that looks good on her will look good on you. And look at this hair!"

At Polly's request, Elly had pulled out all of the pins that were holding up her bun. Her hair was her most prized possession. It was the one thing Elly loved about herself completely. It was long and fell mid-back—when straightened. It was a whole 'nother story otherwise.

"Do you have Indian blood like Jo?"

"Very doubtful," Elly said, standing in front of the mirror. "Far as I know it's white and colored blood."

"This is not permed," Polly said knowledgeably as she gathered a fistful of Elly's hair.

"No. I straighten it with a hot comb."

"A hot comb does this?"

"It does if your hair is trained." Polly's eyes narrowed. "It's not as though I can run or jump or swim." Her hair wouldn't expand right away, but if she sweated or got wet, it was only a matter of time.

Polly grinned. "Girl, this hair got *you* trained. It would never work for Jo. Not with all the dancing she does. We have to perm her hair."

"Doesn't she have a hair product line?" Elly had vague recollections of seeing Jo Baker in advertisements holding a jar of pomade. "Bakerfix! Right?"

Polly's glance was sharp. "That stuff will snatch you bald. It's only a matter of time before Jo loses all the hair on her head. And that's why we thank the good Lord for the invention of the wig. We'll pin your hair up for tonight. Want to try on another dress or do you like this one?"

Elly looked at herself in the mirror. She was wearing an all-black velvet gown. It was sleeveless, fitted at the waist, and expanding at the bottom. Very sophisticated. "I like this."

"You'll need a pair of white gloves to complete the picture."

"Yes."

"Take a seat and let me fix your hair." Elly obeyed, sitting in front of the vanity. They were in Jo's dressing room. She had a whole space in the house dedicated to clothes, shoes, accessories, et cetera. Elly had never seen the like before. "We'll have to look through her jewelry. She has a fabulous pearl set that will go perfect."

"Oh, I have my own jewelry."

"I'm sure you do. I'm also sure Jo's is better. Don't worry, you'll never meet a person more generous than Jo Baker. She won't mind loaning it to you," Polly said as she began to run a comb through Elly's hair. Elly closed her eyes. She loved having her hair combed by someone other than herself. Those school mornings when Aunt Tabitha would fix her hair and ask her about the day ahead were some of the fondest in Elly's memory. But she wasn't Elly Mitchell, niece of Uncle Minor and Aunt Tabitha at the moment. She was Elly Mitchell, cousin to Jo Baker. She opened her eyes. "Polly? How long have you worked with Jo?"

Polly's sigh was loud. "I've known Jo for probably close to ten years. Would you believe I was once a chorus girl?" Polly was not overweight but neither was she as slender as most chorus girls were. "After a few years, I got tired of it but I've always loved shows. Every aspect of them. And I liked France. I didn't want to leave. When I heard Jo was looking for an all-around

114

girl—one who could do makeup and hair and sewing and whatnot? I told her I wanted the job. Can you hand me a pin?"

Elly complied.

"I've had no regrets since. She drives me crazy sometimes but I knew what she was like before I signed up."

"What's she like?"

"Late all the time. She'll argue with an empty house if she wakes up on the wrong side of the bed. And those animals!" Polly shuddered. "I don't mind a dog or a cat. Maybe even two dogs and two cats. But the pig and the goat?" Polly flashed her eyes in exasperation as she extended another hand for a pin. "But all of that aside, you'll never meet a person with a more generous heart and I'm not talking about money. Now, let's see how we're going to do your makeup."

"I usually only wear lipstick. Most foundations either make me look too dark or too light."

"Same with Jo. We usually go lighter. Don't look at me like that! I've mastered the art of using white makeup for colored skin. You won't look like a clown, I promise. But a woman ought not have a bare face. Especially at a swanky event like this one."

Elly grew quiet as Polly began to pluck at her eyebrows and brush at her face with things. "What do you think about all this?" Elly asked through clenched teeth so that her face didn't move.

Polly's hand paused for a second. "I think it fits who Jo is. When she told me that she'd been contacted by the French, my first thought was, of course. She loves this country."

"What about Grant?"

Polly looked away as she reached for some powdery stuff. "Grant, is a relic." She paused as though to say something else and then changed her mind. "I've known him for years and years and nothing about him changes. He's that big brother you hope you don't need but inevitably do. Need money? Ask Grant. Need a job? Ask Grant. Need help with the French? Ask Grant. He knows everything there is to know about everybody and yet he never asks questions. But Jo really likes him. I also think she always wanted an older brother and she's found one in him. I'm gonna be honest, he's probably one of the few men who has known Jo for years and years and has never slept with her. Take a look at yourself. What do you think?"

Elly looked in the mirror. Polly was right. She knew how to wield makeup. Elly was about a shade lighter in the face and it should have looked odd but since the skin on her chest rarely saw sun, it all sort of worked. "You'll have to teach me your tricks."

"Love to!"

Elly sat back in her seat. "How did you get tied up in all of this . . . spy business?"

"I was probably the first person Jo told after the powers that be contacted her. She was gonna need somebody to help her get ready for all these political events that she started going to. And sometimes people need to be available when strange men show up," Polly said, grinning widely. "But I don't want details and I don't ask."

"You're not worried about the war? You don't want to go home?"

116

Polly reached for the makeup tins, closing them. "I was born and raised in Tennessee, honey. The birthplace of the Klan. The way I figure it, we colored folks have always lived dangerously."

CHAPTER 11

In the distance, Elly heard a door open and then male laughter. "That'll be Pierre and Danny. They've come to help me fill you in on the nitty-gritty details of all that is Jo Baker. Don't worry, it's not gossip if it's true," Polly said with a wink.

Jo's butler led Pierre and Danny to the dressing room. One of them knocked. "Come in. We're decent!" Polly hollered as she continued to top up different products.

"Julien gave us a bottle of Jo's finest champagne!" Danny announced upon entering. Indeed, in his hand was said drink and two empty flute glasses. "Jo's twin is here," Danny said tongue-in-cheek.

"Hello, Danny," Elly said as she stood up to greet him.

"Don't know how anyone could have gotten you confused with Jo," Pierre said in that languid voice of his. He was also holding two empty glasses and by the way he was leaning against the doorway he looked as though he didn't have a care in the world. Except his light eyes were focused. Focused on her in particular.

"Pierre!" Polly left Elly's side and flung her arms around her boyfriend's waist—although if Elly recalled, he didn't like labels. Pierre returned the action hugging her tightly, but he was still looking at Elly with an expression that said he was trying to figure her out. She looked away.

"It's like they don't see each other every day," Danny muttered to Elly. "Hold these." Without waiting for a response he shoved the glasses at her while he popped open the bottle of champagne. "If I'm going to spend the next hour talking about Jo, I need all the alcohol I can get."

"Where's Grant?" Elly asked. Since everyone else was there, it seemed odd that he was missing.

Pierre's lips twisted to the side. "Grant caught a train up to Romagne-sous-Montfaucon. He went to visit friends." With affection and a slight hint of possessiveness, Pierre patted Polly's backside. Elly didn't mean to flinch. It was just that she didn't think she'd ever get used to such flagrant intimate public displays of affection. But Pierre caught the movement and his eyes narrowed. "Let's get this show on the road."

Elly returned to her chair at the vanity, but she turned it around first so that it faced the couch in the room that held Pierre, Danny, and Polly. Danny very kindly poured everyone a drink except her since she was working tonight.

"Her mama named her Freda Josephine McDonald," Danny said with authority.

"I thought it was Josephine Freda McDonald?"

"I'm ninety-eight percent sure I'm right and you're wrong," Danny told Pierre.

"Her family calls her Tumpy, something to do with Humpty Dumpty and her being a fat baby," Polly said before taking a sip of her champagne.

"It's unclear who Jo's father is. If she knows, she's not telling. What I do know is that she gives a different story every time the question is asked. Sometimes he's a white guy. Sometimes he's light-skinned Negro," Pierre said, drawing out his words as he leaned back against the couch.

"She's one of three on her mama's side. There's Richard, Margaret, and there was Willa Mae. Willa Mae died a few years back. Botched abortion," Polly whispered even though no one else was in the room. She waved a hand. "Don't bring it up. They were very close."

Elly bit down on her lip to try to keep from reacting. But a thousand questions filled her head. How did Polly know this? Why had Willa Mae taken such a risk when her sister was the most famous woman in the world? Did Elly really need to know about the abortion? Was this not personal, private information that one should keep to themselves?

"You've just shocked the girl's sensibilities," Pierre told Polly in a stage whisper. Elly didn't look in his direction because she knew that was what he wanted. "Poor girl. Probably grew up sheltered. She's not a wild one like you, Polly."

"Well, she's not gonna be sheltered for long if she's spending time with Jo. It's better that I prepare her now than that she be surprised later."

"Anyway," Danny sang. "She's been married three times. The first one . . . I don't even remember the fella's name but she was young. Thirteen? Fourteen? Something like that. The second one was Mr. William Baker. Don't tell anybody I told you, but it's a toss-up as to whether or not they're still married. Jo doesn't always follow the rules. The third husband is Jean Lion who is on his way out the door as we speak . . . which is very sad. I don't know how she walks away from all his money. I, for one, would put up with a lot for Jean Lion's bank account."

"He takes too many trips." Polly tipped her glass at Elly. "Jo does not like to be alone. Some people need to have someone around them all the time."

"And when it comes to lovers, Jo has no preference: male, female, good-looking or ugly. So long as they're warm and breathing, Jo does not mind."

"Danny!"

"Well, it's the truth, Polly. Are we gonna pretend like it isn't?"

"I think it's just rumors and suppositions," Polly said politely but the look in her eyes indicated that she probably knew more than what she was telling.

"Rumors and suppositions have to start somewhere. And you know what she's like. She loves to be adored. She doesn't care who is doing the adoring. Not," Danny was quick to say, "to say she's narcissistic or anything like that. She just loves to be loved by people who love her."

Elly touched two fingers to her forehead, tempted, oh so tempted, to ask them if they had decided to play the game of shock and awe with the new girl although to be fair, they were winning. Her childhood being what it was, she'd never once considered herself to be sheltered or naive. There were days she thought she'd been born an old woman. But the fact of the matter was, there were some topics she'd been raised to simply not talk about and sometimes it seemed that everywhere she turned in this country she came face-to-face with something she'd always thought was best mentioned under the cover of darkness and only in extreme circumstances.

"She's just very lonely sometimes," Polly told Elly, trying to explain. "You wouldn't think so, but it's not easy being at the top."

Elly raised a hand. "Please, can we discuss what's going to be helpful to my role here?"

Pierre was taking a sip of his champagne and smirking at her, apparently amused by her reticence. Whatever. Let him be amused.

"She's been in five movies: *Siren of the Tropics*, *The Woman from the Folies Bergères*, *Parisian Pleasures*, *Zouzou*, and *Princesse Tam-Tam*. Have you seen any of them?"

"No. They're French, aren't they?" She would have had to really search for a theater that would show such films back home and Elly had not had any strong desire to see these movies, which to Elly's understanding had always featured Jo as the exotic other seducing the white man.

"They are French," Polly said slowly, amusement on her face as she eyed the contents of her glass. "Very French."

"Not as French as some of her live shows," Danny

said and then went on to provide Elly with a list of names.

"Jo doesn't have much in the way of schooling. Supposedly she could barely read and write when she first got here in 1925. Either way she has chosen to become more learned," Pierre told Elly. "She has worked with a number of coaches to bring her up to snuff, as they say."

"And she learned French pretty much all on her own," Polly added. "Through sheer will and determination."

"When Jo wants something, nobody can stop her."

"Her most famous song is 'J'ai Deux Amours'."

"She can't drive worth a lick but that has not stopped Paris from giving her license to do so."

"She loves small children."

"She gives a lot to charity."

And on and on it went with them flinging one fact after another at her. And because Elly was trying to hold on to every word, she began to feel the beginnings of a headache. The same sort of headache she got when trying to cram information into her head for an exam.

Then the dressing room door opened. "Are you talking about me, *chérie*?" And Josephine Baker stood there in all her finery.

Polly stood quickly. "You're late."

"You know what Henri is like. He is never satisfied. We must do it again and again. And that Chevalier— do not get me started," Jo said as she entered the room, tugging on her gloves. "How much time do we have before we need to leave?"

"Forty-five minutes."

"Plenty of time!" Jo said with a laugh. "*Bonsoir,*

Pierre," she said as Pierre greeted her in the French way of *faire des bisous*, exchanging kisses on each cheek. "And just how did you get out of rehearsals so close to the raise of the curtain?"

"How do I get out of anything?" Pierre asked, a smile dancing on his lips. "Grant."

Jo slapped an empty glove across his chest. "You'll get him in trouble one day."

"It was his idea."

Jo looked unconvinced as she moved to greet Danny, exchanging kisses with him as well. "I hope you brought your camera, darling."

"Always. It's downstairs."

"Good. Get some pictures of me before I leave."

Jo turned toward Elly and Elly stood up. The older woman paused to take in Elly's hair, makeup, and dress while the most recent facts Elly had learned of Jo spun in her head. "That looks better on her than it ever did on me. You can have it, *ma cousine*."

"Oh no, that's okay," Elly said, taken off guard.

"She protests," Jo said, speaking to Danny and Pierre as she began to unfasten the hooks on her dress. "Everything I say she pushes back on."

"I didn't mean to be rude. I—"

Josephine's dress fell to the ground and there she stood in her undergarments. With two men in the room who were unrelated. Aunt Tabitha got heart palpitations if Elly accidentally entered the living room in a floor-length nightgown and Uncle Minor's winter robe when male guests were still at the house—and they were usually well over the age of sixty. Elly was beginning to see that this was going to be a very high learning curve.

"Thank you, Miss Josephine. Since I'm ready, I'll wait for you downstairs." It would have been a good time to ask Jo any questions she had. But she needed some space. Elly quickly left the room but she didn't get a moment to breathe because Pierre followed her.

"You are not very French are you?" he asked lazily, heavy on her trail.

"What gave me away? The accent?" Deciding to ignore him, she lifted her skirts and glided down the marvelous staircase feeling momentarily like a princess out of a fairy tale. Pierre continued to follow.

"Being French is not a nationality, per se. It is a lifestyle: *liberté, egalité, fraternité.*"

"Okay," she agreed, just to get rid of him. She reached the first floor.

A hand grabbed her arm, pulling her to a stop. Elly looked up at Pierre who still stood a few steps above her. "What you're doing is very important. You cannot mess it up. If your cousin is Josephine Baker, you cannot flinch every time she says or does something that clashes with your upbringing."

Elly placed her hand on his arm and pushed until he released her. "Mr. Roche, it may surprise you, but I do not have to be French to be Jo Baker's cousin. While I can change a few details and adopt a few mannerisms in order for this to work, I cannot be anything other than myself. If you have a problem, tell Grant, and I will happily board a ship back to the States. Now, I'm going to sit over there in that chair and wait for Miss Baker. I suggest you find something else to do with your time besides bothering me."

Pierre blinked once very slowly before raising his

hands in surrender. "I will trust that you know what's best, Miss Mitchell. It's not me you have to convince anyway. It's the Japanese, the Italians, the French, the Germans, and representatives from every other country you come into contact with this evening."

CHAPTER 12

"My dearest friend is going to be here tonight. That's how I got the invitation," Jo told Elly in the car. They'd left Polly, Danny, and Pierre in the house. Jo had given them another bottle of champagne—which from the sound of their gasps had been quite expensive and rare. Elly had no way of knowing. She'd been raised in a teetotaling household. That didn't mean that she subscribed to such thoughts. She very happily enjoyed a glass of wine whenever Madame served it at dinner knowing full well that such an option would be off the table once she returned home. She supposed she could continue the habit if she chose but while she might disagree with Uncle Minor and Aunt Tabitha, she loved and respected them too much to do so— particularly while she still lived in their home. "We met because we're both involved in the same charities. She's married to the ambassador from Japan."

Elly stopped daydreaming and forced herself to concentrate.

Jo's butler had doubled as a driver for the evening and he was escorting them to the embassy.

"Does she know about . . . ?"

"No," Jo said, shaking her head as she tugged on her white gloves. She was wearing a long, silver silk gown that very much flattered her trim figure. Diamonds sparkled in her ears and around her neck. Elly had always thought the Valcourts had wealth. They were nothing compared to the woman sitting next to her. Elly reached up and touched her hands to the pearl necklace draped around her neck. The pearl set that Jo had also tried to give her declaring pearls to not be her taste. "Don't worry about anything tonight. I'm supposed to find out Japan's intentions toward France in specificity and Europe in general. You are just there to take in the show."

Those had been Elly's marching orders: observe and report back. But the part of her who had taken advantage of every extra study session, every extra school assignment even if she was at the top of her class, wanted to do more than just observe.

Their ride pulled into the slow procession of cars that extended from the Japanese embassy's drive, and Elly's heart began to pound as her body flooded with nerves. There was nothing to be stressed out about. She wasn't being asked to discover any secrets. No one was thinking about her at the Japanese embassy. For that matter, no one knew her. But that didn't stop the nervous heat from rising within as the car came to a stop.

"Take a deep breath." Jo's words were a whisper. Elly closed her eyes and obeyed. "Release the death grip on the door handle. It's never done anything to you."

Elly took her hand off the door and placed it in her lap.

"You're just a girl visiting Europe and enjoying the night life."

Eyes still closed, Elly asked, "Are you not the slightest bit nervous?"

"What's one more performance?"

A good point. It was just a performance. The passenger door was opened and Elly was helped out of the car. She and Josephine were escorted into a fancy building that was lit up from the inside out. Through the windows, Elly could see that the embassy was filled with people already. A live band was playing music and Christmas tunes were dancing in the air.

Josephine handed her invitation to someone at the front door and she was announced. It felt as though everyone in the room turned in their direction. Elly took several steps to the right as Jo struck a pose. "*Bonsoir!*"

Looking around, Elly saw faces fill with joy and awe. Behold the power of Josephine Baker.

"Jo!" Elly watched as a slight Japanese woman moved to embrace the famous singer. "You came!"

"I told you I would! Oh, look, I brought my cousin, Elodie. Elodie?"

Elly took several steps forward. She dipped her head in a brief bow, aware that bowing was part of Japanese etiquette. For two seconds, she considered saying, *konnichiwa*, but decided to play the safe route. "*Bonsoir*, madame."

"I didn't know you had a cousin in town! *Bonsoir*, Elodie," the Japanese woman said, very friendly and open and not at all reserved in the way that Elly had assumed Japanese women were. "It's nice to meet you!"

"It's a pleasure to meet you as well!" Elly patiently stood there, being introduced to a number of Japanese officials she'd never thought she'd meet in her life until she found an opportune time to slip away.

She'd wondered if the embassy would be overtly Japanese, but if anything, it was overtly European with small hints of Japanese culture sprinkled throughout. When a server passed with a tray of champagne, Elly took a glass and found a corner in the room. Starting with the waitstaff, she began taking in her surroundings.

A few of the waiters were Japanese but most were French. She took in their looks, their clothes, their posture and who they seemed to hover around. Then her eyes drifted to the French officers in the room. She counted one general, seven lieutenants, and three colonels.

She was careful not to stay in one place. She could not blend into the walls no matter how much she wanted to. She and Jo were the only Negroes in the whole building. It was a feeling she was somewhat used to. One didn't get into higher education without entering spaces where one was a minority.

Elly tossed a glance at her 'cousin' who was laughing at something someone said. Elly might hate the feeling that everyone was sort of side-eyeing her, but Jo clearly loved it . . . if she even recognized such a feeling at all. Remembering Jo's frustration with being treated like a Negro in America, it was very possible that Jo was one of those rare people who really and truly didn't care what color anyone's skin was. A very high ideal to aspire to if rather fantastical.

Not wanting to seem like a creepy person watching, Elly searched the room for someone who reminded her of herself. And then she found her. It was a woman dressed in a colorful kimono, sitting off to the side and alone. The few friends Elly had ever made over the years were girls who had seen her quiet nature and reticence and very gently pushed those boundaries. Because despite Elly's loner ways, she was drawn to those whose natures were opposite to hers.

She took the empty seat next to the woman who looked as though she could be anywhere between twenty-five and forty-five. When they made eye contact, Elly dipped her head, bowing lightly in greeting. To this woman, she said, "*Konnichiwa.*"

"Hello," the woman said kindly. She leaned in Elly's direction. "You will forgive me but my English is better than my French."

"There is nothing to forgive," Elly said quickly. "So is mine." They shared a mutual smile of understanding. Elly reached into her purse and pulled out her fan. She snapped it open. It was black and silk and fashioned into something like a spider's web. "How long have you been in France?"

"Not long. My husband and I just recently arrived from Germany."

"Germany," Elly repeated slowly, careful to tamp down the small thrill that raced through her body.

"Yes, Berlin. Have you ever been?"

"No, ma'am. I hear it's quite cold there."

"Very," the woman said. "And the food is . . . interesting."

"Hearty is what I was told."

"Very hearty," the woman agreed politely. Whispering conspiratorially, she said, "I desperately crave rice."

Elly closed her fan and pointed to herself. "Me too!" It was true. She'd been raised where rice was served at nearly every meal. She had found that to not be the case here in France.

"I told my husband, we're coming just for the food. I expect rice to be served or this place does not reflect Japan at all!"

Elly grinned. "Who is your husband?" The woman pointed to a man in a uniform. Elly had spent the morning learning what the different insignias meant on the Japanese uniforms. This woman's husband was a general and he was speaking to an Italian colonel. "Will you be in France long?"

"No. We are returning home hopefully within the month."

"That has to be a very long trip."

"You would not believe how long it took us to get here. It was so long it nearly justifies the past two months we've spent in Europe. First we were in Italy, then Germany, now France. You are American?"

"I am, yes," Elly said slowly, knowing that America and Japan were not on the best footing right now due to Japan's current invasion of China. "I came with my cousin. Do you see her over there?"

"She's hard to miss. You may call me Mei." The woman held out her hand.

"Elodie, but everyone calls me Elly." Elly nodded in the direction of Jo. "Her new show *Paris-London* opens in two weeks. Would you like tickets to attend?" Jo had given her a few to give out.

Mei's mouth dropped open slightly. She looked both surprised and pleased. "I don't know what my husband's schedule looks like," she began slowly. But then she said, "Forget him. I'll bring a friend if I have to. I'd love to go."

Opening her small purse, Elly handed the woman the tickets. "Did you see many shows in Germany? I hear they have quite an opera house."

"We did not make it. My husband was too busy meeting with Göring and Himmler and . . ." Elly soaked in the names of what she recognized as very powerful German men who surrounded Hitler. Mei was name-dropping, perhaps to show that she knew important people too. Well, name on, Elly thought.

They talked together until it was time for dinner.

"I have to go. It was so lovely to meet you, Elly,"

"Likewise," Elly told the woman. Fanning herself, Elly looked around the room. This was one of those dinners where men escorted women to the table and so she was not surprised to see Jo on the arm of a Japanese lieutenant-general.

Well, she had no problems escorting herself but just when she started to stand, a hand appeared. "Miss Mitchell," Richard Passmore said with one eyebrow raised. "So interesting to see you here."

133

CHAPTER 13

The clouds might have been hanging heavy in the sky and every gust of wind was leaving a chill in its wake, but still Elly and Grant walked les Jardins du Luxembourg. Like the romantic couple they were pretending to be, Elly's arm was looped through Grant's and there was very little space between them.

"I don't think you need to be worried about Mr. Passmore. You probably raised a red flag with him anyway when you decided to stay in Paris after begging to be returned home." She'd had to explain to Grant why and how she knew Richard Passmore. "He escorted you to dinner and that was it?"

"Yes. The tables already had cards where everyone was to sit. I didn't see much of him for the rest of the evening." Although she couldn't help but keep searching for him in the room as though he were some kind of lifeline.

"You promised me good news." She'd started the conversation with the familiar adage of having good and bad news.

"I spoke with a woman whose husband had just been to Germany." Elly went on to describe her conversation with Mei all the while wondering why it was she was trying to please the man who was pressed so close to her. Of course he was looking very handsome in his all black. His scarf today was made up of many different shades of red. "What do you think?" she asked when she finished her recitation. She pulled away slightly to get a glimpse of his eyes, which were shaded by the black hat on his head. The look he slid her was one that indicated that he was thoroughly unimpressed. "But she said—"

"A few years ago, Japan and Germany signed the Anti-Comintern Pact."

"I know that!"

"The fact that they are allies is not news. I imagine they talk to each other regularly." Elly opened her mouth. Then closed it. "But—"

"Now, if the wife was able to tell you what they had talked about, then you might have something there. How about we circle back to the thing you were asked to do? What did you observe?" he asked, sounding very much like a teacher who was irritated with his student.

Annoyed with herself for failing to grasp what was important and what wasn't, and annoyed with him for not letting her off the hook, she started to pull her arm away, but Grant held on tight. He reached over and patted her arm. "My darling, let's not argue today."

Fighting the urge to mumble something rude under her breath, Elly went on to tell him how many French officers had been at the embassy including their respective ranks. She told him about the different nations that were represented at the party and ended with the number of waitstaff she had come across.

"Very good." Grant came to a stop, facing her. He moved his hands to her waist and she could not help but stiffen at the physical contact although she had reluctantly given him permission to play the romantic. Tilting his head to the side, Grant eyed her. "You need to relax."

"Hard to do so when a stranger is touching me."

Grant's grin was rueful. "Reach into my coat pocket. The one inside my jacket above my heart and pull out the sheet of paper there."

"Why can't you reach into your own pocket?" she grumbled even as she carefully obeyed. Trying to touch only his clothes and not him, she found that tucked against his chest was a folded sheet of paper. She opened it. It was a map of a city that she was not familiar with.

"You have thirty seconds to memorize everything you see on that paper and then you're going to redraw it."

"I'm going to what?"

"Twenty-five seconds."

Elly pulled away from Grant, but she didn't get far, because he grabbed her hand, linking their fingers together. Elly had never been in any sort of serious relationship and she wondered if all this constant touching was necessary. But she put a pin in that thought as she focused on the sketch before her. When her time was up, Grant snatched the document out of her hands. "Now, we're going to sit on the bench and you're going to redraw it while also pretending like you're drawing your lover's face."

"Why on earth would I draw my lover's face?" she asked as they took a seat on the nearest empty bench.

"You wouldn't want to have a picture of your boyfriend if you had one?"

"Yes, but the camera was invented for a reason." Ignoring her, Grant reached into the satchel he had slung around his neck and pulled out paper, pencil, and a flat easel-looking thing. "Is this the dark ages? Am I Da Vinci?" It was different with Grant than it was with Jo. With Grant, she felt no need to censor herself.

"You're not a very romantic person, are you?"

"I can be romantic," she countered. "When I know it's real and genuine? Well, there's no one more romantic than me."

"I believe you," Grant muttered. He leaned back against the armrest of the bench as though modeling. "I'll give you two minutes, darling."

Elly made a face but then ignored him as she began to redraw everything she'd seen in thirty seconds.

"Time's up."

Elly handed him her sketch of the map. She watched his eyes scan her drawing and then he balled it up like it was complete, utter trash. "I see we're going to have to try this again."

"That did not look very loverly just now. Anyone watching is probably thinking, that fella is about to get pushed to the side."

137

"I see. In actuality, you talk a lot. Here." He reached into his satchel and handed her another map. A different city. "Thirty seconds starts now."

Elly ended up drafting five city maps before Grant said anything positive about any of them. "We're going to keep practicing this," he murmured as he slipped the last drawing into his bag. "We're also going to work on your French. Starting next week, you will only speak French to me on Mondays."

"Those will be very short conversations."

"What if you have to convey important information to someone who doesn't speak English? You cannot *'merci, beaucoup'* your way through it." Elly raised a hand to her hair, nearly dislodging her hat. Had the semester ended? She was in school all over again. Grant slid across the bench, wrapping an arm around her and tucking her into his side. Not quite like school, she thought, as he gently lifted her face so that their eyes were meeting. She was never going to get used to this sort of intimacy. Never. "Next week is the Christmas party at the Italian embassy. Once again, you are there to observe. But, I also have a task for you."

He reached into his pocket and pulled out an envelope. Then, he undid the buttons of her coat just above her chest and carefully tucked the envelope there. Redoing the buttons, he said, "Recently it came to the attention of the French military that several of their new weapon designs had been misplaced. I have just given you photographs of three men, one of whom is trying to pass on the designs of a new French rifle currently in production to the Germans. Your mission is to figure out which man is the traitor." Elly blinked, starting to feel a wave of incredulity begin to form. "All three will be in attendance at the party. All three will be invited to Jo's next show. If Jo needs to host a holiday party of her own, she will do so and have all three there." He reached out, placing a hand on her arm, rubbing her tenderly. "I'm not saying time is of the essence, but we'd like to know the information before the month of January ends." Elly considered that. That gave her less than six weeks. "Stand up."

Elly obeyed and Grant slipped his hands around her waist. He leaned down to *faire des bisous*. Most *faire des bisous* were not actually lips to cheek, but cheek to cheek while making a sort of kissing noise. Grant brushed his cheek against the right side of her face, sending familiar shivers down her body. *Not real,* she told herself. *Get yourself together.* "Memorize those faces." He pressed his cheek against the left side of her face. "And then burn those pictures. Until next time, *chérie.*" And then he was gone.

Elly felt oddly cold and strangely lost standing there alone in the Luxembourg garden. It took her a minute to remember that she needed to return to the apartment. She nearly pressed a hand to her chest to touch the envelope Grant had placed there, but then decided against it, not wanting to draw any attention in case they were being watched. She shoved her hands into her pockets. It probably was very nice to have a boyfriend. A real one.

Fifteen minutes later she was taking a few steps into the living room and the kitchen, she called out, "Hello?" Again, there was no response. Hurriedly, she removed her coat and grabbed the envelope that Grant had placed there. Then she made her way to her bedroom, closed the door, and pulled out the three pictures inside. How to memorize a face? She thought back to the map-drawing exercise she had done with Grant. She focused on distinctive marks and features. Two of the men had black hair. One was blond. One man had a mole just above his mouth. Another had what looked to be a tiny scar above his brow. Two had thin lips, one had full lips. She categorized their eyes, their noses, their brows. And then she gave them stories to fit their faces. One man had recently left his wife for a woman twenty years younger. Another had a son that he was estranged from but very proud of. The last was in love with a woman who wanted nothing to do with him.

Finally, feeling like she'd recognize these men if they passed her on the street, she left her room and made her way to the fireplace. Getting a small fire started, she got down on her knees and fed each photograph to the fire, watching the men's faces turn into ash.

The door of the apartment opened. "*Bonjour,* Élodie."

"*Bonjour,* Madame," Elly said as she quickly put out what was left of the fire. "Let me help you with those groceries." As Elly had known, Madame had been happy to have her stay for as long as she needed, particularly when Elly had informed her that she would continue to be paid. Elly had reached out to the cousin who had jokingly asked her to stay on as a wartime correspondent. She'd gotten a stern letter back telling her that she really didn't have to. And did she want him to get in trouble with Uncle Minor and Aunt Tabitha who had lectured him no less than five times on how he never should have asked a single young woman alone in a foreign country to do a job most men didn't want to do? But in his postscript, he'd effused much thanks and promised payment to her as well as living expenses. Living expenses she'd pass on to Madame.

"And how was your day?" the older woman asked as she began to remove meats and cheeses and bread from her bags. Elly grabbed the bag that held fruits and vegetables.

"It was good. How was yours, Madame?"

"Fine, fine. Did you see Grant today?"

"*Oui*, Madame." Elly had told Madame and Claire that she had decided to stay in Paris to continue to write for the paper. But they had jokingly teased her that she had decided to stay for Grant.

"A few weeks ago, you could not wait to leave."

"Only because of the war, Madame," Elly said, carefully stacking up the apples that Madame had purchased.

"You were trying to tell me that I needed to leave."

"I still think you should leave. I'm an American. I have a way out." Maybe. She hoped. "This is your country. If Hitler invades, you'll be in real trouble." They'd had this conversation before but to no avail. No one was going to push Madame Auger out of the apartment her many times great-grandmother had earned serving the Duc of something or the other.

"If you honestly believe that, you should not stay here yourself. Not even for a man," Madame said,

141

waving a finger in her direction. Elly sighed, swallowing her frustration. She supposed she did look something like a hypocrite.

"Madame, I promise you that I will never risk my safety for a man. He can risk *his* for me." Madame released a snort. "But please, Madame, think about leaving. This 'phony war' is only phony because Hitler's busy at the moment."

"You don't understand. We are French," Madame said as though that made a difference as to how Hitler would treat them versus the way he'd treated other people in other countries. Or maybe she just thought the French army would be successful. And they might be. It still didn't hurt to have a backup plan.

"Madame, Claire's mother was Jewish, which means she is considered Jewish. The Germans are not treating the Jews kindly. There are reports that they are putting them in camps and anytime the WASPs get to stay in their homes while the others are rounded up, you know things are not about to turn in your favor." Her pronouns had shifted but she knew what it was to be other. The separation of the Jews felt slightly personal. She was certain the Germans would do the same to her kind if they could.

"Élodie!" Madame's voice was sharp.

Elly's sigh was deep. "*Désolée*, Madame." So maybe she could not convince Madame. As much as she hated to go around the woman, maybe she needed to talk to Claire.

142

CHAPTER 14

"Any words of advice?" Elly asked Jo. Once again, they were both dressed to the nines. Elly was wearing another one of Jo's ball gowns. This one was dark blue with feathery accents at the shoulders. Josephine's dress was also a ball gown but it was striped and had a see-through sheer overlay. It was exceptionally pretty and very modern.

"On getting information out of men?" Jo asked, eyebrow raised. Because she knew what Elly's assignment entailed.

Elly did not have to wonder as to why the mission had been given to her and not Jo. Whatever you might say about Jo Baker, she was a hardworking woman. She was in talks for a new film, she was finalizing details on *Paris-London*, which was opening in a week. Tonight she needed to learn Mussolini's intentions toward France—and in her free time she was flying aid to refugees in the Low Countries as part of her duties with Infirmières Pilotes Secouristes de l'Air, which was the aviation section of the French Red Cross.

It meant that the only time Elly could speak to Jo was in the car on the way to events. Like now.

"Some women will say to you that every man is the same," Jo said, punctuating each word with a slight thrust of her hand. "I say to you that every man is different. He is king of his own castle and if you can recognize and acknowledge it? You might get a talker."

King of his own castle. Elly slid her eyes in Jo's direction. "You mean treat him as though he were special?"

"Treat him as though you've been waiting to speak to him your whole life." Elly took that advice and mentally slipped it into her purse.

"Thank you, ma'am," Elly quipped as she fell back against her seat.

Jo's eyes narrowed. "Are you trying to be funny, dear cousin?"

"What? Oh, I didn't mean ma'am like that. It was just an expression."

"Because I hope you realize that what with me being ten years older than you, the fact that people keep getting us confused is a compliment only to one of us. And it's not you."

Elly released a snort because while she understood Jo's point, it absolutely wasn't true. Her snort turned to laughter and then Jo was laughing.

"I will never say ma'am again," Elly promised, her hands raised in surrender.

"We're cousins! You keep talking to me like we're

not. Admit that you don't refer to your older cousins as ma'am."

"I don't," Elly acknowledged. But still for some reason it was far easier to pretend to be Jo's cousin when Jo was not around. It felt a bit presumptuous to Elly to act like the woman was anyone less than the Josephine Baker. But she would try. She had to. She didn't have much time to think about it further because the car came to a stop. They were both helped out, announced, and then welcomed. Elly carefully separated herself from Josephine whose very entrance was like a lit match to gasoline. Around them lights sparkled and women shined in their finery, but Josephine transcended them all.

She was a wonderful distraction, Elly thought, as she looked for a corner to collect herself in. She nearly bumped into a man as she made her way across the room. She hid a rueful smile as Signore Achille passed by her in his haste to greet Josephine. For a second, she glanced back. He did not seem the least bit confused at the sight of the real Josephine Baker.

Elly reached into her purse and snapped open her fan. This one was blue and silver and sparkling. *Become charming. Don't be Elly Mitchell,* she told herself. *Become someone more like Josephine.* Someone with so much confidence, it didn't matter what happened or didn't happen. If there was an awkward moment, it was not her problem. A waiter passed by her holding a tray of glasses, Elly tucked her purse under her arm and reached for the champagne.

Taking a small sip, she scanned the room. Because so many men were in uniform, it took a while to find her targets. But she was very happy to recognize all three of the men whom she was to learn more about.

Make them king of their castle. Convince them that she found no man more interesting than them. With a deep fortifying breath, Elly crossed the room and approached her first target who seemed to have come alone.

Grant was taking her to a crêperie. They'd met near the Champs-Élysées where Elly had provided him with a rundown of the evening before.

"It was boring," she said in conclusion. In some ways it had been a success. Of her three targets, she'd managed to hold the lieutenant's attention all evening. But she had learned nothing of value. Instead, she'd been treated to tales of his wife, who was currently in the south of France visiting family, his ailing mother who refused to leave her home that was less than fifty miles from the Maginot Line. She learned about his children and the gifts he wished he could buy them for Christmas. Happy as she was that he was a family man, she did not know why he felt compelled to share so much with a stranger. But she had smiled and nodded in the right places. She'd held eye contact and by golly, she'd made the man feel like a king.

"You're building trust and that's a good thing. The race is not to the swift." And then he led her to the crêperie.

Most crêperies were slowly disappearing as rationing was becoming the order of the day. But this one was still alive and well although limping a bit by only offering a few selections.

"Order for us," Grant commanded politely as they took their place in line.

"What do you want? Do you want me to pick for you?"

She thought he looked like Toussaint today in his dark clothes. A deep purple scarf was wrapped loosely around his neck.

"Sure. That's fine."

"You want to know something that I did notice yesterday?" Elly didn't wait for him to answer. Standing on her tiptoes a bit, she leaned over and whispered in his ear. "The waitstaff. Three of them were the same from the other party." To this, Grant tilted his head. "Do you think they used the same company?"

"I'll find out." Elly bit down on her lip to stop herself from grinning. Maybe she had accomplished something after all. They didn't speak as the line moved up. And then it was her turn to order.

"*Bonjour. Je voudrais* . . ."

"*Je voudrais?*" Grant whispered as they moved to stand to the side while their crêpes were being made.

"What's wrong with '*Je voudrais*'?" The words translated as 'I would like.'

"There's nothing wrong with it," he said slowly. "It's just not generally used."

"It gets the job done, doesn't it? You wanted me to speak French? Behold! French!"

"Yes, but . . . you read a lot of French, correct? Everyday speaking French is different from . . . reading French."

"I'm sorry but you don't get to be fussy about me

147

not speaking French and then complain when I do speak French."

"Is there no one you practice French with? What about the family you're living with?"

"Madame and Claire want to practice their English. Far be it from me to be so selfish as to deny them."

"Madame?" Grant said, judgment coloring his words. "You do know that to call a woman just Madame is not the same as calling her ma'am?"

"She told me to call her Madame, thank you very much. And I call her Madame Auger in public."

"What about when you were in school?"

"It was an American program. My professors were expats."

Grant blinked. "Of course they were."

"But I've been told my accent is phenomenal." She made an okay sign with her hand.

"I honestly wouldn't know. I've only heard you speak about five words. And I can't imagine that the person who told you that has heard you speak more than three."

Elly rolled her eyes. Seeing that the vendor had just finished wrapping up their orders, she removed her hand from his so she could grab their snacks. She'd decided to step out of her comfort zone and they both had an egg and ham-and-cheese-filled crêpe.

"Have you been to La Tour Eiffel?" Grant asked her in French.

"*Mais oui!*" she said with a grin, proud of herself for the quick response.

Grant shot her a look before sighing deeply. "When we get to the park, I'm going to give you a letter and a cipher. You must decode it," he said, his words very low and in English so she could make no mistake. "You will then use said cipher to write a response back to me. Understand?"

"Yes." After taking a few bites of her food, she said, "Do you know who else I saw yesterday? Richard." They had not spoken although she knew he had seen her too. "I was thinking that maybe we should ask him for help? America is an ally, right?"

Grant didn't respond as he made quick work of the food in his hand. "The Americans helped narrow down the three men. The rest is up to us." He balled up the wrapper that had contained his crêpe and tossed it into the nearest garbage can. "But I don't know what your boyfriend has been briefed on so you should probably leave him out."

"My boyfriend?" Elly's eyebrows rose to the sky. "First of all, he's white and he'd have to be phenomenal for me to even think of breaking that barrier. Secondly, he's married and I don't cross those lines. Thirdly, he's old. Somewhere in his forties. I may as well push him around in a wheelchair."

"A wheelchair?" Grant repeated slowly as he shoved his hands into his pants pockets. "A wheelchair."

"I mean not now, obviously, but it would happen eventually." Finishing her crêpe, Elly stopped in front of another garbage can and tossed her trash. She reached into her purse and pulled out a napkin that she saved for times like these. "Do you need something to wipe your hands?"

"No, but how kind of you to offer to assist the elderly," he said faintly.

Elly glanced over at him. "How old are you?"

"Old enough to be in a wheelchair soon, apparently." He crooked his elbow. "Come on. I don't know how I'll finish this walk without someone to lean on."

Elly slipped her hand through his arm and made the executive decision to needle him further. "Are you really old?"

"Elodie, I am going to ask you questions in French and you are going to answer. Ready?"

She smiled at the change of subject. "They might be very short answers."

"What is your name?" He asked in French.

"Elodie Anne Mitchell." She paused. "I was born," she said slowly, "Elodie Anne Valcourt."

"Where were you born?"

"Valcourt, Louisiana."

"Your parents' names are?"

"My parents' names *were* Louis and Birdie Valcourt."

"Do you have any siblings?"

"One. Albert. But we call him Catau."

"As in Château?"

"Yes. You know what Louisiana is like. French sprinkled everywhere like random seasonings on dishes. Sometimes the words are a bit mangled." She said the last word in English, not knowing the French counterpart. "My father always said Albert made the house a home. You know, because he is a boy. So, everyone called him Catau."

"Younger or older?"

"Younger, by two years."

"Where is your younger brother now?"

"In Washington D.C. studying law at Howard University."

Grant grinned. "*Mais, oui.*" But, of course. "Tell me about the Valcourts of Louisiana."

Elly exhaled. What to say? "*Mon famille de père . . .*" The family of her father, she began, had been free before the war for two . . . Here she paused and Grant filled in the word 'generations.' She didn't have to say what war. He already knew. "They acquired much land and wealth for their time," she told him. "My father was to be a doctor. He wanted to be an actor."

"An actor?" Grant asked, glancing her way.

"*Oui.* Vaudeville. He'd paint his face," she said, waving a hand over her own visage, "to darken his skin. Papa was very fair-skinned." It embarrassed her to disclose that her father thought he'd make more money in blackface. For some strange reason, audiences only ever seemed to find Negroes funny when they were dark and had those bright red lips and exaggerated features. Why on earth her father had bought into such nonsense was beyond her.

"Very common." Grant's voice was low as they reached the Champs de Mars just outside la Tour Eiffel. "Josephine did the same when she was younger."

"Did she?" That surprised her.

"I have learned over the years that those in the entertainment business often go through great lengths for an opportunity to be on stage. A shame that it must be that way." A shame that such things were considered amusing. "Let's sit."

"On the grass?" she asked in English.

"It's not that cold outside. Chicago is colder this time of the year." He was right, but still. "Look at all the other people sitting." A surprising number of people were relaxing on the lawn. Elly looked at him again. "You won't die."

Slowly, reluctantly, she sat down with her legs extended before her. She adjusted her dark blue skirt so that it covered as much skin as possible. No matter what Grant said, it might not be freezing out here but it wasn't balmy either. She could feel the hint of winter in the ground seeping into her clothes. Grant sat down next to her and then to her astonishment, lowered his head onto her lap.

"What are you doing!"

"This is how couples picnic."

"I've never seen such a thing."

"In France," he corrected. "This is how couples enjoy each other's company in France." Elly looked around. "Are you always so literal? Most young men have been drafted, you ridiculous woman. You're not going to see much romance these days."

"What am I supposed to do? Run my fingers through your hair? You barely have any."

"You just do wonders for a man's ego, don't you? You're also not speaking in French. Your father was in vaudeville. Was he a success?"

After a long minute where Elly tried to figure out what to do with her hands, she continued. "Depends on what you call a success," she said slowly. She carefully lowered one hand onto his shoulder. At least he was facing away from her. "Sometimes, he brought money home. Most times, he didn't. Mama was the breadwinner. She was from a different kind of family than my father. They probably should not have married. She was sixteen, he was eighteen. He wanted to . . . escape from my grandmother so . . ."

"What do you mean by different kind of family?"

"Not as educated. Not nearly as much wealth. But hardworking. Very hardworking. When my father did not bring home money, my mama took in laundry. She sewed, she cleaned. Much of my childhood was them arguing. At first, I did not understand why she never left him alone. She was always starting the fights. But after she died, the money dried up. When there was no food to eat, I began to understand." She was stumbling along, grabbing words here and there and trusting Grant to fill in what she missed.

"Fulfilling your dreams does not always put food on the table," Grant commented. His arms were folded across his chest and his eyes were closed. Well, at least one of them was enjoying this experience.

"No. Mama knew how to hunt and grow vegetables and live off the land but we stayed in an apartment. She would take me with her out to land that belonged to someone else and she taught me to hunt and trap and plant and harvest vegetables. After Mama died and I realized that my father didn't have an answer to the hunger in mine and Catau's bellies, I began to return to the swamps. But my father wasn't totally incompetent. One day he made us dress in our best clothes, which were too small at this point, and he took us to Ma Mère's house—that's what we called my grandmother. She agreed to take Catau. He was a very cute little boy and I think it helped that his eyes are blue-gray and his hair is very light brown, almost blond. She would not take me, but she did pay for my schooling at the nearest Catholic institution, my dance lessons, and comportment classes." Several times, Grant stopped her to correct her phrasing.

"You took dance lessons?"

"Ballet."

"Your family is very . . ."

"Bourgeois? They try. From day to day, I attended my lessons but when I wasn't doing that, I was out in the wilds of Louisiana hunting, gathering." Disappearing into fantasy worlds of her own making. "I provided for us as best I knew how. And when we didn't have enough money, I sang on street corners—not in Valcourt—but in the town next to us so it wouldn't get back to my father's family that I was begging for money. If you had asked me back then," she said softly as she began to gently massage Grant's shoulder, "I'd have told you I had a good life. I was so surprised when I came home one day to find my father hanging from the ceiling."

Beneath her hands, Grant stiffened. She wasn't sure why she was telling him this except that it was sort of liberating to share her story with someone who would never know the actors in the play. "I was so angry. We were a team. And he'd just . . . given up." Elly brought her hands to her face, covering her eyes. She didn't cry. Those days were over. But it had been a long time since she'd thought about the details. She lowered her hand back to Grant's shoulder.

"I come from a long line of suicides. My great-grandfather shot himself in the head just after his eighty-second birthday. No one knows why. My grandfather discovered that he had cancer, and went for a long swim in the Mississippi. It's the Valcourt way, I suppose." She leaned down, her lips less than an inch away from Grant's ear. "Catau does not remind me of my father in any way. He is silly and happy and rarely sad. He is also filled with great ambition. Still, I made him promise not to leave me alone in this world." He'd made her promise the same thing. But unlike her, people very easily loved Catau. He collected friends like some people collected leaves. They were plentiful and everywhere. Sometimes she wondered how upset he'd really be if she broke that promise.

"How old were you when your mother died?"

"I was eight."

"How did she die?"

"Having a baby. The baby died as well," she told him. "I was ten when my father decided to leave me. I knew my only options then were to live with Ma Mère or be given to someone on the Valcourt side. I didn't like those choices. The Valcourts . . . they are not warm people. I wrote to my mama's sister. The sister she was so proud of. I explained that my father had died and I asked her to please come and get me and Catau. A week later, Uncle Minor and Aunt Tabitha arrived in Valcourt. Uncle Minor has a college degree. Ma Mère was impressed. She was also, I think, tired. She handed us over. Catau and I have lived with my uncle and aunt ever since."

"Do you like them?"

"I love them. They already had five children and they made room for us. They never made us feel as though we didn't belong. I changed my name to Mitchell to fit in even more and to thumb my nose at my father who was so proud of his Valcourt heritage—little good that it ever did him. Catau has just added Mitchell as another name. He is Albert Louis Mitchell Valcourt." And that was it. That was her life story in a nutshell. She closed her eyes, having developed a bit of a headache. Her brain was hurting from all the mental footwork of translating but she was proud of herself for all that she had said. It was sort of validating to realize that she knew more French than she thought.

Grant sat up, his shoulder briefly brushing hers. Slowly, he reached over, cupping her face. Elly tried to hold his gaze, but she lost the battle, dropping her eyes to somewhere just to his left. Massaging the area just next to her eyes with his thumbs, he murmured, "That wasn't so bad, was it? You cannot have studied as long as you have without soaking something in."

Not sure whether she could handle much more of the feel of his hands on her even if it was just her face, Elly leaned forward, forcing his impromptu massage to end. Resting her chin on his shoulder, and wrapping her arms around his waist, she whispered, "Next week, your turn."

CHAPTER 15

After telling Grant her life story, he'd handed her a map—a much more detailed map than the previous ones—and made her redraw it after viewing it for only thirty seconds. She was getting better at paying attention to the details but she still felt as though she had so much further to go. After he reviewed her copy with a critical eye and gave her further instruction, they parted ways.

Elly returned to the apartment, changed into something more comfortable, and then pulled out the letter and cipher Grant had given her. It was a letter written in French. Was she to translate it into English first and then figure out the code? Or was the code in French? Her brain hurt just thinking about the possibilities. She'd never been all that great at statistics or math, and puzzles typically perplexed her for hours before they made sense.

Nevertheless, she sat at her tiny desk, pulled out a sheet of paper and began to transcribe.

Dear Elodie, it began, *I have lived these years without you and now I feel as though I hold my breath in anticipation of seeing your face.*

Elly paused in her writing, feeling her cheeks grow warm. Whatever you wanted to say about Grant Monterey, he was absolutely, unequivocally committed to whatever task he took on.

I have been in the company of beautiful women. It was not your visage that caught my eye although the more I am around you, the more I realize that there is not a single woman who holds a candle to you when you enter the room. What is it about you that compels me so? My darling, I am not sure. Is it your air of determination? The way your eyes light up first when you see something that fills you with joy? Or the air of pensiveness that follows you around like your shadow with every step you take? You never opened your mouth to say a word, but, my dear, you didn't have to. You'd already spoken to me.

Elly stopped writing, no longer blushing. What a lovely writer Grant was. And all of this hid another message? Elly picked up her pencil and continued to translate. Just when she completed it, she heard the apartment door open and the light footsteps of Claire. Elly lowered her pencil. She was ready to dive into decoding but this might be her only moment alone with Claire for some time.

Leaving her room, Elly met Claire in the kitchen where the younger girl was pouring herself something to drink.

"*Bonjour*, Claire. *Ça va?*"

"*Oui, ça va bien, et toi?*" Claire's abundant hair had been wrestled into a single plait and she was in her school uniform.

Elly could have tried to continue the conversation in French but she had spoken more French today than probably her whole time in the country. A hammer was beginning a slow knock on her brain at the very thought of using it anymore. "I'm good, Claire. Listen, I wanted to talk to you about something important."

"Okay," the girl said quickly. She'd also straightened to her full height, eager to be treated like an adult.

"I know your grandmother does not want to leave Paris. I know she's not worried about the Germans. I believe she should be, if not for her sake, then for yours."

"You mean because I'm Jewish?" Claire's father might be French but Judaism was passed down through the mother.

"*Oui.* I'm concerned, Claire. There are rumors that for every country Germany has invaded, they've searched out the Jews. He's a very strange man, that Hitler. As someone who comes from a people who has had to live side by side with their oppressors, you don't want to do it," Elly said, thinking of her early years in the South. "You will lose every single time and they will laugh about it. They will not be kind to you because your father is French and you are a girl. When people hate your kind—when they think you're not worth the dirt beneath their feet—it doesn't matter your age or your education or your connections." Or your skin color.

159

Claire lowered the glass in her hand onto the kitchen counter. "I am not as ignorant of the situation as you think. My grandmother thinks I do not have much communication with my mother's side of the family and for many years, I didn't. But now that I am older, we talk sometimes. We are aware of the situation."

Elly squeezed her hands into small fists at her sides. Aware of the situation. "They are putting Jewish people in camps, Claire. I don't know what those camps are for, but there is no such thing as separate but equal. Whatever is happening, the Jews are getting the worst end of the stick. Claire, my advice to you is to leave this country. With or without your grandmother. Go to . . . Spain," Elly said, stumbling across the neutral country.

"That all seems very fantastic." Claire frowned, unhappy with the word she'd used. "Like bigger than what I can do," she explained, using her hands.

For the first time ever, Elly understood a bit more about her ancestors. Running away from slavery, running from the South to the North, must have seemed fantastical; bigger than they could do because they were leaving behind the devil they knew for something completely unfamiliar. And if things didn't work out . . .

"Sometimes I think about leaving," Claire said slowly. "But Grandmother . . ."

Elly took a step forward and reached for Claire's hand. She met the girl's brown eyes knowing that the choice before Claire was excruciating. She and her grandmother were very close. And if she had to strike out alone, it was not going to be easy. "Claire, when the Germans invade, I am not going to stay here and let them take me. I am going to run as far away as I can. I suggest you do the same."

Being raised by a reverend meant that Elly had been in her fair share of plays. There was nothing like a holiday to inspire a congregation to take up acting. Elly had seen more versions of Jesuses on the cross and Marys and Josephs knocking on the doors of inns than she ever wanted to see again in life. Those particular Sunday mornings had always been guaranteed to be hectic with last-minute scene changes, actors falling ill, and outfits suddenly not fitting.

None of that even remotely compared to the opening night of *Paris-London*. Elly dipped and dodged dozens of scurrying people as she made her way to the backstage of the theater where the dressing rooms were located.

"If you say one more thing to me!" Jo was yelling at some fellow Elly had never seen. Hair wrapped, barefoot, clothed only in a short, silk robe, Jo stood in the narrow hallway with anger radiating throughout her body. Amazingly enough, no one else around them was paying the least bit attention to the confrontation. "I'll . . ." Jo didn't finish her statement. She raised a fist, shook it in the man's direction, growled, and returned to her dressing room, slamming the door shut behind her. The man that she'd been yelling at—boy really—did an embarrassed turn and disappeared down the hall.

Reaching Jo's door, Elly paused, counting to sixty. Then she knocked. "Who is it?" Jo demanded.

Elly cleared her throat. "It's Elly."

Two seconds later, the door opened revealing Polly. Polly, usually happy and carefree, was carrying a deep frown on her face. "Come on in."

Elly obeyed and carefully shut the door behind her. "What happened?"

"It's that ridiculous man," Polly told her before shooting a glare at the wall in the direction, most likely, of the ridiculous man.

"What man?"

Sitting in front of the vanity, Jo held up a hand. "I don't want to talk about it anymore. If I keep thinking about him, I might hurt somebody."

Polly reached for one of the *Paris-London* fliers and pointed at the name next to Jo's: Maurice Chevalier. Elly knew this French actor. She had seen quite a few of his films because he acted in American movies.

"Rude, insufferable, arrogant . . ." Despite her earlier declaration, Jo continued to fuss. "Who does he think he is talking to me that way! He thinks that just because he is French he's more French than me! I'll show him!"

"Well," Elly said slowly. "I'm sorry I'm late." She'd decided today was a good day to wash and redo her hair, which was always a headache of its own but then her drying machine decided it wanted to do other things rather than working. Realizing the clock was ticking and she needed to hurry to the theater so that she could change, she had decided that having hair that was not wet was going to be the best that she could do. "Polly, can you help me pull my hair into a chignon?"

For the debut of Jo's new show, Elly would be

entertaining a number of people in one of the private balconies. Three of those people were the men suspected of selling the new rifle designs to the Germans.

"Yes. Get out of those clothes. I pulled that red dress for you that's hanging next to the mirror. What do you think?" Polly asked as she returned to Jo's side and began opening her makeup supplies.

It was another ball gown that cinched at the waist and flowed widely in the skirt. In the past month, Elly had been dolled up more than she'd ever been in her life. And while a part of her was loving it, she'd never really been able to enjoy the makeup and the gowns. Each fancy outfit was starting to represent someone who was not quite her.

"It's beautiful," she said as she walked over to touch the fabric of the skirt. And it was. But Elly was also thinking about all she'd have to say and do to convince someone to tell her their secrets. Something in her stomach performed a familiar flip. *You've done this before,* she reminded herself. *You'll be fine.* And truthfully, it was getting easier to socialize with people she had no relationship with and to act as though she were having the time of her life. But she did need to see if she could put more pressure on her targets. December would not last always.

"Look, that's what Jo is wearing," Polly said, nodding at a shiny, feathery thing that was hanging on a hook.

"That's the whole thing?" In her chair, Jo began to laugh while Polly snickered. But there was nothing there, just shiny things and feathers.

"Which part covers . . ."

163

Elly stopped talking as their laughter got louder. Well, at least she'd managed to pull Jo out of her bad mood.

"Think about the audience," Polly explained as she ran a makeup brush across Jo's cheeks. "We're not entertaining ladies and gents."

"Soldiers, you mean?" The whole point of *Paris-London* was to boost morale among the French and British servicemen who at this point were sleeping outside and eating out of cans for seemingly nothing. Elly knew that Jo was planning on performing several British numbers along with her greatest hits from France. It was supposed to be patriotic and supportive and unifying, et cetera.

"Many of them haven't seen their wives and girlfriends in months. We've got to give them something to think about." Elly briefly touched the plumes and rhinestones. And here she'd thought she was doing something with that pink dress she'd worn months ago. "That outfit is for the last number. Rosevienne designed it. It's perfect for '*Mon Coeur est un Oiseau des Isles*'." It did sort of put Elly in mind of a bird.

"You can try it on after me," Jo teased. Elly turned and released a laugh. "Oh, goodness no." If she wore such a thing she wouldn't look alluring and attractive, she'd look ridiculous. The fewer clothes you were wearing corresponded directly to how much confidence you carried and the moment Elly put that on, she knew all confidence would flee.

While Polly put the finishing touches on Jo's makeup, Elly quickly removed her dark green dress and slipped into the red ball gown. She'd already put on the correct undergarments so it took no time at all. Polly came over and zipped her into it. The dress was sleeveless and the only thing holding it up were two straps that tied around her neck and formed a V on her chest. One thing she hadn't noticed earlier was that the skirt was layered. Elly turned this way and that to get the full picture in the long mirror in the room. "You have some gorgeous gowns, Jo."

"Designers give them to me for free more often than not," Jo said as she slipped on her first dress of the evening.

"A shame there's no man to appreciate you in that, Elly," Polly said with a sigh. Elly was thinking the exact same thing. For two seconds she imagined running into Grant—he was here somewhere. But then she stomped on that fantasy. He'd made it clear he wasn't interested in her. And while she was beginning to trust him to a degree, there was still something about him that made her wary.

"I have an idea! Polly, we could find someone for her!" Jo said excitedly.

"Oh, no thank you!" Elly said quickly.

"I'm wonderful at matchmaking! Remember that one couple, Pol? What was that girl's name who danced with Jean? Oh, I know! Danny's currently in the market."

"Oh, that's all right!" Danny was very nice but the more time she spent with him and his optimism, the more she felt like she was with Catau. "I'm not looking for anything serious right now."

"Serious!" Now decked out in rhinestones and shiny pieces, Jo turned to Polly. "Serious," she repeated in disbelief. Jo pointed a finger at Elly. "Let me tell you as someone who has been married three times. Serious is not all it's cracked up to be."

"I'm sure that's true," Elly said cautiously. As Jo and Polly continued to stare, waiting for more, she mumbled, "It takes a lot for me to trust someone."

"Yes, but Elly I think it's like that for everyone," Jo said as she turned her chair around and plopped down into it, resting her chin on the headrest. "You don't have to trust a person to enjoy their company."

Logically, Jo made sense. Why couldn't she enjoy a night on the town with an attractive man just for fun? Did she always have to make that leap to whether or not the man would make for a valid candidate as a life partner? But men aside, she was the same way when it came to plain old friendship. It was not easy for her to be friendly nor to accept an offer of friendship—which was not to be confused with making acquaintances. The flip side of it was that once Elly had deemed you worthy, she was loyal to you for life. She had a feeling that when she finally fell in love, the poor man she rested her affections on wouldn't know what hit him.

"Yes," she said simply. Anything to end this subject because her mind wasn't going to be changed and neither was theirs. "You're right."

Jo and Polly exchanged a look that said that they weren't convinced by her words.

Turning away, Elly reached for the purse she had tucked her jewelry into earlier. She pulled out her fan, double-checking to make sure it hadn't ripped or torn when she'd grabbed it in her haste to get there on time.

"Not that old thing," Josephine called over her

shoulder. "I've bought some new fans. Just for you. Polly, whenever I see Elly whip out one of those things, I know information is being exchanged." Elly looked up, a bit disconcerted that Jo had seen through her one, solitary trick. She walked over to the side table where Jo indicated the fans were. All of them were elegant and beautifully designed. "Thank you."

"Of course, dear," Jo said just before touching the needle of the record player. Elly heard that familiar spinning, and then Billie Holiday filled the space singing about locking her heart away with a key.

"I need to think about something happy before I go out on stage," Jo announced. She grabbed Polly and then moved over to Elly. Then, she slipped an arm around both of their waists. "To the right."

Polly seemed to know exactly what she meant but it took Elly a second to realize they were supposed to be dancing chorus-girl style. Jo started singing the lyrics but then decided that dancing in formation was more important.

"To the right." They moved to the right. "To the left. Kick." They were hopping and skipping and stumbling a bit over each other, giggling all the while. "Spin around. Together again." Polly and Elly obeyed Jo's orders until the song ended and then the three of them collapsed onto the couch together. None of them said anything as they soaked in these few seconds of peace. Because on the other side of the door was war.

CHAPTER 16

Ten minutes later there was a knock on the door.

"Who is it?" Polly asked as she put the finishing touches on Elly's hair.

"Picture time!" It was Danny.

Polly poked Elly in the shoulder, and made her eyes grow wide in the mirror. Elly made sure her expression was dead flat. Polly giggled. "Come on in, Danny! He's sweet," Polly whispered. "You have to give him a chance."

Elly elected not to respond as she stood up, finally good to go.

The door opened, revealing Danny, camera in hand and dressed in a suit. "Came to see if the lovely Miss Baker wanted me to take some photos tonight?"

"Always, Daniel," Jo said, as she stood up and showed off her outfit, which covered quite a lot. The plan was that she'd work her way to fewer and fewer clothes with each costume change. No man would remember Chevalier after the show was over.

Playing with the new white and gold colored fan in her hand, Elly began some very careful breathing exercises, exhaling Elly Mitchell and inhaling Jo Baker's cousin.

"A picture of you, Elly?"

"No, thank you, Danny."

"Danny, Jo and I still need to do a few things. How about you escort Elly to her seat?"

Elly flashed her eyes at Polly who was giggling.

"Sure thing." Danny crooked his elbow. "Come on, Elly." Elly grabbed her gloves and purse and slipped her arm through Danny's.

"Have fun!" Jo called out to their backs. Elly turned to look over her shoulder, tossing Jo a dirty look too. Jo grinned widely.

"Break a leg, Jo," Danny replied, missing everything that was happening around him.

With Jo's door shut, Danny stopped and waved a hand at his nose. "Man, but it stinks over here. I pity the kid who has to clean the zoo." Elly shook her head at herself. She could not believe it, but she was starting to get used to the scent. She knew now that Jo spent her time in there between rehearsals. If not for Polly putting her foot down, there probably would have been a pig or a goat wandering around the dressing room as they got ready. "You look nice this evening."

"Thank you. Where's Pierre and Grant?"

"In the orchestra pit. Most of the folks you met a few weeks ago are gone now. Returned to the States."

"And why didn't you join them? Can we stop for a

second?" Taking a step away from Danny, Elly slid on her long white gloves.

Danny held up his camera. "This is my chance, isn't it? To document what life is like when a country is at war. Maybe I'll be able to sell a photo to a fancy magazine. You never know where life may lead."

"True, but why . . . be involved? There's a risk, isn't there?" Elly asked, trying to delicately probe at his motivations.

"Listen, I'm smart. I have eyes. And I was staying. Do you really think those four could keep anything from me?"

"Yes, but—"

"And when stuff hits the fan—and it will—whose coattails does it make sense to hang on to? That woman's," he said, pointing behind them. "So I'm there when needed. Nothing more. Nothing less."

"Got it." Elly slipped her arm back through Danny's and they exited the underbelly of the theater, entering one of the extravagant lushly carpeted halls.

"In Paris, you can do anything, become anything. And I'm gonna make the most of this time and do something great."

Elly took a look around the exquisite theater they were walking through and caught a quick distorted image of herself in a shiny column as they passed. Yes, it did feel as though they could do anything here.

"Like I could even marry a white woman if I wanted to."

Elly only tripped slightly. "Daniel?" she said after a moment.

"Huh?"

170

"You have an extraordinary gift."

"Oh?"

"With just one comment you can steal all of my words. Once again, I am left with nothing to say."

"My mama always said I was a real charmer."

They reached the front of the theater and parted ways. Elly carefully made her way up a set of stairs and to the private balcony, flashing the card she'd been given. It was a pass that gave her access—as part of Jo's entourage—to any part of the theater.

The show might not be starting for another thirty minutes, but already people were gathered there. "Mei!" Elly said at the sight of the Japanese woman she'd met weeks ago. "*Bonsoir!*" Elly eagerly welcomed the woman and her husband. "It's so good to see you both! Jo will be delighted when I tell her you were able to make it!" All this happiness, all this cheer, all this eye contact and delight. Elly channeled both Jo with her effusive charm and Aunt Tabitha who may have lived up north for nearly thirty years but had never lost her gift of southern hospitality.

"So good to see you again, Elly. Let me introduce you to my husband," Mei said excitedly. A little less emotive than his wife, the Japanese general greeted Elly.

"*Bonsoir!*"

Elly turned to see one of her targets enter the balcony. "Lieutenant! So good to see you!" Elly didn't allow herself to think about it, she just moved forward and hugged the man as though they were the dearest of friends. By the smile on his face, he approved of the action. He *faire des bisous*'d her, planting two light kisses on her cheeks.

171

"Élodie, you are beautiful as always," he said in French. She'd only briefly spoken with this man before but one of the benefits of being one of the few colored women around was that Elly was entirely memorable particularly since Jo was very clearly about to be on stage.

"I don't know what you just said, but I think I heard the word beautiful!" Basic as the tactic was, Elly had decided to pretend that she only understood a little French. There was always a chance one of the men might say something of value in front of her. To be successful, she needed to wield every tool she had. And it wasn't really lying, was it? Not when one was at war. Looking past the man in front of her, Elly beamed as another target joined the party. She waved an enthusiastic hand. "*Capitaine, c'est vous!*"

Elly got everyone settled in their seats but then stood up to face her small party. Fan in hand, she began her prepared speech. "On behalf of Josephine Baker, I welcome you. If you need anything at all, please do not hesitate to tell me. Drinks and appetizers will be served shortly. We so appreciate you for coming!" She grinned excitedly and that was when she saw it. A small piece of paper on the ground with a number. The sort of number one got when one checked their coat in the coatroom. "In fact, I will go arrange for drinks to be sent up right now. Please, what would you like?"

Elly took their requests and made sure to stumble into the captain. "Oh, sorry. Silly me!" She dropped to the ground so that her skirts fell across the small ticket. Reaching under her dress, she grabbed the piece of paper, balling it up in her hand.

"Careful, *chérie*," one of the targets said as he helped her stand. "Do you need assistance?"

"Oh, no thank you." Around them, the lights dimmed and the soldiers who filled the seats below whistled and clapped. "You mustn't miss a second of the show. I'll be right back."

Elly made sure she was far away from the balcony and on the first floor before she looked at what was in her hand. Yes, it was a ticket for a coat. She made a stop at the nearest bar, putting in her order for the drinks requested. "I'll be back to pick them up in a minute," she told the bartender.

Then she made her way to the coatroom where a very young man—a boy, really—stood behind the counter. She noticed, as she glanced around, that most of the other staff had disappeared, probably trying to take in the show themselves.

"Hello!" Be as American as possible, she told herself. Overwhelm this child with foreignness. "Oh my goodness! You would not believe what just happened." Flashing her backstage pass so he could see, Elly continued in a somewhat overenthusiastic Chicago accent. "I am Josephine's cousin, remember? I am entertaining up there." She waved a hand, indicating toward the closest set of stairs. "Very important guests. VIPs. One of them asked me to get his cigarettes out of his coat. I need to go back there," she said, pointing to the room behind the boy, "and do just that."

"Um . . ." the boy began and she knew he was searching for his English. "If . . . give me . . ."

"No, no, no. I work here too." She flashed the pass again. "He doesn't want just any Tom, Dick, or Harry

173

going through his things. VIP. Very important person. I'll do it." Not giving him a chance to protest, Elly moved to the side of the counter and pushed the small door open. She flashed her pass once more. "On staff. Josephine's cousin. Don't worry!" She gave the boy two excited thumbs up as he gaped at her.

A part of her winced because she was doing nothing less than making herself very much memorable. The other part of her reminded herself that she was a colored woman in a bright red ball gown. She was going to be unforgettable no matter how you sliced or diced it. She dived deep into the large closet until she couldn't even see the counter where the child was working.

Moving past row after row, she finally found where she needed to be. For two seconds she wondered if she had the ticket for Mei's coat or that of Mei's husband. What an absolute waste of time if that was how the cookie crumbled. But then she saw the coat. It most definitely belonged to a French officer. Shaking like a leaf on the inside, Elly began to check the pockets. There was a pack of cigarettes, a lighter, and a receipt from a restaurant. She repeated the name of the place back to herself just in case it might have significance. And then she found a folded-up letter.

To her delight, it was not a love letter or a family letter but something military-related. In fact, the contents of the letter had something to do with a supply drop that was occurring in the north of France next week. Perfectly normal information for a French officer to be aware of, but was it normal for him to carry this from whatever military base he was assigned to and bring it to Paris? Praying that she was not destroying her nerves for nothing, she reached down into her bra where she'd tucked away a small pencil and some paper. Then she dropped to the ground and reread the letter— twice—because her anxiety had her mind spinning like a broken record.

It wasn't that she'd never been sneaky before. She had been. But at home, she knew every nook and cranny, every habit of each resident and she had several backup plans in the event things went wrong. Spying here in France was a very different ballgame. It was the difference between church plays and *Paris-London*.

Using the floor as a surface, she jotted down the train routes mentioned in the letter—the trains that would be carrying food, clothing, and weapons from one part of France to another. Perhaps none of this held any value but Elly's gut told her something was off here. Folding her own paper, she returned it to its secure spot in her brassiere along with her pencil. *Please, dear Lord*, she prayed. *Let all of this be worth it.*

Elly stood up and carefully returned the letter to the pocket of the lieutenant-colonel. The coat belonged to the target she knew the least. When she returned to the balcony, she'd make certain to sit next to him.

Hearing clear but low voices near the front desk, Elly stepped away from the coat and headed for the nearest aisle when someone said the magical phrase of 'memorize this and burn it.'

"Come, let us talk more while I explain," a male French voice said.

She could leave. She could walk right out of the coatroom and no one would care.

". . . airplane technology . . ."

Swallowing hard, she backed up and scooted her body between two long coats, mentally juggling whether it would be better to stay where she was or try for a better view.

CHAPTER 17

Snatching coats off the rack, Elly hit the ground and curled into herself like a ball. She flung the fur and cashmere over her, hoping it looked as though coats had fallen off the hangers and landed in a heap. Feeling very much like she was playing a game of hide-and-seek where the seeker would have her shot immediately upon being found, she checked to make sure there were no pieces of red fabric escaping from under the small tent she'd created.

She'd been raised not to fleece God, but the teacher of that lesson had clearly never been in a life-or-death situation before. *Dear Lord,* she prayed, *if you get me out of this sight unseen, I will read my Bible more.* She read her Bible every day because she'd promised her uncle she would. But usually she read a quick Psalm, something short and sweet and easily forgotten a few seconds later.

"When you get back," the voice began in French, moving closer to her aisle.

Lord, I will read one of the big books from the Old Testament: Isaiah, Jeremiah or Ezekiel, she promised God as the men moved closer toward her. *Focus,* she told herself. *Don't let this be for nothing.* Elly quieted her breathing and listened. The conversation about the French airplanes was whispered and hushed, but Elly could still make out the contents. One of the speakers was explaining where the factory was located that would be making a particular plane and how many were expected to be made. It took Elly back to one of her earlier conversations with Grant—several new weapon designs had been misplaced. She had been assigned to learning about the new rifles but she didn't think she should pass this information up.

It felt like the conversation went on for an hour. And just when it seemed to be wrapping up, the thought occurred to her that she needed to know who was speaking. What was the point in having this information if she didn't know whether friend or foe was talking?

Lord? I will pray every day . . .

Were they missing her in the balcony? Were they wondering where exactly she had run off to?

The men were about to leave the coatroom; this, she could tell. And she was running out of time. She flung the coats off of her and swiped at the bead of sweat that was slowly making its way down the side of her face. She had no doubt that her dress was a very interesting shade of wrinkled and that some of her hair had not only escaped the ministrations of Polly's pins but had also risen a centimeter or two.

What would Josephine do? She'd make them the side characters of her story. Elly reached up and took off one of the pearl earrings Uncle Minor and Aunt Tabitha had given her for her twenty-first birthday. She flung it across the room. It made no sound as it rolled across the thick carpet. If this all went badly, she only faced possible torture and death. So. She'd better give it all she'd got.

"Oh my goodness!" she hissed in a stage whisper. She was brushing at her skirts when one of the men came marching around the corner and looked at her, surprise and slight horror clearly written on his face. She stood up, a colored Venus, emerging from unknown depths. She slapped the palms of her hands against her thighs. "I can't find it!" She brought a hand to her mouth as tears filled her eyes. They were remarkably easy to draw up. "It was my birthday gift and I can't find it! I've been looking and looking! I came here to get cigarettes for a guest and now I've lost my earring! Look," she said, pointing to her naked ear. "It's gone!"

Crocodile tears poured down her cheeks. "I've been searching and searching! Can you help me? You and your friend? I thought there were two of you?" Sick. She felt sick. Acid filled her mouth and her stomach churned. *Keep it together, Elodie Mitchell*. She swallowed and pasted a worried smile onto her face. Easy to do.

The man she was speaking to worked at the theater if his outfit was any indication. Most likely he'd replaced the boy who had 'let' her in. But the other man was in uniform. Because of where he was standing, she only got a brief glance of his face: chiseled features,

179

dimpled chin, thick black mustache, black hair speckled with gray, a bald spot at the top of his head, large ears that were a bit too big for his face and a nose the Romans would be proud of. He said something in rapid French. Who was she?

"Excuse me," the theater worker began in slow, stilted English. "Who are you?"

Elly flashed her pass. "I'm Josephine Baker's cousin! From America. I'm supposed to be taking care of her guests—that's why I came down here in the first place. I lost my earring. I've been searching for ten minutes. Look at me! Look at me," she said, waving a hand at herself, knowing it looked as though she'd been crawling around on the floor. "This has to be the worst day ever! I've just made an absolute mess of things!"

She sighed with her whole body, her chest heaving, her shoulders hunching. She was delicate and feminine like Olivia de Havilland in *Gone With the Wind*. The image would never sell back in the States. Colored women were for labor. They cooked meals and then served them. They cleaned and laundered. They raised and mothered babies. They were afforded no inherent protections. They weren't anything remotely precious to behold. But she was in the land of Josephine Baker.

"*N'inquiètez pas*," the theater worker said, raising his hands in a comforting gesture.

"What?" she asked loudly.

"I . . . help you."

The French soldier looked at her once more. She wasn't looking in his direction but she could feel his eyes on her face. "We'll talk later," he told the other man in French and then left.

It took Elly and the usher five minutes to come across her earring. "Mademoiselle!" The man held up her jewelry with triumph.

"*Merci!* Oh, thank you so much! You just don't understand how important this is to me," Elly said as she slipped the earring back on. "You've just made my day!" She reached out and touched his shoulder. "What's your name? I want to tell Josephine about the dear man who rescued my jewelry."

"Matthieu."

"Matthieu," Elly reached into her décolletage and pulled out a very warm bill. "*Merci beaucoup,*" she said, sounding as American as possible. "You've just been wonderful!"

It felt like it took forever to get out of the coatroom. But she did not immediately return to the balcony. First, she ran to the bathroom. "Hello," she called out. She quickly checked the stalls. No one was going to get the steal on her. After making sure the room was empty, she pulled out her pencil and paper and quickly jotted down the few words she had not understood from the conversation and then the highlights of everything she'd overheard.

She flipped the paper over. She was no artist but she still sketched the soldier she'd seen, along with the insignia that had decorated his uniform. She did the same with Matthieu just in case he decided to pull a runner.

Work done, Elly hid her pencil and paper and looked at herself in the mirror. She really did look like she'd been through the wringer. Wisps of hair were at odds and ends, her eyes were still shiny from crying and her cheeks had that hint of rosiness she always got when emotional. Her dress was not as bad as she'd thought but neither did it look like it had when she'd first put it on. She tried to smooth out the worst of it with her fingers and then she left the room.

She stopped at the bar where she was informed by the bartender that he had had the drinks she'd ordered delivered. "Bless you," she told him. She returned to the balcony so full of information that she felt like a balloon overfilled with air. The wrong move might set her to bursting. But she remembered to drop the coat ticket onto the ground so that someone could find it later.

So entertaining was Josephine that no one seemed to have noticed Elly's absence. She grabbed her fan—which she'd left in her seat—and slowly fanned herself until her heart slowed down. It would be nearly three days until she was to meet with Grant. She didn't know if she could retain all that she'd learned for so long and what if it was important? Elly stared down at the orchestra pit where Grant must be. She needed to see him tonight. They were courting, weren't they? It should not be in the least bit odd that she'd want to speak with her boyfriend.

During the brief intermission, she laughed and talked and conversed—particularly with the lieutenant-colonel, filling up with more and more knowledge until she thought she might have to let some facts go in order to breathe.

And then the show was over. Elly stood to her feet. "Thank you so much for coming!" She hugged every-one, *faire des bisous*'ed everyone. She touched their

CHAPTER 18

Four days later, Elly stood on the sidewalk waiting for Grant. She'd spent the remainder of opening night of *Paris-London* in a park with Grant, whispering the evening's events in his ears. She'd given him all of her notes and then he'd walked her home and said they wouldn't meet again until he called her.

He'd called her that morning, told her to wear a pair of pants, prepare a picnic, and plan to travel.

She'd followed his orders to a T. She only owned one pair of pants, which were dark blue, high-waisted and loose in leg. Her shirt was a cream button-down blouse. But most of her outfit was covered by her long, black coat. The hat on her head was black as well.

Just when Elly was about to check her watch again, a car pulled up. She didn't recognize the vehicle—it wasn't one of Josephine's eye-catchers—but she did know the driver. Grant started to get out of the

shoulders and made eye contact. She joked, she laughed, and when the last person was gone, she made her way to the stairs, praying that Grant was in no hurry to leave.

Except the foyer was packed with waves and waves of men. And from the top of the stairwell, Elly soon saw the reason why. Josephine had changed clothes and was standing near the exit. A line had formed. Every soldier wanted to meet her. Swallowing a groan, Elly lifted her skirts and made quick work of the stairs. She was stopped almost as soon as her feet hit the ground.

"*Bonsoir!*"

"Hello!"

"Hi!"

"Nice to meet you," she found herself saying over and over as she tried to make her way through the crowd and down the hall that led to the backstage. "Thank you for coming," she stated as though she'd had something to do with the creation of the show they'd just seen. "Wonderful to have you here."

It felt like everyone on all sides wanted to touch her and some boldly tried to *faire des bisous*. But she put a stop to that. If she made allowance for one, she'd be kissed by men all night long and she was running out of acting juice and patience.

And then she was on the other side. Like Cinderella at midnight, Elly picked up her skirts and ran. Stopping the first person she saw who looked like they knew a thing or two, Elly learned where the men in the orchestra could typically be found. Racing down a flight of stairs and avoiding the nearest crash into a stagehand, she reached the orchestra room. Taking a deep breath, she knocked on the door.

No longer dressed in the black uniform of the musicians, Pierre answered and leaned against the doorway in that languid way of his that showed off his lean body. Per usual, his eyes were hooded as though he were ready to go to sleep at a moment's notice. A smirk danced on his lips. "Well. Look at you."

"Is Grant inside? I need to speak with him about something important."

"I'm here. Maybe you could just tell me."

And just like that her patience snapped. "Listen, little boy—who thinks he's more important than he really is—I need to talk to the adult in the room. Where is Grant?"

Pierre blinked once, his eyes growing wider than she'd ever seen them. "You're really rude. Has anyone ever told you that before?"

Pressing her lips together very tightly, Elly waved a finger at Pierre. It was that or say something she wouldn't regret. His interference was making her literally boil with rage. "Grant!" she yelled into the room behind him.

"He went that way," Pierre snapped as he pointed in a direction. Elly took off. "See if I care if you find him!"

But find him she did and just before he walked out of one of the exits. "Grant!"

Hand on the door handle, he stopped and looked at her. There were a number of people around him who were staring. What a picture she must have made. How frantic she must have sounded. Instead of

stopping, she kept moving. She flung her and he caught her. She wrapped her arms shoulders and buried her face in his neck e lifted her off the ground. Relief flooded he "We need to talk," she murmured against h She'd noticed before and she noticed now: Grant smelled good.

Grant held her tight against his chest for a se before lowering her back down. His eyes searched as he cupped her face. "Okay, *chérie*. Do you h time to change clothes?"

She looked down at herself. She supposed she ough to. "Yes."

"Go change. I'll wait. And then I'll walk you home, and you can tell me all about it."

shoulders and made eye contact. She joked, she laughed, and when the last person was gone, she made her way to the stairs, praying that Grant was in no hurry to leave.

Except the foyer was packed with waves and waves of men. And from the top of the stairwell, Elly soon saw the reason why. Josephine had changed clothes and was standing near the exit. A line had formed. Every soldier wanted to meet her. Swallowing a groan, Elly lifted her skirts and made quick work of the stairs. She was stopped almost as soon as her feet hit the ground.

"*Bonsoir!*"

"Hello!"

"Hi!"

"Nice to meet you," she found herself saying over and over as she tried to make her way through the crowd and down the hall that led to the backstage. "Thank you for coming," she stated as though she'd had something to do with the creation of the show they'd just seen. "Wonderful to have you here."

It felt like everyone on all sides wanted to touch her and some boldly tried to *faire des bisous*. But she put a stop to that. If she made allowance for one, she'd be kissed by men all night long and she was running out of acting juice and patience.

And then she was on the other side. Like Cinderella at midnight, Elly picked up her skirts and ran. Stopping the first person she saw who looked like they knew a thing or two, Elly learned where the men in the orchestra could typically be found. Racing down a flight of stairs and avoiding the nearest crash into a stagehand, she reached the orchestra room. Taking a deep breath, she knocked on the door.

No longer dressed in the black uniform of the musicians, Pierre answered and leaned against the doorway in that languid way of his that showed off his lean body. Per usual, his eyes were hooded as though he were ready to go to sleep at a moment's notice. A smirk danced on his lips. "Well. Look at you."

"Is Grant inside? I need to speak with him about something important."

"I'm here. Maybe you could just tell me."

And just like that her patience snapped. "Listen, little boy—who thinks he's more important than he really is—I need to talk to the adult in the room. Where is Grant?"

Pierre blinked once, his eyes growing wider than she'd ever seen them. "You're really rude. Has anyone ever told you that before?"

Pressing her lips together very tightly, Elly waved a finger at Pierre. It was that or say something she wouldn't regret. His interference was making her literally boil with rage. "Grant!" she yelled into the room behind him.

"He went that way," Pierre snapped as he pointed in a direction. Elly took off. "See if I care if you find him!"

But find him she did and just before he walked out of one of the exits. "Grant!"

Hand on the door handle, he stopped and looked at her. There were a number of people around him who were staring. What a picture she must have made. How frantic she must have sounded. Instead of

stopping, she kept moving. She flung herself at him and he caught her. She wrapped her arms around his shoulders and buried her face in his neck even as he lifted her off the ground. Relief flooded her senses. "We need to talk," she murmured against his skin. She'd noticed before and she noticed now: Grant always smelled good.

Grant held her tight against his chest for a second before lowering her back down. His eyes searched hers as he cupped her face. "Okay, *chérie*. Do you have time to change clothes?"

She looked down at herself. She supposed she ought to. "Yes."

"Go change. I'll wait. And then I'll walk you home, and you can tell me all about it."

CHAPTER 18

Four days later, Elly stood on the sidewalk waiting for Grant. She'd spent the remainder of opening night of *Paris-London* in a park with Grant, whispering the evening's events in his ears. She'd given him all of her notes and then he'd walked her home and said they wouldn't meet again until he called her.

He'd called her that morning, told her to wear a pair of pants, prepare a picnic, and plan to travel.

She'd followed his orders to a T. She only owned one pair of pants, which were dark blue, high-waisted and loose in leg. Her shirt was a cream button-down blouse. But most of her outfit was covered by her long, black coat. The hat on her head was black as well.

Just when Elly was about to check her watch again, a car pulled up. She didn't recognize the vehicle—it wasn't one of Josephine's eye-catchers—but she did know the driver. Grant started to get out of the

two-seater. "Don't. I've got the door." She slid the picnic basket in first, and then followed behind.

When the door was shut and she was settled, she stared at Grant. "Well?"

He glanced over at her for a second. "You did good work on Friday." Turning away so he couldn't see her face, she looked out the window to her right. Her smile was slow but wide. "I can't tell you much more than that, but you were extremely helpful. I . . ." He hesitated for a second. "I'm amazed at how much of that conversation you remembered. It felt word-for-word."

Elly delicately coughed into her fist. "I do try my best."

Two minutes went by. Then Grant took his hat off, reached around the basket, and lightly tapped her knee. Like a balloon being popped by a needle, it was all she needed. "It was horrible! I was dying the whole time. Typically, I write as I eavesdrop on conversations."

"Write?"

"I'm a journalist. Remember? Being able to recount word-for-word what someone says is what I do."

Grant bit down on his lip as though her words had suddenly shined light on something he had been in the dark about. "Well, it was all very helpful. Also, take the lieutenant out of your deliberations," he said, referencing one of her targets. "Focus only on the remaining two."

"The traitor is not the lieutenant?" Elly asked with relief. Grant took his eyes off the road for a second to look at her. "What? He's very much a family man. His wife and children are all he talked about again on Friday."

187

"Family men can be the worst ones."

"Do you know how strange it is to befriend someone for their secrets? To know that you are planning to betray them?"

"They're betraying their country, aren't they? They're willingly getting their own countrymen killed. There's no reason they need to be held with kid gloves."

Elly looked out the window again. "Yes, you're right. But they're still people. I'm still a person. I still have to get to know them to get a job done."

"I can promise you that you'll never get an assignment that requires you to go that deep for that long. But yes, to your point, I'm sure it's not that easy. Don't you want to know where we're going?"

"You're changing the subject, but I'll bite. Where are we going?"

"It's a surprise," he said lightly.

Elly rolled her eyes but then reached for her purse. "Well, since it'll be a second before we get to wherever we're going, I have a few questions for you." She'd taken the time the night before to write everything out in French. "*Comment*—"

"What? Are you voluntarily speaking French to me?"

"*Comment tu t'appelle*—"

"No," he said, catching on very quickly to where she was going. "And who said you could *tu* me? *Vous*, mademoiselle," he said firmly. *Vous* was used for strangers or as a sign of respect to whomever you were talking. *Tu* implied familiarity.

"Don't be ridiculous, Grant. And you said you would answer my questions!"

"I never said that! You," he said, taking a hand off

the wheel of the car and pointing in her direction, "seem to be under the impression that I owe you something."

"You do! Grant, I swear, if you don't answer my questions—"

"You wrote them out?" He reached over and snatched the sheet of paper out of her hand. She reached over and took the paper right back.

"Please watch the road. I don't want to die in a car accident."

"That's cheating."

"It's not cheating. Presumably you'll say something interesting enough that I'll want to follow up on it. And I will. In French. This is an outline."

"I'm not answering those questions right now."

"Grant!"

"Later. There are things—believe it or not—important things that we actually need to address. Now, should something ever happen like last night and you can't reach me, there is a line you can call. But you must speak in code. The code changes daily but there's still a pattern to it."

Grant drove them out of the city and into the country and Elly listened as he explained how to call this number and ask for specific items that really stood for descriptions of various situations. After a half hour, Grant pulled off the main road and onto a dirt road. And then he came to a stop.

"Where are we?" Grant put the car in park and took the keys out of the ignition. "Doesn't matter. Come on, everything is in the trunk."

Elly climbed out of the car, following Grant to the

back of it. He'd already opened the hood. She looked inside and saw a cache of weapons. Folding her arms over her chest, she leaned in his direction. "Are we about to go fight the Germans ourselves?"

Grant slid his eyes in her direction. "How familiar are you with guns?"

"I'm from Chicago. They give us one upon birth and we're required to attend shooting classes after kindergarten."

Grant scoffed. "Have you ever fired a weapon before?"

"Yes. I told you I grew up hunting. Mama had a rifle. One of those long ones." She extended her hands in demonstration. "It had wood on the bottom and metal on the top."

"Wood on the bottom and metal on the top," he repeated slowly. "Okay." She watched him reach into the trunk and pull out a pistol. "This is a French semi-automatic service pistol. Modèle 1935. It's based on the Colt," he said as though that should mean something to her. Grant very slowly pulled the weapon apart and then put it back together. "It feeds from an eight-round detachable magazine. See? Now, I'm going to hand you this weapon and I want to see if you can hit that tree over there."

Elly looked at the tree, which stood maybe twelve feet from her and Grant. She looked at Grant. He handed her the pistol. "This is just practice. But I'm hoping that we can come out here enough for you to be comfortable."

"That tree, right there?" she asked, pointing to make sure they were on the same page. She was used to firing much, much farther away.

"Yes." Elly palmed the gun in her hand. She had never fired a pistol. Only hunting rifles. It was so light. She planted her feet in the ground, raised the weapon, and fired three shots into the tree. Then she handed it back to Grant. Or tried to. He didn't take it.

"You've fired a weapon since you were ten."

"There's lots of deer in Illinois. Uncle Minor goes hunting several times a year. He's a country boy at heart. I always go with him." He used to make the boys go but they complained so much he'd stopped asking. Now, it was just the two of them that made the trip a few hours down south.

"You said wood on the bottom and metal on the top."

"He knows better than to talk guns with me. So long as it works, I'm good. Can I try that one?" she asked, pointing to a fancy-looking weapon in the corner of the trunk. It sort of resembled a Tommy. Grant's eyes were narrowed and he was staring at her. "You know most women raised in the South can hunt." It wasn't as if they had the kind of money that allowed for a trip to the grocery store every week. At least her household certainly hadn't.

"I do know that," he said slowly before dipping his head into the trunk. She watched him take a few minutes to move things around. Then he stopped touching his weapons and lifted his head. "You know, you were made for this. It was like you were dropped into France just for this moment. For such a time as this," he murmured to himself as he returned to searching for whatever he was trying to find.

"What are you talking about?"

"You know Esther, right? In the Bible?"

"Yes, I know Esther. And no, I'm not like Queen Esther." The Jewish queen who was married to the Persian king who had managed to save her people from certain destruction.

"I don't want to hear your ninety-five theses. All I said was that you were made for this. And the way I figure it, if you're willing to risk your life for one or for a million, it's still your precious life on the line. I'll let you get comfortable with my guns but that's it. Since you already know what you're doing we'll work on making plastic explosives. I trust you and Uncle Minor don't blow things up out in Illinois?"

"We thought about it but changed our minds when we realized we wouldn't leave with much meat that way." Grant turned and looked at her. "It was a joke." Elly shoved her hands into her coat pockets and began making a small circle in the ground with her foot. "Is there a reason why I need to learn this particular skill?"

"There is, but in a perfect world, you won't ever have to use this knowledge."

"Oh." Wincing, she continued to work on the hole she was creating. So, she was probably going to have to blow something up one day. "You think I'm going to have to shoot someone?"

Grant finally emerged from the trunk with a rifle and several cartridges. "There's a spy I know, who is French, and he says a good spy never needs weapons. They aren't there to fight or to kill, merely to collect information. If weapons are needed, you've already lost. There is truth to that statement. But the fact is, people do get caught." Grant extended the rifle toward her and she took it. "And I've never known colored men to get taken prisoner."

"Shooting our way out is the only choice we have?" she asked as dread pooled in her stomach.

"That and this." Grant reached into his coat pocket and pulled out something small wrapped in plastic. A piece of candy in a candy wrapper.

"What . . . ?"

"Cyanide. I can't teach you how to survive torture. That is out of my wheelhouse. But I can offer you another way out."

Elly didn't move as Grant closed the distance between them and slid the suicide pill into her coat pocket. His dark eyes met hers. "Don't use that until you know all hope is gone. You understand? All hope is gone."

"Okay."

"Not unless everyone around you is dead and there's absolutely no way out."

"But you said no one would help—"

"I'm not going to repeat myself. I've got one more gift for you."

"I don't think I want any more of your gifts," Elly quipped, her voice a bit weak.

Nevertheless, he reached into his pocket and pulled out something. Something completely unexpected. "Is that a—"

"Moth? Yes. It's a moth."

"I was going to say hairpin." In Grant's hand was a very intricately designed silver and gold barrette. He slowly pulled the wings apart and a blade appeared. Grant handed it to her. It was warm from being tucked inside his jacket, and not as heavy as Elly would have thought. It was essentially a pocketknife just shaped differently. Touching the tip of the blade, she looked down as a bead of blood formed in the center of her finger.

"It's sharp," Grant said, his voice flat. He was looking at her as though she'd just done something stupid . . . which she supposed she had. "I don't suggest sliding your finger up and down the sides of it." Clearing her throat, Elly pushed the metal wings back together and the blade disappeared. She handed it back.

"It is for last-minute situations when the only solution is death and not yours. From now on, always wear it in your hair. Turn around." Elly obeyed. Grant removed her hat, and she took it. She felt his fingertips at the very edge of her hairline as he tried to figure out the best place for the pin. Her eyes felt heavy as he adjusted her bun, his fingers lightly touching her hair. She wondered if he could see the goose bumps that rose on the back of her neck as he very carefully inserted the hairpin at the top of her bun. She was getting a case of the tingles because of the purpose of the hairpin, not because he was touching her. Or so she told herself. "There," he said, pleased. "Now, you're ready."

They worked on weaponry for a good hour before Grant decided it was time for lunch. He drove them further down the road to a park. Elly laid out a blanket and they sat down and ate the sandwiches she'd prepared.

"Are those Cokes?" Grant asked, peering into the basket.

"What else would they be?"

Grant grinned and took one, opening the small glass bottle with expertise. "These are luxuries."

"Don't I know it. But I know people."

"Because you're a journalist," Grant said, his eyes weighty with curiosity.

"Yes." He handed her the bottle and then opened the other. They both drank quietly. "*Comment*—"

"Oh goodness," Grant muttered with a heavy exhalation. "Okay. Hit me. But I'm only answering questions in French with French."

Elly gave one firm nod. Knowing her own situation, in French, she asked him what was the name his mother had given him. "Leslie Grant Monterey."

"Leslie? *Pourquoi?*"

Looking thoroughly unimpressed with that question, Grant still answered. "It was a bad birth but Mama and I both lived. The doctor who saved us was named Leslie."

"Grant for President Grant?"

Grant nodded. Then he turned toward her, his grin rueful. "My older brother is Lincoln. My parents were very creative as you can see."

Were, he had said. "Your parents are not living?"

Grant shook his head, sipping from his Coke. "No. My father died in an accident when I was very young. My memories of him are few. My mama died when I was about twelve. We lived with my grandfather, and he died when I was fourteen. Lincoln is five years older than me. He left Virginia for New York when he was eighteen. After my grandfather died, I packed my things and went to stay with him."

"Which part of New York?"

"Harlem. Lincoln worked . . ." Grant paused. "Lincoln still works at a fancy hotel in Manhattan. He got me a job as a busboy. I loved it. Everything about it. The people, the accents, the busyness, the noise, the food. I love being in a city. I can survive in the country, but I prefer to be where the people are." Grant finished his Coke and tossed the empty bottle back into the basket she'd brought. He scooted over to her and, before she could say a word, he stretched out and lowered his head onto her lap. Just like last time she placed her hand on his shoulder, massaging gently.

"When did you leave New York?"

"Three years later. When I was seventeen."

"Why?"

"Because America went to war." Elly tapped her fingers against his bicep, her mind spinning with this revelation. "New York made me want to see the world. I thought at the time that I might not fight—since they mostly use Negroes for support—but at least I might leave the country. My brother was against it. For the most part, Linc and I get along well. He wanted me to stay, but I had an itch that had to be scratched."

"You were in the Great War? Is that what you're saying?"

"Was there another war I could have been in? I lied about my age as boys often do when they think that they are men."

Grant had fought in the Great War. He was from New York. Harlem to be exact. Elly looked down at the man in her lap. What had Polly called him? A relic. "You were a Harlem Hellfighter, weren't you?"

"Yes."

Lying on her lap was a national treasure. "You have a Croix de Guerre, don't you?" It made sense, didn't it? It was why the French trusted him so much. He'd already spilled his blood for this country. They'd already awarded him their highest honor.

Grant turned and looked up at her for a second. "You're so very quick."

"You're thirty-nine years old."

"Yes." He was fifteen years older than her. Not quite old enough to be her father but close.

He shifted his head, returning to face the grass. She didn't say anything as she tried to determine what to ask next. A Harlem Hellfighter. How much death Grant must have seen. How many men he must have killed to get that French medal. It explained so much.

"Are we done?" He started to rise. Elly pushed him back down onto her lap.

"Just thinking. When did you get married?"

"As soon as I returned home from war. I met my wife before I enlisted. We corresponded the whole time I was away. But she was young and happy and I was . . . not myself after the war. We never should have married but I thought love would cure all. Love is not always enough, in case you're wondering. I regret that the last few years of her life were spent with me."

Gently rubbing his shoulder, Elly watched Grant's chest rise and fall as he took in a deep breath. "We had a child. A daughter named Mary Grace after our mothers." Elly pressed her lips together. A daughter who was probably dead. A daughter who would have been eighteen or nineteen or possibly even twenty were she still living. Only a few years younger than her. "It was the Spanish flu that took them both. I was an empty shell by that point. Death seemed to hit on every side, leaving me stranded and alone. My parents were gone. Most of my unit—made of men who had become very dear to me—was wiped out at Château-Thierry. Quite a few of those who survived the war returned to America only to die of . . . breathing problems."

"Mustard gas?"

On her lap, he shrugged, unwilling to go into details. "I started to wonder when was I last happy. It was here in France, strangely enough. France held both my nightmares and my dreams. I packed my few belongings and crossed the Atlantic. The first place I went to was Meuse-Argonne in Romagne-sous-Montfaucon. The cemetery," he explained, "where most of my friends are buried. Then I came to Paris, roaming around with no real reason or purpose and almost down to my last dime when someone came and sat next to me on a park bench."

"Like you did with me?" Elly's voice was hushed.

"Yes. Just like that. Her name was Josephine Baker. I've been slowly gathering the pieces of myself ever since."

"And here we are in another war."

"I can't return to the trenches. I would rather die," he said simply. "But I can help this way." Grant sat up, looking tired. And Elly didn't think as she placed a comforting hand on his back, rubbing gently. For the first time since she'd met him, he looked every one of his nearly forty years. "Let's pack this up. It's time to return to Paris."

"What do you do when you're not with me or

rehearsing with the band?" Grant hesitated and then looked at her. His body language read reluctance as though he didn't want to disclose another fact about himself to her. "If you tell me, I'll reveal how I got so good at listening in on conversations."

Grant looked away, tilting his head from side to side as he considered her offer. Then he made a strange face and shook his head. She had the distinct feeling he was arguing with himself. "I'll do better than tell you. I'll show you. But first we'll stop at my apartment so I can change."

CHAPTER 19

Elly supposed she ought to feel bad for pushing and prodding Grant the way she had the last half hour. But she didn't. He wasn't going to get to hear her story without revealing his. This was not a one-way street. But also, if she hadn't pressed him, she'd never have known who she was sitting next to.

"Stop looking at me like that," Grant muttered as he drove.

"My brother did a report in school on the Harlem Hellfighters."

"He must have attended a Negro school."

"He did. For months, everything he talked about and did was related to your unit." Catau still had the unit's insignia framed on his bedroom wall.

Grant released a grunt.

"He was so proud of you all. We all were. Are," she corrected. And she knew he knew that when she said 'we' she meant all of colored America and not just her family. Behold the weight and glory of being a Negro in America. There was no such thing as being singular. You carried every colored man or woman's pain and shame. But you also wallowed in their success. Grant made some strange noise in the back of his throat. "And at least now I know you know what you're talking about."

That got Grant's attention. Looking slightly offended, he asked, "You doubted?"

"Grant, I barely knew you from Adam. Here you are—this musician from America telling me how to fight a shadow war on behalf of France. Of course I doubted. But I won't doubt you again," she vowed, meaning every word. Because thanks to Catau, she knew what Grant had been a part of and all that he had done. Grant's only response was to run a hand over his face.

They pulled up in front of an apartment building in a Paris neighborhood that Elly had never explored. It was not as worn down as some areas in Chicago, but it was also not where the Auger apartment was. Elly climbed out of the car a bit heady with excitement and the spirit of rebellion. She was about to enter a man's bachelor rooms without anyone else around. It was a bit thrilling even if they weren't there for romantic reasons. Following Grant up several flights of stairs she said nothing as he pulled out a key and inserted it into the door.

"I won't be too long," he said as he pushed the door open. He let her in first, which was why she got an eyeful of Pierre in a bed lying down and looking like the only thing he was wearing was a sheet.

"Do you know what time it is?" Grant asked Pierre without heat as thought this was a question he'd asked a thousand times. Moving past Elly, he went to close Pierre's door. "I swear he's nocturnal."

"You two are roommates?" Grant waved a hand as though to indicate that that fact was quite clear. "Take a seat." He led her to a small couch that was tucked beneath a window that overlooked the road. "I just need fifteen minutes." And then he disappeared into a room.

The apartment was very clean and very small. The living room only held the furniture she was sitting on, a coffee table, a radio, and a record player. From the sofa, Elly could see the kitchen and the bathroom. Grant's bedroom door opened. She watched him enter the bathroom, clothes and towel in hand. Another door opened and she looked up as Pierre, now dressed, shuffled barefoot into the living space. He flung himself down onto the cushion next to her.

Turning sideways, he placed an arm on the back of the couch, yawned into his hand, and then looked at her. He had sleep lines on his face and for the first time since she'd met him, he looked a bit stripped. He was still exceedingly handsome but gone were the hooded eyes and the sort of playboy charm he draped himself in. "What are you doing here?"

"Grant and I were training this morning and now he's going to show me what he does with his time when he's not playing music or . . . you know." She didn't like to say the word 'spying' out loud if she didn't have to.

Pierre frowned at her as he scratched an itch on his leg. "You mean the restaurant?"

"He works at a restaurant?" She wouldn't have pictured Grant as a waiter.

Pierre's eyes narrowed. "He owns the restaurant—Monterey. Right down the street. You can almost see it from here." Pierre pointed out the window, presumably in the direction of the place.

Elly started to say something and then stopped. Monterey. She'd heard of it. It was a very tiny, hard to get into restaurant that served American food. She'd never been because it only opened for dinner and the line was always down the street. She'd comforted herself with the knowledge that the food probably wasn't all that American anyway. "He's a . . . chef?"

"No!"

"Stop talking to me like I'm stupid! I'm asking because I don't know." For whatever reason, it was easy to be herself with Pierre. Easy to treat him like one of her cousins. Which was very unusual because he was so good-looking and attractive men generally made her cautious.

"Well, you certainly had no problem implying that I was stupid," Pierre snapped, still offended by their small exchange at the theater. "Grant's not a chef. He's a businessman. He hires the chefs and the waiters. You might not be aware of this, Miss Know-it-All, but it's darn hard to get a job in this country in general but especially if you're not French. So, Grant opened his own restaurant and before the phony war, he hired Americans. But you know, most of them have returned to the States."

"Oh." Grant really was settled here in this country.

Pierre lowered his head into the crook of his arm and looked out the window. "How old are you?"

"Twenty-six," he mumbled.

"Danny said you and Grant were like brothers."

"Wrong," he said, his voice flat. "More like . . . uncle and nephew. Brothers imply a level of equality. Grant is definitely in charge around here."

"Not father and son?"

Still resting on his arm, Pierre shifted so he could look at her. "We have both decided that we don't want that sort of relationship. If he's my uncle, he fusses, but he leaves me alone. If he's my father, he interferes with my business."

"How long have you known him?"

"What is with all these questions? Why don't you ask him?" Pierre smirked, a knowing look in his eyes and Elly realized that Grant must not be very forthcoming with most people. Keeping silent, Elly looked out the window. Thirty seconds later, Pierre said, "Grant was good friends with my dad."

"Was your father also with the Harlem Hellfighters?"

Pierre raised one eyebrow. "Congratulations to you if you got that out of him. Yes, they served in the same unit. Dad is buried here in France. Grant came to see me and Mama after the war ended. I was about seven. He'd pay our rent every few months. He'd make sure I went to school. I met his wife, played with his daughter. Went to their funerals. I hated when he left, even though he kept sending us money. I love my mama but we don't always see eye-to-eye. I turned seventeen, made my way across the pond, hunted Grant down. Been here ever since."

The bathroom door opened, and Grant stepped out, dressed in brown pants and a crisp white shirt. "You didn't offer our guest anything to drink?"

Pierre looked at Grant and then looked at her. Pointing a finger in her direction, he said, "I thought women aren't allowed in the apartment?"

"She doesn't count."

"How does she not count?"

"She's here for work, not pleasure," Grant muttered before walking into his bedroom and slamming the door.

"The rules are never the same for him," Pierre murmured like a spoiled little boy. Then he grinned. "You thirsty?"

"Yes."

"You're supposed to say no." Nevertheless, Pierre stood up and made his way to the kitchen. "Juice, okay?" he called over his shoulder.

"Yes, thank you." A few seconds later, Elly entered the spartan kitchen that held only the absolute necessities. "You all don't cook much?"

"He owns a restaurant. It's just easier to eat there." Pierre plunked down a glass of what looked like orange juice onto the table.

Elly took a sip of the tart drink that was not orange juice. "Why have you stayed?"

"Why have *you* stayed?" Pierre asked as he poured himself something to drink.

Elly hesitated only for a second. He'd been straightforward with her for the past few minutes. "I think I'm still trying to figure that out but it came down to doing something I can be proud of when I look back on my life."

"Yeah, it's not like that for me at all." They looked at each other and then laughed. "You really came here to study French?"

"And to write articles, remember?"

"Your family rich or something?" Pierre asked, evidently moving past the polite phase and into the honest one.

"No." They were solidly middle class. "The newspaper paid for me to come out here."

"What's your family think about you staying?"

"They're not terribly keen on the idea." That was putting it mildly. First, the letters from her aunt and uncle had been demanding, telling her to come home. Now, the letters were emotional, packed with how much the family missed her. Catau's last letter was not so subtle. It had ended with 'bring your black butt home.'

"What's your mama think?"

Pierre gave her an exaggerated shrug. "I wish I could tell you that I write my mama every week but I don't. Either way, I doubt she has a clue what's happening over here. She wasn't much of a news follower, if you know what I mean."

"Hey." Elly turned to see Grant, leaning against the doorway displaying his long legs, his narrow waist, and his slender but muscular frame. For a moment her breath caught. She'd been seeing him so much lately that she'd almost forgotten that he was such an eye-catching man. "You ready?"

Walking down the street, Grant explained that his first job in Paris was as a waiter. "Jo got me the job. She told me to learn an instrument and she'd get me another job. Lucky for her, and me, I've always loved music. I grew up playing the guitar. At the hotel in Manhattan, they had a live jazz band that would come in and play every Friday evening. I got to know some of those guys well and they'd let me fool around in the horn section. I saved up, bought a sax, and taught myself how to play because just being a waiter wasn't going to cut it. Meanwhile, my boss at the restaurant started thinking about getting out of the business. I came up with this great idea, why not let me revamp the place and slowly buy it from him? Two years ago, I bought him out."

"So, this is yours," Elly said, as they came to a slow stop in front of the setup that was before them. Like most restaurants in Paris, there was a small enclosed space for eating outside although none of the tables and chairs were set up yet.

"Not anymore," Grant said with a sigh. He placed his hands on his waist and eyed the place. "The day war was declared I began to look for a buyer. I sold this place last month. I'm staying on to help with the transition." He looked down at her with a rueful smile and she read the sadness in his eyes. "I've long since learned not to hold on to anything too tightly. When the war is over, I'll come back and start over with something fresh and new. Come on," he said, reaching into his pocket for keys. "We need to talk about what you're going to be doing next anyway."

Elly pointed to the outside menu. "Can we talk over food?"

"I'm sorry, ma'am, but I don't think you have a reservation. The famous Jo Baker dines here once a month, you know. We don't feed just anybody." He elbowed her teasingly. "What do you want? I'll make it happen. It's the least I can do considering all the work I'm about to get out of you."

CHAPTER 20

Time passed. Christmas came and New Year's followed right behind. Elly made her deadline, fingering the French officer who had turned traitor. She was then given the mission of finding where a specific French officer was hiding the money he'd made from selling the designs of the new French tanks to the Germans. The Deuxième Bureau wanted to make sure the money filled their coffers before arresting the man. Josephine continued to perform show after show for the French and British troops while Elly allowed herself to be wined and dined by the French officer until he fed her one small tidbit that led to a raid on a great-aunt's home in the suburbs of Lyon.

When Elly wasn't listening in on conversations or starting her own, she was walking the streets of Paris hand-in-hand with Grant as he tested her French and her memory. Every Saturday they went to a matinee but not before playing an elaborate game of who could trail the other without being spotted. They dined on Thursday evenings at different restaurants where Elly had to be able to describe the layout and everyone who filled the space all the way down to the waitstaff who brought them their drinks.

And then flowers began to bud again. Trees grew leaves. The chill of the air was chased off by the warmth of the sun. And Germany invaded Belgium, Holland, Luxembourg . . . and France.

"This has all happened before," Madame explained to Elly and Claire over breakfast. They were sitting at the kitchen table with Elly nibbling on a sweet roll and drinking a cup of coffee while Claire very intently buttered and jammed the piece of toast in her hand. Madame was holding up the latest newspaper. "In the Great War it looked like we were losing but then there was Clermont-Ferrand and the Germans got no further."

Elly's eyes narrowed on her cup. The very fact that this had happened before should have been the first clue that the Germans wouldn't let it happen again. That she was now in a country that was currently being invaded made her break out in cold sweats at the most random moments of the day. But she said nothing. Madame wasn't leaving this apartment. She was born here. She'd die here.

"Well," Elly said after a minute. "I need to go. I'm sure the others are probably already at the church."

"L'Église de la Sainte-Trinité?" Madame asked.

"Yes, that's where the Red Cross has set up." Elly, along with Jo, had started volunteering with the Red

Cross as refugees began pouring over the border. The church had been commandeered by the organization and was now a feeding center for those in need. It was also a place German spies might be infiltrating. Grant had told Elly the other day that the Germans were using different ones on the ground to see the war from their enemies' eyes. Jo and Elly were to keep an eye out for men who looked to be fit, hearty, and hale and more importantly not at the front lines but trying to hide behind women and children. Elly finished the remainder of her breakfast and stood up. "Don't wait for me for dinner."

"Take the métro if you need to, Élodie," Madame told her. "I heard the buses and taxis are no longer running."

Elly looked down at the older woman and then at Claire who seemed to be disappearing into a cloud of depression with each day that passed. She needed to try again. One more time. If Madame took great offense, Elly could always throw herself on Jo's mercy. "D'accord." She paused. "Madame, would it be all right if Grant came over for dinner?"

Madame's eyes lit up with delight and even Claire looked up from her plate. "Oui. Yes! When?"

"I'll ask him and find out which evening works best. And thank you." Madame was from a different generation. Perhaps if she wouldn't hear it from Elly, she'd hear it from a man. And Elly knew if she asked, Grant would come and charm them both before also hitting them with a heavy dose of reality.

Grabbing a light jacket, a matching hat, and an orange, Elly slipped down the stairs of the apartment.

Exiting the fenced courtyard, she stepped out onto the sidewalk. In the past few weeks, the streets of Paris had changed. Initially, the refugees had been a small trickle, arriving on trains that were pausing in Paris and heading further south. Then the trickle morphed into a steady stream. You could not walk down the street without seeing displaced folks lingering on every corner. And Elly always recognized these non-Parisians. It was in the heaviness of their footsteps, the sagging of their bodies, and the sorrow and slight shock that was stamped on their faces. These were a people who had not expected to flee as they had.

Deciding against the métro, Elly walked the few miles to her destination. The church that was sharing its space was large and by European standards, very young. It was a beautiful white building, tall and ornate and majestic as Catholic churches often were. Wrapped around the building was a long line of people waiting patiently to get in.

Elly slipped around to a back door where a woman wearing an apron was carrying a box filled with glass jars of milk.

"Let me help you," Elly said in French. The words came quickly, a result of spending several days a week speaking to Grant in the language. After opening the door for the young woman, Elly then followed her inside.

The pews had been removed from the sanctuary and stacked against the walls, piled high and covering the stained-glass windows. Tables and chairs had taken their place. Elly hung up her jacket and hat, grabbed one of the Red Cross aprons, and slipped it on. In the corner of the room, she quickly peeled the orange before making her way to where Jo already stood behind a counter, serving eggs.

"I saw two men who don't belong here," Jo whispered under her breath just before smiling brightly at the family that came to stand in front of her pan.

"Where?" Elly asked through her teeth as she waved at the family. They were frozen, gaping at the sight of Josephine Baker serving them breakfast.

"*Bienvenue à Paris!*" Jo told them, her voice bright. She leaned back toward Elly. "Look toward the table in the back. The one next to the statue of Mary. That's where one of them is. The other is sitting just to our left."

"Got it. Here." Elly placed the peeled orange in the pocket of Jo's apron. "Eat." In her haste to save the world, Jo Baker often forgot herself. Jo took a second to slip an orange slice in her mouth. Her eyes lit up from the burst of flavor. "*Merci, beaucoup!*"

Grabbing a tray, a pitcher of water, and several cups, Elly began making rounds at the tables. "*Bonjour.* Where are you from?" She always got a few surprised looks that pulled people out of the deep thoughts of their mind. Another American colored woman in Paris? There were two?

Smiling gently, Elly eventually reached the tables with the men that Jo had found to be suspicious. She knew instantly what had caught the other woman's eye. They were too young to not be in uniform and too old to be schoolchildren and yet here they were sitting among the elderly and the defenseless. She'd gotten much, much better at memorizing faces and she was careful to do so now. "Hello, where are you from?" After serving water and taking time to listen to stories, Elly made her way to the church office where she placed a phone call to the Bureau requesting more butter and eggs, which was code for two suspicious men in the church.

"Your order has been placed. Thank you," the person on the other line said calmly. Elly hung up the phone knowing that someone would come from somewhere to scope out and follow the men and determine whether they were truly German spies. From that point, Elly had no idea what would happen next. That was for the French to decide.

"Are you sure you don't want me to drive?" Jo asked as she slid into the passenger seat of her car, purse in hand. They'd stayed at the church for a good five hours.

"No, no. I can drive. I know you must be tired. Let me do this for you." It was that or die in a car accident. Jo drove as though she expected all the other cars to very kindly move out of her way and she was utterly surprised when they didn't. "What time is everyone else coming to your house?"

They were having a little meeting: Grant, Polly, Pierre, Danny, Jo, and her. A what-to-do-now-that-Germany-had-invaded-France meeting. "In about an hour, which means we have time. Can we make a stop?"

"Of course. Where to?" Jo said and Elly made a turn, heading south. "Other than the Red Cross, have you been able to rest lately?" Jo was always so busy,

214

always moving this way and that, and it did not seem that she ever looked after her own health. And Elly knew it was draining to serve and never pause. On more than one occasion Aunt Tabitha had burned the candle at two ends and then fallen sick for a month.

"Because I'm not doing a show right now? Or going to any parties?"

"Yes," Elly said, answering both questions.

"I don't know what resting means." That was probably a very true statement. In all the time that Elly had known Jo, she'd never seen her in a state of non-movement. "I've been working on projects for after the war." Elly made another turn. It seemed strange to make plans for after the war ended when it had only just begun. But Elly supposed one could not live as though the war was the end of all things. "And I still have the restaurant."

Chez Josephine was Jo's restaurant. It also contained a stage. She was there nearly every night greeting and performing for the few guests who still came. Not that the place was empty. It just wasn't what it was a few months ago.

"Right there. Stop."

Elly looked around but saw no building. "You want me to pull up to the corner?"

"Yes." Almost before the car stopped moving, Jo was out of it, an air of eagerness surrounding her. Elly watched as a man materialized out of nowhere and greeted Josephine, *faire des bisous*'ing her in a way that implied they were intimates rather than acquaintances. Elly couldn't hear a word they were saying, but she'd spent the past few months learning how to watch. And she watched their body language now. Jo leaned into the man as she spoke to him with excitement. The man placed his hand tenderly on Jo's lower back. Jo reached up and brushed his hair. The conversation lasted maybe five minutes and then Jo was back in the car.

"That was your handler, wasn't it?" Elly asked as she pulled into traffic.

"He's very handsome, isn't he? When I was first approached to be an honorable correspondent, I expected an old balding man who would look like a bulldog and maybe smell like one too," Jo joked as she dug through her purse. She paused and looked up, a wide, happy day-dreamy grin on her face. "And then Jack arrived with that golden hair and those blue eyes."

Elly was pretty sure Jo was still married. For whatever reason, the divorce had yet to be finalized. On the heels of that thought, Elly wondered if Jack, of the blond hair and blue eyes, was also married. "Is he French?"

"Yes. He was born in the Alsace region."

"That's right on the border of Germany, right?"

"Yes." Jo pulled out a tube of lipstick and a small mirror. "He speaks German, French, English, and I think Russian. He's the smartest man I've ever met." Jo wrinkled her nose in good humor. "And you know how I feel about smart people."

"Does he . . . have family here?"

"He sent his wife and children to America. Because of the war, you know." Jo pouted her lips at the mirror, applied another layer of color, and then closed the small tube.

They were sort of friends, having spent the past seven months working with each other. "Does it not bother you at all? That he pledged his life to one woman and . . ."

Jo looked at her for a second as she lowered her purse to the floor of the car. "You can't police love, Elly. When it comes, you have to grab it with both hands."

Elly squinted at the traffic before her. She should let the topic go. But what kind of logic was Jo trying to sell here? "How can you even begin to trust a word he says if the moment his wife is out of the picture, he's with you? I mean, look at it from her point of view. Is it fair?"

"Elodie." Jo's voice was sharp as she shifted in her seat toward Elly. "You've only got one life to live. One." Jo raised a finger in demonstration. "You've got to do what's best for you because no one else will do it for you."

"I was not raised that way." Elly knew it was the wrong thing to say as soon as the words exited her mouth.

"Who says the way you were raised is the right way? The only way?"

"I . . ." Elly nearly said that she was raised to think of others first and to think of herself last. But Jo lived like that too. There was no one more giving or more selfless than Jo Baker. Except when it came to relationships. "When I give my word, I follow through on it. And when someone else gives their word, I like to think they too will follow through with it. The world breaks down the moment we decide promises, vows, and integrity doesn't matter."

"Would you like to know what I believe, Elly?" Not waiting for a response, Jo continued. "I believe what you put into the world is what you get out of it. I put a lot of goodness and light into those around me. I want to make this world a better place. Maybe you think I'm selfish—"

"I don't think you're selfish. I just . . . quibble with the way you define love." Yes, that was it. "Love is self-sacrificing. It's a willingness to put the other person's needs and desires above your own. You cannot boil it down to mere touch and affection."

Jo nodded in that way people did when they in fact did not agree with you. "I'm curious. How do you feel about Grant?"

"I . . . what?"

"Unlike you, I'd rather not live in a state of denial, thank you very much. If there's one thing I've learned in this life of mine, it's that I never regret the times I take a risk. It's those other times I sat on my hands wishing and hoping that I lament. Live your barred-up and jailed life if you want to and leave me to the freedom of mine."

CHAPTER 21

Elly placed an elbow against the window ledge of the car. Well, she guessed she'd been told. She had known good and well that she probably could not change Jo's mind so why on God's green earth had she tried? Barred up and jailed. She supposed that was one way to describe how she approached relationships. But it was a jail cell that Elly held the key to. It kept her from some things but it also protected her from other things. Things Elly was just fine being protected from. Jo's sort of freedoms would drive Elly mad.

And why had Jo brought up Grant and how Elly felt about him? It wasn't complicated. Grant had become a very good friend and a sort of measuring stick. When everything felt crazy, if Grant said it wasn't that bad, she believed him.

Elly closed her eyes for a second and sighed. The tension in the car was thick and Elly broke more than one traffic rule in an effort to get them both to their destination with the utmost haste. Pulling onto the graveled road of Jo's yard, Elly came to a stop parallel to the car that currently held Grant and Pierre. Grabbing her purse and hat she wondered if she shared with Grant the details of her argument with Jo whether he'd agree with her or not.

"Hello," she called out as she exited the car.

"Hey, Elly," Pierre said, sounding less than enthused as he slammed the passenger door shut behind him.

"You look tired," Elly told him when, to her surprise, he extended an arm for a side hug. She took several steps forward, hugging his waist. For the merest second, she closed her eyes, feeling just a little bit of comfort from this man who usually irritated her. She was just that frazzled on the inside.

"You always give the best compliments," Pierre mumured, gently patting her back. "Hey, Jo. I think Polly and Danny are already inside." Leaving her side, Pierre went to greet Josephine.

Elly walked around the Renault to where Grant was leaning against the driver's door, thinking deeply. The scarf wrapped loosely around his neck was gray this morning. Like his mood. Elly was becoming quite proficient in reading his temper.

"What's happened?" she asked when they were only a foot apart. At her question, Grant shifted and glanced over at Pierre who had one arm slung around Jo's shoulders as they walked in step to the front door. "Did you two have a disagreement?" He looked at her. "If it makes you feel any better, Jo and I had a . . . disagreement as well."

"About what?"

Elly shrugged. "Don't want to talk about it."

Grant eyed her for a second, waiting to see whether she'd change her mind. When she didn't speak, he took a step toward her, extending his elbow. Elly looped her arm through his, leaning into him ever so briefly. If Pierre's touch provided a little bit of comfort, being close to Grant was almost like making a visit home. "Arguments are a way of life, especially when you're around someone for any length of time," Grant said sagely. Lowering his voice, he bent down slightly so that his mouth was at her ear. "I still want to strangle that boy."

"What did he do?"

"You're about to find out."

They gathered in one of the small parlor rooms where Jo's butler had set up drinks, small sandwiches, and little bowls of fruit.

"How have you been?" Polly asked Elly, arms open wide for a hug. They'd gone from seeing each other weekly to seeing each other every now and then. Polly looked happy as always. But today she seemed to be almost glowing.

Elly had been better but she wasn't about to go into that. "I'm good. And you?"

"Better than ever. As a matter of fact, Pierre and I have an announcement to make. Can I have your attention, please!" Polly's voice broke up the small huddle that included Pierre, Danny, and Grant. Jo was lounging on one of her couches with a dog lying across her lap. She looked up at Polly's words.

Polly crossed the small room and moved to stand by Pierre's side. She looped an arm through his. Pierre smiled down at her although his body language was a bit stiff. Elly snatched a small grape off the table and popped it in her mouth. "We're pregnant!"

Elly's eyes went to Grant who was reclining against the wall behind him. He looked less than pleased and she knew this was what he and Pierre had been discussing in the car. She glanced at Jo, but Jo didn't look surprised at all. Of course, Polly was her personal maid and dresser so she'd probably been one of the first to know. That meant that only Elly and Danny were learning something new today. She didn't know why that made her feel a bit left out.

"That's not surprising at all," Danny said with a shake of his head. "But this is just about the worst timing."

"No, it's not the best timing," Polly said, looking up at Pierre for some sort of reassurance. He was not looking at her. Elly tugged on another grape, snatching it from the stem's tight grasp. "It does mean that we're returning to the States."

Elly popped the grape into her mouth to keep from saying the words 'take me with you.'

"Well, I for one am very excited even if that means I'm losing you," Jo said, coming to her feet. Elly watched the two women hug. Looking like she was about to cry, Jo continued. "I know I can get on without you but I'm still not sure how." Polly began sniffling and wiping at her tears.

"Will you be getting married here or in the States?" Grant asked pointedly, sounding very much like a man born at the turn of the century. Pierre shot him a look but it lacked heat. Pierre looked too ill to be angry.

"Here!" Polly said excitedly, either missing Pierre's mood entirely or ignoring it. Probably the latter, Elly thought as she grabbed another grape.

"You're gonna hop on a boat to the States just like that?" Danny asked as he moved to the food table, joining Elly in picking at fruit.

"Well, it's a little complicated," Polly admitted as she turned to look at Grant.

"Do we want to eat first and talk later or talk now?" Grant asked.

"Now," everyone in the room said.

Grant still took a moment to look at Jo. She waved a hand in his direction, giving him silent permission to proceed. "It looks like we'll be heading south. Jo has rented a house for us to stay in. Julien and Margo are leaving soon to get the place ready." Jo's butler and housekeeper. Elly glanced over at Jo. Once again, they were all relying on Jo's money and resources.

"If you have any big items that you must keep and cannot carry in a single bag, make sure they're in that car."

"How can you all play your little spy games in the country?" Danny asked, nibbling on a piece of cheese.

Grant shrugged. "I'm not sure we can. We'll regroup and touch bases with the French government and take it from there. But our safety comes first, I've always said that. As for Pierre and Polly returning to the States, it is my understanding that there are still ships coming in and out of Marseille. It's not going to be a direct trip to the U.S., but if you can get to England or Spain or Portugal, the hope is that eventually you'll find a ship that is returning home."

This was not terrible news. "When do you see us leaving Paris?" Elly asked.

"Within the next two weeks. We'll help the Bureau as long as we can. You and Jo should keep volunteering with the Red Cross. Keep picking out the German agents until the day we drive out of here."

There wasn't much to say after that.

"Congratulations," Elly told Polly as she gently placed a hand on the other woman's arm.

"Thank you, Elly. I'm ready to be a mother . . . I think," Polly said with a laugh.

"You'll be a good one, I'm sure." As for the father, well, Elly had her doubts. Fixing a small plate of fruit and sandwiches, Elly made her way to Grant who had yet to leave the wall he was holding up. She held up the plate and he took a slice of an apple.

"I take it that this was what had you bothered?"

"Children are a gift from God," Grant said politely as he tossed the fruit in his mouth. Then he said, "Parents, on the other hand, may not be. Polly will make a wonderful mother. I have no doubts about that," he said under his breath. He reached for another slice of apple. "I'm free today," he murmured.

"Oh, that's nice." Nibbling on the edges of a small sandwich, Elly said, "But I'm not." There were two days a week that she tried to put time in for her articles. This was one of those days where her plans were fairly set.

He elbowed her. "Free between two and four. On a Tuesday or Thursday. I believe those were your instructions." They had yet to get around to Elly showing Grant how she came across the information she did when writing her articles. Between him tying up loose ends at the restaurant, the weather being cold, and her missions, they'd never found the time.

Elly hummed as a feeling of delight filled her stomach. She'd been wanting to bring him along for a while now and had pretty much given up hope of that happening. Keeping her voice cool, she said, "All right. You don't need to bring anything but yourself."

"Are Grant and his shadow making plans over there?" Pierre asked, his voice loud as it carried across the room.

Danny, Polly, and Jo looked up from the table where they were standing around and talking.

Next to Elly, Grant stiffened. "Pierre." There was a warning in his voice.

"It's like he can't go a day without her."

Pierre Roche was such a child sometimes. "Don't get us confused with you and Polly," Elly told Pierre. "We send all the happiness and felicitations your way."

If Pierre could have blanched, he would have.

"You know, Pierre," Danny said, failing to note the elephant in the room, "I can teach you how to take and develop photos. For the baby. Wouldn't you like that, Polly?"

"I'd love it!"

Grant and Elly didn't stay at the house for much longer. They returned to the city and parked where Elly instructed.

Together they walked to Elly's place of rendezvous.

"Wait a minute," Grant said, pulling Elly to a stop as they reached the riverbed. "Are you about to try to get me on a boat?"

Fingers intertwined with his, Elly looked out over the river. She could see that her favorite captain was heading toward them. Crossing Paris by boat was still an option of transportation. And Elly, for one, was glad.

She looked up at Grant. To her surprise, he was eyeing the water with great distrust. "You don't like water?"

"I like drinking water. I like washing up with water. I do not like . . . that," he said, pointing to a small rowboat that passed them.

"Do you get seasick?"

Grant raised his eyes to the sky. "It's more like the world starts spinning and my head starts aching and then every now and then something in my stomach flips."

Elly looked out on the water, a bit disappointed but she understood. "You don't have to go."

"Getting on this boat is critical to how you write your articles?"

"Yes."

A pained expression crossed his face. "I'll get on."

The large riverboat pulled up to the small pier. Elly and Grant climbed aboard and Elly paid their fare. Walking along the perimeter of the boat, Elly found her favorite bench—which was empty. They took a seat. When the boat began to move, Grant closed his eyes and brought a hand to his face. Elly tugged on his coat. When he glanced at her, she patted her shoulder. Grant looked at her hand and then at her, his eyes filled surprisingly with suspicion. Did he think she was making fun of his weakness? She would never do that. "What?"

He started to say something but then the boat rocked. He lowered his head onto her shoulder. "Would you please explain to me how this helps you get information from all of those sources you have?"

"Be patient," Elly whispered. She did not smile even though that one question had revealed that he still read her articles.

"*Bonjour*," an older woman said, smiling at them as she passed by. "Must be nice to have your husband?"

"*Oui*," Elly quipped, returning a quick grin. Grant lifted his head, staring at her with an odd look in his eye. She felt herself blush. "It's easier to say yes than to explain." Choosing to change the subject, she said, "I thought all good southern boys made rafts and had adventures on the river?"

"I'm sorry but my life was not a Mark Twain novel." He returned his head to her shoulder.

Elly laughed. "You mean you didn't grow up Jim to someone's Huckleberry Finn?"

"Ain't nobody tryin' to be Jim to Huck Finn."

"Well, I grew up next to a river. Only way to get some good fishin' is by boat."

Grant grunted. "In Surry, you can fish from land."

"You must have hated crossing the Atlantic."

"I still have nightmares."

Hearing the weight in his words, Elly stopped talking, figuring that it might be easier for him if he didn't have to think too much about anything. Looking behind her, Elly was able to see directly into the cabin. A few people were seated inside and looking out the windows. No one was seated next to the window beside her yet. Seeing that the window wasn't all the way closed, Elly slipped a finger into the small gap, pushing the pane slightly but not too noticeably. Then she turned, returning her gaze to the view before her. The boat drifted up to another stop.

"You don't have to open your eyes, but just in front of us are several government buildings. For some strange reason, bonfires are going." Elly felt Grant tense. "It is my theory that the French government is burning papers in anticipation of German arrival."

Grant sat up then and she pointed to where you could see a steady stream of smoke. "I noticed the fires two days ago. It's May. No one is doing that because they're cold. Have you heard anything about it?"

Grant looked at her for a second. "I just know things are a bit chaotic at the moment." When the boat started moving, he returned his head to her shoulder. Elly reached into her purse and pulled out her small notebook and pencil. It took a few minutes but then the conversation started behind them. Elly quietly took notes that made it plain that the French government was very much thinking of packing their bags and running quietly into the night.

They rode the boat for two more stops before Elly tapped Grant's knee and they got off. On land, Grant was taking deep, deep breaths. "So. Did you hear?"

"How often does the Secretary of Transportation ride that boat?"

"Twice a week. Every Tuesday and Thursday. He gets on around two p.m. Sometimes he rides alone, which is always a disappointment, but lately he's been on a roll with inviting different people to come with him. Naturally, they discuss the war." Recently, her articles had been extremely on point. Because she mailed them and did not telegram them—the paper she worked for could not afford the expense—her revelations were almost always two weeks behind. But that was a good thing because that meant she was not leaking any information of value to the enemy. The very last thing she wanted was for her stories to somehow play the role in getting someone killed. Despite the time delay, her insight as a soldier on the ground still made her articles highly sought after. Several had been picked up by bigger papers across the country. She could have a real career in this business when she returned to the States. If only she liked it.

"I see. You've always been an eavesdropper." Seeing that he was regaining his equilibrium, Elly reached for his hand, but before she could grab it, he slipped it into his coat pocket. No doubt, he was still trying to collect himself.

"Well, sometimes I'm granted interviews and sometimes I can get what I need just by listening. It's amazing the number of people who do not understand what should be kept private. Grant," Elly said, turning to face him. Catching sight of a tiny leaf on the shoulder of his coat, she reached up to brush it off. He jerked back slightly, startled. She held up the leaf so he could see it before she let it go. "I was wondering if you could do me a favor?" Not waiting for a response, she continued. "Not tonight, but maybe tomorrow? Madame is being very difficult. I know she is from a different generation—"

"We are not dating."

"What?"

"I just want to make sure that you understand that all of this is fake."

CHAPTER 22

Elly blinked once before shoving both her hands into the pockets of her jacket.

"This is not real," Grant continued, wariness in his eyes. "None of it is. I just want to make sure that you're not confused about that."

Elly had felt embarrassment before. No one lived to the ripe old age of twenty-four without experiencing at least one moment of complete shame and dread. But this single minute in time had to be one of the worst of them. Thousands of questions flooded her brain. What had she said or done that made him think she thought it was real? What had she said or done that had repulsed him? Was she that unattractive? Was there something about her that just made no one want to be around her? *Had* she lost sense of what was fake and what was real over the course of the past few months? Could Jesus come back right now so she could be a part of the rapture?

Her heart was pounding, and her blood felt like it had turned to ice, so numb were her fingers. But her voice was impassive. "I'm not confused. I'm sorry if it appears that I crossed the line somewhere. I'll just head on home."

Without waiting for a response, she turned on her heels and left Grant.

"Elly! Elodie." He jogged up to her. "You said you had a favor to ask."

"Don't worry about that. I'll take care of it." She'd find another way to get Madame's attention.

Grant's sigh was deep and heavy. "Elly."

"I'll see you around. Take care." She picked up her pace and didn't look back as she left Grant behind.

It took her until she reached the gates of the apartment to realize the truth. Somewhere along the line, it had stopped being pretend to her. The moments from a half hour ago flashed through her mind. The way she expected to hold his hand as they walked, the way she easily stepped into his space to touch him. He was the first person she went to when something bothered her and he was one of the few people she rarely policed herself with. And she loved it when he reciprocated in kind. In all their time together she'd discovered that he was naturally reticent, sarcastic, and perpetually annoyed but he tried not to be. Which meant perversely that Elly loved when he was.

Lord have mercy. At some point, Grant really had started to feel like her boyfriend. And to think that he'd picked up on that. And chosen to confront her about it. She was going to die of shame.

Opening the door with more force than it deserved, Elly entered the apartment. She took a quick glance around. Neither Madame nor Claire were home yet. It allowed for her to release the sob that rose in her throat. For no reason she could name, she was crying when she hung up her jacket.

She never should have stayed. Was she living? Was she even accomplishing anything? She felt like a tiny drop in a bucket, barely making a sound and providing no splash.

She made it to her room and shut the door. Grabbing her pillow off her bed, she hugged it to her chest trying to find comfort.

In the distance, she heard the door to the apartment open and shut. "Élodie?"

It was Claire. Looking around, Elly grabbed at the first loose piece of fabric she could find—a shirt she had decided not to wear that morning—and wiped her face. She cleared her throat. "Here, Claire."

Elly opened her bedroom door as Claire bounded down the hallway with all the enthusiasm of the young.

"Elly, my family, they are leaving France," the girl said excitedly.

"Your mother's side of the family?" Elly guessed.

Claire nodded. "*Oui.* I am not going with them. I cannot leave my grandmother. But I have made arrangements."

"Arrangements?"

"Grandmother has a cousin who lives near Aix-en-Provence. I have written her a letter asking if we can come and visit for the summer. She has agreed to take us in. We are leaving Paris, Elly, whether my grandmother wants to or not." Claire sliced the air with a hand.

Feeling a bit relieved, Elly sagged against the bedroom doorway. "Claire, that's wonderful news. We're going to get your grandmother out of this apartment if we have to knock her out to do it."

"*Oui*. I think of what you say. When the white people get to stay home, you have to leave."

That pulled a reluctant laugh out of Elly. "Just for now. In the meantime, you regroup, figure out your resources, and then fight back."

"*Exactement*," Claire said, anger and determination written in every line of her face. "We live today. We fight tomorrow." But then Claire's body language softened. "I'm glad you are here, Elly. I feel like I am not so alone. Between the two of us, we will get Grandmother out of Paris."

"*Oui*, Claire."

"And you will leave soon?"

"Yes. Plans have already been made." She was going to be fleeing Paris to live in the same house as Jo, Danny, Grant, Polly, and Pierre. The very thought of it gave her a headache.

"Thank you for staying," Claire said, nodding at the floor. "Thank you for telling the world about what is happening here."

The words bolstered Elly, making her stand a little taller; making her square her shoulders with pride even though she doubted the world was reading her words.

Nevertheless, someone was. Her splash might be tiny but it was still wet and it was still filling the bucket. She was playing her role in this game well. And that was not anything anyone could take from her.

"Thank you, Claire."

The girl shifted from one foot to the other. "If you are still here in France when the Germans come, please tell the world what they do to my people. We don't really know exactly, but whole families are disappearing." The last sentence was a whisper.

"I will," Elly promised as the sudden rise of tears began to fill her eyes. "I will tell everyone what I see." When Germany invaded, the likelihood of her being able to send anything to America would shrivel up completely. But that didn't mean she couldn't keep writing. Her articles just might be delayed by months rather than weeks. "Everyone deserves to have their story told."

Claire beamed and then reached into her back pocket. "You received a letter. If Grandmother asks, I am going to visit Gabrielle."

"What about homework?"

Claire's only response was a look that asked who did homework when one's world was ending.

When the apartment door shut behind Claire, Elly opened the letter. It was from her cousin at the newspaper. The message was clear, leave France now. Elly tossed the letter into the nearest trash can. She was still needed here. If she could save one life, then her time here was not in vain.

At breakfast the next morning, Madame asked Elly when Grant would be coming over for dinner.

"He won't be able to make it," Elly told her. She

was proud of herself for releasing only the merest of flinches. That wound was going to hurt for a good minute but she wasn't here in France for him. She wasn't here in France to make friends. She was here in France to make a difference; to use her life to help others. If she focused on that, everything else was like water rolling over a duck's back.

"Grandmère, I have been thinking that it might be nice to visit Cousin Mathilde. We did not see her last year." Madame looked at Claire, unimpressed. "We do not have to stay very long," Claire said, her voice placating although Elly knew that Claire's intention was to never return to Paris as long as Germany was a threat.

"Maybe in July."

Claire's sigh was deep and she looked across the table at Elly, a plea in her eyes.

Elly gave a small nod. She'd think of something. Finishing her cup of coffee, she stood up. "I have to go. I'm running late as is."

The line to get into the church seemed twice as long as the day before. Elly only had a few seconds to speak to Jo and the other woman didn't have much to say except to indicate that it was so busy it was hard to take time to scrutinize everyone who entered the sanctuary.

Elly realized the truth of that as she stood behind a table serving thin slices of ham. It wasn't that she didn't notice men who were suspicious. It was that there was no time to do anything about them.

But she still tried. When she found a free minute, she made her way to the church office and dialed the number she'd been given. "*Bonjour*, we are out of ham and flour today."

"We have no time for deliveries." Elly frowned and then looked at the phone in her hand. That was not an answer she'd ever been given before.

"I'm sorry. What?"

"We cannot help you today."

"But . . . the ham and flour."

"Ham and flour is out everywhere." And then the person on the other end of the phone hung up. What did that mean? They were so completely overwhelmed by German spies that they could not help? Or was the Deuxième one of those government agencies that was so busy burning things in their backyard they didn't have time to help? Elly set the phone onto the receiver. How very odd.

Returning to her spot at the serving table, Elly continued to fill plates and look over different ones and that was when she saw him. The young man would not have been particularly noticeable except that Elly had seen him before . . . months ago. He'd been a waiter at the Japanese embassy and then again at the Italian embassy. He was French. Or at the very least, he was not a refugee.

Excusing herself once again, she went to the office and placed another call.

"*Bonjour*." The person who answered sounded tired and frustrated and as though they were already done for the day.

"*Bonjour*, I am requesting sugar." This matter was of great importance.

"There will be no deliveries today," the person said,

237

enunciating each word as though Elly did not understand the language. "None. Zero."

"But—"

"We cannot help you. You must take care of your needs yourself." And then there was nothing. Elly slowly hung up the phone. Take care of her needs herself? What on earth did that mean?

Leaving the office once more, Elly did not return to her spot in the serving line. Instead, she found Josephine. Tension between them or not, some things were more important. Whispering in her ear, Elly explained all. Jo smiled briefly at the person standing in front of the bin of potatoes.

Breakfast in France was toast and jam and coffee and sweets. But that was not going to fill refugees who had been traveling—many by foot—to get there. So the Red Cross was serving whatever they could cook. What these people needed, Elly had thought time and time again, were some grits and eggs. That would fill everyone's stomach.

"I don't know that there is anything we can do. I'll try to call Jack when I get a second."

Elly looked at the line that was before Jo. She was not going to have a free second for a long time. She glanced over at the man she was certain was a spy. He was leaving. He'd finished his food and was about to go on his merry way. *You must take care of your needs yourself.* Elly reached behind herself, untying her apron. "I'm going to follow him."

Jo, who was trying to juggle three things at once, dropped several balls. She stared hard at Elly, ignoring everything else around her. Elly could see that there were a number of things she wanted to say that all started with 'that's a bad idea' except it was literally their job to sniff out spies.

Elly touched a hand to her arm. "I'll come back once I know what he's about. But I've got to hurry, he's almost out the door."

Careful not to sprint across the room, Elly reached the small closet where her jacket and hat were hanging. She'd left her purse at the apartment that morning, opting to keep her keys and a few francs in her pockets instead.

Leaving the church, Elly looked both ways, caught sight of her target and began to follow. Grant had spent the month of January teaching Elly how to trail after someone without getting caught and how to know when someone was trailing her. The thing was, he'd told her, as a colored woman she was never going to blend in. So, she needed to not be seen in the first place.

She stepped off the sidewalk and into a group of women who were slowly making their way somewhere in the same direction as the spy. When that group scattered, she ducked into the shadows of a doorway, waiting for the man to turn a corner before continuing to follow him.

He led her on a twenty-minute walk to a door tucked into a building that rested in the very center of an alley. In Chicago, people with wisdom did not walk down those narrow paths between buildings. It had taken Elly literal months before she felt even remotely comfortable traveling down such small, often darkened spaces. But in Paris, it was down those very passageways where you'd find the best restaurants and the most extravagant homes.

The spy disappeared into the building. Elly walked backwards to see the front of the building. There was nothing special about it. Several stores littered the face of the structure: a grocery store, a bakery, a shoe store. But above them were dozens of windows. It was most likely an apartment building of sorts. Elly made note of the address. She'd give it to Jo and Jo could pass it on to blond-haired Jack.

Just when she'd made that decision, the door in the alleyway opened and the spy exited. Well, she'd come this far. The spy walked deeper into the alley and Elly let him disappear from sight before following. Pulling her hat down low, Elly was careful to mute her steps. With no one else around, and everything as narrow as it was, it'd be easy to be caught.

She turned at the same corner he'd taken very slowly and it was a good thing she did because he stood right there waiting for her. When their eyes met, she knew in that moment that only one of them was going to walk out of this situation alive.

CHAPTER 23

"You're not Josephine Baker's cousin," the man said in heavily accented English.

Elly released a slow breath. She'd neither confirm nor deny that fact. Besides, she had bigger things to think about like how she was going to survive this encounter. The only weapon she had on her person was the moth switchblade in her hair. But, like she always did when she walked down these stupid little paths, she'd made note of other things she could use as a weapon. She was pretty sure someone had dropped a crowbar on the ground about ten feet back. She took a small step backwards.

"It begs the question of why Josephine Baker needs a false cousin anyway," the man continued. He was young. Maybe her age or younger. He had a mother and a father. Maybe sisters and brothers. Or a wife. But Elly couldn't think about that. Whatever he knew or thought he knew needed to disappear along with him. The very thought of it sent her heart to racing but not with fear. She didn't have time for that emotion just yet.

"I think the bigger question is how you can spy for a country like Germany when you are clearly French." She needed to be certain she was talking to the enemy. She took another tiny step backwards.

"I am thinking about France. And it will be a better country under Hitler." He reached into his pocket and Elly did not wait to see what he was trying to grab. She ran to where she'd seen that heavy piece of metal.

But he was faster than she expected, and he grabbed her from behind, one of his hands going to her mouth and the other around her neck. She stomped hard on his foot, relaxed her muscles so she slumped, and then elbowed him in the stomach. All of it made him loosen his grip but he did not let go of her. She reached up for the pin in her hair, pulled it out, and stabbed blindly behind her.

The man yelped and released her long enough for her to escape his grasp. She didn't get far before he grabbed her around the waist. She lashed out with her switchblade, wondering why she had never thought to practice using it. The man brought his hand down on hers with such force, she dropped the blade and it skittered across the pavement.

He was stronger than her and she was losing this fight. And that was when fear began to flood her veins. Elbowing the spy in the stomach, Elly was able to turn slightly. She threw a punch. He caught it with his hand. She threw another. He caught that one too. Then, as though she were a small child, he hoisted her up by the fabric of her coat and slammed her against the brick wall of the nearest building. Pain ratcheted up the back of Elly's head, but she still dug her fingers into his wrists, trying to dislodge his hands. Releasing a grunt, the man jerked on her lapels once more and this time tossed her to the ground. Elly's shoulder hit the cobblestones and pain shot up her arm like lightning but there was no time to think about it.

Scrambling forward on hands and knees, the only thought in her head was escape. But she paused when she heard the telltale click of the cocking of a gun. Elly looked over her shoulder just in time to see a flash of metal. And then suddenly there was a shadow, a thud, and the man hit the ground.

Heart pounding so hard Elly could barely catch a breath, she met the eyes of Jo Baker who stood there with a large piece of wood in hand. Jo looked at the wood she was holding like it had betrayed her and then she dropped it. For thirty seconds, neither of them said anything. Finally, Elly pushed herself to her feet. The ground dipped and blurred beneath her.

"He's still alive," Elly said, breathing heavily. Feeling like she'd just spun in circles, Elly's unsteady feet carried her over to the gun the man had dropped. Crouching down, she picked it up.

"If we let him go, he'll lead them right to us." Jo's voice was low and sad but resolved. She was also right. For one, everyone knew Josephine Baker. For two, sometimes it felt like they were the only colored women in all of Paris. They'd be easy to find no matter what. The gun in Elly's hand suddenly felt ten pounds heavier.

If they shot this man, they would draw attention. It was probably why he hadn't shot her in the first place. She slipped the weapon into her coat pocket. Then, she caught sight of her switchblade, silver and gleaming on the pavement. It would be like killing a deer, she told herself. Jo drew in a loud breath as Elly crawled over to her knife, turned the man over, and then slit his throat without allowing herself to internally debate for another second.

Warm blood gushed out and she watched him until she was sure he had left to meet his maker. Almost as though she were handling a sleeping baby, she gently tucked him face first against the wall so that people passing would think he was sleeping off a night of debauchery. "I don't think we should waste time trying to hide his body."

Elly's words came out cool and calm even as her body had a sudden attack of the shakes. She was proud that her brain was still moving, still working. But this was all going to hit her like a ton of bricks at some point. *You are a soldier and you are at war,* she reminded herself.

And they needed to disappear.

"Let's go," Elly told Jo. The two women headed down a different path, walking quickly but not running. "You followed me."

"While you are without a doubt one of the most self-assured people I've ever met, I thought to myself, she might have trouble."

The alley spit them out into the bright beautiful sunny Paris day. It felt incredibly incongruous to the past ten minutes Elly had just lived. "I was in over my head and I'm very grateful you made the decision you did."

Jo turned a corner and Elly followed. She didn't know where she was and she didn't think she had the willpower to muster up the desire to find out. "You looked like you were handling it."

"Did I?" What a thought. The man she'd killed would have said otherwise. She looked down at her hands, about to shove them in her pockets when she saw blood. For a second, she stopped, about to have a Macbeth moment.

Jo slipped an arm through hers and Elly sagged against her shoulder. "You had the right idea. Put your hands in your pockets." Elly obeyed and they strolled down the street arm in arm. "So it did bother you?"

"Of course it did! I did what I had to do because it was him or me. He knew too much." It had sounded like he'd been keeping an eye on them all this time. Elly told Jo this.

Jo squared her shoulders. "*We* made the right decision. There's no point in second-guessing it."

"Can you tell your handler?" For two seconds she'd considered trying to find Grant's apartment. Elly craved Grant's presence in the same way that she had desired Aunt Tabitha's after realizing her aunt bore echoes of her mother. She needed someone who would hold her while she cried and calm all of her fears. And he'd made it abundantly clear that he wasn't there for any of that. So she'd rather just go through Jo's boyfriend.

"Yes."

"Jo?"

"Yes?"

245

"Thank you. Thank you for following me. Thank you for saving my life. Thank you for this," she said, nodding at Jo's arm, which was linked to hers. She needed the comfort of physical contact. She needed to know she was still alive although the soreness in her arm was a very strong indicator.

"Well," Jo said after a moment. "We're cousins, aren't we? Families argue and disagree all the time and it's not the end of the world. Besides, you're still young even if you feel like an old soul. I can't expect you to understand everything, can I?"

Elly didn't quite grin—her emotions were still a bit too raw for that. But she almost did. "Is that right?"

"When you've lived as long as I have," Jo teased, "you might see the world differently."

"Doubtful." There was almost cheer in Elly's voice.

Jo released a huff of air. "You're very annoying but I would be lying if I didn't say I'm glad that if I had to experience such a moment it was with you. I've come to realize that in times like these the world needs people able to make quick decisions. That's what Jack told me when he first recruited me. I can reach out for help or advice but at the end of the day, I have to be able to weigh a situation and come to a solution on my own."

Elly took the words for the reassurance they were.

"Just focus on all the lives you've saved."

"Like ours?"

"Who's more important than us?"

Jo's words made Elly smile. She tugged on Jo's arm, feeling strangely connected to the woman in a way she hadn't felt before. "Do you have dinner plans? Would

246

you mind coming to meet the French family I'm staying with? I'm trying to convince them to leave Paris, but I think they need to speak to someone with a bit more pizzazz."

Jo patted her arm. "If anyone knows how to bring the pizzazz, it's me."

"We're having a guest for dinner?" Madame asked that evening as Elly and Claire set the table.

"Yes, she should be here any minute." Neither Jo nor Elly had returned to the church. Instead, they'd walked the streets of Paris like tourists. Or rather Elly had been the tourist while Jo had been the tour guide, telling her stories of different places she'd been and famous people she'd encountered. Even though Jo was doing most of the talking, it had felt like they both needed it. They both needed to escape the war if only for an hour. But eventually, they came across a payphone. Elly had waited outside the booth while Jo placed a call to Jack. Then they'd split up. Elly returned to the apartment while Jo went to rendezvous with her handler. But she had promised to come for dinner.

"Oh, good, a female friend. I'm glad it's not Grant. Dinner is a simple affair." Indeed. Dinner was a spaghetti omelet and a salad. A very strange combination. Before France, Elly had never had eggs for dinner unless it was because she had a craving for breakfast. And certainly she'd never make an omelet and toss cooked noodles into it. And then add a salad. But Madame had fixed it before and it was quite tasty. Elly briefly imagined making this meal for Uncle Minor and Aunt Tabitha when she returned to the States. She found

247

herself grinning already at the look they'd give her when she served them.

There was a knock on the door. "I'll get it." Elly opened it. Jo stood on the other side dressed in a long black and white gown, a feathered hat, a pair of white gloves, and a pure white mink wrap. In one hand was a champagne bottle.

"You said pizzazz."

Elly clapped her hands lightly. "So, I did. Thank you." Elly moved out the way to let Jo enter, but then stopped the other woman as she passed. "Jack said . . . ?"

"All taken care of. Don't think twice about it."

The load of bricks that had been resting on her chest fell off. Or at least half of them did. Now that she did not have to worry about being caught, she could simply worry about the fact that she'd killed a man. It would only take her about fifty years to recover. "Madame, Claire, may I introduce you to Josephine Baker?"

She was absolutely terrific at this, Elly thought as she scanned the kitchen table an hour later.

"I am so sorry." Madame was apologizing again for the simple fare they'd eaten.

"Please don't be," Jo said, somehow managing to look both haughty and down to earth. "It was exactly what I was craving. And so delicious. I can't make an omelet to save my life. The things the French do to an egg." The whole conversation was in French. Madame and Claire were too starstruck to try their English.

"I have some fresh raspberries for dessert."

"And I'm looking forward to them," Jo told Madame. "But please don't get up yet. Elly asked me here for a reason." Madame and Claire both looked at Elly for a brief second. "Nearly ten years ago, if you can believe it, I was asked to do a tour that encompassed Germany and Austria. I thought nothing of it. I had been there before." As Jo began talking, Elly stood up to gather the empty dinner plates. "I knew some people were not fans of my show. You can't expect everyone to love you—although Lord knows I try!" Jo released a small self-deprecating laugh. But then she sobered. "I was greeted with newspaper headlines that called me the Black Devil or Jezebel. I was followed by strange men who were most assuredly not fans. I had to hire guards. I was heckled and harassed constantly. Mobs of horrible people would form outside my hotel. The show was to last six months; it lasted weeks. Their hatred of me was a thing of frenzy and nothing like I've seen anywhere. And that's saying something."

Elly quietly turned on the faucet, running water so she could wash the dishes.

"Whatever is happening in Germany you cannot reason with no matter how hard you try. I have loads of friends in high places. And they're all saying there's a chance the Germans may enter Paris—I'm not saying France is going to lose the war. I'm saying, in the fighting, the Germans may reach as far as here. Elly says Claire is Jewish. Is that right?"

"*Oui*," Claire said softly.

"I can tell you from personal experience that you don't want to be 'other' when they arrive. It is a sad state of affairs that humanity seems to always look for a scapegoat. One day I pray that the world is accepting of all kinds. I want to do everything I can to create that kind of place. But even I know that if I want to live to see tomorrow, I need to leave this city."

"You know, it was like this during the Great War," Madame said, trotting out her familiar line.

Jo raised one shoulder in a lazy shrug. "Perhaps. But what does it cost you to take a trip to the south for the next few months? If I'm wrong, you've got a vacation out of it. If I'm right, you're not worrying about Claire's life. Madame Auger, I am from America. The land of the free, they call it. The land of great hatred, I call it. I have fled in the night with nothing but what I could carry in my hands as white men shot at us like rats in the street," Jo said, her voice hard and rough with emotion. Elly paused in her dishwashing to look at Jo. "Trust me. You don't want to let it get that far."

"My son," Madame said and, for a second, her lip quivered. Her son. Elly had been so focused on Madame and Claire that she hadn't given much thought to the man between them: Claire's father. It used to be that they received a weekly letter from him but Elly could not remember the last time Madame sat down with a cup of coffee while she memorized her son's words. "I have not heard from my son in a few weeks. What do we do if he comes looking for us?"

"I wrote to Papa," Claire told her grandmother. "I told him we were trying to go south. Don't worry. He'll be able to find us."

"I suppose," Madame said softly. "We could visit my cousin in Aix for a few weeks."

Claire, whose shoulders had been hunched with

tension as she listened to Jo, straightened in her seat. "*Oui*, Grandmère!"

"There's a train leaving in three days," Elly murmured from her place at the sink.

"I should write to her first," Madame said with a shaky laugh.

"I already have," Claire informed her. "She can't wait to see us."

Elly was grinning at the fork in her hand when the telephone rang. "I'll get it." Snatching a drying towel off the kitchen counter, she dried her hands before picking up the receiver. "*Bonjour?*"

"May I speak to Elodie Mitchell?" The male voice asked politely and in perfect French. It was familiar.

Elly frowned for a second. "Pierre?"

"Elly," Pierre said, his voice flat as he lost the French accent. "I don't know what you did, girl, but Grant wants to see you asap." His voice lowered but came across crisper as though he had cupped a hand around the mouthpiece. "You in trouble," he sang out like a little kid.

Elly ignored the way her stomach flipped. "All right. I'll be there in a half hour."

CHAPTER 24

Elly walked with Jo out of the apartment building and onto the street. "Thank you so much. I think she's going to listen to you."

Jo had said things differently, adding her own history and background to the situation but she hadn't said anything new. Elly shook her head. Regardless, if Josephine Baker could get Madame and Claire moving then it didn't matter whose words worked. "You're welcome. How's your head?"

Not wanting to put hands in her hair, which had been spotted with another's blood, Elly had waited until she returned to the apartment to wash before taking inventory. "Head is fine." Surprisingly enough there was no open wound, and she hadn't felt a knot. Her shoulder, on the other hand, was a massive shade of purple.

"Want a ride?" So happy was Elly that she took Jo

up on her offer and ten minutes later when the car screeched to a stop in front of Grant's apartment, she made a vow to never ever do something so foolish again. "I don't know what Grant wants, but I wouldn't worry too much if I were you. He's all bark and no bite . . . nine times out of ten."

"Got it," Elly said, her voice and legs a bit shaky as she climbed out of the car. Never again, she told herself, as Jo sped off for her next engagement, barely dodging the nearest parked car. After entering Grant's apartment building, she made her way up and up, wondering for the third time why on earth he had insisted that she come to his place? She'd gotten the impression that he wasn't really one for inviting people over.

Elly reached the door and pounded a fist against it. She'd talk to him about what was important and then she'd leave. There would be no dilly-dallying or daydreaming. He'd stood on all ten of his toes and told her exactly how he felt about her and she'd more than honor his thoughts on the matter.

Pierre cracked the door of the apartment open. "What did you do?" he asked her, his voice low as though afraid of being overheard.

"What are you talking about?" She'd admit nothing to this man in front of her.

"He's been fussing ever since he got home about the most ridiculous things. It took me two hours to figure out it had something to do with you," Pierre said pointedly, his eyes narrowed on her.

"He's the one who asked me to be here. Why didn't you ask him?"

Pierre pressed his lips together and raised his eyes

to somewhere just above her head. "Well. Technically, he didn't ask you to be here. I did. Because I need peace in my house and you've destroyed that."

"What?"

"He doesn't know you're here. I was very surprised you didn't question the story I was telling. It isn't exactly Grant's MO to invite women to the apartment at night no matter what. He's a gentleman that way," Pierre mocked even as he rolled his eyes.

Elly took a step back, unamused. "I'm going home."

"Elly! Don't go home! Come in here and take your medicine so he'll stop growling at me."

"You had me leave my warm, comfortable apartment, risk death with Jo behind the wheel—"

"Now that I am sorry about. I thought you knew better."

"To come out here to chase a man who doesn't want me—"

"Whoa. Coming to our apartment does not equate to whatever you think it does in that head of yours. This ain't the Victorian era. And as for Grant wanting you, that's . . . I never . . . I am so confused . . . and also strangely intrigued."

"And now I have to return to the apartment in the dead of night because you're selfish!" Elly turned on her heels and started down the stairs.

"Elly! Elodie!"

"Who are you yelling at? What is wrong with you?" Grant's voice. Elly picked up her pace.

"Elly came to visit!" She paused on the step, turned around, and glared at Pierre. She was going to hurt the Negro.

"Elodie!" It was Grant. He replaced Pierre in the doorway, moving the other man out of the way. Elly raised a hand in greeting.

"I got my wires crossed about something. No worries. I'm headed home."

"Come back," Grant ordered, beckoning her. "There's something we need to talk about."

Like a little kid, Pierre was sent to his room while Grant and Elly talked in the kitchen. She sat at the small table with a small cup of coffee while Grant stood in front of the counter next to the stove and butchered an already butchered chicken. Pierre had not been lying. He was not a chef.

"What did you come here for?" Grant asked as he began to season the mess on his cutting board.

Elly took a small sip of her coffee, thinking about how to reply. Well, it wasn't as though she owed Pierre a dime. "Pierre told me you wanted to see me."

"That boy," Grant muttered under his breath as he scraped the meat into a hot pan on the stove.

"What are you making?"

"Pasta."

"Shouldn't you be boiling water?" She didn't know if he was muttering in French or English as he somehow managed to slam open a cupboard and grab a pot. She watched him fill it with water.

"Tell me about today."

Elly glanced toward Pierre's room.

"If he's listening, it doesn't matter. And he's probably listening."

Slowly, hesitantly, Elly ran through the facts. She

was very careful to keep all emotions out of it. "You were in over your head."

"I know."

"You're lucky that Jo had the God-given sense to follow you."

"Yes, I know."

"Your instincts were right, but you didn't have the skill set to follow through."

"I agree."

"But killing that man, that was the right decision." Grant slammed another pot onto the stove causing Elly to jump as he reached for different ingredients. "Not taking the time to call me was also the right decision." He slammed his container of noodles onto the kitchen counter.

"It *was* the right decision?" she repeated for clarification because she was unsure whether he believed that or not.

"Yes," he bit out.

"I suppose that's a good thing because it never crossed my mind once to call you."

Grant turned away from the stove for a second and stared at her. The room, already weighty with his anger filled with a different sort of tension. "You would not have called me?" he asked repeating her words in a voice so low it was almost hard to hear him. "Me, who has spent the last umpteen months pouring my time and energy into you?"

"You didn't train me to call you in times of trouble. You trained me to handle whatever's thrown my way. So, no, I didn't think to call you," Elly said, suddenly feeling as angry as he apparently was.

"You could have been killed!" He pointed this out as though she wasn't well aware of that fact.

"Yes, I know," Elly said through clenched teeth. Hadn't they gone through this already?

"And you have the nerve to sit there nonchalantly as though you just went for a walk in the park."

What was he talking about? "I'm not sitting here nonchalantly—"

"Looking at me as though you don't have a care in the world while I feel like I'm about to lose my doggone mind."

"Grant—"

"What was I supposed to do if Jo had arrived thirty seconds too late and come across your dead body? Tell me, Elodie! Explain how I was supposed to keep going knowing that you—" He stopped talking, cutting himself off as he turned his back to her to scrape at something in the pan.

Elly looked down at her hands. Now, she understood. In his forty years on this earth, the man before her had lost a lot of people and she was officially his mentee. "I should have let you know. I'm sorry."

"I don't care," he tossed over his shoulder. Elly lifted her eyes to the ceiling even as the strangest thought fluttered through Elly's mind. Irritated Grant might be the most attractive version of Grant that she'd come across. Not because she liked moody men but because she knew she was with the real Grant Monterey. Not the charmer, not the patient but dedicated teacher, not the Parisian caricature he'd created for their 'dates.' This person standing in the kitchen burning something at the stove was Leslie Grant Monterey of

Virginia, New York, the Harlem Hellfighters, and now of Paris.

Underneath the table, she pinched herself. No daydreaming. No wondering what it would be like to really be pursued by Grant. "May I leave then?"

"Am I holding you prisoner?"

Elly rolled her eyes. An easy thing to do with his back to her once again.

"We'll meet up in three days."

"Can't," she said quickly. She could not do it anymore. She could not do the hugging and the touching and the talking about their lives knowing all of it culminated into nothing for him past training or simple friendship. Now that she'd realized how much she liked him, she could not pretend anything else. No matter how much better she'd gotten at make-believe.

"What do you mean can't?" Grant turned around, vexation in his jaw and a challenge in his eyes. He was daring her to bring up something so unprofessional as hurt feelings.

She glanced away and then remembering her cup of coffee took a sip. "I have plans."

"Plans."

"I'm helping Madame and Claire leave Paris for Aix. They catch the train in three days." She glanced at him out of the side of her eye, watching him tilt his head to the side as he considered her words. "Then we can meet after."

"I still have to be at the Red Cross with Jo. We never know what can happen there." Elly didn't exactly want to return to the church and the Red Cross—it was forever going to be tainted by the fact that she had killed a man. But it was safer than walking the streets with Grant. "And then I have to pack up for leaving Paris. So much to do."

"So much to do," he repeated, his voice dull.

"People to see." Not exactly true. "Things to wrap up." She didn't know what that meant but it sounded good. "Articles!" she said, suddenly remembering her day job. "So many articles to write. If we're both honest, I've learned everything I can from you. I don't much see the point in meeting anymore."

"Because you know everything?"

"No. I don't know everything. Today proved that to me clearly enough. But we're leaving Paris soon. I think my job as a spy is pretty much done here."

"You can't know that."

"Then let me take a break, Grant," she snapped as she flashed her eyes at him. "I need a break." To her horror, her voice broke and her eyes welled up with tears. "Your food is doing something strange." Not waiting for him to stir it, Elly stood up, made her way to the stove, and turned down the heat. Reaching over, she snatched the spoon out of his hand. "The water is boiling."

"I'll take you home before I cook the noodles." He was standing just behind her, his breath warm on her neck.

She both wished him away and wished him closer. "I don't need you to take me home." Doing her level best to ignore him, she scraped the spoon against the bottom of the pan. Things were not quite burnt yet.

When Grant reached for the spoon, cupping his hand around hers, she dropped it and turned around so quickly, her right hand brushed against the boiling pot of water. "Ouch," she hissed and shook her hand out.

"Let me see."

"No!" Grant grabbed her hand and lifted it, eyeing the small red mark on the side of her palm. He dragged her over to the sink, turned on the faucet, and ran cold water over the small burn. "I can do this," she hissed as she tried to pull her hand from his grasp. But he would not release her.

"Let me help you."

"I don't need your help."

"You can't do everything alone in this life."

"Who said I wanted to do everything alone? When have I ever said that I wanted to do everything alone? But no one is ever going to accuse me of being somewhere I'm not wanted. Can we turn the water off? I'm freezing."

"I never said you weren't wanted." Jaw ticking, Grant reached over and shut the water off. For the space of two heartbeats they stared at each other. "Sometimes," Grant began softly, his thumb gently stroking her hand and sending unwanted little zings throughout her body, "it's not a matter of want."

He dropped her hand and turned back to the stove, shutting the fire off. "Come on. Let me take you home."

Feeling a bit jittery, Elly rubbed the mark on the palm of her hand. "I don't need you to take me home. If you insist that I can't walk home alone, Pierre can come with me. But Grant, I mean it. Our time working together is over."

CHAPTER 25

The last words she'd flung at Grant danced in her head. If he hadn't known for sure how she felt about him, he had to know now. How embarrassing. His focus was on keeping her—and probably everyone within their small group—safe. While she was too busy imagining them together without the war in the background. But if not the war, what would be in the background? France? Or the U.S.? It didn't matter, she told herself sternly.

"You okay over there?"

Elly looked up. She and Pierre were in the car. "I was not in trouble."

"Hmm. I suppose it's all a matter of perspective." Pierre started the engine. "Thank you, by the way, for volunteering me to take you home. I was sitting in my room just hoping that when it was time for you to leave, you'd think of me."

"I was there because of *you*."

"I'm just making sure you understand that all of this," he said, waving a hand in a circle toward himself, "is taken."

"Oh, you're taken all right."

"Don't be rude."

"When's the wedding?"

"Nobody asked you to toss out insults. What's going on between you and Grant?"

"There's nothing going on between me and Grant."

"All this time I thought you were his happy little protégée. His stand-in for Mary Grace. Don't take this the wrong way but I thought you hated men."

"No. I don't hate men. Just you."

"I thought your plan was to be one of those spinsters who works at the library and yells at children having a good time."

"I thought your plan was to be one of those men who dates women and leaves babies in their wake. Oh wait, you are one of those men."

Next to her, Pierre grinned, not the slightest bit offended but instead looking rather tickled. And he wasn't the only one. Their exchange was a strangely comforting thing to her.

"You didn't answer. Is there something else going on between you and Grant? I, honest to God, never considered it. Grant likes his women older."

"Shut up. And no, there's nothing going on."

Pierre hummed. "All this time I thought you were trying to become like my cousin or something and you're trying to be my auntie."

"I'm not trying to be your anything!" Pierre pulled

up in front of Madame's apartment building, but Elly did not exit the car. Next to her, Pierre fiddled with a lighter and a cigarette. "I have a question for you."

"Maybe I have an answer," he countered with sass.

"Do you think Grant would ever leave France?"

Pierre's grin was more of a smirk. "So you do like him!"

"I was just curious," she snapped.

"Uh-huh. I believe you." Pierre brought the cigarette to his mouth, inhaling. "No."

Pierre said it so decisively that Elly was startled. "I know why he returned to France, and he has a life here so I can understand why he's stayed but you don't think he'd return to the States after all is said and done?"

"Nope." Pierre popped the p in that single word.

Another thought occurred to her. "Is it because of the lack of racism? Like Jo? Did he want to escape all of that?"

Pierre looked unimpressed by the question. "The day every chocolate baby is born, they come into the world with fingers and toes and the weight of being the lowest in the caste system. You can't escape racism. It's here in France. It just manifests a bit differently. You should see how they treat Africans. It is a big fricking deal that we're Americans. These white people might like the idea of the exotic but I've never seen a dark-skinned woman with an accent from the motherland on their stages performing the Charleston. I will belt out the 'Star Spangled Banner' if it means they'll treat me with dignity and respect and we'll all pretend like we're on the same page. No, honey, it's not racism. Especially because he was living in New York where you can disappear into neighborhoods white folks don't go in and if you're lucky you won't run into any that will call you boy."

"So what is it then?"

"Nothing in this life is free. If you expect me to share my wisdom, you will owe me." Elly considered that. She couldn't think of a single thing that she had or could do that he'd want. Still, she eyed him warily. "I wouldn't ask for anything criminal. Like say, killing anybody." Elly's eyes turned icy. Pierre pulled on his cigarette and exhaled smoke. Waiting.

Elly released a huff of air. "Fine. I'll owe you."

In the shadow of the car, Pierre's grin was swift. "Fear."

"What?"

"Grant is afraid."

That made Elly pause. "Of what?"

"Of living. Before the war, if he wasn't working, he was visiting the cemetery. It's creepy. I went there once. He made me visit my dad's grave. There were hundreds of men out there. Thousands. Why in the heck do I want to spend my free time sitting amongst the dead? He's not all right here," Pierre said, tapping a finger against his head. "And he knows it. And he also knows that the love of a good woman isn't going to change that. He walked that road before and his marriage was a disaster."

"Even now, you think?" Elly whispered.

"Even now," Pierre murmured, the weight of the past twenty-two years in his voice.

"I'm sorry you lost your father in the previous war." Elly wished there was another way to express one's sadness over someone else's grief. But the English language seemed peculiarly failing in this aspect.

"Hmm? Oh, well. I barely knew him," he said lightly. He cleared his throat. "Grant cannot sleep unless he's exhausted, which means it isn't unusual for him to walk the streets of Paris until his feet have blisters. He can stare out the window for hours, lost in his own head. And do not make the mistake of surprising him. Ever. I've known him for ages. I'm the closest person to him and he still refuses to share parts of himself— not because he's afraid of vulnerability. But because the more he knows a person, the more it'll hurt when they leave. So he gets to know people only up to a certain extent before he withdraws."

Elly looked out the window, next to her, seeing nothing.

"That war messed him up. You don't get all the medals he's got without losing a part of yourself in the getting. He has learned how to make it from day to day and leaving Paris would require him relearning all over again. That's why I don't think it'll ever happen." Pierre sighed deeply. "We all have our demons but his are just too much."

"I don't have demons. *You* might have demons," Elly said, pointing at him even though she knew exactly what he meant. She knew what it was to live with certain voices in your head that had to be ignored on a daily basis. But this was Pierre and she was going to take advantage of every opportunity to needle him. "I'm saved, sanctified, and filled with the Holy Ghost. No demons. But you . . . ?" Elly spread her hands in uncertainty.

"You're crazy. Do you know that? Absolutely bat—"

"Anyway," she said, cutting him off. "I do thank you. I did not expect you to be so insightful."

Pierre rolled his eyes. Hard. "I love Grant. He's the only family I've had all these years. Of course, I've tried to figure him out."

"What do you think would ever make him want to try again?"

Pierre rolled down the window of the car and tapped his cigarette against the side, creating a small flurry of embers. "I told you the love of a good woman ain't gonna do it."

"Yes. What will?"

Pierre shrugged dramatically. "I don't know. He has to be more afraid of not living than living. He's got to recognize that life is about taking risks and challenging yourself and being willing to get hurt in the process. And that the people who love you don't need you to have it all together first before they accept you. They just do, flaws and all. Of course you have to be willing to work on those flaws. Everybody gets tired of crazy after a while."

"Layers," Elly said, nodding seriously as she eyed him. "You are a man of infinite layers and wisdom."

"I know. I'm practically King Solomon." Pierre slapped the wheel of the car. "Well, not trying to push you out of the car or anything but some people have things to do and places to be."

Elly opened the car door, stepping out onto the sidewalk. "Thank you, Pierre."

"Always happy to help. Although, if I'm well and truly honest, prettier women than you have tried to crack the nut that is Grant."

Leaning down, Elly waved a finger. "In case it's not clear, I don't like you."

"Uh-huh. Love you too, sweetheart. *Bonsoir!* Looking forward to cashing in my favor!"

Elly slammed the car door behind her.

Madame may have agreed to leave Paris for the south of France but that did not mean that she made things easy for Claire and Elly.

"This is my wedding dress. I cannot leave it behind."

"I'm going to leave her behind," Claire muttered under her breath. They'd been trying to convince Madame to treat her leaving as though taking a holiday but the older woman wasn't fooled. She was well aware that there was a chance she might not be able to return to the home she'd lived in her whole life and Elly kept stumbling over her as she cried into old clothes and over items she hadn't seen in years.

It was all making Elly feel restless. She had been the type of student who never could take all of the allotted time a teacher gave for an exam. Once the first student turned in their test, it was time for Elly to wrap things regardless of whether she was ready or not. She was starting to get that same itch as Madame and Claire packed. She too should be packing. She too should be walking out of the door in three days.

"Let her say goodbye," Elly told Claire. Elly didn't know what it was to leave a home that had housed family for generations. But it wasn't a great leap to place herself in their shoes. How hard it would be to have to flee the home she'd been raised and loved in with Uncle Minor and Aunt Tabitha. Yes, it was all just things but they were things that represented your very life. Such thoughts set Elly to weeping and it wasn't unusual for her to take a momentary break to collect herself.

Despite all of their packing and maneuvering, the apartment still looked lived in and loved. There was so much that Claire and Madame were leaving behind, all of them knowing that it might be years before the Auger family returned . . . if they ever did.

And then the day came.

"Grandmère, we will be late," Claire said from the doorway of the apartment. She stood there with her schoolbag slung across her shoulders. Elly knew it carried her journal, photographs, jewelry—including the lucky necklace—and snacks for the road.

Madame stood at the sink, washing dishes despite knowing that Elly would be staying in the apartment for a bit longer. "All right, all right," the older woman said as she dried her hands on the nearest dish towel. Madame raised her eyes to the ceiling of her home and stared as though taking mental pictures of the space. "I lost my only brother in the last war. We used to argue about who would inherit this place and then suddenly there was no longer a discussion. When I got married, your grandfather moved in. I refused to live anywhere else. Why pay rent when we own this place right next to the river Seine? Champs-Élysées is just down the street. This place was given to us because of my grandmother. How she must have pleased the duc."

Neither Elly nor Claire said anything as they stood by the door.

"We managed to pass it down from generation to

generation knowing that we would not sell one brick." Madame's voice broke. "I raised Bernard here. I used to do my homework over there like Claire. I . . ."

"It's just a holiday, Grandmère," Claire said quietly. "We're leaving for a little while. But we'll come back."

Madame's smile did not reach her eyes. "I thought I would die here like my parents before me."

"Holiday," Claire stressed, her voice calm, even as her eyes filled with emotion. And hers weren't the only ones. It wasn't fair that this was happening; that one country's greed was destroying the lives of so many people who had never done anything to anyone. Elly blinked back tears and discreetly coughed into her hand. She'd cried more in the past week than she felt like she'd cried in all of her life.

Madame sighed. "Holiday," she repeated. "One day this will be your home, Claire."

"*Mais, oui.*"

Elly watched Madame place two fingers to her lips and then touch them to one of the walls as though blessing the home. Then she squared her shoulders. "Let's go."

No one was able to flag down a taxi anymore and so Madame, Claire, and Elly joined the masses of refugees who were also carrying their whole world on their shoulders and trying to get as far away from the war as possible.

Elly and Claire had spent hours in the train station tag-teaming in the long line to get tickets out of Paris. The place was filled with the bodies of desperate people of all ages, and reeked with the scent of uncleanliness and anxiety. Babies wailed while parents looked on with

269

worry. The elderly leaned on anything they could, only one stiff wind from falling over. Everyone clutched their bags and suitcases knowing good and well that if they lost it they would have nothing. And every single person carried with them a little pocket of hope that they'd make it into a car that would take them far away from Paris.

"What is this? There cannot possibly be enough tickets for all of these people," Madame muttered under her breath. Madame was right. The trains filled first with those who paid and then secondly with those who couldn't. No train left Paris with empty seats. And just like in the house, the fear and worry was catching. Elly suddenly wished that she too had a ticket so she could leave this city.

"The train leaves in fifteen minutes," Claire said, alarm in her voice as she looked over the crowd they had to cross to get to their car.

"*Quel est le problème?*" Elly asked. The French had never had a problem shoving her to the side when she was in the way. And God forbid they say excuse me. If anything, it went against *her* upbringing to rudely knock people over but desperate times and all of that. Extending a hand toward the sea of people, Elly said, "Darn the torpedoes. Full speed ahead."

And then, before Elly could dive into the fray, Grant was there.

"*Bonjour*, Madame Auger. Claire. Give me your suitcases. Come on. Let's get you on this train." They barreled through the horde with Elly and Grant saying, *pardon*, every few seconds as they pushed Madame and Claire along.

Elly had imagined one last hug, one last goodbye,

but there was no time for that. Madame handed the conductor their tickets while Grant opened the train door and shoved their bags through. With one hand, he kept it open for the women. "*Merci*! *Merci*." Madame and Claire were both crying as they climbed into the car.

"*Au revoir*," Elly yelled as she jumped and waved from the crush of people that was threatening to swallow her. "*Au revoir* and *merci!*" Claire and Madame disappeared for a brief second and then Claire was at a window, tugging it open.

"Be careful, Élodie!"

"If it stays bad, Claire, keep running! You have your very precious life to live! Keep running and don't stop!"

"I won't," the girl promised as she waved. "I won't."

Elly was bumped from behind and she felt her feet slip. And then her hand was snatched out of the air. Grant. She didn't argue as he pushed and pulled and dragged her through to an empty side of the train station. Neither of them spoke as they climbed the stairs up to the street and back to fresh air.

Elly rubbed a hand across her face. "I'll probably never see them again."

"Very unlikely," Grant agreed as he moved toward her and reached for her arms. He rubbed her gently, comfortingly while she stood there trying to stop her nose from itching with emotion. When she knew she was no longer in danger of crying she took a step back and Grant released her. Without discussing anything, they started walking, heading in the direction of Madame's apartment.

"How did you know where we'd be?"

Grant released a huff of air. "It was not a hard thing to figure out, Elodie. Only so many trains are headed to Aix-en-Provence today."

Neither of them said anything for a long moment leaving plenty of time for the last words that Elly had flung at Grant to rise to the surface. Shoving her hands into the pockets of her jacket, she watched traffic pass by as embarrassment filled her cheeks.

"Thank you for coming," she murmured as she looked at her feet. She still sort of wished he'd disappear and leave her alone. How was she going to let him go if he was everywhere she turned?

"You're welcome." There was another pause. "I've spoken with our superiors. There's no point in going to the Red Cross anymore unless you want to help. Enjoy what you can of Paris because we'll be leaving soon."

"Are we taking the train?"

Grant shook his head. "Two cars. I'll drive one and Pierre will drive the other. He'll call you when the time is set but have your things packed. Live out of a bag you can snatch and grab."

She nodded. She was already down to the bare essentials, having sent a suitcase and her typewriter to Jo's house so it could be delivered to wherever they would be staying once they left Paris.

Elly listened quietly as Grant waxed on about the ramifications of leaving Paris. He was just going to ignore it, she realized. All of those pesky feelings. Her initial reaction was relief but as he continued to talk she felt herself undergoing a change of sorts. It was in her nature to want to be pursued. To want to be absolutely certain the other person wanted her before she opened herself up. But, he'd made it clear he absolutely wasn't going to go down that route. Because he was afraid of living if Pierre was to be believed. And Pierre might be full of malarkey half the time but she didn't think he was lying. How odd. Grant was afraid of living and she was afraid she would never live.

She glanced over at the man next to her who was comfortably rambling on about something. Thoughts began to run through her head. All sorts of thoughts.

CHAPTER 26

The waiting was interminable.

When she heard of Belgium's surrender to Germany, of the collapse of the French line, of the disaster at Dunkirk, and then felt the vibrations from the bombings of the airports just outside of Paris, she worked hard to drown out the fears that yelled at her in the quiet moments by cleaning. Not that the apartment was dirty. But scrubbing everything down felt like the only action she could take at the moment that would accomplish anything. And yet, no matter how hard she worked, no matter how hard she cleaned, eventually her mind always found itself reaching the same conclusion: she could be in Chicago right now.

And then the call came.

She'd obeyed every word of instruction she'd been given. All of her things were in one bag she could carry. She was wearing a loose gray sweater over her most comfortable dress: a dark cotton number she'd brought with her from the States. Her shoes were walking shoes. Shoes she'd broken in some time ago with her long, meandering journeys through the Jardin du Luxembourg and up and down the Champs-Élysées.

She opened the door expecting Pierre. It was Grant. But not the Grant who wore tailored clothes that made him look as though he'd stepped off the cover of a men's magazine. This Grant still wore dark clothing, but his pants were loose and wrinkled. There was no scarf in sight. This Grant hadn't shaved in a few days.

"I'm sorry," Grant began, his voice low and polite. "Do you think we have all day?"

Elly smiled before she could think about it. She'd missed him these past few days. Missed his lectures. Missed his company. Missed being with someone who just . . . understood. And seeing him standing right there was confirming some things. What those things were, she was going to have to figure out. "Of course not."

Leaving Grant still standing in the doorway, she walked over to the couch in the living room and moved it a few inches over as Claire had shown her. She pressed down on the loose piece of wood and the other end popped up. She dropped her key to the apartment into the hole. Then she smoothed out the wood once again. If Grant weren't hovering some feet away—clearly anxious—she'd probably pronounce a benediction of sorts, a sort of parting farewell like Madame had. But it was time to go.

She replaced the couch, grabbed her bag, the picnic basket, and returned to the door.

"What is that?" Grant asked, eyeing the second item in her hand as though he'd never seen it before.

"Food. Drinks. I've seen the refugees." At that, his expression grew thoughtful, and he must have realized it wasn't a terrible idea to have food because he dropped the subject and extended a hand. She handed him her bag and closed the door behind her silently, saying goodbye to the life in Paris she had once lived.

"Where is Pierre?" she asked as they made a slow, hesitant trip down the stairwell. Each stair seemed to contain at least one thing that the neighbors had dropped in their haste to leave. Elly carefully stepped over toy soldiers and a cotton nightgown that would probably never be worn again. She paused at the sight of books stacked neatly to the side. Someone had come to the conclusion, at the last minute, that they weren't necessary.

If she'd thought there were a lot of things left on the stairs, it was nothing compared to the tiny courtyard.

"Pierre's running late."

Elly looked up. "Is that what's got you . . ." Upset? Irritated?

But she didn't need to spell it out because he knew what she was talking about. "I told everyone that if you had to bring something with you that was larger than what you could carry in one hand, send it ahead of you. But does anyone listen to me?" Without waiting for an answer, Grant continued. "Now, there's barely any room in the cars. You'll have to keep that basket in the trunk. It's either that or pray that Poppy, Mignonette, and Luca aren't hungry."

Elly came to a stop. "Are they the—?"

"Dogs? Yes. Josephine was supposed to send all of the animals down south weeks ago. But she just couldn't live without the . . ." He paused. Her mind filled the space with the expletives that she knew he wanted to say but didn't because whether he wanted to be or not, he was still Grant Monterey of Surry, Virginia. "Dogs." The word was practically hissed. "Because nothing says run for your life like packing up your zoo."

Deciding she'd think about Jo's animals later, she said, "But there's only six of us."

"Eight," he interjected. "Jo's made room for refugees." She heard the frustration in his voice. "You won't survive this thing by being a bleeding heart." He fussed at her, but she knew the words for Jo. They finally made it out of the apartment complex and to the street.

Leaning against her dark Renault, and looking nearly unrecognizable in slacks and a shirt, with a scarf wrapped around her head and a dog in her arms, was Jo. A strange feeling washed over Elly that wasn't quite déjà vu but felt similar to it. To think that someone had once mistaken Elly for Josephine Baker's lithe, statuesque form.

Grant held out his hand and Elly passed him the picnic basket. Then he made his way toward the trunk of the car and tried to squeeze Elly's contributions in with the rest of the things.

Elly moved to stand next to Jo who was watching the procession of people passing by with a narrow, concentrated look in her eyes. It was like a slow, delayed parade. Parisians traveled by foot, looking as though they'd already crossed thousands of miles that morning. Grandparents were being pushed in wheelbarrows— their children and grandchildren unwilling to leave them behind. In the distance, wagons pulled by horses moved south, packed full with things and children. It was a jarring sight for such a modern city like Paris.

"This is not the first time," Jo said softly, stroking her dog, "that I have fled in the face of hatred."

Elly watched as Grant rearranged one more thing in the trunk and then slammed it shut. He looked tired already and they hadn't even left yet. "You're referring to the race riot?" The incident Jo had brought up when she'd been trying to convince Madame and Claire to leave Paris. Although the words 'race riot' weren't fair. A riot implied destruction of property to make a point although there was some of that too But that was not the goal of a 'race riot.'

It was a massacre where whites could kill Negroes at will, knowing full well they would never suffer the consequences of the law. Race riots destroyed families and knocked out generations of wealth that would never be acquired again.

"Have you ever lived through one?" Jo's question was filled with the bitterness and rage of someone who had caught a glimpse of hell. Elly side-eyed Jo. She didn't know why it always felt like the woman had sprouted from thin air but of course Jo must have come into contact with some ugliness. You could not be colored in America and escape it.

"No," Elly said simply.

"We ran that day," Josephine said under her breath, rocking her dog like it was a baby. "Left everything and fled as they shot at us. And we never returned to the place that had been our home."

Not having any pockets, Elly clasped her hands behind her back. "And yet you're still optimistic?"

Josephine smiled down at her dog before meeting Elly's gaze. There was determination and steely coldness she'd never seen in the woman's face before. "You know, I do believe this is the first time I'm fighting back. It's the first time I've decided that I'm not going to just sit there and take it. I might be leaving Paris now. But I can promise you, I'll return."

CHAPTER 27

Before Elly could respond to that comment, Pierre pulled up driving another Renault. Sitting next to him in the passenger seat was Danny. Polly was spread out in the back.

"Time to hit the road." Jo gave Elly a finger wave and climbed into her car. Elly saw that there was an elderly couple in the back seat: the refugees Jo had decided to bring along. Catching their eyes for a second, Elly raised her hands in greeting before making her way to the other vehicle. Pierre got out of the car.

"Have we got everybody and everything?" Grant asked Pierre as he walked over to the younger man. His voice was low and uninviting, not wanting anyone else to take part in their conversation. Clasping her hands together, Elly was careful not to make eye contact as she listened.

"As far as I know we do. If we don't, it's too late."
The two men exchanged quick, decisive nods.

"Good. You take two of the dogs—"

"Uh-uh."

"Uh-huh."

"Grant."

"Pierre."

"You're the one who likes dogs."

"Sure. But where I grew up, they slept outside and they certainly didn't ride in cars." Elly grinned, her gaze on her feet.

"Well, I've never liked dogs." Pierre's voice was stubborn.

"Are you kidding? The last time Jo had one of those fancy lunches, you were kissing the dog on the mouth. I'd never seen such a disgusting display of—"

"That is not true, Grant! If it starts running around and barking while I'm driving, I might hit somebody. What if it pees in the car? That's hours of smelling urine."

Danny, who had also been listening to their conversation, rolled down the window of the car. "Look at it this way, food's probably scarce right now. At least we have the dogs." Grant and Pierre looked at him. "It is survival of the fittest out in these streets."

Grant sighed. Deeply. "Fine, whatever. I'll keep the dogs for the first leg of the trip. Follow me the whole time. If you decide to go off on your own, I'll kill you myself."

Grant made his way to the other car while Danny opened his door and helped Elly inside. Polly was sitting sideways with her back pressed up against the window of the car. She tucked her legs to the side as Elly sat down. She had one hand on the small bump of her stomach.

"You look miserable," Elly told her. Polly looked like she was battling both nausea and a headache.

"I feel miserable, but I'll be all right. Maybe I'll be lucky enough to fall asleep."

The car doors were shut, Grant pulled into traffic, and Pierre followed.

It seemed as though it took forever to get out of Paris because there were so many people spilling over from the sidewalk and into the street, forcing vehicles of every kind to match the pace of walkers.

"I guess everyone and they mama decided today was the day to leave," Pierre muttered from the driver's seat.

It didn't get much better as they left the city limits. But Elly was still thankful she wasn't making this trip by foot. And yet, she felt guilty. It was hard to look out the window and see the elderly struggling and the children looking tired and here she sat almost in the lap of luxury on her way to a pre-planned destination. She understood, now, why Jo had two refugees in the car with her. She also understood Grant: they couldn't help everybody. The longer they drove, the harder it was to look out the window although that didn't stop Danny from snapping the occasional picture.

"How long is it supposed to take us to get there?" Danny's question pulled Elly out of her thoughts. She looked down at her watch. They'd been in the car for over an hour and yet no one had said anything since they left. The exodus before them didn't invite commentary.

"I think six hours with no traffic. I'm going to go out on a limb right now and say it will take us eight. I do think the traffic will clear up soon." A bit of a hard-to-believe statement as the cars on the road were bumper to bumper.

"What about the restroom?" Polly grumbled.

"Gonna have to pull over to the side of the road, darling. I should have talked to Grant about it so we could time our stops together."

Elly and Polly exchanged brief wide-eyed glances. Pulling over to pee on the side of the road was easy for one particular gender.

"What about gas?" Elly asked.

"We've been hoarding gas since March. We have like, sixty champagne bottles in the back full of it. If we still run out of gas we've got bigger problems than I thought."

"Did Pierre tell you?" Polly asked Elly, nudging her with a toe. She'd long since kicked off her shoes. "We're only going to stay with y'all for two days and then Pierre and I will keep going south."

"You were able to find a ship?" Elly asked her, remembering that Polly had said she and Pierre were going to get out of France as soon as they could now that the baby was coming.

Polly nodded once. "It's leaving for Spain out of Marseille. Once we get there we'll try to find a ship that takes us to America or a ship that takes us to a country that will get us to America."

Elly reached over and touched a hand to Polly's knee.

"I'm gonna miss you. I don't know about that other person you're leaving with."

"Ha, ha, so funny," Pierre muttered from the front of the car.

"We're going to get married in Marseille before we get on the ship. Jo helped me reach out to some friends of hers and it's all set."

Elly flicked her gaze to Pierre. He was looking straight ahead. Elly was usually a fan of marriage, particularly when children were involved but maybe in this instance marriage might backfire. Of course, Pierre might surprise them all and turn into a family man. Greater miracles had happened.

"When you get settled, you'll have to find me in Chicago," Elly said as though it was a confirmed thing that she'd be back in the States soon.

"Yes! Don't let me leave without getting your address."

"Of course. Are you hoping for a boy or girl?"

"It doesn't matter. I want one of each."

"What's the baby's last name going to be?" Danny asked, eyes on Polly.

"Roche," Pierre said, pronouncing the word in perfect French.

"The question was for Polly."

Polly released a tired giggle. "I still don't know what his name is." Elly felt her whole face scrunch up in slight horror. Polly's laughter grew louder. "It doesn't matter, Elly. I love him the same whether he's Pierre or Tom."

"So when he dies and you try to go to the bank to get the money—"

"And just like that, you killed me off."

"And they won't give it to you because he is, in fact, not Pierre Roche but John Smith . . ."

Still grinning and absolutely undeterred, Polly said, "I think he'll tell me at the wedding. We have to get married under our legal names."

Polly was so happy and so light-hearted that Elly swallowed the other questions that danced on her tongue because she certainly was not the sort who found secrets to be romantic.

Feeling a small rumble, Elly scooted closer to Polly as military vehicles honked and tried to zoom down the road past them. Elly had thought it strange to see wagons drawn by horses smack dab in the middle of the Champs-Élysées but there was something a bit breath-catching about seeing soldiers and guns and weapons up close. All lightness and humor fled as she was once again reminded that they were in fact, running from the Germans.

"Bet you're missing Chicago now?" Danny muttered, momentarily catching her gaze.

"Just a little."

"It's probably a lot like New York," Pierre said, his eyes still on the military trucks. "You know, where I'm from."

"Actually, it's better."

They spent the next hour trashing each other's hometowns as they tried to take their minds off of what was happening around them. Pierre was also beginning to pick up speed as traffic let up and the roads cleared somewhat because people who had left their houses in eagerness that morning were running out of steam.

285

Elly was two seconds from falling asleep when another military convoy drove past, causing the road to vibrate. And so at first, she didn't think anything of the popping noise behind her.

"Oh my God!" The car jerked to a stop. And Elly heard screams. She turned around and what she saw took her brain too long to comprehend: a plane, people running, blood. "Get out!" Pierre yelled. He started to open the door of the car but then they heard it, the ping-ping of bullets hitting the hood. He slammed the car door shut and he and Danny tried to burrow down as machine-gun fire rained down overhead. The Germans were shooting at them.

Just like Danny and Pierre, Polly and Elly fell to the floor of the car. Elly curled into herself wishing she had something she could use as a shield besides her hands.

It lasted maybe thirty seconds. But it felt like an hour had passed. Even when the plane was gone, and not even a dot in the sky, no one moved in fear that it was going to come around again. Or that there would be a second one behind it.

"Is everyone okay?" Pierre asked after a moment. Elly didn't move but she heard him sit up. "Guys!"

"I'm alive," Danny muttered, his voice weak. "Somehow . . ."

"I'm fine," Elly said, after touching different parts of herself to make sure. She lifted her head from where she'd buried it in her lap—as though that would protect her from a bullet. She looked across the back seat at Polly. Polly raised a hand, and it was covered in blood. "Polly's been shot!"

"What?" Elly heard the car door open, and Pierre was moving his seat to get to Polly.

"Everyone okay?" The voice was Grant's and a wave of relief washed over her. He sounded hale and hearty. "Elodie? Pierre?"

"I'm okay," Danny said stiffly.

"Polly's been shot," Pierre told him. Danny opened his car door and Elly climbed out as Pierre and Grant pulled Polly from the other side of the car. Elly looked around and saw the military convoy turned on its side with bloodied soldiers crawling out of it, she saw bags and things tossed into the middle of the road by people who had run for cover into the trees. She saw bodies. The shadow war was over. Bloodshed had replaced it.

"Fix it, Grant!"

"I'm trying!"

The words snapped Elly out of her trance, and she ran to the center of the road where Pierre was holding Polly across his lap and Grant was up to his arms in blood trying to do something. Jo stood there, holding one of her dogs so tight against her chest it may as well be a pillow.

"Grant! Fix her!" Pierre's voice was hard and demanding but also boyish in the way that it broke.

Grant sat back on his haunches. He'd lost his jacket. No, Elly saw that it was wrapped tightly around Polly's stomach. Elly slowly dropped to her knees. "I can't . . . Ralph . . . I can't . . ."

"Grant." Pierre's voice was hoarse, and he extended a bloody hand toward Grant. "Fix it."

It had been nearly a lifetime since Elly had stood on the other side of the door while her mother struggled to bring a new person into the world. Years since she'd watched the midwife and their neighbor race back and forth from the room, each towel in their hand bloodier than the last. But the pungent scent of iron filled her nose and she was back there again, waiting patiently as someone dearly loved slowly died in front of her. Grant seemed to come to the same conclusion—that there was nothing that could be done here. "Polly, honey," Grant said, his voice comforting and the merest whisper as he leaned toward her. He grabbed her hand, taking it in his. "Polly, we love you."

"No!" Pierre screamed. "No!" Placing a bloody hand on Polly's cheek, he turned her face to him. "Think about the baby, Polly. We're going to get married." Polly was looking at him, her mouth moving but no words forming. Jo dropped to her knees and her dog leaped out of her arms. Crawling, she grabbed Polly's other hand. "My Paulina, Paulette, Polly . . ."

Elly heard it, that rattling gasp, and then a long deep sigh. She swallowed the bile in her throat and pressed a fist to her chest. Just like that, life was gone. For a long minute, nobody moved as they all tried to come to grips with the fact that in less than ten minutes they'd lost a member of their group.

Danny took several steps back and slumped against the car. Jo pulled Polly from Pierre, cradling the dead woman's face against her chest. Pierre was thunderstruck, unmoving except for the silent tears making their way down his cheeks. Grant stood up on shaky legs and walked to the vehicle that Pierre had been driving. He reached into the car for something and then made his way to the trunk. Elly heard him digging around. When he slammed the trunk shut, she stood up.

He walked toward them, shovel in hand, Polly's blood streaked across his shirt. She saw his eyes sweep over a weeping Jo who was rocking Polly's body, over Pierre who was frozen in shock, over Danny who looked like one stiff wind would knock him over. He closed his eyes for one second and then turned and walked into the trees that were gathered along the side of the road.

Elly blinked a few times as though that might help stabilize the ground beneath her feet. Her eyes drifted off to where Grant was most likely digging out a grave for Polly. Of course they would have to bury her here in what felt like no-man's land on the side of the road. Who would visit Polly's grave? Who would even know where she had been laid to rest?

Voices and wailing began to fill Elly's ears as she exited the mental tunnel she'd been in. She saw that people were returning to their things. Those who had survived were slipping on their bags once more, determination in every step as they continued south.

Elly sighed once. Then she snatched the keys Grant had left dangling from the trunk and went to crank up the car. Bullet holes marred the metal and she gave a silent prayer of thanks when it still started up. Elly moved the Renault to the side of the road so that they wouldn't block traffic as everything and everyone continued on their journey. She made her way to the vehicle Grant had been driving and did the same. The elderly couple that Jo had picked up stood awkwardly on the side of the road as Jo's dogs danced around them. When the second Renault was parked, Elly dug through the trunk of that car until she found a shovel in the very back.

She walked into the forest, following the path Grant had taken. She found him about one hundred feet away from the road and digging Polly's grave with all the expertise of someone who had done this before. She came to a stop a few feet down from him and got to digging and she didn't stop even as her hands cramped and ached and sweat dripped down her temples and pooled under her arms.

When Grant paused, leaning on his shovel and looking in her direction, she stilled. "It's enough," he said tiredly. He climbed out of the hole they'd created and then extended a hand. She grabbed it and he pulled her out. "Wait here. I'll go get Polly."

Breathing heavy and thirstier than she could ever remember, Elly waited. She didn't have to wait for long. Grant returned shortly with Polly strewn across his arms. "Check her pockets," he said, his voice low. "Take out anything of value."

Elly looked at him for a second. His voice was shaky and heavy and there were light-colored trails on his face from where tears had rolled down his cheeks. She hadn't even realized that he'd been crying as they worked.

"Elly," he said simply, reminding her to get on with it. There was something grim in his voice. He'd done this before. He'd stripped his friends of things the living might need before planting them in the earth.

Taking a deep breath to staunch everything—emotions, nausea, thoughts—she began digging through

290

Polly's pockets, which were soaked with blood. She tried not to think of how only a half hour ago, they'd been laughing and teasing each other. She found a few francs.

"Take her earrings and her necklace."

Elly obeyed, pocketing the items. And then Grant jumped into the hole and reverently lowered Polly's body onto the soil. Together, they covered her with dirt. Grant took a moment to smooth the ground out and then dropped to his knees. "Know ye that the Lord he is God: it is he that hath made us, and not we ourselves. Father, we commend Paulina Godfrey and her child into your hands. Amen."

And this was it: the final act of Polly.

CHAPTER 28

The pair of them sat at Polly's grave, lost in their own thoughts. Elly wanted nothing more than to crawl somewhere, close her eyes, and pretend like none of this had happened. But she knew they needed to go. Not only could the Germans return at any second, but lingering wasn't going to get them any closer to their destination.

That said, Pierre and Jo were probably going to have a hard time getting back in the cars and only one person could make them.

"I'll be right back." Elly returned to the cars where Jo was sitting in the passenger seat of one of them, looking as though she'd gone through the wringer.

Danny was leaning against the side of one of the vehicles while Pierre was sitting on the ground, his shirt pulled up and covering his face. Upon seeing her, Danny took a few steps forward, taking the shovel out of her hand.

"Is it done?"

"Yes."

"Pierre begged Grant not to take her. I've never seen him like that," Danny whispered, looking less like a young man in his twenties and more like a boy in need of comfort from his mother. "He kept saying she might not be dead."

Elly glanced at Pierre who was doing his best to hide where there was no place to hide. "Keep an eye on him."

"I will," Danny said quickly even though he looked like he wished he could be anywhere but here. He hesitated. "We had to bury her quickly, didn't we?"

Very gently, as though she were talking to Catau, Elly asked, "What was the alternative?" In response, Danny shuddered. Elly placed a hand on his shoulder before making her way to the trunk that held the picnic basket. She dug around and took out the blanket and a jar of water. "We won't be much longer." Returning to Polly's makeshift grave, Elly unsealed the water jar, took several gulps and then sat down on the ground next to Grant. She offered him the jar. "Don't drink it all. You'll need some to clean your hands."

For a long second, he didn't move. Then, obeying her, he drank several swallows, leaving a third of water in the jar. Elly took it from him, poured the water on his hands, and then wiped him down with the blanket.

"Thank you," he said after a moment.

"You're welcome."

"Jo and Polly have known each other for years . . . like sisters . . . It was too hard . . ."

"I understand."

"Pierre is . . ."

"It's fine."

"And Danny is like a schoolboy . . ."

"Grant. I get it." Elly inspected his arms. There were still streaks of Polly's blood that refused to leave the crevices of his skin but at least she'd gotten most of it.

"Next exit we see, we take. It'll take us longer to get to Castelnaud-Fayrac but we'll be less likely to run into Germans. Elodie, I should have known this was a possibility. We never should have taken this road."

Running the blanket over his arms, once more, she said, "Are you Jesus, Grant? Do you hold life and death in the palms of your hands?"

When he lifted his eyes to hers, she saw wildness in them. She didn't know how she knew but he was losing his grip now. Something about burying Polly was taking him back to the trenches of the north of France. She made sure her gaze was cool. "Are you?"

"No."

"Then shut up."

Grant blinked and this time when he opened his eyes, she knew she had him. "Not the time to be maudlin?"

"Absolutely not."

His response was a weighty sigh. "Pierre's not in any condition to drive and Danny will tear up an engine faster than you can say Jiminy Cricket."

"I'll drive," she said as she folded up the blanket.

"I hate to ask that of you." Grant's voice was shaky.

"It's not a problem," she said determinedly despite wanting to take a very long break from ever being in a car again.

"Stay on my tail. Keep an eye on the road and the air. If you see something, stop and hustle everyone else out of the car. The Renaults are a target."

She nodded once and because she was looking at the ground, she missed Grant leaning toward her. She didn't move as he very slowly, very gently lowered his head onto her shoulder. His arm found her waist, pulling her closer. Elly reached over, placing a comforting hand on his neck. She closed her eyes. She could do this. They would get to where they needed to be.

"Thank you," he said softly against her ear. For a second, she leaned into him, and then, without words, they pulled apart and stood up.

They took the back roads the rest of the way as they made their way south. It added hours to their traveling time and they used far more bottles of gasoline than Elly knew Grant would have liked but that was preferable to being shot at again. They stopped every few hours for bathroom breaks and then once to eat although no one was very hungry. It was amazing how your body kept right on needing things even though your mind wanted to be left alone. There was very little conversation—not that Elly could have thought of a single thing to say. Sitting next to her in the passenger seat, Pierre leaned against the glass window with one hand covering his face. Every other hour, his body would shudder with renewed grief and Elly would find herself wiping away tears until it seemed she had no more.

The sun dipped below the earth and darkness settled over the sky as they finally turned onto a path that was more dirt than road. Crossing a stone bridge, Elly saw a large house in the distance. No, not a house: a castle.

"Oh, my dear goodness," Elly muttered under her breath as she continued to follow Grant up the twisty lane. His car came to a stop in front of two enormous wooden gates that were just as effective at blocking their progression as a drawbridge. And then, the gates began to slowly swing open.

"Lesson learned," Danny said quietly from the back seat. Pierre was slumped over. He hadn't moved for the past few hours. Danny had volunteered to sit in the back—most likely so that Pierre did not have to view Polly's blood, which had soaked into the interior of the car.

"What do you mean?" Elly asked as she followed Grant through the gate.

"A house with a name is not a house. It's something else entirely."

"What's this place called again?" She was sure someone had told her.

"Château des Milandes." It loosely translated to house in the middle of the woods—which meant that when Elly had first heard the name, she hadn't thought much of it. Now, she gasped as a medieval castle took shape before her.

Grant's vehicle came to a slow stop as a door opened revealing two people: Julien and Margo. Jo's butler and housekeeper.

Elly climbed out of the car and took several steps back so she could take it all in. She almost couldn't wait until the daytime so she could really see the place. A castle. She was about to sleep in a castle.

"Come on," Grant was saying. "We'll deal with the cars tomorrow."

Elly didn't say much as she grabbed her bag and entered the massively old building. The moment her feet crossed the entrance, she paused and looked around at the high ceilings and the Latin inscribed in stone. The castle was built in 1489. She gasped.

"I wanted to feel like Cinderella," Jo said with a tired sigh as she reached Elly's side. Cinderella! Touching a hand to her shoulder, Jo continued, "Let's talk tomorrow. It's been a day." Without waiting for a response, Jo headed down the hall, already familiar with the place.

Elly waited patiently until Julien led her to a small bedroom that already held the items she'd sent ahead including her typewriter, which sat on a small desk. Julien pointed her in the direction of the nearest bathroom where she washed, changed, and then crawled into the bed. She'd think about everything tomorrow.

Elly awakened the next morning with the sun. The first few images that flashed through her mind were of Pierre cradling Polly, of Grant digging a grave, of Pierre sobbing for hours next to her. She lay there for how long, she didn't know until she remembered she was lying in a castle. She chose to think about the castle. Tossing back the covers, she ran to get ready for the day.

She spent the next hour exploring every nook and cranny. She ran her fingers across stained-glass windows that featured scenes that put her in mind of Chaucer's

Canterbury Tales. She got lost in the intricate designs of the ceilings that curved above her head as she made her way to a turret. She leaned out over a high window and fought the urge to yell for Rapunzel. She—a colored girl from Chicago—was in a real-live castle like a princess or something. She thought of Jo's comment from the night before. Cinderella, indeed.

She finally made it outside, walking along the gravel. There was a small chapel about one hundred yards from the château. She'd visit eventually but for now she'd look over the gardens. She was probably very wrong when it came to garden architecture but the place put her in mind of a tiny version of the gardens of Versailles. There were layers as the garden sort of dipped, taking you further and further down the way. And it was perfectly symmetrical—like looking at two mirrored halves.

Elly walked through the park until she reached the edge of a river. Around her birds sang and butterflies flew. Flowers released their extravagant perfume and she felt a bit as though she'd been invited to visit the Garden of Eden. Finding a nice spot on the grass next to the riverside, she sat down listening to the gentle rush of water.

And then she pulled her knees to her chest and cried. She cried for Polly who would never hold her baby. She cried for Pierre who had lost someone he loved. She cried for Jo who had lost a sister. And she cried for France because Polly's death seemed like a harbinger of things to come. After her cries turned to hiccups and her hiccups to silence, she stood up, brushed off her backside and started back for the castle.

She was somewhere in the middle of the garden when she caught sight of Pierre sitting on the ground, his long legs stretched out before him, his back against a tall tree. She walked over to his side. The only form of comfort that Elly knew how to provide was 'Job's friends' kind of comfort. She could sit with those who grieved in very easy silence. And if the situation warranted it, she could start an argument to allow the person to release the emotions that had been sitting on their chest.

Elly sat down next to Pierre, looped her arm through his, and rested her head on his shoulder.

"I didn't want to get married," Pierre said, his voice low. Elly's only response was a hum. "I'm not ready to be a father either or to leave France for that fact but I was gonna do it." She squeezed his arm. "I didn't want her to die." His voice broke.

"We know, Ralph. You're not to blame for her death."

There was a moment's hesitation. "Ralph?"

"Pierre *is* better. You do look like a Pierre."

"Who told you my name was Ralph?"

"Grant called you Ralph yesterday. What's your last name?"

There was another long moment of hesitation and then a deep sigh. "Roach."

"Ralph Roach," she repeated.

"Very American."

"Actually, I was thinking German."

"Bite your tongue!" But then he released a small snort, and a sort of reluctant hiccup of laughter. Someone had been doing some crying himself.

"Your parents didn't love you, did they?"

"Shut up, Elodie," he said, stressing the syllables of her name as though it were strange and weird. "I'm a junior if you must know." He raised a finger. "And do not call me that name."

"You realize Pierre is incredibly unoriginal."

Pierre blew a raspberry. "I realize that now, yes. But it's my name."

"Okay, Pierre. I won't call you Ralph."

"Thank you."

"Unless—"

"No, unless!"

They both quieted. Neither of them really wanting to talk about the previous day. "Isn't this place amazing?" Elly whispered. She had been told before she left for France that living in a foreign country was a little like being married. You would love it at first, have a bit of a honeymoon period, then get tired of it, then hate it, then want to go home, but then you would come across something and suddenly you'd love it again. A cycle. Elly had fallen in love with France again. This place was making her feel like she was always supposed to be here, if only for this moment.

Beneath her head, Pierre shrugged. "Not really my sort of thing."

"It's like I'm a princess."

Pierre released a small huff of air. "Sorry, but standing in a castle no more makes you a princess than standing in a garage makes you a car."

Ignoring him, Elly continued. "I would settle for duchess or countess or marchioness."

"This ain't England, sweetheart. Titles aren't the same here."

"Don't care. For the duration of our time here, you can call me Lady Elodie."

"The day hasn't come—"

"And I will call you Peasant Pierre."

"You are so rude!"

"There you two are." Elly lifted her head off Pierre's shoulder as Danny took a seat on the ground next to her. "Mom and Dad are arguing. I came out here to get away from it."

Elly frowned but Pierre knew exactly who Danny was referring to. "You made the right decision. When Grant and Jo go at it, it's best to be nowhere around. What are they fussing about?"

"Jo wants to open the château's gates and allow refugees in. Grant said why not hang a sign that says all Germans welcome. You know, the usual. Also . . ."

"Also?"

"We're having a memorial service for Polly this evening before dinner."

The five of them dressed in black and formed a circle around a recently dug up plot in the garden that held a stone that read *In Loving Memory of Paulina Godfrey, friend and mother*. Elly didn't know how Jo had gotten something commissioned so quickly.

Grant read several scriptures from a small black Bible and then invited each of them to say something. Elly was silent as memories were shared and tears were formed. She had not known Polly nearly as long as the others and didn't feel as though her words would add

301

anything. But when Jo began to sing, she found herself joining in. Her voice was deeper than Jo's and she sang alto to Jo's soprano as familiar lyrics about a balm in Gilead making the wounded whole filled the park.

Pierre and Danny fell in line with tenor and Grant with bass. And together they sang all of the verses of the old spiritual until there was no more to sing.

"Jo," Grant began as the last notes died off. "This is your home, do what you want with it. But I trust these people standing before me. Do you understand?"

"Yes," Jo said quickly. "I understand. I'm not saying we take anyone into our confidence. But I cannot just stand by and do nothing. I recognize that Germans are possibly flooding this area but so are ordinary French people."

Grant looked around, meeting the gaze of everyone. "We live like every person who walks through that gate is the enemy. We know nothing; we help nobody. Like every Parisian, we're here to escape the Nazis. Take some time to rest," Grant said tiredly as his gaze drifted to Polly's small headstone. "Because the fight's nowhere near over."

But still, Danny followed Elly and Pierre down the stairs. There was no light except that which came from the flashlight in Elly's hands.

Beneath their feet was stone and the walls were made of bricks. Elly was pretty sure that this part of the house had not been touched during the renovations. They slowly moved down a dark, eerie tunnel.

"I cannot believe you have us down here waking up spirits."

"I did not realize you were into mysticism, Danny."

"I'm not. But anyone could be walking around this place. How many people do you think died down here?"

"They gonna come get you tonight, Danny. They gone be like who this black man in my house."

"Shut up!"

"Look!" Pierre said excitedly. Before Elly could turn, he snatched the flashlight from her hand and switched it off.

"I will kill you," Danny said after a long minute in darkness. Elly very nearly said the same thing as her heart began to pick up speed. She had not been afraid earlier but fear was catching and Danny's emotions were spreading.

Pierre turned the flashlight back on just under his face, giving him a ghoulish expression. His laughter was wicked.

"Pierre? What's that on your shoulder?"

"Do not even try it, Elodie."

"Okay."

Pierre looked over his shoulder and screamed as a large spider ran across his arm. He dropped the flashlight and Elly scooped it up. "This is a terrible place! Why are we down here?"

Elly ignored them as she continued down the tunnel to where empty cells rested. Something in the corner caught her eye. "Is that another door?"

"No, Alice. We are not going down the rabbit hole. Correction, I am not going down the rabbit hole with you."

Feeling mildly disappointed but also unwilling to keep going deeper into the castle alone, Elly merely frowned. "All right, let's go back upstairs."

They returned to the main floor just in time to run into Grant. For the past few days, she'd noticed that whenever she caught sight of him, he was wearing white undershirts and dark pants as though he were back in his military days. All he needed was a pair of dog tags dangling from his neck.

Placing his hands on his waist, Grant sized them up and then shook his head. "I don't want to know." Elly looked down at herself and then at Danny and Pierre. The three of them were covered in dust. "I got the radio working." It had been damaged in the commute and Grant had been tinkering with it all afternoon. "We've got it set up and running on the terrace. Nazis have jammed most of the stations, but we still get BBC."

News. Elly wasn't sure she wanted to hear any of it. She much preferred the fantasy of her thoughts and this place. But she nodded. "I'll get cleaned up and join you all."

A half hour later, Elly was sitting in one of the chairs

on the terrace drinking a cup of coffee. Grant, Pierre, and Danny were there. Jo, Julien, and Margo were there. The older couple—the Belgian refugees were there. And then there were the French that Jo had accumulated.

Mostly Jo gave out food and allowed people to rest a minute before sending them on their way. Except not everyone had a place to go. Like the French deserters who had effectively moved in. They too were currently drinking coffee under the terrace and sitting next to several of the local families that had been invited to visit. This was not the first time Jo had rented this castle and she was not a stranger here.

Everyone was silent as they listened to the tinny words coming out of the radio. They learned that Italy had declared war on France and Britain. Elly stirred her sugarless coffee a little hard at that. Norway had surrendered to Germany, with the King of Norway fleeing to Britain. And Paris was currently occupied by the Germans. They'd left just in time. And then, Elly heard French.

"Charles de Gaulle?" someone murmured.

Elly squinted in the distance as the Frenchman, a general supposedly, began to speak not to the British but to the French. *Is defeat final? No!*

They all listened intently until the French general's voice was replaced by someone British.

"He's right! It's not over," Jo said excitedly and indeed most everyone under the terrace looked as though they'd just been given the gift of hope. Elly looked at Grant. His arms were folded over his chest and he was looking at the ground. Pierre had shifted his chair so that he was looking at the sunset and Danny was fiddling with the camera in his hand. "We're going to win this war. It's just the beginning! America is going to get involved. I know they will."

On that point, Elly agreed. She didn't see how America could continue to stay neutral while Europe was turning into something out of a nightmare.

"And this *is* a world war. Even if France can't hold out right now, it's not the end."

Jo was repeating the general's speech and Elly wondered if the words were for the guests or herself. Either way, she was ready to celebrate and she ushered everyone inside for drinks. Neither Grant, nor Pierre, nor Danny, nor Elly moved. And Jo came back out a few minutes later.

"We'll never win the war with this attitude."

Pierre reached into his pocket and lit a cigarette.

"This is going to be, um, quite the uphill battle," Danny said lightly.

"But we can still win it. Good always triumphs over evil."

"In what world!" Pierre exploded. "Jo, if good always triumphed, Polly would still be alive!"

At that comment, Jo exhaled and looked away. "I can't afford to be anything other than optimistic," she said quietly. "I believe if given the chance, people will always choose to do what's right."

Pierre grunted. But then turned in his chair in Elly's direction. "How about you, Elly?" Elly flashed her eyes at him. "Do you think people always choose to do what's right?"

She did not want to answer but everyone seemed to be looking at her. "Unfortunately," Elly began slowly, her eyes on her cup, "I rather subscribe to Hobbes's philosophy."

"Who is Hobbes?" Danny demanded.

"A man who believed that human nature is fundamentally corrupt. He believed that people were greedy and selfish and their motivation is ruled by their self-centeredness."

"Wow," Danny said, sitting back in his seat. "And you're the religious one."

Elly raised her eyebrows. She'd never ever had a conversation with Danny about religion. She was more than a little curious as to what had led him to that conclusion. "It is precisely because of my faith that I believe that. Born sinners, saved by grace. I think it's much more natural for people to be evil and selfish than to be kind. All you need to do is look at a homogenous society. Even they will find reasons to separate and demonize the 'other'."

"I don't believe that," Jo said forcefully. "I believe not everyone is raised right."

"Nature versus nurture," Grant muttered and Elly nodded once. Exactly so.

"I believe that if everyone was raised to love and to be kind, they would do so."

Elly didn't know whether to marvel in awe or be thoroughly exasperated. Here was a woman who had been and was still being exposed to the very worst of mankind and yet, she clung so tenaciously to this hope in people. Choosing to swallow the rest of her argument, Elly merely said, "Sure, you can teach people to behave.

I absolutely believe that. But folks aren't born inclined to think of others." Elly waved a hand. "None of this matters."

"The Nazis are going to lose," Grant announced. And everyone looked in his direction. "One way or the other. But it's going to be a very long war and one fought not quite like we've ever seen before."

A few days later, their group was once again sitting on the terrace drinking coffee and munching on small snacks as they soaked in the news from the world. And then they heard the voice of Philippe Pétain, president of France. Elly felt her eyes widen as they learned that the war between Germany and France was over; an armistice had been negotiated. The north of France would continue to be occupied by the Germans while the south would be under Pétain's government. Pétain would be operating out of the town of Vichy. France was to free all German captives and to turn over all refugees who were on the run from Germany. France was to pay four hundred million francs a day to Germany and any resistance was to be met with death.

No one said anything. Everyone looked north to where the Germans were gathered only a few hours' drive away.

Grant flipped the radio off. No one wanted to hear any more.

"I didn't expect Gettysburg," Danny said softly, "but I didn't think France would turn belly-up that quick."

Elly kicked his chair and tossed her head in the direction of the actual French who all looked like the rug had been pulled from underneath them. She too had expected more of Sherman's March to the Sea but now wasn't the time to say anything.

"I feel like taking a walk," Grant said randomly and abruptly stood up. "The river is beautiful this time of evening."

Twenty minutes later, they were all there: Jo, Danny, Pierre, and Elly. They stood tall, their shadows staring back at them from the small, lapping waves.

"We cannot just hole up in this castle and do nothing," Jo said quietly, once again refusing to play it safe.

"I thought that you'd lost contact with the handlers?" Danny asked. As far as Elly knew, everyone had been too busy fleeing Paris to really stop and exchange new contact information.

Jo and Grant exchanged a long look before turning to face them.

"Rest one more day," Grant said softly. "Because tomorrow it's time to get back in the thick of things."

CHAPTER 30

She was dressed in all black: dress, stockings, shoes, gloves, hat, and a fairly long veil that was so covered in designs you almost couldn't see her face . . . which was exactly the point. If she was seen making her way through town and to the church, no one would know who she was. Bonus points if they didn't realize she was colored.

But it also meant she was relying a great deal on her memory to get her to where she was going. It was twilight and she didn't dare lift the veil to check which road she was on. Good thing Grant had made her take long walks around the town to familiarize herself with the area and create a mental map of sorts. Of course, walking around in the daytime, she'd stood out like a sore thumb. Colored women in Paris seemed far and few between. Colored women in Castelnaud-la-Chapelle consisted of Jo and Elly.

This plan belonged all to Grant. It was a card he'd been carrying in his back pocket since before they left Paris.

"Last week, I was told that my contact in this area was a priest who had been recently placed out here," Grant had said as they stood by the river. "I was told that if and when we made it to safety to reach out to him for next steps."

"A priest?" Danny had asked, skeptical.

"A very unusual priest. He fought in the Great War before joining the priesthood and then suited up again for this war. When things looked like they were going south, the Deuxième arranged for him to leave the Front to take up his position as priest again."

"Why here?" Elly had asked Grant.

"There's a railroad about ten miles that way," Grant had said, extending his hand east. "It crosses paths with several factories so although it does carry passengers, mostly that train moves *things*."

"Weapons?" It was always weapons with Grant.

"Yes. As far as I know, Father Laval was sent here to keep an eye on the situation. We need to contact him without making it known to the public that we are associates. Jo, in the morning, you should make your way about town and end at the church. When you speak to Father Laval, let him know we're here."

"Is there some kind of code word already in place?"

"Yes. Once you say it, he'll know something's up. Tell him that he'll get a visit in two nights from someone else who will be there to learn of any tasks the Bureau needs accomplished. You know the drill. Don't speak to him long. You're too closely watched, and we don't want you or this castle linked to Father Laval. Or vice versa." Grant had turned to Elly then. "Are you familiar with the Catholic church?"

"I was born Catholic."

Grant's smile had been wry. "Of course you were. You'll make a visit to the church two nights from now as a regular parishioner. Find out what it is that Father Laval needs us to do in this fight. You'll speak French the whole time, although it's my understanding the Father can not only speak English, but he's spent a significant amount of time in the U.S. Regardless, as far as he knows, you've come from nowhere. You have no past and he doesn't need to know your present. I meant it when I said I don't trust anyone but you four. I believe Father Laval to be a patriot but all the more reason not to burden him with too much information."

And that was how Elly wound up crossing this small town about ten miles south of the château in the near dark to make a visit to the church. In her meandering walks earlier in the day, she'd had a clear view of the building. It was one of those majestic stone structures that had probably been around since long before the U.S. had even become a nation. She had not gone inside because she did not want any of the natives staring at her to put two and two together. And they had been staring.

Approaching the church, Elly reached down, lifting her skirts slightly as she climbed the stone stairs. The doors to the church were closed but she knew they weren't locked. Father Laval should be expecting her.

And yet, as Elly crossed the foyer and entered the sanctuary no one was there. Or rather no priest was

314

anywhere to be found. There were a few older women sitting in the pews and praying. One lady was lighting a candle. The confessional was open, and empty.

Elly made her way to the center of an empty pew and sat down. The utter silence of the space and the dimness of the room that was only lifted by the candles that were flickering made the church feel other. Almost like the Château des Milandes, it felt like a place that was a tiny pocket of escape from the chaos that was happening around it.

With a sigh, Elly shifted to get a better look. Still no priest. Maybe she needed to make herself a bit more noticeable. Standing up, Elly walked over to the stone planks where one could kneel and petition heaven. Lowering herself very carefully onto the plank, she rested her forearms on the extended panel and bowed her head. So quiet this church was. It was easy to get lost in one's own thoughts so she began praying again but this time for Uncle Minor and Aunt Tabitha, for Catau and her cousins. Had it really been over a year since she'd last seen them?

Just thinking about it made her chest ache. Who was double-checking Uncle Minor's facts before he stepped into the pulpit? Who was helping Aunt Tabitha cook Sunday dinner when guests were invited? Who was making sure Catau didn't get distracted by the latest flashy thing when he needed to be focused on his studying? How in the world were they getting on with a whole ocean between her and them? A wave of homesickness washed over her.

"How long wilt thou be drunken? Put away thy wine from thee."

Elly's jump was only slight. She'd let her mind run crazy, allowing her sense of focus to drift. Terrible thing to do when one was about to do something illegal. Elly didn't move as Father Laval lowered himself onto the kneeler next to her.

"No, my lord," she began hesitantly, recognizing instantly which story in the Bible he was quoting from. Continuing in Hannah's words, she said, "I am a woman of a sorrowful spirit: I have drunk neither wine nor strong drink, but have poured out my soul before the Lord."

"You are not French," the priest said bluntly.

"Neither am I German," she said, knowing her accent was perfection. She tried to tilt her head to get a better view of the man next to her. Was he Grant's age? Just under forty? Was he tall or short?

"British?"

"Does it matter?" To move either to the right or the left was to also give him access to discover her identity. If she could not see him, he could not see her and she was just going to have to be satisfied with that.

The priest hummed. "I suppose it doesn't. In the confusion of everything somehow I managed to get my hands on some . . . weapons."

"How did you manage that?"

"Does it matter?" Beneath her veil, Elly smiled. "They are hidden within this church's bowels but they cannot stay here. I need to move them as soon as possible to somewhere safe. Please return tomorrow with instructions."

Elly dipped her head. "How big is this cache?"

"Large. A wagon will be needed to transport them."

Elly didn't see how that was going to work but that wasn't her job. "I'll be here tomorrow at the same time."

"And what shall I call you?"

"*Le papillon de nuit*." The Moth. "*À bientôt, Frère Laval.*"

CHAPTER 31

Elly slipped out of the church as quickly and quietly as she could. It surprised her not at all when Grant stepped out of the shadows, appearing at her side. When he crooked his elbow, she looped her arm through his. They had about a fifteen-minute walk to the car.

"What are you thinking about?"

"Home." Her mind had taken her right back to where she'd been before the priest had spoken to her. What were her uncle and aunt doing tonight? Was Catau studying as he should?

"You mean we haven't convinced you to stay?" Grant teased, his voice unusually light.

"No." She brought a fisted hand to her chest, tapping her heart. "When I think about my family being so far away from me sometimes it's like I can't breathe." A strange dichotomy, she recognized. Particularly when compared to those mornings where she woke up and was certain her family could get on without her. "And I don't think I was meant to live life on the edge for too long."

She wasn't sure she liked what the war was doing to her. What had Grant said? She was made for this? Perhaps. But it felt like being a soldier—whether fighting in the dark or the light—was appealing to all of her worst attributes. She was becoming more cynical, less trusting, and she was already a suspicious person by nature.

"You're going to leave when your year commitment is up." It was a statement not a question.

"If it's a possibility, I'm going to grasp that chance with both hands." She had committed to spying for France in November of the previous year. It was now May.

"Do you regret it?"

What a question. Her worst moments flashed before her: the constant anxiety, killing the spy, Polly dying in the middle of an unknown road. But then she thought of the things she'd learned and the ways she'd grown that she never would have had she returned home. She spoke fluent French, she knew who she was in times of danger, she found great joy and satisfaction in knowing that she was helping others. She could safely say that she was friends with Jo, Pierre and Danny. They did not always agree. They did not always get along. But she knew them and, more than that, she trusted them. She briefly glanced in Grant's direction. She had done what she hadn't thought was possible: she'd met someone who stirred both her mind and body. Not that she knew what to do with that information. "I have no regrets."

"Tell me this," Grant said softly. "If France weren't at war, would you stay?"

"No." She didn't even have to think about it. "France without war is a beautiful place. But it's like a dream. And you can only dream so long before you're ready to return to reality."

Grant hummed. "It's been well over a decade since I've been in the States. Jim Crow still alive and well?"

"Yes," she said after a hesitant moment.

"Lynchings still a part of the natural order of things?"

She may have been away from her country for over a year now but this was not something she had to think about. "Yes."

"That's not a reality I would like to wake up to." His words were gentle and not the least bit argumentative.

"Fair enough. But things will never change if you just walk away." Kudos to Jo Baker. The woman had managed to do something few could: she'd changed Elly's mind. Particularly on how to approach life. "Problems do not suddenly stop existing because you are not there. I bring something of value to the table," Elly said, coming to the realization as she spoke. "I have worth and merit. That is what France has taught me. I cannot then refuse to share it with the world."

"Does someone now have a hankering for civil rights?"

"I think I do." It was the first time she admitted it to herself. Why was she here trying to save lives in France and had never thought to try to do it back home?

"I'm almost from a different generation than you." Elly looked at Grant. Well, as much as she could in the dark. "There's a huge part of me that says you can't change what has happened in America. I've never known of someone who held power who was willing to share it and white folks have been in power a very long time."

His comment surprised her. "Well . . . they didn't want to give up slavery either."

Grant tilted his head in her direction. "True. But they were willing to sacrifice a lot of people to hold on to it."

"You really don't think things can change? You're really willing to accept the status quo?"

Grant sighed. "When I think of America, exhaustion fills my bones. It's like returning to visit family you can't stand. You're probably right, Elly. With enough pushing and prodding and patience, eventually things will change. Very doubtful that either of us will live long enough to see it."

"I disagree," Elly said adamantly. "I absolutely do. Do I think we'll live long enough to see white people pass us the equality baton? No. But this Jim Crow business won't last always. Each generation since slavery is gaining monumental grounds. You should meet my brother. The things he says they're learning in law school are things our parents would have never considered."

"Elodie Mitchell, is this optimism I'm hearing in your voice?"

Elly opened her mouth and then shut it. "I guess it is. If we can be optimistic about this war then what

321

can't we be optimistic about? I don't suddenly believe good will trample evil just because it's good. But I think . . . evil can't last always. It can last a heck of a long time. But not forever. The fight in America is something akin to a hundred years war. But if there's anything I've learned here, it is that small drops of water do eventually fill the bucket. I don't know what my role will look like in that fight but if it makes life better for one person, then I did what I was supposed to do." Of course, Elly could say all of this now very easily because she didn't know what the fight for civil rights actually looked like.

Grant hummed but she heard the humor in it. "You're going to return home a revolutionary. Uncle Minor and Aunt Tabitha won't know what to do with you."

She nearly tripped. Grant, referring to her uncle and aunt, with such familiarity, did something to her on the inside. Almost, almost, she told him that he should come with her.

Didn't he miss it? Yes, there certainly were problems where they'd come from but there were good things too. And then she remembered that he'd owned a restaurant that had served only American food and before things had gone south in the war, he'd hosted those small concerts that were designed to bring people together and remind them of home. He did miss it. Just not enough to return. But still, in a small voice, she found herself saying, "You could be one too."

"Europe is an absolute mess right now," Grant said gently. "But I have no desire to ever return home."

They met in Jo's bedroom, which was the master suite of Château des Milandes. Jo, Elly learned, had a real desire to leave the castle in the most natural state possible and it had nothing to do with the fact that she was renting and everything to do with the fact that she genuinely loved the château. It was a feeling Elly understood completely.

But that meant that Jo's bedroom felt like something frozen in time with its stone flooring, large thick rug that only partially covered said floor, and fireplace that was even now going despite the warmth of the evening.

Elly and Danny sat on the lounge chair in the room. Pierre was sitting on the ground in front of the fire watching the wood pop and disintegrate. If left alone, Pierre was often found sitting somewhere and staring into the distance, smoking cigarette after cigarette and missing meals. So they all did their best not to leave him alone. Grant was standing sentinel, looking out one of the windows in the room. And Jo was stationed in the center of her bed with a skinny little monkey in her lap.

Elly did know that next door to this room was the zoo. She'd poked her head in there for only a second and caught sight of two more monkeys, some mice, and a parrot. She'd backed away very quickly. To each his own.

"There's plenty of room here to hide weapons," Jo said as she fed the monkey a grape.

"That's my thinking as well." Elly had reluctantly changed clothes. The long black gown made her feel as though she'd stepped directly from the pages of a Regency novel but they weren't the only ones staying in the castle and Grant was becoming paranoid about someone potentially revealing their activities to the wrong party. So she'd exchanged her spying dress for a regular cotton dress.

"Maybe in those dungeons you dragged us into," Danny offered.

"How would we get them here?" Grant asked, his attention on whatever had caught his eye out the window. He was so tall and handsome. Could she change his mind? Could she convince him to return to the States and live?

"I think," Jo said slowly, her words pulling Elly out of her ridiculous thoughts, "that we have to work with the soldiers." She was referring to the small group of men currently bedding down in the main hall of the château. Men who were supposed to have turned themselves in to the Germans but had made the executive decision not to. "They have as much to lose as we do. More so. And I think they'd like the idea of sticking it to the enemy. You or Danny or Pierre garner a lot of attention everywhere you go." They all did. "Those men might not be from around here but they've got a much better chance of blending in."

"And we don't have to tell them everything," Danny said pointedly.

"Also," Jo said, now boring holes into Grant's back. "Remember the blacksmith?" Elly couldn't hardly believe it when she'd heard that someone still practiced such a profession. A blacksmith working next to a medieval castle. But she did remember the blacksmith and his family. They often joined them on the terrace to listen to news on the radio. "He told me today that he has access to a radio transmitter." Grant turned then, looking at Jo. "One that can reach as far as Great Britain. Think of the possibilities."

The possibility was that they wouldn't be so isolated and alone out here. But if they used the radio transmitter, they'd most likely have to take the blacksmith into their confidence. "We can't work alone, Grant. We're going to have to take a risk and trust that some of these people hate the Germans even more than we do."

"Okay," Pierre said, interrupting the staring contest between Jo and Grant. "Suppose we can communicate with the British. What are we going to be communicating exactly? 'The Germans aren't here. Thank God'?"

"I was thinking," Jo began as she turned away from Grant and toward Elly. "What if I agreed to perform at the nearest theater? Germans are men. I'm sure they'll want to come to the show."

"The Germans hate your show," Grant reminded her.

Jo shrugged. "They didn't really watch it. And besides I could tailor this one to their preference."

"With what musicians?" Pierre demanded, no longer looking at the flames. "Me and Grant? Danny on set design and Elly as your . . . maid." Pierre's voice broke on the last word.

"We can hire from the town," Jo said breezily.

"Oh, do they have jazz players hiding under rocks here?"

Ignoring him, Jo continued. "And Elly wouldn't be my maid. She'd be on the stage with me."

Elly's eyebrows shot to the top of her head as Danny

coughed into his hand and Pierre's eyes filled with sudden delight. "What now?"

"You would be on the stage with me. That way we both could mingle among the enemy. Just like we did back in Paris."

The idea had merit. Elly had no faith in the execution. "No."

Pierre began to snicker. Loudly. Grant returned to looking out the window.

"I know, I know," Jo said quickly. "Your first reaction to anything is no. Think about it."

"I don't need to think about it. I hate to break it to you, but every colored woman cannot dance. You want me to get up there and make a fool of myself?" Elly heard the pitch of her voice go high. The very thought of performing in front of an audience was giving her heart palpitations. This was a terrible idea. A horrible one.

"We wouldn't just throw you up there. I'd teach you. We have time. It's not as though I could do a show tomorrow."

But Elly was shaking her head before the words exited Jo's mouth. "I'm sorry, but no."

"So," Pierre said, still overcome with a case of the giggles. "Dance rehearsal starts at noon?"

Elly picked up the couch pillow on her right and threw it at him.

"The weapons," Grant stressed after eyeing both Elly and Pierre as though he expected better, "appear to be coming from the factory that had those leaks."

"They're new technology?" Elly asked, understanding

what he was referencing immediately—and also not feeling the least bit chastened.

"To a degree, we have been protecting them all this time." The room went silent.

"I guess that answers the question," Jo said firmly. "We'll hide the weapons here and do whatever it takes to keep them out of German hands."

CHAPTER 32

It turned out that the little room that Elly, Danny, and Pierre had found in the dungeons led to a cellar. At least Elly thought it was a cellar. Perhaps it was something else. Either way, the space was certainly perfect for the weapons they began to slowly attain and conceal over the next month.

After much back and forth, the French soldiers who were hiding from the Germans were recruited and over the space of several weeks Father Laval asked them three more times to come and collect weapons that the French would rather let sit and rot than hand over to the enemy. And the weapons *were* just sitting if not quite rotting. It wasn't as though they had an army to hand them to.

Jo had come down once to see what they were storing and then she hadn't returned. The rest of them inspected every box. Elly knew the items had fancy names but in layman's terms, they boiled down to machine guns, rifles, pistols, hand grenades, and bullets.

"Guess we'll be ready if they ever come for us," Danny muttered as he tapped the crate of the newest arrival of rifles.

"Have you ever heard of John Brown's raid on Harpers Ferry?" Elly asked him in the darkened space. What had once been creepy was now familiar. Grant released a small snort. He was standing in a corner holding the only flashlight in the room. She wasn't surprised he knew what she was referencing. Harpers Ferry was somewhat in his backyard. He took a sudden step forward.

"Put that down, Pierre!" Pierre, who had been fondling one of the grenades, quickly released it and jumped back. "Pierre!"

"I was just looking!" Pierre raised his hands in surrender. Then he shifted toward Elly. "Are you talking about that guy in the 'Glory, Glory, Hallelujah' song? *John Brown's body lies a molderin' in the grave*," Pierre sang aloud.

"Yes, that John Brown. He took over an arsenal and still very much had his behind handed to him on a silver platter. In case you're wondering where I'm going with this, we would not be ready if the Germans ever came for us."

"I bet we'd take a lot of 'em out with us though," Danny countered.

"This is not the Alamo. If you want to die in a blaze of glory, please do that elsewhere," Grant told him. "Besides, if I was German, I would retaliate on the innocent to make it something less likely to happen again. They have to. It's the only way to keep a tight hold on people who hate you."

"So you don't think they should fight back at all?"

"I didn't say that. But I think it would be foolish not to count the costs first."

"How long are we going to stay here in the dark playing with guns? Can we leave now?" Pierre grumbled.

In a single-file line, with Elly in the lead, they exited the room, entering the dungeons themselves.

"How's that dancing going, Elly?" Pierre asked, taking a moment to poke her in the back.

"Oh, shut up." With great—great—reluctance, Elly had started meeting Jo in the 'music' room on a daily basis to learn the choreography for a fast up-tempo number that Jo had performed in *Paris-London*. It was going as well as Elly had known it would . . . which meant that it was going badly. Elly didn't care what anybody said, performing in front of people had to be one of the most vulnerable things a person could do and she'd never been one to turn over and reveal her underbelly.

Whenever she felt herself even getting remotely comfortable with the footwork, she just remembered that there was a real possibility she'd have to perform these same moves in front of possibly a hundred people that she did not know, and that thought was enough to have her stumble over her feet again. Jo was doing her very best not to get frustrated.

"I got a brief glance of you two practicing the other day," Danny began, "and I meant to ask you, Elly, if you could cook?"

Nearly tripping on the first stair that led out of the basement, Elly asked, "What do you mean you caught a brief glance of us practicing?" The door was always shut. If she was going to embarrass herself, Elly preferred that very few people saw her.

"Well, there are windows." Elly glared at the space in front of her. And then she frowned as his question hit her. "Did you ask me if I could cook?"

"How did you tie those two things together?" Pierre asked. He was snickering as though he already knew Danny was going to say something ridiculous. And if Elly knew Danny, he would.

"Well, I'm still confused as to how Elly was taken for Jo. I mean, Elly is bigger." Elly, at the very top of the stairs, stopped, turned around and stared at Danny while Pierre's laughter grew louder and Grant sighed deeply. "Hey," Danny said, bringing his hands to his chest. "I like bigger girls. Don't get offended. It's just that you look like you eat cornbread and black-eyed peas every now and then. Jo's been on that grapefruit diet for ten years. There's very little meat on her bones."

Elly pushed the door open, blinking as the light from the hall filled her eyes.

"I was just thinking." Because Danny wasn't done yet. "It's been an awful long time since I had soul food. And you look like you know how to cook it. It'd be real nice if you fixed us something. Man can't live on quiche and omelets alone."

"This may surprise you, Danny, but men can cook."

"True. But none of the men in this castle can. You know what would be nice? Some collard greens and mac and cheese."

331

"Sweet potatoes," Pierre offered, his voice holding a dreamy element.

"Yes, all of these things can be found in France," Elly said sarcastically as she started down the hall.

"You're right. What part of the South are you from again?"

"Louisiana," Grant said, answering for her. "The land of Cajun and Creole."

"Hmm. That is a bit hindering." Because Cajun and Creole food mainly consisted of seafood and while there was a river not too far from here, you wouldn't be pulling out any crawfish, shrimp, or catfish anytime soon. "I'm not cooking," Elly yelled over her shoulder.

"Oh, I know. Jambalaya!"

"No!"

Elly made her way down the hall to the music room where she knew Jo was already running through her paces. Their rehearsal wasn't scheduled for another half an hour but sometimes the best part of practice was watching the master of performing do what she did exceptionally well. After all, Elly was only learning the choreography for one dance. The rest would all be danced alone by Jo—should there ever be another show.

Elly heard the music playing before she even reached the door. Benny Goodman was filling the air. It was the song that Elly was trying to learn to dance to. She entered the room just as the horns cut off and the drums took over. And Jo was hitting every beat, every note with every shake of her hip and tap of her foot. Elly parked herself into a corner as Jo danced up and down the room, exaggerating gestures so every part of her could be seen. Beautiful, but the moves made Elly tired just looking at them.

When Jo caught sight of Elly, she went over to the record player and lifted the needle. Wiping at the sweat on her brow, she asked, "Is it that time already?"

"No, no. I'm early. Please don't mind me."

"Early?"

"It was dance or cook Danny jambalaya. I chose dance."

Jo rolled her eyes. "He can cook his own jambalaya. Since you're here, let's get started. I'm supposed to meet Jack by the river anyway."

Jack. Jo's boyfriend and handler had showed up a few weeks ago, boxes and boxes of papers in hand. In his car had been almost all of what was left of the Deuxième Bureau. The rest of it was somewhere near Marseille. That meant they were not only hiding weapons but French secrets. When Jack wasn't up in the highest tower trying to communicate with allies, he was kayaking on the river. A nice man, but naturally somewhat distant. Except where Jo was concerned.

Elly stood up and made her way to the windows. She released the curtains, making the room darker.

"We need that light."

Elly imagined Danny peeking his head through the window to laugh at her. "Let's close this one and leave the rest open."

Elly already had on the pair of dancing shorts that Jo had given her and so she removed the pants she was wearing and slipped on the dance heels.

"Remember," Jo said as she began stretching from

side to side. "Lengthening your legs makes your derrière look better."

Elly's only response was to shake her head. She was never going to get used to such talk. They'd briefly discussed costumes. For her, Jo had volunteered for something more modest. Elly had been most grateful except that they both had different ideas on what modesty looked like. It had come down to what a bathing suit would cover. The question was would it be a two-piece bathing suit or a one-piece? They had both decided to pick the discussion back up, if and when it became necessary.

"Let's run through it first without any music. On my count. One, two, three, four." These moves were something Elly practiced every evening before she went to bed. Sometimes she practiced them as she made her way through her morning walk around the gardens. Intellectually, she knew them. They weren't hard. They were repetitive. And more than that, they were made up of steps from different swing dances that Elly knew from back home. It was just that sometimes when practicing with Jo, she got lost in her own head.

"You're doing it again, Elly," Jo said as they turned and met in the middle and then swung away from each other.

"I'm trying not to."

"Well, it's not working. You're thinking too much. I can always tell because those frown lines appear on your forehead. Stop. Let's stop. Elodie." Jo formed a fist with one hand and slammed it into the palm of her other hand. "If you don't think you look good dancing, no one else will."

"Yes." Jo had explained this before.

"If you don't think you're the best thing since sliced bread out there on that stage no one else will. You cannot sell a product you don't believe in."

"Understood." Everything Jo was saying made absolute sense.

Jo's eyes narrowed. "You can make a mistake."

"Not on a stage with hundreds of people looking at me!"

"Yes! Even on a stage with hundreds of people looking at you. Elly, I make mistakes all the time. All the time. And you know what? You never know it because I learned at a young age that if you keep going, they won't know it either. Once, I was supposed to be lowered onto the stage from the ceiling by this metal contraption thing." Jo pointed up and then to the ground. "The thing broke opening night and I dangled above everyone for the whole show. I had to improvise and entertain from the air. And no one in the audience had a clue that that wasn't how the show was supposed to go. We got rave reviews. Sometimes mistakes make things better. I've learned to cherish them."

Having folded her arms over her chest, Elly tapped a finger against her bicep. Cherish a mistake. What a unique idea.

"There's no mistake you can make that I cannot cover you for. None. So take that weight off your chest, Elodie. And remember, dancing is fun."

There was a knock on the door and Danny poked his head in. "We found sausage." Danny held up the meat so Elly could see. "And I have confirmed that the garden out there is growing the Holy Trinity."

"Danny!"

"Remember every shake of the hip is a fight against the Nazis." He gave them a thumbs-up and then he shut the door.

Elly didn't want to smile. Particularly because she knew she would now be cooking dinner.

"So annoying. Okay, where was I? Right." Jo held up her hands in a gesture of surrender. "Make mistakes. From here on out, we're not going to stop if you trip over your feet or forget the next step. I want to see you turn that problem into a solution. All right? Let's try it with the music."

CHAPTER 33

The confessional was small and slightly cramped. It was a beautifully crafted box with woodwork that depicted small stories all along the sides of it but it was not designed with a person's comfort in mind. Whoever had put it together had not wanted people to stay long. Either that or Elly simply was not someone who could linger in enclosed spaces for longer than she had to.

"I must place some very important information into your hands. Forgive me, daughter, but I know no one else who I can trust."

Already feeling stiff as a board on the slight wooden pew, Elly tensed. "I'm listening."

"There is a freight train bound for Paris carrying weapons and supplies to the Germans. It will pass through here in two days' time."

Elly considered his words. "I do not know that we can find a place to hide so much."

"I do not ask you to hide it, my child. I ask you to destroy it." Destroy it? "The train must never reach Paris with those items on board."

For ten seconds, Elly said nothing. Grant's conversation with Danny danced in her head. "Such an action invites the scrutiny of the Germans." As it was, their small town had been left alone, a little pocket of heaven in the midst of hell.

"Then we must be very careful not to lead them to us."

"Someone will pay the price, Frère."

"*Oui*. One always does in war," he said tiredly as though he too would prefer not to go down the route he was ushering her toward. But Elly understood. They could not simply sit back and do nothing. The small slot between them opened and a piece of paper dropped onto her lap. "The times and different stations that the train will pass through."

Elly did not take a second to look at the paper. She folded the already folded note again and reaching under her veil, she tucked the paper between her breasts. Feeling the intensity of the moment in her body, Elly rotated her neck under the large, heavy veil. Then she lifted her head. "I will convey your requests. You will know your answer in two days' time."

"*Merci*, my dear. May the Lord bless you and keep you. May the Lord make his face shine on you and be gracious to you. May the Lord lift up his countenance to you and give you peace."

"Frère Laval, please keep your death benedictions for someone who needs them."

*

Once again they met in Jo's room while Jack the boyfriend was upstairs in one of the towers trying to communicate with his counterparts in Great Britain.

"He's asking us to blow up the train, isn't he?" Danny was sitting on the floor rubbing Luca's belly.

"Well, we certainly have the weapons to do it," Pierre said with a sigh. He too was sitting on the floor, but he was holding up a wall, tapping the back of his head against the stone every now and then.

"Can it be done?" Jo asked Grant. This time she had a small cat in her arms. Elly had no clue where she'd even gotten it from. And she thought it was a bit counterintuitive considering that Jo kept mice for pets.

Grant was sitting on the couch next to Elly. He leaned forward resting his elbows on his kneecaps. "It's not a matter of whether it can be done—not that that would be easy in the slightest. It's how do we get in and get out without being seen and without leading anyone back here? Two days? I'd prefer more time to scout out the train station."

"Are we going to do it?" Elly asked quietly. It was, after all, the most important question.

"I don't want to say yes or no until I see what we're working with. I hope no one was planning on getting any sleep."

While Danny and Pierre worked on constructing plastic explosives, Elly, Jo, and Grant pored over maps until they narrowed down the train station, a rudimentary plan for getting the explosives onto a car, and a way of escape.

Because they were up until the wee hours of the

morning, Elly waited until noon before she knocked on Pierre's door. It still took him a while to answer. "What?"

Cracking his door open, Elly peeked in. Pierre was looking at her through slitted eyes and tangled sheets. "I need to talk to you. Get dressed."

"No." He turned away, burying his face into his pillow.

"It's very important."

"My beauty sleep is very important," he mumbled into his pillow.

"It's about Grant," she whispered. And then she waited.

He punched the pillow next to him. "Fine!"

Ten minutes later, Pierre was still in bed but dressed and smoking a cigarette. Elly sat at the other end of the bed with her legs tucked under her.

Elly watched him lean over and tap his cigarette against an already filled ashtray. "What is it that you want?"

It had taken her a while to come to the decision to speak to Pierre. But she had very few options here. "I need to ask you something. I need you to promise me this conversation won't leave this room."

Pierre returned the cigarette to his mouth, his light brown eyes glittering. "You're very lucky I'm extremely curious right now."

"Yes, yes." Elly lifted her pinkie finger. "Promise me."

"Are we ten?"

"Promise me."

Pierre blinked three times. Then he scooted forward and wrapped his pinkie finger around hers for two seconds before returning to sit back against his pillows.

"Several times you've said something along the lines of 'the love of a good woman will not change Grant's mind.' Are you implying that he does like me as a . . . potential romantic possibility?" Elly needed to be sure that it was fear keeping Grant away and not . . . distaste. She could only try to change his mind if certain things were an option.

The cigarette in Pierre's hand froze on its way to his mouth. His eyes went wide as he tilted his head, looking at her. "Definitely expected you to be a bit more circumspect."

"Why? There's nothing circumspect about me."

"If that were true, you would be asking Grant about his thoughts, not me." Elly opened her mouth to refute this. And then closed it. Some things very much made Elly hesitant no matter how bold and straightforward she was built. Like rejection. "It's okay," Pierre said, a hint of a smile dancing on his lips. "It's nice to know that you too have human emotions."

"Oh, please."

"In answer to your question, we don't talk about that kind of stuff. Grant is a very private person and a southern gentleman with a capital G. The most he has ever said about you was before he actually met you. He watched you before he recruited you to be a spy. You know that?"

"Yes."

"I recall him once saying that he could probably watch you all day and be content. I thought he meant because you put him in mind of Mary Grace. But let's just say, I no longer think he thinks of Mary Grace when he's with you. That's all I got."

Mary Grace? His daughter? Elly almost shuddered at the thought. When she glanced over at Pierre, he was watching her so intently that she felt as though he'd read every thought that crossed his mind. Removing his cigarette from his mouth, and tapping the side of his ashtray, he said, "I've decided that I'm going to be nice. I'm going to call in that favor you owe me."

"What favor? Oh."

"Yes. That one. You seem like a very nineteenth-century kind of woman."

"Oh, hush up."

"You know the sort. Those kinds of girls who won't say boo to a man unless he speaks first."

"Pierre."

"Now, there's a place for that. Sometimes there's a reason he ain't speaking first but here's the favor I'm calling in: when the time comes, ask him to go with you."

"What?!" She didn't have to ask Pierre for clarity. She knew what he was saying. She stared at him in bewilderment. Cool eyes stared back.

"You owe me, darling. And I'd like to think you don't renege on your word. Ask him." Pierre smashed the butt of his cigarette into the ashtray. "I'll know whether you do it or if you flake. C'mon, Grant's little moth isn't afraid, is she?"

She never should have come here. Elly tossed him an annoyed look as she swung her legs over the side of his bed.

"It's been fun!"

She slammed his bedroom door behind her. Ask him, he said. As if Pierre wasn't demanding that she reveal the whole kit and caboodle. *Ask him*. Elly stomped down the stone stairs. How did Pierre know that there was nothing more she wanted than to ask Grant to come home with her?

CHAPTER 34

A few hours later, Grant, Elly, Danny, and Pierre drove out to the train station, parking several miles away and hoofing it to a hill that overlooked the tracks to see whether their plan translated from paper to reality.

"There are no guards or people on watch in this area," Grant whispered from next to Elly as he looked through binoculars. They had split up. Danny and Pierre were on one side of the hill and Grant and Elly were on the other. No one else seemed to be around—the station was fairly deserted—but still Grant and Elly were in the grass on their bellies. Best not to be seen, if possible. Elly held out a hand and Grant gave her the binoculars. Lifting them to her face, she saw what he had seen.

This particular station was chosen because the town was barely a dot on the map. There would be few people lingering around at night. Next to her, Grant pulled out his notes and the sketch he'd made. He leaned in close enough to her that she got a whiff of his cologne. "We have to assume the train stops for no longer than thirty seconds."

"Why does it stop here at all?"

"People from three towns frequent this station," Grant said, showing her the map. His shoulder brushed against hers, sending wonderful shivers across her skin. She'd missed these light touches that reminded her she was alive. "They don't all live here but they are close enough to this area to warrant the train coming through."

"There will be civilians on this train?"

"Most likely. We'll target the freight cars. Preferably the one furthest away from the passenger cars." It just didn't even seem real what they were about to do. She looked through the binoculars again and tried to picture a train exploding. Dear goodness, this life that she was living. Grant cleared his throat and she lowered the binoculars. "You can always ask me if you have questions."

"What?" she asked, confused.

"I understand that you spoke with Pierre. About me." Elly's blink was long and slow. She would never, ever speak to Pierre Roche again.

"What did he say?" Her voice was cool. He had pinkie promised!

Resting on his elbows, Grant eyed her suspiciously. "He wouldn't say. I did not realize the two of you had become such good friends."

"We're not," she said quickly, relieved. "I am curious, though. What was his father like?"

345

Grant frowned, thinking. He slid his eyes over to hers. "He was very different from Pierre. Quiet, unassuming, bookish. On the one hand he'd be appalled at Pierre's lack of education. On the other hand his son can read, write, and speak two languages, play three instruments, and has traveled the world, so you take what you can get. Were you talking about the war with Pierre?"

Elly thought about the question. "We've talked about it."

"He doesn't know anything. If you have questions, Elly Anne, ask me." Elly jerked back, surprised by the nickname. Grant smiled, wide and free, pleased with himself. "You know so goodness well, yo mama ain't never call you Elodie. In Valcourt, Louisiana, you was Elly Anne." With that, he reached for the binoculars and returned to looking out at the station.

Elly slowly returned her elbow to the ground. She glanced at Grant out of the side of her eye before returning to look ahead. "Where are you going to place me?" She'd seen a spot for Pierre, Danny, and Grant in this planning, but she hadn't come across her job.

"You're not coming."

Elly frowned. "Why not? You know you can rely on me to do whatever needs to be done."

"I do know that. But you're still not coming."

This wasn't making any sense. "I can probably outshoot both Danny and Pierre."

"While that may be true, we're not planning on shooting anybody."

She hated when he got this way—all high-handed and knowing. "You would rather have those two at your back than me?"

Grant lowered the binoculars once again. "Elly, you're not coming and that's it."

"Is it because I'm a woman?" As she was living in a world where being colored was the worst offense a person could commit, she rarely reached the point where she was discriminated against simply because she was a woman.

"I have placed you in dozens of dangerous positions. What does your being a woman have to do with anything?"

"You just answered my question with a question—"

"Yes. It has everything to do with you being a woman."

They looked at each other for a minute. Elly felt a thrill for about two seconds until she recalled Pierre's words, which had been echoing in her head even if he had refuted the charge. "Do you think of me as your daughter?" Grant blinked once. If she wasn't mistaken, he looked slightly horrified. Thank God. "Pierre made a comment that got me thinking."

"Pierre rarely says smart things. My daughter . . . how old are you?"

"Twenty-four," she said reluctantly. "But I'll be twenty-five in a month." She grimaced as soon as the words exited her mouth. "You're the one who said something about being old enough to be my father."

Elly's gaze dropped to the grass beneath her. "For what it's worth, I do not think of you as my father." Louis Valcourt, God bless his heart, had always felt like a child to her; unable and unwilling to do the hard things in life. And then there was Uncle Minor who had stepped in where her father had failed, becoming everything she'd needed as a girl and even now as a woman. She did not need another father.

"That's good to know, Elly. I am at peace," Grant muttered before looking away. His hands were shaking a bit as he returned the binoculars to his eyes once again.

"Now, you're not coming with us tonight. There will be plenty of opportunities for you to live dangerously. Let us handle this, this time. Okay?"

With an irritated huff, he returned to his map.

He'd changed the subject. Fine. But he'd answered her question so she wouldn't push it. Returning her gaze to the station below them, Elly said, "Don't you come whining to me if they upset you."

Grant raised his eyes to the heavens. "I wouldn't dare."

Nearly twelve hours later, Elly was pacing in front of the small fireplace in one of the parlor rooms. She never should have let Grant distract her with his flattery. She should have insisted on going.

"You're giving me a headache." Jo was dressed for bed and wrapped in a long silk robe. Her hair was covered and she was sitting in an oversized armchair with her feet on a footstool, cradling a dog in her arms. Elly was dressed and ready for battle in a pair of dark pants she'd gotten from Danny and a dark shirt. "Grant said to expect their return by midnight. We still have a half hour to go."

"Do you think that noise we heard ten minutes ago was the train exploding?" Elly was sure she had heard something.

Jo shrugged, lifting one delicate shoulder. "I don't know about that but I do know that all this back and forth is making me dizzy."

"I can't sit still when I'm nervous. If I was back at home . . ."

"If you were back at home?"

"We'd be pacing and praying until dawn." That was how they dealt with anxious moments in the Mitchell household.

"Like a watch night?"

"Yes," Elly said, pausing to look at Jo. "Exactly like that." Watch night had roots going all the way back to December of 1862 when American Negroes had gotten word that Abe Lincoln was planning to free the slaves on January 1, 1863. It was Frederick Douglass who had asked that everyone go to church the last night of the year to beseech God on behalf of those enslaved. And it had become a tradition after that. Most churches still held service on December 31st. "Have you been to watch night?"

"My grandmother used to take me every year. It was so hard to sit in those pews. I'm a mover and a talker. Not the best combination for all-night prayer at church. I thanked God when I was finally old enough to go to a party on New Year's Eve."

If Elly didn't go to watch night, she brought the New Year in, in bed. Usually reading a novel. Except for this past year where she'd been trying to sniff out another mole in the French military while also acting as though she were having the best time of her life. It had been thoroughly exhausting and she had no desire to repeat it.

"That's the thing about working hard," Jo was muttering to herself. "The payoff is that you can do whatever it is that you want and Lord knows I've worked hard all my life."

"Dancing?"

"Yes, but even before that. I was about seven when I got my first job as a maid."

"A maid?" Elly had thought she'd grown up poor— hunting and gathering for her next meal. Singing on street corners when she needed coins. But in her youth, she had never worked for anybody.

"I worked for some crazy white people. Crazy." Jo stroked her dog—Elly was pretty sure it was Poppy. "One lady I worked for had chickens. And you know me, I made one of them my friend. Took care of it. Slept with it, 'cause room and board was a part of the deal. I fed it. Talked to it. And that woman found out and told me I had to kill it." Closing her eyes, Jo reached up, massaging the stress of the memory from her brow. "This other lady I worked for didn't like my work and she took my arm and laid it on a hot stove as punishment." Jo raised said appendage. "You can still see the marks from the burn if you look close enough. Were you ever in service?"

"No," Elly said abruptly and returned to pacing. "If I had been born eighty years ago, they would have probably killed me. I would have been the one very slowly poisoning them."

Jo tossed her head back, laughing. Elly grinned. But she was serious. Being treated like that would have broken her. But it clearly wouldn't have broken Jo. Nothing that had happened to Jo had even remotely

350

dampened the optimistic way in which she approached life. Before Elly could say any more, they heard the door open from down the hall. Jo came to her feet, Poppy diving off her lap with a leap.

Pierre appeared first, looking jittery and excited. "It was like boom!" He made a dramatic motion with his hands. "Did y'all hear it?"

"I think so," Elly told him as Danny and lastly Grant entered the room. She scanned all three of them. They looked hale and hearty. "How did it go?"

"Well, there weren't any guards or anything so we weren't exactly in danger," Danny said as he rested his backside on the arm of the nearest couch. "We just ran to the freight car, attached the bombs, ran off, and watched it explode."

"Like fireworks," Pierre offered. "The railcar must have had some ammunition inside because the explosion was bigger than it should have been and set off the next car. Look at my hands. They're still shaking. I won't be able to sleep an inch tonight."

"Well, I have some photos I need to develop. Why don't you come with me?" Danny asked Pierre.

"Sounds boring." Still he followed Danny out the parlor room, leaving just Grant, Jo, and Elly.

"Where are you supposed to be going?" Grant asked, nodding in Elly's direction as he made his way to the armchair directly across from Jo.

"Don't worry about me," she said politely.

"She was in here trying to stress me out," Jo said as she sat back down. Grant wrinkled his nose at Elly, and then released a mischievous grin. It was so unexpected and such a rare sight that she grinned back, feeling like she could float on air. And then there was a tug on her heart. For how much longer would she be able to see him? *Ask him.* The echoing of Pierre's demand had Elly's eyes dropping to the ground and she lost her smile. "What happens next?"

Grant sighed deeply as he looked across the room at Jo. "I guess we'll find out."

They found out three days later when a convoy of German soldiers arrived.

CHAPTER 35

Once again, Elly sat in the church where Father Laval couldn't be found anywhere. She did note that there were more people there—men *and* women—silently filling the pews. It probably had everything to do with the Germans who had commandeered the only hotel in the area and set up a rotation of patrols. 'Twas as good a time as any to petition God. Elly knew this firsthand. She'd been born in a sundown town herself.

With the Germans watching everyone's movements, these visits to the church were no longer practical. Elly was there to wrap things up. If only Father Laval would do as he ought.

Deciding to stay in the role she was playing, Elly tugged on the cross at her neck. Pierre had found the white-stoned rosary under one of the benches in the chapel at the château and grandiosely gave it to her.

Making the sign of the cross and holding the crucifix,

she began to mutter under her breath in French. "I believe in God, the Father Almighty, Creator of Heaven and Earth . . ."

By the time Father Laval lowered himself next to her on the bench, she'd finished the Apostles' Creed, prayed the Our Father, and said ten Hail Marys.

"You have fought the good fight." He was facing straight ahead and his words were low so only she could hear him even though they were sitting in the middle of an empty bench and the nearest person was two pews away.

"And finished my course?"

Father Laval hummed and that sound made Elly lift her head and look in his direction. "Just because evil has crawled its way here, doesn't mean that we're done yet."

"Frère." She was not here to listen to another request. She was here to tell him he'd be getting no more help from their group, small as it was.

"The items I asked you to hold must now be transferred elsewhere. There is a home for them."

"Frère. We cannot—"

"You can. And you must," the priest said, his voice harsh and icy. "Lives are relying on it." He reached for her gloved hand and slipped a small piece of paper against her palm. Grasping her hand tightly, he bowed over it as though praying. "One does not get to choose which battles to fight in a war." He squeezed her hand one last time before standing. "Go in peace, my daughter."

And then he exited the pew and went to sit down next to another parishioner.

With great irritation, Elly slipped the note into her purse and continued praying the remainder of the rosary although her mind was far, far away. Making a final sign of the cross, she walked down the center aisle of the church, leaving. She would probably never make for a good general. She did not think she had it in her to send people to their possible deaths, even for the sake of the greater good. Exiting the church, Elly stopped and inhaled, taking in a French summer night. It should have calmed her nerves. Instead, it made her wary.

Lifting her skirts, she made her way down the few stone stairs and headed for the path that she and Grant had agreed on earlier that day and so she was neither startled nor surprised when he materialized from the shadows to walk alongside her.

They didn't speak for the first few minutes, mostly because Elly's mind was on all that she wanted to tell him but could not say.

"Last time we made this trip, you said you hated journalism. Why?" Grant asked in French. Their conversations on their walks to and from the church had started to drift more into the personal as they were too worried about possible eavesdroppers.

"There is nothing wrong with journalism, per se, but it makes me feel like a voyeur and a gossip."

Grant released an amused grunt. "That's probably because of how you get your information."

"It probably is," she admitted. "I think I want to go into academia. I could happily teach literature and the written word every day of my life." Elly found something very comforting in the thought of becoming an expert in one field and teaching the same subject for years and years. "And as soon as you can, you're opening another restaurant?"

"Probably. I like it. I'd like to have more than one so they could play off each other." Their conversation was light and easy. Comfortable.

But there was something about the night that lent itself to bravery. And if there was any chance that she was going to change his mind—particularly without having to directly ask him—she needed to hurry. She was running out of time. "Do you ever think you'll get married again?"

She heard the slight misstep he took.

"Me? No."

Honestly? She'd expected that answer. "You don't want any more children?"

"Do *you* want children?"

"Five or six of them."

"Five or six . . . !"

"I'd be a good mother," Elly said defensively. She would be. She might lack some of that natural nurturing that Aunt Tabitha possessed but that didn't mean she wouldn't be able to raise some very fine people who would then go on to contribute to society.

"I thought you wanted to go into academia?" Grant asked, sounding slightly aghast. She didn't know what had surprised him more: that she wanted to be a mother or that she wanted so many children. But the little girl who had not had much of a childhood wanted very much to create the kind of home she had craved. The kind of home she'd experienced when she'd moved in with her aunt and uncle.

"Motherhood is a season. I'd like to think they wouldn't take over my whole life. You haven't answered the question."

"But I did answer the question. I have no desire to ever get married again."

"Listen, I'll be the first person to say that you don't need a spouse to be happy. I've seen my share of disastrous marriages and I'd rather be a spinster than have those problems. But what about the ones that work?"

"Elly Anne, what in the world are you talking about? Marriage simply isn't for me."

Elly's mind raced, catching and releasing different responses. "Grant, I know why you don't want to get married."

"Is that right?" Grant sounded bored with the conversation.

"Yes.. Pierre and I talked about this too."

"Oh, dear Lord."

"I know what it's like," Elly began, ignoring his sarcasm. "To go to sleep at night and wonder if it's worth it to wake in the morning. To be absent with the body is to be present with the Lord." Elly snapped her fingers. "Just like that, it could all be over." The only way they'd have a real conversation about this was if she were willing to be vulnerable and take a risk. "Especially when you don't feel like there's any rhyme or reason why you're supposed to be here in the first place. It's a fearsome thing to go through each day and feel like this is all there is to life." It was hard to admit this aloud and Elly realized that she felt very near to tears.

Grant's footsteps slowed to a stop and she felt his eyes on her. "Just when I think I know you, you surprise me. Elodie, you have your whole life ahead of you." His voice was almost pleading. "Why would you think that way when you know how special you are?"

"How special am I really?" She teased half-heartedly trying to lessen some of the tension that filled the air.

"Elly—"

"The reason I stayed here was because I wanted to live." Physically, emotionally, mentally. "I needed to take a risk." She'd needed to figure out her own value. "I chose life, hard as that might be to believe—all things considered. I do not have the history you have. I have not seen the things you have seen or done the things you did. But from one person who has struggled to get through the day to another, I understand," she said gently. "I understand how hard it can be to take that step of faith to believe that goodness just might be around the corner."

Grant stilled. "Did we switch to talking about me? Who said I struggle to get through every day?" Elly frowned. So, he was going to deny it. "Is this what you and Pierre were talking about?" he demanded, his voice cool.

"Fine, Grant. Don't be honest with me or with yourself. But let me just tell you, you can't break free if you don't acknowledge the prison that's holding you."

"Break free from what?"

Elly reached up, touching a finger to her brow. Men. They'd rather walk off a cliff than acknowledge that they were lost. "Never mind, Grant. Never mind."

So distracted was Elly that it completely caught her

off guard when Grant grabbed her arm and started hauling her across the road. "Hey! What is wrong—"

He nearly slammed her back up against the wall of the empty store they were passing but stopped just shy of contact being made. Before she could protest, his hand covered her mouth. "We're being followed."

She stilled beneath him and he lowered his hand from her mouth to her waist, tugging her a bit closer to him. "There was time for you to open your mouth and say something," Elly hissed.

"And hear you go on some more about how broken I am?" He leaned in, his breath warm against her ear, the bristles of his beard tickling her cheek. And her body reacted as it always did when she was near Grant no matter how irritating he was being.

"Grant, everyone is broken to some degree." Her words were soft. She slipped her hands around his waist, possessively as though he were hers.

"In two minutes, you're going to walk down the road on our right for another half mile, get into the car, and return to the castle. But take the long way home."

"What about you?"

"Don't worry about me."

"It doesn't work that way," she warned.

"You have to trust me. It's the best way to get out of this situation. If they have to choose, they're much less likely to follow a woman."

Elly was silent for a moment. "If you don't return home, I'll have to go looking for you." She'd never forgotten what he said about how if they were caught, they were on their own.

He lowered his chin onto her shoulder and she heard him exhale. His other arm wrapped around her back. "I cannot be fixed."

Elly's breath caught for a second and she squeezed him tight. "Last time I checked, I possessed no divinity and no magic powers. I'm not trying to fix you. You can't fix me. I'm saying I can live with your failings. Assuming you can live with mine. Grant, I don't like this idea of leaving you." Of leaving him here in this moment. Of leaving him here in France.

Grant lifted his head and pressed the softest kiss to her cheek. Then he gently grabbed her chin, turned her head, and placed another tender kiss on her other cheek. *Faire des bisous.* "The sooner you leave, the sooner we'll both be home with a story to tell."

Elly leaned forward and touched her lips to his. Grant's hand moved to the back of her neck, pulling her closer. He parted her lips with his own, kissing her slowly as though wanting to savor every taste of her, and making her feel like she could do this forever. Then he lifted his face, separating their mouths and leaving Elly with a heart that was pounding, lips that were swollen, and a body that wanted more. "Be careful," she whispered.

"I will. But the only thing I'm afraid of right now is you."

CHAPTER 36

Father Laval's instructions were plain and straight-forward. The weapons were to be delivered to a train station about thirty minutes away from them. There, the stationmaster would make sure they were loaded onto an empty car and sent north. Very simple. In and out. But this was not just one or two small boxes. It was more like ten very large ones. And the Germans were patrolling. Jo and Grant went back and forth about whether to take on the job but there was no heat. They both knew it had to be done. Especially if it meant keeping the weapons out of German hands. But it did mean that in order for this to work, they were once again going to have to make use of the French deserters they were hiding.

Elly knew almost immediately that the plans being tossed out around her didn't include her in the least. She still found a corner in the dining room, listening as the men talked in quick, careful bursts and scrutinized maps that were spread across the long, marble table. She eavesdropped quietly as she finally got around to hemming some clothes.

Pierre entered the room, looked around, saw her, and then turned in her direction. "You can do mine next," he said as he lowered himself into the chair next to hers. He and Danny had gone out earlier to take pictures of the area. Danny was developing the film now.

"Thanks, but no thanks. I don't even like to do my own sewing."

"You talk a big talk but you're nothing but a softie inside. I bet you would fix my clothes." He wasn't completely wrong. Elly was beginning to discover that a part of her really liked to feel needed.

"Still not doing them."

"I bet you would do Grant's."

Grant. She looked across the room at him where he was talking easy French with these soldiers as he must have done twenty years ago. They had not been alone once since the night before. Pierre had insisted on waiting up with her for Grant. And when Grant had arrived in the wee hours of the morning after giving the Germans something of a chase, he'd just nodded in her direction before heading for bed and leaving Elly with dozens of questions. "Well, we both know I won't do yours."

Unoffended, Pierre lowered his head onto her shoulder. She should have been annoyed. She did not particularly like being touched, even when she missed being touched, unless, of course, it was Grant Monterey doing the touching and yet, she did not tell him to move. "I'm beginning to see how this war is going to be fought in France now."

"Yep," Elly said as she pulled the needle through a seam.

"I don't think it's going to get better."

"Nope," she said as she snipped a long piece of thread.

"I would like to go home. I just don't know where home is."

"Fun has worn off?"

"Wore off a long time ago," Pierre muttered and she knew they were both thinking of Polly.

Danny appeared in the doorway, photos in hand. He eagerly passed a handful to Grant before shuffling over to Pierre and Elly. He brought a hand to his mouth, yawning. "Boy, I'm tired. But I do think that those are some of the best photos I've ever taken if I don't say so myself. Here," he said, handing several to Elly. "I made copies."

Elly lowered her sewing onto her lap and began flipping through the photos. This train station was just below a wooded hilly area, offering a lot of places to hide. Every time she finished looking at a photo, she passed it to Pierre who was still resting on her shoulder. "You do good work, Danny."

"I know," he said with all the confidence of someone who knew his craft. "It's nice to be able to do my part in this thing."

Elly hummed, acknowledging his comment.

"Now it's just Pierre who's a deadweight."

Pierre lifted his head off of Elly's shoulder. ". . . what?"

"How have you contributed? You could at least play the banjo. Then we'd have something to listen to while we work," Danny muttered, inspecting his fingernails, which were an unusual color due to all the chemicals he used in developing film.

"I was literally just in that dark room helping you."

Elly stood up, grabbing her sewing. Danny and Pierre could really nitpick at each other when they wanted to. "I'll see y'all later. I've got dance rehearsal."

After several months of rehearsing with no possible performance in sight, Elly was beginning to think that it was highly unlikely that she was ever going to be on a stage performing. The situation here in France was just too volatile. Elly didn't see how it could be done. Nevertheless, she kept showing up on time for her practices with Jo.

"There you are!" Jo said excitedly, already going through the paces. Elly changed into her dance uniform and then she began stretching as Jo had taught her to. She was here for Jo. Because Jo seemed to look forward to dancing and rehearsing and if that meant Elly had to play along then so be it. Besides, she *was* developing into a better dancer. And how many people could say that they had been given exclusive one-on-one dance lessons from *the* Josephine Baker? So, she'd keep going to her practices.

"Okay," Jo declared as she fiddled with the record player in the corner. "I've figured out your problem."

"I thought you did that already."

"Well, yes. It's probably more accurate to say I've figured out a solution to your overthinking problem."

"I cannot wait to hear it."

Jo shot her a dark look that brightened two seconds later. "You're dancing for the wrong people. When you think of dancing, you see a faceless crowd. You need to pick one person and dance for them." Jo tapped a finger against the side of her head. "Preferably someone in here and not an actual audience member. So, think of the one person you want to see you dance, and dance for them."

Elly frowned, considering her words. Who would she want to see her dance? Her thoughts went immediately to Grant and she felt her face grow warm. Thinking of him did suddenly make her want to lengthen her legs the way Jo always stressed and to shake with a little bit more oomph. She thanked God the heat in her face was barely discernible.

"If you dance for one single person, everyone in the audience will think you're dancing for them. All right, up on your feet. Let's go."

There were twelve of them going: Grant, Pierre, and Danny, of course. Along with all nine of the French deserters they were currently housing. The weapons were going to be taken to the train station using their two Renaults and one wagon. They'd unload the weapons and then their group would ride into the night. An easy task unless one considered the Germans.

Elly knew that they had planted a few men at the station whose sole purpose for the past two days was to watch the movement of the Germans. The only thing was, two days was not exactly long enough to establish a pattern. They were going to have to be very careful, very quiet, and very quick so as to not attract attention.

Elly had listened to the plan over and over until it danced in her head. She was going to be able to watch the clock and know exactly where each man was and what he was supposed to be doing. Three of the French soldiers had already left with the wagon and a wagon bed filled with boxes. They were taking the long, circuitous route to the station. There was no help for it. The main routes were much more likely to be frequented by the enemy. The remaining men would leave in the two cars, arriving at the station hopefully at the same time as the wagon. The stationmaster was prepped to have the very last train car unlocked and empty. Seven men would move the weapons and ammo inside the car while the rest remained on guard. Then they would leave by car and fetch the wagon at a later time. All in all, it should take an hour max.

"I've made a decision," Grant was saying to the remaining men. "About the weapons. I know we're supposed to turn all of them over but I don't like going down there knowing we might face the enemy and have nothing."

"We're going to take some?" one of the men asked eagerly.

Grant nodded and a wave of relief seemed to wash over the face of every man. "Just a rifle and a few rounds of ammunition. What we don't use, we can ship later."

Appearing before them with three rifles in hand, Grant handed one to Danny, one to Pierre, and then he held one out to her.

"For me?" Elly asked, surprise filling her voice as

she carefully took the weapon from him. They'd had no time to speak to each other in the past few days. None.

"You would think he'd given her a pair of diamond earrings," Pierre muttered to no one in particular as he began to check his weapon with easy expertise.

"Thought you might want to come along for the ride. We don't have anyone to keep lookout for the cars." Lookout for the cars.

"Are the cars planning on going somewhere?" Danny asked. A stupid question but the same one that was running through her mind.

Grant ignored him, his dark eyes on Elly. "You want to come or no?"

And that was how she found herself squished up front next to Grant who was driving one of the Renaults. He drove slowly with no lights on.

"Just stay with the vehicles," Grant explained. "Make sure they're running and ready to go in case we're moving in a hurry."

"Okay." It was not a meaningless job. These particular cars needed cranking. You couldn't just hop in them and go.

"Lay low."

"Yes," she said quickly, her grip on her rifle tight. She did not know why she wanted to go with them except that she hated sitting on her hands and waiting.

They parked the cars on the side of the road at the top of the hill that overlooked the train station. The wagon was going to be coming around from below. It was carrying most of the weapons but Elly watched as the men popped the trunks of the car, hefted boxes and started into the forest. And then it was just her, alone with the cars, and her rifle in hand.

Not wanting to be seen standing in the middle of the road—although she thought that might be hard to do considering it was night and she was wearing all black—she still crouched down behind one of the cars and waited.

A cool breeze blew through the countryside carrying with it a hint of lavender. Elly closed her eyes, inhaling deeply. She'd loved Paris. It was such a beautiful city. But she was beginning to think that she preferred the countryside of France. There was just something about being in a town where everything around her was a little bit trapped in time. It was that fantastical element that made her feel like France was not quite real.

So lost was Elly in her daydreams that the first pop of a weapon made her fall forward to her knees. Freezing in that position, Elly strained her ears. And then she heard it again. The sound of a gun firing, several times in rapid succession.

Elly looked down at the rifle in her hand as a wave of iciness began to crawl over her. Just who was doing the shooting and who was being shot down there?

And then the sound of many weapons being fired at the same time filled the air. There was a battle taking place.

"Watch the cars, Elodie Anne Mitchell," she whispered aloud to herself. "They'll need them."

But the shots kept firing. "And just what are you going to do if you go down there? Hunting deer is different than being a part of a gunfight." But what if they needed her? What if Grant or Pierre or Danny were in serious danger?

She would just go check. And then she'd race back. Happy with that decision, Elly took off, bent slightly over. *Step lightly,* she reminded herself as she crossed ground. *Breathe deeply.* She still managed to trip over unseen foliage a few times. But at least with her sitting in the dark as she had, her eyes had adjusted to the night sky and so it wasn't as hard to see where she was going.

Elly followed the sound of the firefight until she knew she was just above it. She looked down the hill at the station, which was lit up, giving her a clear view of everything. And the first thing she saw was bodies. French bodies, lying twisted and unmoving just outside of the last freight car that was hooked up to the unmoving train. It looked as though her group had gotten the weapons onto the train and then been ambushed. Which probably meant that somewhere along the line they'd been betrayed.

CHAPTER 37

From where she was crouched down, hidden behind a wide tree, Elly began to count the bodies below. Scattered on the ground, in a near-perfect half-circle in front of the open train—as though they had just delivered the last few boxes of weapons—were the bodies of five of the French deserters. That meant that at least seven men were trapped at the bottom of the hill fighting it out with what appeared to be twenty German soldiers. But the Germans had taken a few losses themselves. Elly counted seven uniformed men lying on the gravel, looking like bloodied rag dolls.

The living German soldiers were lined up almost parallel to the train, shooting and firing and occasionally taking cover from behind a railcar if needed while Elly's group was tucked behind the small wooden station itself. Elly had no doubt that more soldiers were probably on their way. They were going to die down there: Grant, Pierre, Danny, and the others. Even if it was only because they ran out of ammo. More than anything, she wanted to peek over the ridge to confirm that Grant, Pierre, and Danny were still standing. But there was no time for that.

Elly dropped to the ground, tucking the butt of the rifle into her shoulder. The others were behind the station not only for protection but also because there was a direct path up the hill from that point. And yet, to take that first step was to put oneself at a huge risk of being spotted and killed. She had to give them a chance. She was going to have to take the heat. Which meant she was going to have to kill a few men. Her first round hit one of the Germans right between the eyes. Because of her nerves, the second round hit another in the neck. The Germans paused, turning, searching. Her third round hit a man in the chest and then she picked up her gun and ran fifty feet to the right.

Ducking behind a large tree, she took a second to wipe at the sweat on her face but she didn't waste time thinking. Snipers were effective because if they kept firing, they could pin entire units to the ground. This knowledge came courtesy of her brother. Thank heaven for little boys. Elly raised the rifle again. Having caught on, the Germans were playing a bit of hide-and-seek. Most of them had disappeared behind the railcars. Elly's eyes darted to the station. One of the French deserters took off at a run for the path that led up the hill. A German soldier stepped out. Elly shot him, killing him instantly. Her grip on the barrel slipped and she took a second to wipe the sweat on her hands onto her pants.

If they would just please come on, she silently prayed. Another French soldier ran up the path. Where was Grant? It might be dark, but Elly would recognize his form. Her heart thudded a reply. It would be just like Grant to be the last person to run to safety. He was the captain who would go down with his ship. Elly fired at the German who stepped out but her bullet grazed him at most. Another person ran up the hill but Elly didn't have a chance to see who because one of the Germans was firing in her direction. So, she ran. No one needed to explain to her that a sniper who stayed in the same spot invited death.

Finding another location that offered a better view of the Germans, even the ones tucked behind the railcars, Elly began firing and moving and firing and moving, all the while getting slapped in the face by more than one tree branch but also taking on the attention of all of the German soldiers. She barely winced as a bullet sliced into her arm. The others had to climb a hill. She would hold the Germans off. And she did until she heard feet running through the forest.

Elly kept shooting, not looking in the direction of the runners. And then Grant was at her side, firing off rounds with absolute precision. "Fall back."

"I can stay."

"You need to get the cars started. Fall back—that's an order, Mitchell. And for goodness' sake, hurry." Elly turned and ran through the woods, boundless with adrenaline flooding her veins. Grant was alive. And if he had made it to the top then so had Pierre and Danny.

This thought infused her with a burst of energy. She easily passed the wounded and the limping, reaching the road in record time. The cars were still there untouched. Elly opened all of the doors and then cranked up both engines just as the first few survivors entered the small clearing.

"Take the first car and go," she ordered.

"Elly. Help." It was Pierre and he had Danny strewn across his back. Elly jumped into action, helping Pierre lower Danny onto the back seat of the car as others filled the front. Danny was strangely still, unmoving. But there was no time to see what was wrong.

"Get in the driver's seat," she told the Frenchman who had limped alongside Pierre.

"I can't leave Grant," Pierre growled.

"Yes, you can. I've got him. Go." Elly pushed Pierre into the passenger seat, which was an unusually easy feat. She tried not to let herself think what that meant. He was alive. That was all that mattered. She closed all of the doors and the car was off, quietly puttering down the road.

Rifle still in hand, Elly turned to her right where there was still the sound of gunfire and just when she was about to move toward the forest again, in the distance, a ball of fire rolled into the sky, filling the night and shaking the very ground beneath her feet. The sound of it had her reaching for her ears. And that's when she saw the shadows of figures running. She made her way to the driver's seat of the car and slid in. Three men climbed into the car, Grant included. Elly took off down the road before the doors were shut.

"What was that?"

"I blew up the train," Grant said calmly although his chest was moving up and down at a rapid pace.

"You all did get the weapons into the car?"

"Yes. They waited until everything was loaded before they opened fire. Very smart," Grant clipped.

"Who . . . ?" Who had betrayed them? Who had said anything?

"Other side," one of the French soldiers said from the back. "I think. Most of our men are dead," he said bitterly.

"Other side . . . you mean from the receiving end? Grant, do you think . . ." Elly stopped talking, not sure what to say or who to say it in front of but it seemed to her that the French soldier was correct. If everyone on their end was supposed to be killed then there must have been a leak on the receiving end. She glanced at Grant, but he was looking out the window. Nobody said anything as she carefully navigated the twists and turns before finally circling up to the castle. The gate was already opened, waiting for them.

Elly brought the car to a stop just behind the other Renault where Julien, Jo, and Margo were trying to help the wounded into the house.

Grant and the others rushed out of the car and into the château. Within minutes only Elly stood outside, lingering in the dark. The adrenaline was wearing off and her arm was starting to ache. Her body was racked with sudden shivers.

Elly carefully lowered the rifle she was still clinging tightly to with one hand, onto the ground. She sank down next to it, bringing her hands to her face. It had been so easy, killing those men. And there had been so much death. She'd tried to separate herself from the French soldiers who had been staying with them but she was suddenly hit with a kaleidoscope of memories of each man whose body they'd left behind. The thought of entering the castle, the thought of finding out more heart-wrenching news made her chest ache and before she knew it, she was pulling, tugging at her shirt and sobbing.

And then Grant was there, his arms around her. He said nothing as he held her while she wept.

"Pierre?"

"He was shot twice but they're flesh wounds. He'll be fine." Grant's voice was soft, gentle.

"Danny?"

"He was dead before he knew what hit him. But the only way to get Pierre moving was to make him think Danny had a chance."

"Grant." Elly fisted the fabric of her shirt that rested above her heart. The boy she'd begun thinking of as an echo of Catau was gone, this war having taken everything that was uniquely him away forever.

"I know," he said quietly, his arms tightening around her to the point where she wasn't sure who was comforting whom.

She didn't know how long they stayed out there, but at some point she forced herself to stand. She forced herself to enter the castle. She forced herself to walk up the stairs, shower, and bandage her own small wound. Then she forced herself to sleep.

When Elly woke up the next morning, the sun was shining brightly through the glass windows. Birds were singing. Had the events of yesterday really happened? Like a silent film, pictures flashed through her mind, ending with her last sighting of the unmoving Danny. Elly lay on the bed suddenly wishing with everything in her that she could go home. She was tired of this. Of all of it. The weight of this war was becoming too much to bear and it was only just starting.

Flinging the covers off of herself, she checked the makeshift bandage she had wrapped around her arm. She didn't think she needed stitches but she'd disinfect it again. She'd heard of the horrors of gangrene. And then she'd visit Pierre. After she had some coffee.

Dressed in her simplest outfit and wearing a long sweater despite it not being cold, Elly made her way down the stairs and poked her head into the dining room where the three remaining French soldiers were convalescing on makeshift pallets. Three out of nine. Elly turned on her heels and made her way to the kitchen where Jo stood at the stove stirring a big pot of something that smelled like chicken soup.

"Good morning," Elly said as she crossed the room to the cabinet that held the cups.

"Did you sleep well?" Jo asked. Her hair was still wrapped up tight as though she had just rolled out of bed and she was wearing a cotton robe.

"Did you sleep at all?" Elly asked as a sudden thought hit her. She lowered her empty cup onto the counter with a thud. "I should have helped with the wounded."

"I heard you helped enough. Elly, what would have happened if you weren't there? We'd have lost all of them," Jo whispered, her eyes watering as she turned away to swipe a tear.

Elly was glad she'd been there. The only regret she had was that she hadn't helped them sooner. But she was still ready to go home.

"It's just too much. Isn't it?" Jo asked as though reading her mind. She reached into a drawer, grabbed a spoon, scooped up some broth, and held it out toward Elly. "Have a taste. I haven't cooked chicken soup in years."

"Where's Margo?"

"Sleep. We were up half the night learning how to be doctors."

"I'm so sorry."

"Nothing to be sorry about. Taste."

Elly sipped the broth. "It's good!"

Jo nodded, a pleased look on her face. "This is my granny's recipe. I know I'm missing something but it still works. Listen, I'm thinking it's time to leave France."

"You're reading my mind."

"We can still help France from some other safer location."

"Yes. Absolutely." Because Elly felt like a ball of glass that had just rolled to the very edge of a table. She was mere seconds from falling and crashing. And for her that didn't mean having a meltdown, it meant that she was on the verge of losing a piece of her humanity. She had cried yesterday in part because of how easy it had all been. If she stayed here any longer, she was worried that one day she wouldn't recognize herself in the mirror.

"Losing Danny . . ." Jo began and then stopped, unable to say more.

"Where is he?"

"Grant buried him this morning. He's probably still out there in the garden."

Elly released her grip on her empty coffee cup. "I'll be back."

Outside, the sun was still shining, the flowers were blooming and Grant was planting Danny next to Polly's memorial. Elly stopped just short of looking into the grave. "Do you need help?"

"No," Grant said as he continued to shovel dirt on top of Danny's body.

"Are you all right?"

Grant straightened and then leaned onto the handle of the shovel. When Elly looked into his eyes, she saw that they were clear. "I'm fine. How are *you*?" he asked pointedly.

Elly looked away, rubbing her arms. "I might be ready to go home," she admitted.

"I can imagine." He returned to his work. "You were excellent, yesterday. Thank you, Elodie."

"You'd have done it for me," she said quietly.

Grant glanced over at her for a second. "I don't want to have to do that for you." Elly stared at him. What on earth was that supposed to mean? "I was talking to Jo this morning and . . ."

Grant stopped talking, looking past her at the closed gates of the château.

Elly turned around as the sound of vehicles nearby filled the air. Grant stepped past Danny's grave, moving to stand next to her. They both heard the engines of the cars die down. They both heard the sound of someone's footsteps and then banging on the gate. German words filled the air. Elly brought one hand to her mouth in disbelief. It wasn't over yet. They'd found them.

CHAPTER 38

Elly and Grant exchanged a look that required no words. He hurried back to the grave and she took off running. Reaching the entrance of the castle, she nearly ran into Julien. "Hold them off for two minutes."

Nearly sliding into the kitchen where Jo still stood at the stove, Elly paused to take a breath. "What's wrong? Who is doing all of that banging on the doors?"

"Germans," Elly hissed. Jo's eyes widened to nearly the size of saucers. "Here. Outside. I'll get the men out of the dining room. Go change."

"Library," Jo called over her shoulder, taking a second to turn the stove off before running in the opposite direction.

Elly booked it to the dining room where Margo had come down and was checking wounds. "Germans are here. Head to the dungeons, now. Margo, can you get Pierre?" Elly hadn't seen Pierre yet but that was most likely because he was convalescing in his room.

She did not need to repeat herself. Wounded though they might be, everyone scrambled while Elly chased after them, putting the room to rights and erasing all evidence that anyone had slept there.

When the room looked untouched, Elly slowly made her way to the castle foyer where Julien had just opened the door for six German soldiers. Before her was an officer, a non-commissioned officer, and four infantrymen.

Elly clasped her hands together and realized that she was shaking. She dipped her head not only in greeting but also to take a deep breath. *You've done nothing wrong. You're in the middle of making soup. You're Prissy in* Gone With the Wind. *You don't know nothin' 'bout birthin' babies.*

Lifting her head slowly, Elly took in the polished black boots of the man directly in front of her. She noted the balloon flare of the pants, the silver emblem of the eagle holding the Nazi symbol on the man's chest, the Wehrmacht collar and the braided officer's cap. Before her was a colonel. She did not notice his appearance or the appearance of his men. They were all the boogeyman to her. "Welcome to the Château des Milandes," she said very calmly in English.

"*Heil* Hitler!" someone said and the men snapped their boots together and saluted.

Elly took a startled step back. It was even more disconcerting in person. "Yes, well, um, this is the current home of Josephine Baker. She should be in the library—just this way." Elly extended her hand toward the staircase.

"And you are?" the officer asked in heavily accented English.

"Her personal maid. You may call me Elly. Your name, sir?"

The colonel eyed her for a long minute as though deciding whether to answer. "Colonel Hahn."

"Very nice to meet you, Colonel Hahn. Right this way, please." Elly once again motioned in the direction of the library.

"Elly," Julien called before she could leave. She stepped over to the butler. "We are completely surrounded," he whispered. "They are guarding every exit."

"Coffee would be wonderful. Thank you, Julien." She patted the man on the shoulder and with her eyes told him to go to the kitchen.

"My men will stay down here. Only I will go to speak with Ms. Baker," the colonel stated firmly. Elly nodded in agreement before leading the colonel up the stone stairs and down the hall to where the library was located.

She opened the doors for him, carefully stepping away as he entered. Jo was there, reclining in an armchair with her hair wrapped in an elaborate blue silk turban. She had on sparkly earrings that matched the long, brightly colored gown that enrobed her. She looked as though she had been dressed and sitting for a portrait for hours. The colonel bowed, clicked his heels together, and made the salute once again. "*Heil* Hitler."

Jo said nothing, merely flicked her gaze to Elly. Elly stepped forward. "Ms. Josephine, may I present to you Colonel Hahn. Colonel Hahn, Josephine Baker."

"Please do take a seat, Colonel," Jo said, waving toward the armchair opposite hers.

Elly closed the library doors but did not leave the room. Instead, she found a corner to hover in.

"Madame," the colonel began, switching to French. "I am a member of the Armistice Commission. My job here is to overlook the transportation of weaponry from this area to the north. I bring with me a search warrant."

Elly forced herself not to make any movements as the colonel reached into his coat and pulled out a sheet of paper. He laid it on the small coffee table that rested between him and Jo. Jo didn't even glance at it. Instead, she rested her elbow on the armchair and touched a tired hand to her face. "Do you think I'm hiding weapons here, Colonel? Are there guns in my shoe closet and grenades in my underwear drawer?"

There was gentle knocking on the door and Elly opened it as Julien appeared with a coffee tray.

The colonel removed his warrant, returning it to his coat as Julien laid cups on the small table.

"You'll have to excuse the lack of sugar. We have very little," Jo told the colonel. That was true. There was sugar in the castle; Julien had simply brought none.

"A shame what war does," the colonel said as he reached for his cup.

Jo looked at the man with slightly annoyed eyes. "Yes."

When Julien left, the colonel began again. "Do you miss the stage?"

"Not enough to perform while others are suffering."

"Things did not have to be this way, Ms. Baker," the colonel said, taking a sip of his coffee.

"Germany did not have to invade France, you mean? I agree. There is still time for you all to leave."

"If only life were that simple. Ms. Baker, are you telling me that if I have this place searched, they will find no weapons?"

"They might find my kitchen knives."

"We are not here for nothing, Ms. Baker. Someone notified us that there are weapons in this castle."

Elly released a silent breath of air. So. Someone *was* watching them and had reported them to the Germans. Grant had been right to be paranoid.

Jo blinked, bored with this conversation. "Do you believe everything you hear?"

"We are in war, Ms. Baker. We cannot afford to ignore reports."

"You might be at war, Colonel. But I am not. This is a place of peace. Of love. Of joy. Of friendship that morphs into family." Even from where Elly stood, she could see that Jo's dark eyes glittered with emotion. Elly clenched her fists at her sides, digging her nails into the flesh of her palms so that she would not cry. "Can you imagine what the world would be like if we all sought love rather than hate?" It was Jo's rallying cry. The message she delivered regularly and sincerely from her pulpit. And in that moment, Elly realized that while she may not always understand her, she'd forever love Josephine Baker. "Look out of the window, Colonel. What do you see around you? Life! It's everywhere and never more than in this country. That's why I love France. *Vive la France*! Why would I want to be a part of something that brings only death?"

The colonel lowered his cup of coffee onto the saucer, a look of bemusement and pity on his face that suggested he thought the pair of rose-tinted glasses Jo wore daily were idiotic. "All right, Ms. Baker. I will trouble you no longer. But I suggest you be very careful from here on out." The colonel slowly stood up and it was Elly's turn to blink. That was it? He wasn't going to search the castle? Elly looked at Jo who had not moved an inch. The colonel offered one last salute and Elly escorted him to the foyer where his men were still gathered. Julien took them the rest of the way to their cars.

When the castle gates closed, Elly sagged against the doorway.

"Are they gone?" Jo asked as she made her way down the stairs.

"Yes," Elly said even as she double-checked behind her and in corners just in case a German soldier had decided to linger. Seeing her movements, Jo did the same. They both wandered around the nearest rooms in case someone was hiding in a closet.

Finally at ease, Elly turned to Jo. "Marvelous. You were absolutely marvelous."

"I was absolutely terrified."

"You didn't look it."

"We're leaving," Jo said resolutely. She placed a hand to her heart. "I can't take that sort of thing. My heart still feels like it's going to burst at any minute. You know it's not just the soldiers below or the few weapons we're holding on to. Jack has all those papers up in the tower. We have that radio transmitter that reaches the British. A nightmare, Elly. An absolute nightmare. Where's Grant?"

They went out to the garden where Grant had uprooted numerous plants, replanting them on top of Danny's makeshift grave. He was stretched out on the ground, leaning back on his elbows. "I don't know what you two did to get them out of here but whatever it is, I'm more than impressed. I'm grateful."

Still elegantly dressed, Jo dropped to her knees and touched a hand to the fresh dirt. "Daniel?"

"Yes."

"He was going to be famous, you know," Jo said lightly as she ran her fingers through the soil. "He was going to take pictures that were going to be everywhere."

Elly carefully dropped down to her knee between Jo and Grant.

"Sometimes, I feel like a motherless child," Jo began to sing. Having been a motherless child, Elly quite hated this song. But Jo sang it as it was supposed to be sung. In lament. Every note, every inflection was more a prayer of sorrow prompting Elly to think of the unfairness of Danny's life being cut short; of his dreams that would never be realized. "Sometimes I feel like a motherless child." Elly blinked, holding back the tears that threatened, her eyes still slightly swollen from all of her crying the night before. Grant was looking away from both of them. But silent tears ran down Jo's cheeks. "Sometimes I feel like a motherless child, a long way from home."

And then they were quiet, each lost in their own thoughts.

"I got us visas," Jo said, breaking the moment of silence. Elly and Grant looked at her. "I didn't want to say anything until I was sure I could get my hands on them but they arrived yesterday after you all left. I have a friend in the Brazilian embassy who got them for us."

"Brazil?" Elly asked.

"Yes, the idea would be that I'm leaving France to do a tour in South America. The visas will get us into Portugal."

Portugal . . . which also had boats that still went to England . . . which had boats that went to America. Elly's heart fluttered as she realized that home was within grasp.

"I thought we might finish out the summer here but now . . ."

"We should leave yesterday," Grant said, finishing the statement.

"Yes. I would like to be on the first train that leaves tomorrow," Jo said definitively. The Germans appearing at their gates had really scared her. And rightfully so, Elly thought. They all stood up. "We can't take the French soldiers with us but I can give them a car, some money, and directions to the safe house in Marseille. It's time to say goodbye to France. For now."

Everyone spent the remainder of the day packing although Julien and Margo had declared that they were staying in the castle and in turn with all of Jo's animals. As a butler and housekeeper, they felt as though they'd be safe. Grant and the remaining French soldiers wrapped the rifles they had retained and stuffed them into the trunk of one of the Renaults. They returned the radio transmitter to the blacksmith and Jack burned all the papers he could but with the ones he couldn't, he transcribed the intelligence onto Jo's score sheets using invisible ink. It was information they would have to pass on to the British once they reached Lisbon.

It was a remarkably easy thing to pack her bag to leave. Elly had no problem leaving behind clothes and items that wouldn't fit like her typewriter—which she had used more than she had thought she would that summer. She had been asked to transcribe the speeches de Gaulle had given over the radio. Her writing had then been copied and passed around to those who didn't have access to the air waves. She'd also written a number of articles on life in occupied France. She did fold those and bury them in her dresses. She'd mail them off once they reached safety.

With all of her things ready, Elly finally made her way to Pierre's room. "Knock, knock," she said as she slowly opened his bedroom door.

"Is that Elly? Finally remembering I'm alive?"

Smacking her lips together, Elly entered Pierre's room and shut the door. He was lying in the bed on his back, looking slightly miserable. They were going to have to be very careful with him as they traveled. Elly knew now he'd been shot near his shoulder and on his side. What a very blessed boy he was as the bullets had missed all the important parts.

"I was going to come by sooner," Elly swore as she sat down gingerly onto his bed, next to him.

"Grant said Danny died." Pierre blinked up at her like a small child.

"Yes," she said simply, looking down at her hands.

"I hate this."

"I do too."

"You handle it well."

"Do I?" She heard movement and then Pierre's hand was grasping one of hers.

"The Germans suspect us."

"Yes."

"We're leaving in the morning."

"Uh-huh."

"I'm tired," he said, exhausted from more than just his wounds. "Stay with me."

"All right." Elly held Pierre's hand until his breathing deepened and he fell asleep. Then she tucked him in and returned to her room.

She barely slept and she was awake with the sun the next morning. Grabbing her things, she left her room after taking in one last lingering glance. For all of her enthusiasm to leave, she'd never forget that she'd once been a princess in a medieval castle.

Elly closed the door behind her and then she saw him. Grant, sitting on the top stair of the staircase. "Are you waiting for me?" Elly asked as she lowered herself down to sit next to him.

Grant turned, facing her. He reached for one of her hands, stroking it lightly. "When you get to Portugal—"

"When *I* get to Portugal?" What was he saying?

Grant lifted his eyes to meet hers. He looked exhausted, as though he hadn't slept a wink the night before. "I'm not going with you and Jo."

A feeling of complete dread washed over her. It wasn't as if she hadn't known they'd be having this conversation. She'd just assumed it was going to be on the shores of Portugal. She'd thought she'd have more time. "You're staying here?"

"Not at the château. I'm going to Marseille. I'm not leaving France." He was not leaving France. The words settled like a weight in her stomach. "I told you from the beginning—"

"Don't," she warned. "Don't you finish that sentence." But he was right. He'd never lied to her. He'd never led her on. Pierre had told her he wouldn't leave. None of this should be a surprise to her and yet it was. That familiar iciness started in her fingers, slowly creeping up her skin. Her voice turned cool. "It's not safe here. You're that devoted to this country you've already shed blood for? Have you not sacrificed enough for France?"

Grant's expression was unchanging. "France has done a lot for me."

"Oh? Does France love you as much as I do?" Elly asked, knowing her eyes were blazing with all sorts of emotion. There, she'd said it out loud. She'd broken her own rules for him again and again, being vulnerable first. And look what it had gotten her.

Grant was still holding her hand and he looked down at it now, his thumb stroking her gently. His Adam's apple bobbed as he swallowed. When he spoke, his voice was hoarse. "If I thought love was enough, I'd go with you."

Elly blinked back tears. "This would not be the same as your first marriage. We would approach life together, the way we have always done since you've known me. What we have is more than love, Grant. It's respect, trust, and understanding." What was that Pierre had asked her to do? Ask him. "Grant, this is me asking you to come with me. Please." When Grant lifted his eyes, she knew not a single word she'd said had moved him and she felt something die inside of her. "You'll die here."

"Maybe. Thoughts of my death do not scare me."

"And that somehow makes it better?"

His grip on her hand tightened because she was shaking. She tried half-heartedly to pull out of his grasp, fighting with the notion that this was the last time she'd ever touch him. "You're going to return to America and you're going to become a professor. You're going to get married. You're going to have your five or six children. You're going to join the fight for civil rights. And you're going to live long and die in your sleep after having held your great-grandchildren."

Elly jerked her hand out of his. She reached for her bag. "Tell yourself whatever story you need to tell. But you have no right to dictate to me how I'm going to live or die in the future. You just gave that up, Grant Monterey. I hope when they bury you in Meuse-Argonne, it was worth it."

Elly stood up and made it down one step when she felt his tight grip on her arm. She stopped and looked over her shoulder. She didn't know how long they stood there, memorizing each other's faces. "After the war," he said, his voice low, his eyes almost pleading. "You can come back."

Elly looked away. She supposed she could come back but she already knew in the depths of her heart it would never happen. She met Grant's dark gaze. "This is not my home." This was not where her heart was.

But this was Grant's home. His heart was buried in the cemetery with the rest of the 369th Infantry Regiment. And so as much as she felt like she was being ripped apart, she could not be angry with Grant. Leaning forward, she placed one lingering kiss on Grant's right cheek and then a second one—this one mixed with tears—on his left cheek. "*Au revoir.*"

CHAPTER 39

December 1940

Four months later

The neighborhood of Alfama was Elly's favorite place
to explore in Lisbon, Portugal. Daily, while Jo was
entertaining the press or meeting with dignitaries, Elly
climbed the town that went up in something of a loose
spiral. And each time she walked through it, she came
across a different sight on her journey to the top of
the hill that overlooked stacked red rooftops and a
magnificent view of the ocean. Having reached the top
once again, Elly parked herself on a nearby stone ledge.
Had it really been four months since she'd left France?

She shivered a bit as cool December air tried to make
its way through the openings of her coat. Lisbon was

393

nowhere near as cold as Chicago in December. But there was still a definite chill that hung in the air, particularly on days when the sun was playing hide-and-seek with the clouds. Elly looked out at the ocean as she always did. To think she had thought it would be easy to jump on the first ship that was headed to London or America. A nice idea, but there just weren't that many. However, she'd been informed that one should be coming in before the new year and Elly would make sure she was on it. At least, she thanked God, she wouldn't have to take a plane.

They'd left France by train. Elly played Jo's maid while Jack, the boyfriend and handler, played Jo's tour manager. Looking back on it, Elly could see how surreal it must have been. Jo dressed in a fancy pink suit with a matching wide-brimmed hat and a white fox fur stole wrapped around her shoulders while Elly and Jack each carried two of her suitcases plus their own amid refugees running for their lives.

They'd arrived in Spain and then been given the option of getting to Portugal by train or plane. Jack had opted for the plane because it would not present as many opportunities for them to be stopped and checked. It had been Elly's first flight ever. And the less said about it the better.

But even still, Elly had not quite been in the moment. She'd literally done whatever Jack or Jo told her to do, her mind a million miles away trying to grasp and hold on to any thought that did not contain Grant Monterey. Or even Pierre.

"I told him this was one decision he was going to regret for the rest of his life," Pierre had told her when she'd gone to say goodbye. They had been the first words out of his mouth when she appeared in his bedroom doorway.

He'd been sitting up this time, trying to put on a white button-down shirt and struggling mightily because he was only using one hand. Elly had moved to his side to help him. "I don't wish to discuss it."

Pierre had ignored her. "I told him one day he'll wake up and look at all the time he's wasted. He'll realize he could have been in a home with his wife and a baby by now and all he has to show for it is more dead bodies."

"Pierre," she had warned. "Besides, you're staying too." She hadn't even needed to ask him. She'd just known that if Grant was staying, so was his 'nephew.'

"That's different. I don't have any other really good options," Pierre had said, finally slipping his other arm into the sleeve of his shirt.

"Pierre," she'd said, feeling a bit guilty. "You have other good options. Come to Chicago and I'll take care of you."

"Live with your religious family, you mean? Honey, that's prison. That's not an option."

"Who said my family was religious?"

"You did. With every look of shock and awe that crossed your face those first few times I met you. Remember that, Elly?"

"Hush."

"It's okay. Believe it or not, once upon a time, I was the same way."

That had pulled out a reluctant snort from Elly. "It's not a prison. Stand up so I can button your shirt."

"If you say so. But you're talking to a boy who grew up COGIC."

Elly had felt the tugging of a grin as she finished helping him dress. His upbringing explained a few things. "They do church all day, don't they?"

"Only stopping to eat lunch."

"But nobody does music better," she'd said, patting his chest and indicating that she was done. "Well, I can promise you that no one will imprison you in the Mitchell household. They'll feed you, and clothe you, and care about you until you wonder how you ever lived without someone looking over your shoulder."

Pierre had shuddered. "Not for me."

"Pierre."

He'd taken her hands in his. "Leave me your address. When this war is over, I'll need to be able to wave it in his face."

"Don't."

Bringing her fingers to his mouth, he'd kissed them before pulling her into a tight hug. "*Au revoir, ma chérie*. And I absolutely mean that. We will see each other again. I did promise my mother I'd come home for my thirtieth birthday. When I get back to the States, we'll meet up and paint the town red."

"I can't wait," she'd said through tears.

"I'm serious," he'd said, his own voice sounding shaky. "We'll hit all the clubs in Chicago."

"Yeah, okay."

"No church services though."

"Oh, shut up."

They'd hugged one last time and then that had been it.

Elly stood up and took one last look at the ocean before slipping her hands into her pockets and starting the trip down the mountain. She missed Pierre. If he were here right now, they'd find something to laugh about until their sides ached. She wondered what he was doing and how he was healing. And then she allowed herself to wonder for two seconds about Grant. He was probably very happily assisting the French Resistance, laying his life on the line for the country that had provided him with a home in a time of need.

"I hope you're happy," she whispered aloud. She was not happy but she was learning to be content despite trying not to think of him constantly. Every day there was something she wanted to ask Grant, something she wanted to experience with him. Every day she woke up and he was the first person on her mind. And every day she had to comfort herself with the knowledge that she probably wasn't on his. But she wasn't embarrassed about that fact. Jo had helped her reach that conclusion.

Their first night in Lisbon at the fancy hotel they were staying in, the woman herself had come knocking on Elly's door. "Let me in!"

Dressed for bed, Elly had obeyed, opening the door as Jo slipped into her room with her hair wrapped up and a silk robe quivering in the wind behind her.

Jo climbed onto Elly's bed and patted the mattress. "Let's talk. Like sisters do after a breakup."

"There's been no breakup," Elly countered as she shut the door and very tentatively sat on the edge of the bed.

"Here," Jo said, patting a spot. "I said sit here."

With great reluctance, Elly lifted her legs onto the bed and scooted next to Jo. Jo slung an enthusiastic arm around her shoulder. "I always hate to be alone but especially after a fight."

"I love to be alone," Elly said just to be contrary.

"I knew you were going to say that." Jo hugged Elly's tense shoulders to her side, forcing Elly to inhale something sharp and citrusy. "Listen, the first rule of thumb is, you can't count on anybody but yourself."

"That's . . . not what I thought you'd say at all."

"Men are disappointing."

"I mean, some of them are, yes. But some aren't," Elly said, thinking of Uncle Minor and Catau. And was it really Grant's fault that he felt as though he belonged in France?

"Excuse me, but we're having a men-bashing moment right now."

"Are we?"

"Haven't you ever done this before with a sister or something?"

"I don't have any sisters but I get where you're going. Continue."

"I could have told you that chasing after Grant was a bad bet. I know men. I know when they're pliable— even if they say they aren't. I know when they're made of steel. Grant has iron in his bones. You were never going to move that mountain. I would have told you that if you would have ever admitted aloud what was obvious to all."

Elly straightened so that Jo's hand fell off her shoulder and she stared at the woman.

"You were offering Grant something he not only

didn't want but the very thing he's spent the last twenty years running away from."

Put that way, Elly could only look down at the white bedspread as embarrassment washed over her.

"If there's one thing I've learned in this life it's that try as hard as you might, you can't control anybody. You can only control yourself."

Elly's response was a grunt.

"So when you look back on your life, the only thing you can possibly regret is what you did and didn't do. The rest is out of your hands. Do you know what you did do? You tried." Elly looked up. Jo's eyes were soft and understanding. "You tried, Elodie. And you'll never have to wonder what would have happened if you had only tried. And sure it hurts now, but one day you'll look back on this moment with pride. Because you will have no regrets. You saw something you wanted—a life with Grant Monterey—and you did all you could to make that happen. So lift your chin and hold your head up. You took a risk. It failed. But you still did your part."

Jo was right. She'd stopped feeling embarrassed about being rejected. She'd stopped feeling like there was something wrong with her. She was okay and she'd continue to be okay. And she'd never have to look back on this time and wonder if things would have been different if she'd only done something differently.

With a sigh, Elly looked up at the sky. She'd stayed up top a bit too long. It was starting to get dark and she did not want to be outside in Lisbon at night. They'd stumbled into a country of spies. With Portugal being neutral as it was, there were hundreds of foreigners gathered here for the sole purpose of collecting and exchanging information. Elly didn't want to be caught in any of it, accidentally or on purpose.

And then she looked up from the cobblestones she was carefully navigating and saw him.

CHAPTER 40

Richard Passmore raised a hand in greeting and pointed to the chair opposite his. Elly hesitated only for a second before turning off the path leading to the bottom of the hill. She quickly made her way to the small enclosed outdoor space of the restaurant where Richard sat alone.

The restaurant seemed empty, a little hideaway tucked into a crevice. It begged the question of why Richard was there. Elly watched him light a cigarette. "Richard, as I live and breathe," Elly said politely as she took her seat.

"Elodie Mitchell." His eyes were thorough and searching as he pulled on his cigarette and exhaled smoke. "How are you, my fellow American?"

"I'm well. How are you?" she asked as she lowered her elbows onto the table and leaned forward. He looked the same, except a bit tanner.

"I'm good."

"Have you been here awhile?"

"Longer than I would have liked."

"Why haven't you returned home?"

"The same reason you haven't." Richard grinned and Elly pressed her lips together, refusing to do the same. Sobering, Richard asked, "How did you get out of France?"

Spreading her hands, Elly said, "I have no idea why you'd need to know that information."

"We're on the same team, Elly."

"Of what team do you speak, Richard?"

Richard's eyes narrowed as he brought his cigarette to his mouth. "Imagine my surprise when I saw you here the other day. I thought I must be dreaming."

"I thought you were going down with your ship in Paris?"

"I thought so too but then I was given other orders. What are you doing in Lisbon?"

"Waiting for a ship to London."

A waiter appeared, asking them if they wanted something. "Tea, please," Elly said in English. Her Portuguese consisted of hello, goodbye, and thank you.

"The cod here is delicious."

"If I eat any more cod, I'll turn into a fish."

Richard's grin held the knowledge of someone who had been in Lisbon a bit longer than they would have liked. They said little as they waited for the waitress to return with Elly's tea and a coffee refill for Richard. He leaned forward when they were alone. "Elly, I need you to do me a favor."

It was the way he said it. Elly stirred her tea.

"Richard, you've always been very kind to me but I don't do favors for people in foreign countries. Ask me that again when we get back to the States."

"I'm being watched."

Elly lifted her eyes to his for a second. Then she continued stirring. "That's terrible."

At her cool response, Richard's eyes lit up with a flash of delight as though he'd stumbled upon the exact thing he was looking for. "I have information that must be passed to SIS." The British.

"Richard, are you sure you should be telling me this?"

"I thanked God the moment I saw you. This information must be delivered asap. It's time-sensitive."

Elly raised her cup to her lips. "You don't know anything about me."

"I know you're not working for the Germans. They don't exactly like your kind." Elly glared at him, unamused. "What? I like to think we've never been anything less than honest with each other. If you help me, I'll get you on the next ship to London or wherever. That is a job I'm still performing, even here. And Elly, it's not just me you'd be helping."

"Please," she said, stopping the rest of his words. She was tired of that chorus. "If you're being watched, how do I get out of this alive?"

"You're a woman."

"Richard—"

"A colored woman. The maid of 'The Black Angel'." Elly recognized that the Portuguese title for Jo was supposed to be endearing but she still found it rather degrading. Wouldn't it be nice if these white people were a bit more original?

"Elly, find a way," he said, frustration lacing his words. She wasn't that worried about being killed and she knew Jack was talking to the British almost daily. All she needed to do was hand the information to him.

"Fine. But you get me on the next ship out of this country."

"Deal," he said firmly. "There's a ship leaving in two days. I'll have a ticket for you tomorrow."

Elly leaned back, startled. She hadn't expected him to follow through that quickly.

"Have you finished your tea? It's getting late and you shouldn't walk home in the dark." Richard stood up and Elly followed. When he leaned in to hug her, she kept herself still as an envelope was slipped down the opening of her coat. "I'll find you tomorrow."

Elly nodded and then continued down the path to the hotel. It took her only five minutes to realize she was not alone. If she was a person who cussed, she'd release a long stream of words. Well, it was a good thing she'd been making this climb nearly every day for the past few months.

Elly ducked into the nearest alleyway, one hand in her hair. Grabbing the moth clip, she placed it in her coat pocket so that it was there for easy access. Picking up speed, she turned down another path and entered a very small shop where the owner looked up from the counter in surprise. "*Olá.*"

Elly looked around. She was in a pastry shop. They were opened rather late. "Two *pastéis de Nata, por favor.*" If she was going to eat the small custard pie, she preferred the ones in Belém like most people but she'd happily eat these too. Pulling out her purse, she paid for the desserts even as she kept her eyes on the door. Laying another bill on the counter, she asked the owner, "Do you have another exit?"

Elly arrived at the hotel, alone and intact. She climbed the stairs up to the fourth floor where Jack and Jo shared a room just across from hers. She carefully knocked on the door. "It's me."

The door opened before she could knock a second time. "Hello, Jack. I've got a present for you."

"He's American?" Jack asked her for the third time as the running water for the shower stopped.

"Richard Passmore from Ann Arbor, Michigan. He worked for the embassy in Paris while I was there. Do with that information whatever you will," Elly said, nodding at the heavy envelope that was now in Jack's hands. "What is going on here?"

Around the hotel room, clothes and things were scattered everywhere.

"Orders came down. We're leaving. We were just going to fetch you."

Elly straightened. It looked like she wouldn't need Richard at all. "We're headed to London?"

Jack's lips thinned. "Afraid not. If this is as important as you say, I've got to run." And with that, he walked out of the hotel room just as Jo entered, wrapped in a robe and rubbing a towel over her short hair.

"Did Jack tell you?"

"Where are we going?"

"Marseille."

"Marseille! France?!" Jo sat down on the bed amid

a pile of her things. "Back to the place we've just fled?" Back to where Grant was?

"There are three reasons why I've agreed to go and three reasons why you should come with me." Elly was shaking her head before Jo finished talking. Still, Jo held up three fingers. "There is information that we must pass on to the agents still there. I've been asked to return to the stage to create an atmosphere that allows for other agents to do what needs doing. And I'm all out of money."

The last bit was startling. "Really?"

"Yes. Really," Jo's grin was wry.

"But you had the castle and jewelry and cars and . . ."

"Let me correct myself. I'm all out of cash and I have no way to liquidate the rest of my assets. Now, here's why you're coming with me." Jo raised three fingers again. "We've got to convince Grant and Pierre to leave." Elly shook her head. She'd tried that already even as her heart leapt with readiness at the thought. "You agreed to dance with me should I do another performance."

"You've got to be kidding."

"You owe me money."

Elly's mouth dropped slightly open. That was probably true. She'd been living off Jo for months now.

"Josephine."

"Jack's not coming. Are you, my only family on this side of the world, going to let me enter enemy territory alone?"

Elly licked her lips not liking where this was going at all. "What's your escape plan?"

"There are ships in Marseille."

"There were supposed to be ships here!"

"Then I guess we better figure it out. Elodie Mitchell, I am asking you to march back into the lions' den with me one last time. Not for France, but for me. Will you help me?"

CHAPTER 41

Elly watched the albatross surf on the air above the harbor of Marseille, bringing to mind a line from the *Rime of the Ancient Mariner*. The Château d'If loomed in the distance, making her want to search for Edmond Dantès of *The Count of Monte Cristo*. Every place in France was magical.

"Excuse me, miss. Are you American?" Elly rocked on her heels slightly as she slid her eyes to her right where Pierre was approaching. "Is that how Grant does it?"

"No, that's not how I do it." Elly nearly jumped out of her skin. He was right there, standing on her left. Elly and Jo had been back in France for nearly a week and a half. Jo had immediately put out feelers to find them. They'd been told the two men were on a mission and expected back any day now. Today, apparently.

Making a quick decision, Elly turned in Grant's

direction first. He was once again wearing all black, with a burnished gold scarf wrapped loosely around his neck. He'd lost weight and shaved his beard because that was most definitely gray peppering his cheeks. Grant dipped his head, his dark eyes scanning her just as much as she'd scanned him. "Elodie."

"Grant."

She turned away from him and opened her arms. "Pierre." Pierre pulled her to him, hugging her tight. "Are you feeling better?"

"Yes. It's been, like, four months."

Elly took a step back, her hands still on his arms. He too looked thinner. "How did you find me?"

"We got word of Jo's clarion call."

"Where were you?"

"Near Nice." Pierre lowered his voice, but amusement danced in his eyes. "Is it true? Will you be dancing on the stage with the one and only?" Elly let her eyes do the talking. Pierre threw his head back and laughed. "Oh, man. This is the one time I wish I was not in the orchestra. What are you wearing?"

Elly punched his arm as he continued laughing.

"Pierre, go take a walk." Pierre looked past Elly, saluted Grant, winked at her, and then headed for the nearest bench.

Not looking at Grant, she said lightly, "I hadn't caught up with him yet."

"He's not going anywhere. But I am."

"Oh? Where are you going?" she asked, still not looking at him. Why was he doing this? Hadn't they said all they needed to say? "This is your home, is it not?"

"France has been what I needed when I needed. But I've been running away from home for years." The admission made Elly blink in surprise. Grant's voice was gruff as he continued. "You asked me to go with you and I'd be lying if I said I hadn't considered it before but returning to America with you scares me. Elodie, we are very similar. When I'm in, I'm all in and the thought of losing another wife or child . . . that's very frightening to me." Elly bit down on her lip for more than one reason. "I don't know if it's fair to say that I love you more than my first wife. But sometimes it feels that way. Sometimes it feels like I knew you from the moment I saw you marching down the Victor Hugo with determination and self-assuredness in every step. I didn't want to bring you in as a spy because you intrigued me so. But it was also for that very reason that I didn't want you to one day disappear. I decided to leave it to God. That first day we met, I gave you those tickets as a sort of test of chance, not sure if I wanted you to show up or not." Grant paused, briefly glancing down at his feet.

"You were right. Living the rest of my life tending the graves of the deceased is not living. It's its own form of suicide. Will you—"

"Yes." She really had no self-respect, did she? A bunch of pretty words and she was ready to toss all of her principles out the door.

"It was a dual question," Grant said after a moment, a grin tugging on his lips. "For forgiveness and marriage."

"I thought you weren't getting remarried." She

couldn't help it. "And you looked horrified at the thought of having five children."

"Five or six, you said. I am horrified. It's been over twenty years since I've held a baby. But I've decided to live the rest of my years challenging myself."

"You might like them." Elly blinked back tears. They did not have to have five or six children. Just having Grant was enough.

"Maybe. So long as we do it together, we'll manage." The look they exchanged was pure delight mixed in with a bit of shyness.

"What if you regret it?" Elly asked quietly.

Grant scoffed, shooting her a familiar irritated look that made her want to grin. "Elly Anne, trust me to know my own mind."

"Well," she said slowly. "I only have two tickets for the next ship that leaves Marseille for London." Richard had been more than a little put out when she'd told him to exchange the ticket he'd brought her for two out of Marseille. But he'd done it. "You'll have to be the one to tell Jo she's got to find another way out." She wasn't worried about Jo. Jo had already declared that she didn't want to go to London if Jack wasn't there.

"We ran into her first. Jack's back. With tickets to Casablanca."

Elly frowned, alarmed. "Where is Casablanca?"

"Africa." Grant elbowed her. "Did you want to go?"

"No, indeed."

Next to her Grant laughed, light and free. And then she felt his arm around her shoulders. He pulled her to him, pressing his lips against the top of her head.

She closed her eyes, inhaling the scent of him. "I love you, Elodie Anne Mitchell. No matter what happens, don't you ever doubt that."

"Smile!" Pierre demanded, holding up one of Danny's cameras in his hand.

Elly raised a finger. "You are not taking a picture of me in this outfit. What if my grandchildren see it?"

"They won't," Pierre said dismissively. "The things you worry about. Hurry up. I have to get back to the pit." The orchestra pit where Grant already was. He'd tried to make her promise that she'd give him an encore performance when they were alone. It was, after all, their wedding night since the two of them had hastily married in a civil ceremony at the tiny headquarters of what was left of the Deuxième Bureau. She'd promised nothing.

"Come on, Elly," Jo said, hip-bumping her. She was wearing the equivalent of a brassiere with shorts that stopped high on her thighs. Elly's outfit was more like a one-piece bathing suit, shiny, and flashy, and showy. It matched the color of Jo's shorts. With a deep sigh, Elly removed the robe, tossing it onto the couch of the changing room.

"Behold. All has been revealed," Pierre began in an announcer's voice.

"Shut up!"

"Smile!" Wrapping an arm around each other, they smiled. Pierre snapped the photo, the flash slightly blinding them.

"Yes, yes, get out of here." Jo all but pushed him out of the room before turning to face Elly. "Hands."

Elly was dancing in the opening number. Fluttering in her stomach were numerous butterflies and she felt like she was going to be sick. She touched her palms to Jo's. Jo looked down at their clasped hands. Elly wondered what she saw but Elly saw the same skin color, the same long, thin fingers. The similarities that had brought them this far in the first place. "Thank you."

Elly, who had been expecting words of encouragement, was momentarily thrown. "For what?"

"Your friendship these past few months." All the wrinkles had been ironed out. Jo and Pierre were headed to Africa, Pierre having declared that it was time to stand on his own two feet. Elly and Grant were America-bound. "I know I've changed for the better simply because you were around."

The feeling was absolutely mutual. Elly was not the same person she'd been before she'd met Jo. "Are you trying to make me cry?" Elly asked, her voice dry. But really, she was mere seconds from tearing up. She was leaving more than just a country, she was leaving family. Family she'd be unlikely to see again for quite some time, if ever again.

"Let's do this for each other? Yes? Just like in practice."

"Well, in practice I wasn't really doing it for you."

"Elodie Mitchell!"

"Yes, Josephine Baker. Let's do it for us." And then there was a knock on the door. The contents of Elly's stomach instantly tumbled. "I'm going to be sick."

"No, you aren't."

An amazing number of people who had performed

413

with Jo in the past in one capacity or another had made their way to Marseille to help this production come to life. She'd very loudly declared her return to France with the intent to perform and artists arrived—even those who had been in hiding for one reason or another. The orchestra pit was filled to capacity. An old costume designer had created several new outfits for Jo to wear on stage. Some incredible person had put together a striking but simple set that brought each number to life. The only real difference between *Paris-London* and this show was the audience. German soldiers filled the seats.

Behind the curtain, while the master of ceremonies droned on, Jo and Elly posed as they had practiced. "Remember, smile," Jo said through clenched teeth. "You're having the time of your life. It's just us. Not them."

Except as the curtain rose, Elly did see them. White faces, brown uniforms and all seemed to be looking at her. It was her worst nightmare come to life. The advice Jo had given her in the château returned. *You need to pick one person and dance for them.* So, she found a blur in the back of the audience—someone whose face she could not make out—and she imagined it was Grant. And the thought calmed her nerves.

The drums started, and because she'd practiced this one song so much, her hips started shaking without a second thought. They kicked on beat, rocked, and Jo, being an expert, occasionally winked at Elly, making her smile as they moved up and down the stage. And indeed, sometime after the first thirty seconds, the audience did disappear, and it was just the two of them.

The first time she met Jo flashed before her, their meeting at Le Beau Chêne, the Japanese embassy, dancing in the dressing room with Polly, hiding the dead spy's body in Paris. On and on it went, a montage of their moments together filled Elly's head as she hit every beat and matched every step. As Jo passed her on stage, she smiled, bittersweetly as she performed this last swan song with all of her heart, a tribute from the moth to the butterfly.

EPILOGUE

Gwen's family was all gathered in the house of her oldest uncle, Joseph Mitchell, listening to the tales of Elodie Mitchell Monterey from Ange Marie Preston. In the wide-open living room space, her uncle Jay was sitting on the largest couch next to his sister Leslie Anne, his brother Paul, and the twins, David and Darcy. Across from them was their guest of honor.

Scattered around the room in chairs and on the floor were their spouses, their children, and their grandchildren.

"This picture . . ." Ange Marie began from her seat in front of the fireplace; she held up the infamous photo of Miz Elly and Josephine Baker ". . . was the first photo my grandfather, Pierre Roche, developed. He credited it as the start of his career."

Ange Marie was about Gwen's age and she had that dusky coloring of a biracial woman. Her curly hair was pulled back into a bun and in her lap sat a large envelope. "After Gwendolyn sent me a photo of Dr. Monterey, I found her again." Ange Marie held up another photo. In this photo, Josephine Baker was wearing a uniform with several medals pinned to it. She looked older, around sixty. Miz Elly was hugging her, a large smile on her face. Next to her was Papa Grant and next to him was another man. Pierre, Gwen presumed.

It had been both enlightening and heart-clenching to learn about her grandparents. In so many ways, Gwen felt like she didn't know them at all. She regretted that they were gone from this world, unable to answer any questions. And yet she was so thankful to Ange Marie for reaching out to share this part of their lives.

"That's the March on Washington, isn't it?" Uncle Paul asked. A retired lieutenant-general who missed nothing, he peered at the photo that contained the familiar Washington Monument.

"*Oui*. Josephine spoke just before Dr. King. She was there and so was my grandfather, here," Ange Marie said, confirming Gwen's guess. "Did the Montereys go on to fight in the Civil Rights Movement?"

"Had you asked me that question a day ago, I'd have told you they didn't do anything more than the average black family. But now, you've got me thinking and rethinking. They took an awful lot of vacations when we were little," Uncle Jay said as he eyed his siblings.

"Did you know about their activities in France?"

"I knew Dad fought in WWI. That's him in the uniform in the picture above your head." Gwen looked up at the photo of her seventeen-year-old grandfather in his U.S. Army uniform. Below that photo was one of her grandparents on their honeymoon—as Miz Elly had described it. Gwen recognized the Marseille harbor behind them. "I knew Dad returned to France for a few years and that's where he met Mama who was studying abroad. Uncle Minor always said she shocked the socks off of him when she walked through the front door with a quiet, serious man in tow. They often talked about French culture but you would have never known they were there in the beginning of the second war."

"Daddy wasn't one for talking about the past," Aunt Leslie Anne told Ange Marie. A professor of French literature, her short hair was perfectly coiffed as always and she never went anywhere without a silky scarf wrapped elegantly around her neck. "To talk to Daddy was to hear about the here and now. He'd talk your ears off about business."

"He started two restaurants," Gwen's father, David, said, chiming in. "Le Papillon is a French restaurant and Le Papillon de Nuit is Cajun/Creole." Restaurants that Uncle Jay and Aunt Darcy currently ran. "He and Mama did that together for years. Then Mama took up teaching. I do remember," David said, turning to his siblings, "when Josephine Baker died."

"Mama cried," Aunt Darcy offered. She was a chef who had studied at Le Cordon Bleu in Paris. "Daddy told her there was no reason to; Josephine died doing exactly what she loved."

"How did she die?" Aunt Leslie Anne asked Ange Marie.

"Josephine Baker had money issues. She was a big spender, a big giver, and not always willing to listen to her financial advisors."

"Didn't she have something like twelve children?" Aunt Darcy asked, interrupting.

"She adopted twelve children with her fourth husband. They were all different races and religions. She called them her Rainbow Tribe. It was her way of proving to the world that if people are raised in love, they won't hate. She purchased the Château des Milandes after the war and raised her children there until she lost the castle to creditors. Which takes us back to her death. In need of money and I think because she just liked to entertain, around the age of sixty-nine, Ms. Baker signed on for a new show. She danced all night, outperforming everyone on stage and then died a few days later in her sleep."

Ange Marie held up another photo. "I came across this picture." Smiling at the camera were Pierre and Miz Elly. They had to both be in their eighties. Behind them was the Eiffel Tower.

"I know where I have seen your grandfather before," Uncle Jay said, leaning forward. "When Daddy died, Mama insisted on having him buried in France. Your grandfather was at the services. I was confused why Mama let this stranger hold her hand the whole time."

"But Mama is buried here," Aunt Leslie interjected. "She said it didn't matter where they were buried on earth, they'd find each other in heaven. She said Daddy had given a lot to France and if they were willing to honor him there, then she would leave his ashes with the men who had meant so much to him."

Sitting on the floor between her husband and her sister, Gwen played with the moth hair clip her grandmother had given her just before she died.

"This is a reminder, dear girl, that if you do the things you were placed on this earth to do, you will die, knowing that you lived."

Gwen tugged on one of the wings and very slowly, almost reluctantly, a blade appeared. Her sister gasped and so did her husband. Everyone else in the room was focused on the conversation before them, missing this display. Gwen pressed the wings together and the blade disappeared.

"She was an inspiring woman. No?" Ange Marie said, once again looking at the photo of Elly Mitchell and Jo Baker. "They both were."

ACKNOWLEDGEMENTS

Life has a way of combining the tiniest moments over the years and producing the strangest results. Twenty-three years ago, I asked God whether I should study French or Spanish and then a Tresemmé commercial appeared on the television. So, French it was. Sixteen years ago, I packed my bags and went to live in Aix-en-Provence, France for a semester, hoping to return to the United States like Audrey Hepburn's character in the film, *Sabrina*. Things did not quite turn out that way. Nevertheless, it was an adventure all on its own and one that has stayed with me all these years—sometimes I think just for a moment like this. The girl who rented an apartment for a week in Paris with three other college students—several blocks from the Sacre-Coeur—never would have pictured writing any sort of historical novel about that time. To Janine, Kaia, and Summer, I say thank you. As you probably noted, I cherry-picked from our adventures in France and gave some of our memories to Elly.

This novel is not in the least bit autobiographical (naturally) but I did find myself pulling, unusually from my personal history. And so I would like to acknowledge that much of Elly's stories about her French Creole family are very similar to that of my own French Creole ancestors that lived in Louisiana. I even gave Elly my many times great-grandmother's name: Elodie Mitchell.

Writing is very much an alone pastime but I have discovered over the years that one does not write a novel in a vacuum. I would like to thank the wonderful team I worked with at HarperCollins, specifically Rachel Hart who has kindly held my hand through this process.

I would be especially remiss if I did not mention my personal writing team. There's my father, who will watch every documentary with me and discuss different historical points of views at the drop of a hat. There's my sister Jannett who is just as much a history lover as I am and will often lead me to exactly the right source when I'm stuck. It's because of Jannett that I created Grant's back story. If I haven't said it before, I say it now: I appreciate you. My youngest sister, Victoria, is my romance aficionado, always telling me when something works and when it doesn't. She told me to fix Grant and Elly's relationship. I hope it's fixed, my dear. I greatly value your input. To my aunt (Tee) Jannett who gives me her honest feedback, thank you so very much. And to my mom, who reads and rereads and rereads again—everything that I write—never tiring of each draft I wave at her, I am so grateful.

To my readers, time is such a precious commodity. Thank you so much for spending some of it with my characters. As always, I hope you were both blessed and entertained. *À beintôt!*